A Walk Along the Beach

"Macomber scores another home run with this surprisingly heavy but uplifting contemporary romance between a café owner and a photographer. Eloquent prose . . . along wi[th] [a] charming supporting cast adds a welcome dose o[f] and hope. With this stirring romance, Macom[ber] strates her mastery of the genre."
—*Publishers Weekly* (starre[d review])

"Highly emotional . . . a har[d]-own page-turner, yet, [a] strength and love of family throughout all the heart shines throug[h]." —*New York Journal of Books*

Window on the Bay

"This heartwarming story sweetly balances friendship and mother-child bonding with romantic love."
—*Kirkus Reviews*

"Macomber's work is as comforting as ever." —*Booklist*

Cottage by the Sea

"Romantic, warm, and a breeze to read—one of Macomber's best." —*Kirkus Reviews*

"Macomber never disappoints. Tears and laughter abound in this story of loss and healing that will wrap you up and pull you in; readers will finish it in one sitting."
—*Library Journal* (starred review)

"Macomber's story of tragedy and triumph is emotionally engaging from the outset and ends with a satisfying conclusion. Readers will be most taken by the characters, particularly Annie, a heartwarming lead who bolsters the novel."
—*Publishers Weekly*

Any Dream Will Do

"*Any Dream Will Do* is . . . so realistic, it's hard to believe it's fiction through the end. Even then, it's hard to say goodbye to these characters. This standalone novel will make you hope it becomes a Hallmark movie, or gets a sequel. It's an inspiring, hard-to-put-down tale. . . . You need to read it."
—*The Free Lance–Star*

"*Any Dream Will Do* by Debbie Macomber is a study in human tolerance and friendship. Macomber masterfully shows how all people have value." —*Fresh Fiction*

If Not for You

"A heartwarming story of forgiveness and unexpected love."
—*Harlequin Junkie*

"A fun, sweet read." —*Publishers Weekly*

A Girl's Guide to Moving On

"Beloved author Debbie Macomber reaches new heights in this wise and beautiful novel. It's the kind of reading experience that comes along only rarely, bearing the hallmarks of a classic. The timeless wisdom in these pages will stay with you long after the book is closed."
—SUSAN WIGGS, #1 *New York Times*
bestselling author of *Starlight on Willow Lake*

"Debbie dazzles! A wonderful story of friendship, forgiveness, and the power of love. I devoured every page!"
—SUSAN MALLERY, #1 *New York Times*
bestselling author of *The Friends We Keep*

Last One Home

"Fans of bestselling author Macomber will not be disappointed by this compelling stand-alone novel."
—*Library Journal*

ROSE HARBOR

Sweet Tomorrows

"Macomber fans will leave the Rose Harbor Inn with warm memories of healing, hope, and enduring love."
—*Kirkus Reviews*

"Overflowing with the poignancy, sweetness, conflicts and romance for which Debbie Macomber is famous, *Sweet Tomorrows* captivates from beginning to end."
—*Bookreporter*

"Fans will enjoy this final installment of the Rose Harbor series as they see Jo Marie's story finally come to an end."
—*Library Journal*

Silver Linings

"Macomber's homespun storytelling style makes reading an easy venture. . . . She also tosses in some hidden twists and turns that will delight her many longtime fans."
—*Bookreporter*

"Reading Macomber's novels is like being with good friends, talking and sharing joys and sorrows."
—*New York Journal of Books*

Love Letters

"Macomber's mastery of women's fiction is evident in her latest. . . . [She] breathes life into each plotline, carefully intertwining her characters' stories to ensure that none of them overshadow the others. Yet it is her ability to capture different facets of emotion which will entrance fans and newcomers alike." —*Publishers Weekly*

"Romance and a little mystery abound in this third installment of Macomber's series set at Cedar Cove's Rose Harbor Inn. . . . Readers of Robyn Carr and Sherryl Woods will enjoy Macomber's latest, which will have them flipping pages until the end and eagerly anticipating the next installment."
—*Library Journal* (starred review)

"Uplifting . . . a cliffhanger ending for Jo Marie begs for a swift resolution in the next book." —*Kirkus Reviews*

Rose Harbor in Bloom

"[Debbie Macomber] draws in threads of her earlier book in this series, *The Inn at Rose Harbor,* in what is likely to be just as comfortable a place for Macomber fans as for Jo Marie's guests at the inn." —*The Seattle Times*

"Macomber's legions of fans will embrace this cozy, heart-warming read." —*Booklist*

"Readers will find the emotionally impactful storylines and sweet, redemptive character arcs for which the author is famous. Classic Macomber, which will please fans and keep them coming back for more." —*Kirkus Reviews*

"The storybook scenery of lighthouses, cozy bed and breakfast inns dotting the coastline, and seagulls flying above takes readers on personal journeys of first love, lost love and recaptured love [presenting] love in its purest and most personal forms." —*Bookreporter*

The Inn at Rose Harbor

"Debbie Macomber's Cedar Cove romance novels have a warm, comfy feel to them. Perhaps that's why they've sold millions." —*USA Today*

"Debbie Macomber has written a charming, cathartic romance full of tasteful passion and good sense. Reading it is a lot like enjoying comfort food, as you know the book will end well and leave you feeling pleasant and content. The tone is warm and serene, and the characters are likeable yet realistic. . . . *The Inn at Rose Harbor* is a wonderful novel that will keep the reader's undivided attention." —*Bookreporter*

"The prolific Macomber introduces a spin-off of sorts from her popular Cedar Cove series, still set in that fictional small town but centered on Jo Marie Rose, a youngish widow who buys and operates the bed and breakfast of the title. This clever premise allows Macomber to craft stories around the B&B's guests, Abby and Josh in this inaugural effort, while using Jo Marie and her ongoing recovery from the death of her husband Paul in Afghanistan as the series' anchor. . . . With her characteristic optimism, Macomber provides fresh starts for both." —*Booklist*

"Emotionally charged romance." —*Kirkus Reviews*

BLOSSOM STREET

Blossom Street Brides

"A wonderful, love-affirming novel . . . an engaging, emotionally fulfilling story that clearly shows why [Macomber] is a peerless storyteller." —*Examiner.com*

"Rewarding . . . Macomber amply delivers her signature engrossing relationship tales, wrapping her readers in warmth as fuzzy and soft as a hand-knitted creation from everyone's favorite yarn shop." —*Bookreporter*

"Fans will happily return to the warm, welcoming sanctuary of Macomber's Blossom Street, catching up with old friends from past Blossom Street books and meeting new ones being welcomed into the fold." —*Kirkus Reviews*

"Macomber's nondenominational-inspirational women's novel, with its large cast of characters, will resonate with fans of the popular series." —*Booklist*

Starting Now

"Macomber understands the often complex nature of a woman's friendships, as well as the emotional language women use with their friends." —*New York Journal of Books*

"There is a reason that legions of Macomber fans ask for more Blossom Street books. They fully engage her readers as her characters discover happiness, purpose, and meaning in life. . . . Macomber's feel-good novel, emphasizing interpersonal relationships and putting people above status and objects, is truly satisfying." —*Booklist* (starred review)

"Macomber's writing and storytelling deliver what she's famous for—a smooth, satisfying tale with characters her fans will cheer for and an arc that is cozy, heartwarming and ends with the expected happily-ever-after." —*Kirkus Reviews*

CHRISTMAS NOVELS

Jingle All the Way

"[*Jingle All the Way*] will leave readers feeling merry and bright." —*Publishers Weekly*

"This delightful Christmas story can be enjoyed any time of the year." —*New York Journal of Books*

A Mrs. Miracle Christmas

"This sweet, inspirational story . . . had enough dramatic surprises to keep pages turning."
—*Library Journal* (starred review)

"Anyone who enjoys Christmas will appreciate this sparkling snow globe of a story." —*Publishers Weekly*

Alaskan Holiday

"Picture-perfect . . . this charmer will please Macomber fans and newcomers alike." —*Publishers Weekly*

"[A] tender romance lightly brushed with holiday magic."
—*Library Journal*

"[A] thoroughly charming holiday romance." —*Booklist*

Merry and Bright

"Warm and sweet as Christmas cookies, this new Debbie Macomber romance is sure to be a hit this holiday season."
—*Bookreporter*

"Heartfelt, cheerful . . . Readers looking for a light and sweet holiday treat will find it here." —*Publishers Weekly*

Twelve Days of Christmas

"Another heartwarming seasonal Macomber tale, which fans will find as bright and cozy as a blazing fire on Christmas Eve." —*Kirkus Reviews*

"*Twelve Days of Christmas* is a delightful, charming read for anyone looking for an enjoyable Christmas novel. . . . Settle in with a warm blanket and a cup of hot chocolate, and curl up for some Christmas fun with Debbie Macomber's latest festive read." —*Bookreporter*

"*Twelve Days of Christmas* is a charming, heartwarming holiday tale. With poignant characters and an enchanting plot, Macomber again burrows into the fragility of human emotions to arrive at a delightful conclusion."
—*New York Journal of Books*

Dashing Through the Snow

"This Christmas romance from Macomber is both sweet and sincere." —*Library Journal*

"There's just the right amount of holiday cheer. . . . This road-trip romance is full of high jinks and the kooky characters Macomber does so well." —*RT Book Reviews*

Mr. Miracle

"[Macomber] writes about romance, family and friendship with a gentle, humorous touch."
—*Tampa Bay Times*

"Macomber spins another sweet, warmhearted holiday tale that will be as comforting to her fans as hot chocolate on Christmas morning." —*Kirkus Reviews*

"This gentle, inspiring romance will be a sought-after read."
—*Library Journal*

Starry Night

"Contemporary romance queen Macomber (*Rose Harbor in Bloom*) hits the sweet spot with this tender tale of impractical love. . . . A delicious Christmas miracle well worth waiting for." —*Publishers Weekly* (starred review)

"[A] holiday confection . . . as much a part of the season for some readers as cookies and candy canes."
—*Kirkus Reviews*

Angels at the Table

"Rings in Christmas in tried-and-true Macomber style, with romance and a touch of heavenly magic."
—*Kirkus Reviews*

"[A] sweetly charming holiday romance."
—*Library Journal*

DEBBIE MACOMBER

A Bright New Day

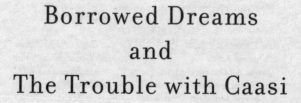

Borrowed Dreams
and
The Trouble with Caasi

BALLANTINE BOOKS
NEW YORK

A Bright New Day is a work of fiction. Names, characters,
places, and incidents are the products of the author's imagination
or are used fictitiously. Any resemblance to actual events, locales,
or persons, living or dead, is entirely coincidental.

2023 Ballantine Books Mass Market Edition

Borrowed Dreams copyright © 1985 by Debbie Macomber
The Trouble with Caasi copyright © 1985 by Debbie Macomber

All rights reserved.

Published in the United States by Ballantine Books,
an imprint of Random House, a division of
Penguin Random House LLC, New York.

BALLANTINE is a registered trademark and the colophon
is a trademark of Penguin Random House LLC.

Borrowed Dreams and *The Trouble with Caasi* originally
published separately in paperback in the United States by
Silhouette Books, New York, in 1985.

ISBN 978-0-593-35988-4
Ebook ISBN 978-0-593-59881-8

Cover illustration: Diane Luger, based on images:
© monkeybusinessimages/Getty Images (couple),
© RomanKhomlyak/Getty Images (mountain and meadow),
© chinaface/Getty Images (clouds)

Book design: Edwin Vazquez

Printed in the United States of America

randomhousebooks.com

2 4 6 8 9 7 5 3 1

Ballantine Books mass market edition: March 2023

Dear Friends,

One of the many advantages of a long publishing career, and the advances in technology, is that my early books have been given a new life. I've read through *The Trouble with Caasi* and *Borrowed Dreams* in order to tweak them here and there and update the two stories to current times. Nevertheless, as we know, the years have brought about a lot of changes from when I first penned these stories. That said, a good story will always remain a good story, no matter when it was written. My hope is that you will find that to be so with these two books.

One of my greatest joys as an author is hearing from my readers. You can connect with me in a number of ways. You'd be surprised by how friendly I am! You can log onto my website at DebbieMacomber.com and leave me a message. You can get in touch with me on Facebook, too. If you're so inclined, write me at P.O. Box 1458, Port Orchard, WA 98366. I look forward to hearing from you.

Warmest regards,

Debbie Macomber

Borrowed Dreams

Chapter One

"Don't worry about a thing," George Hamlyn stated casually on his way out the door.

"Yes . . . but—" Carly Grieves interrupted. This was her first day on the job in Anchorage, Alaska, and she was hoping for a few more instructions. "But . . . what would you like me to do?"

"Take any phone messages and straighten the place up a bit. That should keep you busy for the day." He removed his faded cap and wiped his forearm across his wide brow as he paused just inside the open doorway.

All day! Carly mused irritably. "What time should I expect you back?"

"Not until afternoon at the earliest. I'm late now." His voice was tinged with impatience. "A couple of drivers will be checking in soon. They have their instructions."

Fleetingly, Carly wondered if their orders were as vague as her own.

"See you later." George tossed her a half-smile and was out the door before she could form another protest.

Carly dropped both hands lifelessly to her sides in frustrated displeasure. How could George possibly expect her to manage the entire office on her own? But, apparently, he did just that. On her first day, no less. With only a minimum of instruction, she was to take over the management of Alaska Freight Forwarding in her employer's absence.

"Didn't Diana warn you this would happen?" She spoke out loud, standing in the middle of the room, feeling hopelessly inadequate. Good heavens, what had she gotten herself into with this job?

Hands on hips, Carly surveyed the room's messy interior. George had explained, apologetically, that his last traffic supervisor had left three months ago. One look at the office confirmed his statement. She couldn't help wonder how anyone could run a profitable business in such chaos. The long counter was covered with order forms and a variety of correspondence, some stained with dried coffee; the ashtray that sat at one end was filled to overflowing. Cardboard boxes littered the floor, some stacked as high as the ceiling. The two desks were a disaster; a second full ashtray rested in the center of hers, on top of stacked papers, and empty coffee mugs dotted its once polished wood surface. The air was heavy with the smell of stale tobacco.

Forcefully expelling an uneven sigh, Carly paused and wound a strand of rich brown hair around her ear.

Straighten the place up a bit! Her mind mimicked George's words. She hadn't come all the way from Seattle to clean offices. Her title was traffic supervisor, not janitor!

Annoyed with herself for letting George walk all over her, Carly got her desk in reasonable order and straightened the papers on the counter. She grimaced as she examined the inside of the coffeepot. It looked like someone had dumped chocolate syrup in it. She guessed it had never been washed.

When the phone rang, she answered in a brisk, professional tone. "Alaska Freight Forwarding."

A short hesitation followed. "Who's this?"

Squaring her shoulders, she replied crisply, "Carly Grieves. May I ask who's calling?"

The man at the other end of the line ignored the question. "Let me talk to George."

It seemed no one in Alaska had manners. "George is out for the day. May I ask who's calling?"

Whoever was on the line let out a curse.

"I beg your pardon?"

"When do you expect him back?"

"Well, Mr. Blanky Blank, I can't rightly say."

"I'll be there in ten minutes." With that, he abruptly severed their connection.

Sighing, Carly replaced the receiver. Apparently Mr. Blanky Blank thought she could tell him something more in person.

A few minutes later, the door burst open and a man as lean and serious as an arctic wolf strode briskly inside and stopped just short of the counter. Dark flecks sparked with interest in eyes that were wide and deeply set. He was dressed in a faded jean jacket and worn jeans, and his Western-style, checkered shirt was open at the throat to reveal a broad chest with a sprinkling of curly, dark hair.

"Carly Grieves?" he questioned as his mouth quirked into a coaxing smile.

"Mr. Blanky Blank?" she returned, and smiled. His lean face was tanned from exposure to the elements. The dark, wind-tossed hair was indifferent to any style. This man was earthy and perhaps a little wild—the kind of wild that immediately gave women the desire to tame. Carly was no exception.

"Brand St. Clair," he murmured, his friendly eyes not leaving hers as he extended his hand.

Her own much smaller hand was enveloped in his calloused, roughened one. "I'm taking a truck," he announced without preamble.

"You're what?" Carly blinked.

"I haven't got time to explain. Tell George I was by—he'll understand."

"I can't let you do that . . . I don't think . . ." Carly stammered, not knowing what to do. Brand St. Clair wasn't on the clipboard that listed Alaska Freight Forwarding employees. What if one of the men from the warehouse needed a truck later? She didn't know this man. True, he was strikingly attractive, but he'd undoubtedly used that to his advantage more than once. "I can't let you do that," she decided firmly, her voice gaining strength.

Brand smiled, but the amusement didn't touch his dusky, dark eyes. Despite the casual way he was leaning against the counter, Carly recognized that he was tense and alert. The thought came that this man was deceptive. For all his good looks and charming smile, it could be unwise to cross him.

"I apologize if this is inconvenient," she began, and clasped her hands together with determination. "But I've only just started this job. I don't know you. I don't know if George Hamlyn is in the habit of lending out his trucks, and furthermore—"

"I'll accept full responsibility." He took his wallet from his back hip pocket and withdrew a business card, handing it to her.

Carly read the small print. Brand was a pilot who freelanced his services to freight operators.

"A hiker in Denali Park has been injured," he explained shortly. "I'm meeting the park rangers and airlifting him to British Columbia." The impatient way he spoke told Carly he wasn't accustomed to making explanations.

"I . . . I . . ." Carly paused, uncertain.

"Do I get the truck or not?"

She unclenched and clenched her fist again. "All right," she finally conceded, and handed over the set of keys.

He gave her a brief salute and was out the door.

She stood at the wide front window that faced the street and watched as Brand backed the pickup truck onto the road, changed gears, and sped out of sight. Shrugging one shoulder, she arched two delicate brows expressively. Life in the north could certainly be unnerving.

"A pilot," she murmured. Flying was something that had intrigued her from childhood. The idea of soaring thousands of feet above the earth with only a humming engine keeping her aloft produced a thrill of adventure. Carly wondered fleetingly if she'd get the opportunity to learn to fly while in Alaska.

She paused, continuing to stand at the window. Her attraction to the rugged stranger surprised her. She preferred her men tame and uncomplicated, but Brand St. Clair had aroused her curiosity. She couldn't put her finger on what it was now, but it felt as real and intense as anything she'd ever experienced. He exuded an animal magnetism. She'd been exposed to those male qualities a hundred times and had walked away yawning. Whatever it was about him, Carly was intrigued. She found she was affected by their short encounter. She stood looking out the office window, watching the road long after the truck was out of sight.

Once the Formica counter was cleaned, the orders piled in neat stacks, and the boxes pushed to one side of the office, Carly took a short break. The phone rang several times and Carly wrote down the messages dutifully, placing them on George's desk. A warehouse man came in and introduced himself before lunch, but was gone before Carly could question him about the truck Brand St. Clair had taken.

With time on her hands, the afternoon dragged, and Carly busied herself by sorting through the filing cabinets. If the office was in disarray, it was nothing compared to the haphazard methods George Hamlyn employed for filing.

When George sauntered in around five he stopped in the doorway and glanced around before giving Carly an approving nod.

"I'd like to talk to you a minute," she said stiffly. She

wasn't above admitting she'd made a mistake by moving to Alaska. She could cut her losses and head back to Seattle. If he needed someone to clean house, she wasn't it.

"Sure." He shrugged and sat down at his desk. Although George possessed a full head of white hair, he didn't look more than fifty. Guessing his age was difficult. George's eyes sparkled with life and vitality. "What can I do for you?" he asked as he rolled back his chair and casually rested an ankle on top of his knee.

Carly remained standing. "First off, I'm a freight traffic supervisor. I didn't cart everything I own thousands of miles to clean your coffeepot or anything else."

"That's fine." George's smile was absent as he shuffled through the phone messages. "Contact a janitorial service. I've been meaning to do that myself."

His assurance took some of the steam from her anger. "And another thing. Brand St. Clair was in and took . . . *borrowed* a truck. He said it was an emergency and I wasn't sure if I should've stopped him."

"No problem." George glanced up, looking mildly surprised. His thoughts seemed to have drifted a thousand miles from her indignation. "One of these days that boy will come to his senses and give it up."

"'Give it up'?" Carly repeated, amused that she'd verbalized the thought.

George nodded, then set the mail aside. "I've been after Brand to join up with us. He's a good pilot." His eyes moved to Carly and he lifted one shoulder in an indifferent shrug. "Not likely, though, with all those medical bills he's paying off. He can earn twice the money freelancing."

"Medical bills?" Carly asked, curious to find out what she could about the man.

George appeared not to have heard her question. "Any other problems?"

"Not really."

He shook his head, his eyes drifting to the stack of mail. "I'll see you in the morning, then."

There was no mistaking the dismissal in his tone. Already he had turned his attention to the desk.

Carly left the office shortly afterward, wondering how much longer George would be staying. The man was apparently married to his job. There was little evidence in the office that he had a wife and family. And the hours he seemed to keep would prohibit any kind of life outside the company.

The apartment Carly had rented on Weimer Drive was a plain one-bedroom place that was barely large enough to hold all her furniture. Some of her things were being shipped from Seattle and wouldn't arrive for another month. Diana—dear, sweet Diana—couldn't believe that Carly would give up a good job in comfortable surroundings on the basis of a few phone conversations with George Hamlyn from the parent company. Her friend was convinced Carly was running. But she wasn't. Alaska offered adventure, and she'd been ready for a change.

Hugging her legs, her chin resting on her bent knees, Carly sat on the modern, overstuffed sofa in her new living room. She hadn't expected to find Alaska so beautiful. The subtle elegance, the immensity had enthralled her. Barren and dingy was what she'd been told to expect. Instead, she found the air crisp and clean. The skies were as blue as the Caribbean Sea. This state was so vast it was like a mother with her arms opened wide to lovingly bring the lost into her warm embrace.

"A mother . . ." Carly smiled absently.

The nightmare returned that night. For years she'd been free of the terror that gripped her in the dark void of sleep, but that night she woke in a cold sweat, sitting up in bed and trembling. Perspiration dotted her face, and she took several deep, calming breaths. The dream was so vivid. So real. What had brought back the childhood nightmare? Why now, after all these years?

As she laid her head against the pillow and closed her eyes, Carly attempted to form a mental image of her mother. Nothing came but a stilted picture of the tall, dark-haired stranger in the photo Carly had carried with her from foster home to foster home.

She woke the following morning feeling as if she hadn't slept all night. After the nightmare her sleep had been fitful, intermittent. Dark images played on the edges of her consciousness, shadows leaping out at her, wanting to engulf her in their dusk. Half of her yearned to surrender to the black void that beckoned, while the other half feared what she would discover if she ventured inside.

———

Brand St. Clair was sitting on the corner of her desk, one foot dangling over the edge, when Carly walked into the office later that morning.

"Morning." His greeting was casual.

"Hi." Carly's response was equally carefree. "Come to borrow another truck?"

"No. I thought I'd bring you coffee and a Danish as a peace offering."

Her gaze went to the white sack in the center of the desk. "That wasn't necessary."

He opened the sack and took out a foam cup, removing the plastic lid before handing it to her.

"Thanks."

Brand removed a second cup for himself. "I don't suppose you do any bookkeeping on the side?"

The question took her by surprise. "My dear Mr. St. Clair, I am a traffic supervisor, not an accountant." A thin thread of humorous sarcasm ran through her voice. "I haven't studied bookkeeping since high school."

Amusement flashed across his handsome features. "I'd be willing to pay you to take a look at my books. The whole accounting system is beyond me."

"You're serious, aren't you?"

He smiled. Carly studied him and speculated that the crow's-feet weren't from smiling.

"I couldn't mean it more."

Carly took the chair and crossed her long legs, hoping he'd notice her designer nylons with their tiny blue stars. "Unfortunately, I've only had a few courses in bookkeeping. I'd only make matters worse." *Dear heavens,* Carly mused, stifling a laugh. She was flirting. Blatantly flirting! She hadn't done anything so outrageous in years.

Her first impression of Brand yesterday was accurate. He was a wolf, all right, and more sensual than just about any man she knew. She guessed there was more to him than met the eye—and her response to him proved that there was more to her than she'd realized.

Whistling, George sauntered into the office, carrying a steaming mug in one hand.

"Good morning," he greeted in a cheery singsong voice. He seemed surprised to see Brand. "Good to see you, St. Clair. How did everything go yesterday?"

The glance Brand threw to Carly was decidedly uncomfortable. "Fine." The lone word was clipped and impatient.

"I talked to Jones this morning," George continued. "He explained the situation. I would have hated your losing that commission for lack of a truck."

"Commission?" Carly's dark eyes sparked with anger. "Was that before or after you rescued the poor injured hiker off Denali?"

"Hiker?" George's gaze floated from one to the other.

"You wouldn't have given me the truck otherwise," Brand inserted, ignoring George.

"You're right, I wouldn't have."

"I got a message that you wanted to see me." Brand directed his attention to George.

"As a matter of fact, I did." George adopted a businesslike attitude. "Come into the warehouse. I want to talk to you about something." He turned toward Carly and grinned sheepishly. "I don't suppose you'd mind putting on a pot of coffee? We're both going to need it before this morning's over."

Carly opened and closed her mouth. Coffee making

hadn't been listed in her job description, but she complied willingly, rather than argue.

The two men were deep in conversation as they headed toward the door. Brand stopped and turned to Carly. "Think about what I said," he murmured, and smiled. It was one of those bone-melting, earth-shattering smiles meant to disarm the most sophisticated of women. But the amazing part of it all was that he didn't seem to recognize the effect he had on her. The gesture should have disarmed her; instead, it only served to confuse her further.

She was busy at her desk when Brand returned alone a half hour later.

"I meant what I said about paying you for some book-keeping."

"I'm sorry," she returned on a falsely cheerful note, "but I'm busy. There's an important rescue I'm performing in Denali Park this weekend."

Brand didn't look pleased.

To hide her smile, Carly pretended an inordinate interest in her work, making a show of shuffling papers around. "Was there anything else?"

Slowly, his gaze traveled over her. When he didn't answer right away, Carly looked up. She had been angry at his deception, disliking the way he'd gone about borrowing the truck. But one look and she had to fight her way out of the whirlpooling effect he had on her senses.

"Think about it," he said in a slightly husky voice.

"There isn't anything to think about," she returned smoothly, her tone belying the erratic pounding of her heart. When he walked out the door, Carly was shocked to discover that her fingers were trembling. "Get a hold of yourself, old girl," she chastised herself in a breathy murmur, half surprised, half angry at her reaction to this man. Brand St. Clair had an uncanny knack for forcing her to recognize her own sensuality. And Carly found that highly disturbing.

As the week progressed, Carly couldn't decide if she was pleased or disconcerted when she didn't see Brand again. Her job was settling into a routine aside from a few minor clashes with George. He gladly surrendered the paperwork to her, preferring that she handle the collection and claims while he took care of the routing.

On Friday afternoon Brand strolled through the office door and beamed her a bright smile. "Hello again."

"Hello." Carly forced an answering smile. "George is out for the day."

"I know. It's you I wanted to see."

"Oh." She swallowed uncomfortably, disliking the way her heart reacted to seeing him again.

"I just stopped by to see if you'd be interested in going flying with me tomorrow."

Carly stared at him blankly, confronted with the choice of owning up to what she was feeling or ignoring this growing awareness. In all honesty, she'd prefer it if he walked out the door and left her alone.

"Why me?" She didn't mean to sound so sharp, but she wanted to know what had prompted him to seek her out. Had she been flashing him subliminal messages?

His eyes narrowed fractionally. "I want your company. Is that a crime? Come fly with me."

Carly hesitated. His challenge was open enough, and

she found that the answer came just as easily. She wanted his company, too. True, Brand possessed a dangerous quality that captivated as well as alarmed her. One flight with him could prove to be devastating. But she'd love to fly. "How long will we be gone?" Not that it mattered; she hadn't planned to do anything more than unpack boxes.

"Most of the day. We'll leave in the morning and be back in time for me to take you to dinner." His faint drawl enticed her.

"What time do you want me to meet you?" she asked. Red lights were flashing all around her, but Carly chose to ignore their warning. Brand St. Clair was a challenge—and she'd never been able to resist that. In some ways it was a fault, and in others it was her greatest strength.

The next morning, as Carly dressed in jeans and a thick jacket, she wondered at the wisdom of her actions. Only when she was strapped into the seat of the Cessna 150, her adrenaline pumping at the roar of the engine, did she realize how excited she was. She started to ask Brand about the panel full of gauges when she was interrupted by the voice of the air traffic controller, who gave them clearance for takeoff.

Brand turned and gifted her with another of his earth-shattering smiles before taxiing onto the runway and pulling back on the throttle. Then, with an unbelievable burst of power, they were airborne. Her stomach lurched as the wheels left the safety of the ground—but with exhilaration, not alarm.

Looking out the window, Carly watched as the

ground below took on an unreal quality. She had flown several times, but sitting in a commercial airliner was a different experience compared to floating in the sky in a small private plane.

"This is fantastic." She shouted to be heard above the roar of the engine. The skies were blue, with only a few powder-puff clouds, the view below unobstructed. "Will we see Mount McKinley?"

"Not this trip. We're headed in the opposite direction."

Carly responded with a short nod. She was anxious to view North America's highest mountain. Mount Rainier, outside Seattle, and the Cascade Range featured distinctive peaks, but from what she'd read about McKinley, the mountain was more blunt, less angular than anything she'd seen.

"It's so green," she shouted, and pointed to the dense forest below. When Carly had made up her mind to take this job, her first thought had been that she would be leaving the abundant beauty of Washington behind. "I'm really impressed," she said with a warm smile.

Brand's gaze slid to her. "What would it take for *me* to impress you?"

Carly threw back her head and laughed, refusing to play his game. There wasn't much he could do that would impress her more than he had already.

Brand took her hand and squeezed it. "What did your family think about you moving north?"

Carly was reluctant to admit she didn't have a family. "They didn't say anything. I'm over twenty-one." The lie was a minor one. She'd never known her father, and only God knew the whereabouts of her mother. The longest

Carly had ever stayed in one foster home was four years. With only herself to rely on, she'd become strong in ways that others were weak. Carly didn't need anyone but herself.

"How long have you been flying?" She discovered that the best way to defuse questions was to ask one of her own.

"I've flown since I was a kid. My dad owned an appliance business and traveled all over Oregon. I took my first flying lessons at sixteen, but by that time I had been in the air a thousand times."

"Are you from Portland?"

He answered with an abrupt nod.

"What made you come to Alaska?"

He didn't hesitate. "The money."

Carly remembered George saying something about heavy expenses. "Medical bills, right?"

Brand turned to study her. Carly met his gaze. "Yes," he answered, without elaborating. Carly didn't question him further.

His attention returned to the sky, and Carly watched as a proud mask came over him, letting her know that this subject was off-limits. The transformation in him confused her. She was unsure of Brand, but he didn't intimidate her. In some ways she sensed that they were alike. Each had buried hurts that were best not shared so early in a relationship. Sighing, she glanced away. His attitude shouldn't bother her.

They were both quiet for a long time. "What do you think of Alaska?" Brand asked her unexpectedly, as if he were attempting to lighten the mood that had settled over them.

"I love it," Carly responded freely. "Of course, I haven't survived an Alaskan winter yet, so I might answer your question differently a year from now."

"A lot of people see Alaska as big and lonely. Its appeal isn't for everyone." His smile was wry.

"Alaska is isolated, that much I'll grant you. But not lonely. I've sat in a crowded room and been more alone than at any time in my life. Alaska demands and challenges, but not everyone is meant to face that—"

Abruptly, Carly broke off and bit her lip. This was the very thing that had attracted her to this frozen land of America's last frontier.

Brand studied her, his expression revealing surprise at her answer. "George purposely hired someone in early spring," he told her. "Only a fool would move to Anchorage in winter."

"That bad?" She, too, hoped to lighten the mood.

"You have to live through one to believe it." The edges of his mouth deepened to reveal a smile.

"I'll make it," Carly returned confidently. She wasn't completely ignorant. Diana had taken delight in relaying the fact that temperatures of twenty degrees below zero weren't uncommon during the winter months in Anchorage. Carly had known what to expect when she'd accepted the job.

"I don't doubt that you will." His dark gaze skimmed her face. "I like you, Carly Grieves," he admitted, his voice low and gravelly, as if he hadn't meant to tell her as much.

"And I trust you about as far as I can throw you," she teased. "But then, I'm stronger than I look."

———

Once they returned, they ate in a restaurant not far from the Anchorage International Airport. A companionable silence hung between them. The men Carly had dated in the past were talkers; she preferred it that way. The experience of sharing a meal with a man she had seen only a handful of times and feeling this kind of communication was beyond her experience, and that excited her.

They rode back to the airport, where Carly had left her car. "Come into my office and I'll show you around," Brand invited. "I'll put some coffee on."

"I'd like that."

He opened her door for her, and she followed him into the small building that served as his office.

A flicker of uncertainty passed over Carly's features as she entered the one-room office. The area was too private, too isolated. Once inside the darkened room, Brand didn't make any pretense of getting coffee. Instead, he turned her into his arms; a hand on each shoulder burned through her thick jacket. He seared her with a bold look as his eyes ran over her.

"I'm not interested in coffee," he muttered thickly.

"I knew that," she answered in a whisper.

His hand cupped the underside of her face as his thumb tested the fullness of her mouth. When his hand fell away, Carly involuntarily moistened her lips.

She watched, fascinated, as a veiled question came into his eyes. He looked as if he were making up his mind whether to kiss her or not. His fingers slid into her hair, weaving through the dark strands and tilting her head back. Although her heart was pounding wildly, she continued to study him with an unwavering look. His eyes were narrow and unreadable.

With a small groan, he fit his mouth to hers. Carly opened her lips in welcome. The kiss was the most unusual she had ever experienced: gentle, tender, soft . . . almost tentative. Gradually, he deepened the contact, his arms pulling her closer until she was molded tight against him. His hands roamed her back, arching her body as close as possible as his mouth courted hers, exploring one side of her lips and working his way to the other in a sensuous attack that melted any resistance.

He broke away, his mouth mere inches above hers. His warm breath fanned her face as his fingers worked the buttons of her coat. Again his mouth covered hers in long, drugging kisses as he slipped the coat from her shoulders and let it fall unheeded to the floor.

Carly fought for control of her senses. This was too much too soon, but she couldn't tear herself away. The throbbing ache his mouth, his hands, his body were creating within her was slowly consuming her will.

She moaned softly as he buried his face in the curve of her throat. Her eyes closed as she tangled her fingers in the hair that grew at the nape of his neck.

"Brand." Breathlessly, she whispered his name, not sure why she had.

Instantly he went still, as if the sound of her voice had brought him to his senses. His hand closed over her wrists and pulled them free.

"What's wrong?" she pleaded.

He took a step in retreat. His eyes no longer met hers, but were cast down at the floor as he took in deep breaths. When he looked up and ran a hand along the back of his neck, Carly saw something flicker in his eyes that could be read as regret or guilt or perhaps shock.

The world came to a stop as she realized what must have happened. How could she have been so blind not to see what was right in front of her? All the clues were there. She'd been so stupid. A coldness settled over her as a hoarseness filled her throat.

"You're married, aren't you?"

Chapter Two

"No." Brand issued the single word with a vengeance.

"I'm not entirely stupid—" Carly's voice became a whisper.

"I'm a widower," Brand interrupted harshly, wiping a hand across his face.

It doesn't matter, Carly's mind screamed as she retrieved her coat. If she hadn't been so blinded by her pure physical attraction to him, she would have recognized those blatant red lights for what they were. His wife might be dead, but it didn't make any difference.

"Carly, listen."

She ignored him, irritated with herself for her own stupidity. "I had a great time today," she murmured.

"Carly, I want to explain."

She could hear the frustrated anger in his voice. The anger wasn't directed at her, but inward. Every dictate of her will demanded she turn around and run from the building. Both hands were tucked deep within her pockets as she took a step backward. "Thank you for dinner. We'll have to do it again sometime." Not waiting for his response, she hurried from the office. By the time she reached her car, Carly's knees felt as though they could no longer support her.

When she arrived back at her apartment she had an upset stomach. *Brand had been married.* Forcing herself to breathe evenly, she deliberately walked around the living room, running her hand over the back of the sofa. Everything she owned had been purchased new. She wouldn't take second best in anything. Not clothes, not cars, not jobs. After a life filled with secondhand goods and a hand-me-down childhood, she wasn't about to start now—especially with a man. All right, she was being unreasonable, she knew that; Diana had taken delight in telling her so a hundred times. But Carly didn't see any reason to change. She liked herself the way she was—unreasonable or not.

Three days later, she was still unable to shake the confusion and disappointment that Brand's announcement had produced. She'd made up her mind not to see him again. Yet her mind entertained thoughts of him at the oddest times. She forced his image from her brain, determined to blot him from her life completely.

Thursday evening, when the phone rang, Carly stared at it in surprise. The telephone company had installed it at the beginning of the week and, although she'd made several calls out, she had yet to receive one.

"Hello."

"Carly?" The voice reverberated, sounding as if it came from the moon.

"Diana?" The soft echo of her words returned over the line.

"I couldn't stand it another minute. I had to find out how everything's going. I miss you like crazy," Diana said softly. Then, as if she'd admitted more than she'd wanted to, she quickly changed the subject. "How's Alaska? Have you seen any moose yet?"

"No moose, and I love Alaska," Carly responded enthusiastically, knowing that her friend was uncomfortable sharing emotions. "It's vast, untouched, beautiful."

"That's not the way I heard it," Diana said, and released a frustrated sigh. "How's the job and the mysterious George Hamlyn?"

"We've had a few minor clashes, but all in all everything's working out great."

"After all I did to convince you to stay in Seattle, you wouldn't admit anything else," Diana chided. "How's the apartment?"

"Adequate. I'm looking into buying a condo."

"I knew it." Diana didn't bother to disguise her friendly censure. "I wondered how long you'd last in a *used* apartment."

"It's not that old," Carly responded with a dry smile. Her friend knew her too well.

"When are you going to get over this quirk of yours?"

"Quirk?" Carly feigned ignorance, not wanting to argue.

"No, it's become more than that." The teasing quality left Diana's voice. "It's an obsession."

"Just because I happen to prefer new things doesn't

make me obsessive. I can afford the condominium." But barely. The payments would eat a huge hole in her monthly paycheck.

"How's Barney?" Carly quickly changed the subject. "Have you got a ring through his nose yet?"

Diana's laugh sounded forced. "So-so. If I'm going to marry again, you can bet that this time I'm going to be sure."

"I've heard love is better the third time around."

"Love maybe, marriage never. Besides, that's supposed to be the *second* time around."

"In your case I had to improvise."

Diana gave a weak snort. "I don't know why I put up with you."

"I do," Carly supplied, with the confidence of many years of friendship. "I'm the little girl you've always wanted to mother. Problem is, I'm only six years younger than you."

"I'm feeling every minute of thirty-one. Why'd you bring that up?"

"Good friend, I guess."

"Too good. Listen, sweetie, I'm worried about you. Don't let your pride stand in the way if you want out of that godforsaken igloo."

"Honestly." Carly released an exasperated breath. "I'm perfectly capable of taking care of myself. So straighten up, crack the whip over Barney's head, and quit being such a worrier. I'm doing fine on my own."

"True. You don't need me to louse up your life, especially since I've done such a bang-up job of screwing up my own. You'll keep in touch, won't you?"

"A letter's already in the mail," Carly assured her.

"I suppose I should go."

"It's good to hear your voice, my friend."

Diana sighed softly. "You're the best friend I've ever had. Take care of yourself and let me know when you've come to your senses and want to head home."

"I will," Carly promised. But she wouldn't be moving back to Seattle. In fact, she doubted that she ever would. Alaska felt *right*. In a few short weeks it seemed more like she thought a home should be than anything she'd known as a child.

Late Friday afternoon, as Carly was working on a claim, George sauntered into the office, an oily pink rag dangling from his back pocket. He'd been working with a mechanic. It hadn't taken Carly long to discover that George was a man of many talents.

"Get Brand St. Clair on the line for me," he said on his way to the coffeepot.

Carly's fingers tightened around the pencil she held. As much as she'd fought against it, Brand had remained on her mind all week.

Flipping through the pages of the telephone directory, Carly located Brand's number and punched the buttons of the phone with the tip of her eraser. She would be polite but distant, she decided. He hadn't made any attempt to contact her this week, so apparently he was aware of her feelings toward him.

With the receiver cradled against her shoulder, Carly continued working on the claim.

"No answer," she told her employer, hoping the relief in her voice was well disguised.

"Leave a voicemail and try again in five minutes," George returned irritably. "That boy wears too many hats. He's working himself to death."

Carly had punched out Brand's number so many times by the end of the afternoon that she could have done it in her sleep. At five-thirty she straightened the top of her desk and removed her purse from the bottom drawer. George was talking to a mechanic when she stepped outside to tell him she hadn't been able to reach Brand.

"I never did get hold of St. Clair." The brisk wind whipped her shoulder-length hair about her face until it stung her cheeks.

George glanced at Carly with a smile of chagrin. "Since it isn't out of your way, would you mind stopping off at his office and leaving a message on the door?"

Carly swallowed tightly. "Sure."

"Tell him I've got a couple of jobs for him next week and ask him to give me a call."

"Consider it done." She turned before he could see her reaction. She didn't object to doing George a favor. What she wanted was to avoid Brand. If someone were to see her and tell him she'd been by, he could misinterpret her coming.

The portion of the airfield that housed Brand's office was only a mile or so from Alaska Freight Forwarding. As Carly eased her vehicle into the space nearest his office, she noticed him walking toward her from the airfield. He'd obviously returned from a flight and had just finished securing his aircraft. Carly groaned inwardly and climbed out of her car.

Six days had passed since she'd last seen him, but

time had done little to wipe out the pure physical impact of seeing him again. His glance was dry, emotionless, as he moved closer, his face lean and weathered from the sun. Mature.

"Hello." He stopped in front of her, revealing none of his feelings. The least he could do was look pleased to see her!

"George sent me over with a message." It was important that he understand she hadn't come of her own accord.

His nod was curt.

"He wanted me to tell you he has work for you next week if you're interested." She prayed the slight breathlessness in her voice would go undetected.

"I'm interested."

A shiver skipped over her skin at the lazy, sensual way he studied her. Carly had the crazy sensation that his interest wasn't in the flying jobs.

"You're on your way home?" he asked her unexpectedly.

Her eyes refused to meet his. "Yes. It's been a long week." Goodness, she shouldn't have said that. He might think she'd been waiting for his call.

"Have you got time to stop someplace for a drink?"

"No." The word slipped out with the rising swell of panic that threatened to engulf her.

"Why not?" he demanded.

"Let's just say that I consider married men off-limits. Even widowers. Especially widowers who have eyes that say, 'I loved my wife.'"

"I can't argue with you about that," Brand agreed easily. "I did love Sandra."

"That's the way it's supposed to be." Carly was sincere. She couldn't imagine Brand not having loved . . . Sandra. Her mind had difficulty forming the name. It was easier to think of Brand's wife as a nonentity. "Well, it was nice seeing you again." She fumbled in her purse for her keys.

"Do you have anything against friendship?" Brand's features suggested a wealth of pride and strength. In the shadows of early afternoon, they appeared more pronounced.

"Everyone needs somebody." Reluctantly, she turned back. She was thinking about Diana, the only true friend she'd ever had.

"Are we capable of that, Carly?" He refused to release her gaze.

Unable to find the words to answer him, she shrugged.

"Surely a drink between friends wouldn't be so bad."

She remained unsure. "I won't date you, Brand." Making that much clear was important.

"Not to worry." He beamed her a dazzling smile. "This isn't a date. Friends?" He extended his hand to her.

Her mind was yelling at her, telling her this wouldn't work. But it didn't seem to matter as she held out her hand to him for a curt shake.

Mentally chastising herself every block of the way, she followed him to a lounge, parking her car in the space beside his. Together they stepped into the dimly lit room.

Brand cupped her elbow, but when Carly involuntarily stiffened, he dropped his hand. "Sorry, I forgot we're just friends," he said, as they walked across the room.

No sooner were they seated when a waitress appeared. Carly was undecided about what she wanted to drink, and while she was making up her mind, Brand took charge and ordered for her.

"I prefer to order for myself," she said after the waitress had gone, disliking the way he had taken control. She wasn't his date. He went still, then shrugged. "Sorry, I keep forgetting."

He was strangely quiet then, Carly thought, considering the way he'd pressed the invitation on her. After a few minutes of small talk he settled back in his chair, seemingly content to listen to the music.

"I don't know what to make of you," Carly said, uncomfortable with the finely strung tension between them.

"Little wonder," he said with a wry grin, and took a sip of his Scotch. "You've been on my mind all week."

Carly sat upright and leaned forward. "I don't think friends are necessarily on one another's minds."

He discounted her words with an ardent shake of his head. "Some friends are. Trust me here."

"The last man who asked me to trust him trapped me thirty thousand feet in the air and demanded that we make love."

"What did you do?" He straightened slightly, the line of his jaw tightening.

Carly smiled, taking a sip of her wine before she spoke. "Simple. I jumped. He was my skydiving instructor."

"Did everything turn out all right?"

"Depends on how you look at it. I wrenched my ankle

and landed a mile off target. But on the other hand, it felt good to outsmart that creep."

"My goodness, you live an adventuresome life."

"That's nothing compared to what happened to me the weekend I climbed Mount Rainier."

"I don't think I want to hear this," he murmured, nursing his drink. "Have you always had this penchant for danger?"

"It never starts out that way, but I seem to walk blindly into it." She leaned against the back of the chair, a hand circling her wineglass.

"Have dinner with me?" Then he quickly added. "As friends, of course."

Carly knew she should decline, but something within her wouldn't let her refuse. "All right, but I have the feeling I was safer on Mount Rainier."

He smiled as he rose and led the way into the restaurant that was connected to the lounge.

Once they were seated at the red upholstered booth, a middle-aged waitress in a black skirt and peasant blouse handed them each a menu.

Quickly, Carly surveyed the items listed, mainly a variety of seafood and steak dishes. "If you don't mind, I'll order for myself this time," she teased, keeping her gaze centered on the oblong menu.

"Red wine was Sandra's favorite drink." Brand's words seemed to come out of nowhere.

"Oh." Carly shut her eyes tightly and set the menu aside. "I wish you hadn't told me that."

"I was just as shocked as you when it slipped out."

Carly half slid from the booth. "I think I'd better leave."

"Don't go. Please."

Carly had the impression he didn't often ask something of anyone. She stopped, her heart beating at double time.

"Did I ever tell you about the time I came face-to-face with a Kodiak?" he asked.

"A bear?"

His gaze was intent as he studied his water glass. "Crazy as it sounds, I'm more frightened now here with you."

Carly exhaled, releasing her breath in a rush. "Good grief, we're a fine couple."

He smiled. "We're only . . ."

"Friends." They said it together and laughed.

"All right," Brand said, and breathed in a wobbly breath. "I'll admit it. This is the first time I've been out with a woman since Sandra died. She's been gone almost two years now. But the past is meant to be a guidepost, not a hitching post. I need a . . . friend."

Carly had been unsure this friendship would work from the moment he'd first suggested it. He seemed to confirm her suspicions every minute she was with him. "Brand, I don't know."

"You're not even trying. At least hear me out. It's been a while since I was into the dating scene. I realize you don't want to date me. I don't understand why, but apparently it's an issue with you. But I was thinking that maybe I could practice with you. We could go out a couple of times until I see what kind of action there is." His tone was suddenly light, casual.

"Not on dates." Her fingers surrounded her wineglass, and a chill moved up her arm and stopped at her heart.

"No, these wouldn't be *real* dates."

"Just practice, until you find someone who interests you?" Something deep inside her said she was going to regret this. Diana should be the one he was talking to. Diana was the rescuer. Not her.

Brand lifted his gaze until their eyes met, granting Carly the opportunity to study his face. His mood had shifted again, and now she realized that the look she had recognized earlier wasn't maturity but pain. Without him saying a word she realized he'd been through hell. His wife's death had brought him to his knees and nearly broken him. Carly's first response was a desire to ease that pain. Such intense feelings were foreign to her.

"I can't see how it would hurt, as long as we both understand each other," she said cautiously.

The waitress came and took their order.

"How'd we get so serious?" Brand's smile was forced, but the effort relaxed the planes of his face, and again Carly found herself responding involuntarily.

"I don't know."

"Let's talk about something else. As I recall, women like to talk about themselves."

"Not this woman. I'd bore you to death," Carly returned, with a weak laugh. "I was born, grew up, graduated, found a job . . ." She hesitated, her eyes smiling into his. "Shall I continue?"

"Seattle?"

"Mostly." The tip of her index finger circled the rim of her wineglass. "What about you?"

He answered her question with another of his own: "What about men?"

"What about them?" Carly shot back.

"You've never married?"

"No." Her laugh was light. "Not even close."

"Sandra and I were barely out of college . . ."

Carly sighed with relief when the waitress returned, delivering their meals. She didn't want to hear about Brand's wife. Yet in another way it was good that she did, because it reminded her that it would be a colossal mistake to fall in love with Brand.

Carly's salad was piled high with crab. Lemon wedges dipped in paprika decorated the edges, and thin slices of hard-boiled eggs defined the bowl. "This looks wonderful." Picking up her fork, she dipped into the crisp lettuce leaves. Brand followed suit, and they ate in silence. Several times during the meal Carly felt Brand watching her, his gaze disconcerting, making her uncomfortable.

"Did I commit some faux pas?" she asked, setting aside her fork as she met his eyes.

"No. Why?" Brand glanced up curiously.

"The looks you've been giving me make me think I've got Thousand Island dressing all over my chin."

"No, you haven't." Brand's chuckle was low and sensuous.

To avoid his look, Carly glanced into the lounge. Couples with arms wrapped around each other were dancing on the small polished floor to the slow music. Dancing had never been her forte, but the thought of Brand holding her produced a willful fascination. She shook her head to dispel the image.

"Do you dance?" she asked, but frankly she hoped his response would be negative.

His fork paused midway to his mouth as he gave her a startled glance.

Carly looked away. "Don't look so shocked. My interest was purely academic. It wouldn't be a good idea for us to dance."

"Why not?"

"Because—" She swallowed. He was enjoying her discomfort. "Well, because of the close body contact . . . I just don't think it would be a good idea . . . for us, seeing that we're only friends."

"But I'll need to practice a few times, don't you think?"

"No," she said, wishing now she'd never introduced the subject. "Dancing is like riding a bicycle. It all comes back to you even if you haven't gone riding in a long time." She pushed her plate aside, indicating that she was finished with her meal.

Brand mumbled something under his breath. Carly didn't catch all of it, but what she did hear caused hot color to warm her cheeks. He'd said something about hoping that the same was true when it came to lovemaking.

While Brand paid for their dinner, Carly wandered outside. With hands thrust deep into her jacket pockets, she stared at the dark sky. The stars looked like rare jewels laid out on folds of black satin. The moonlight cleared a path through the still night. With her face turned toward the heavens, Carly walked past their parked cars and down the narrow sidewalk. Alaska was supposed to be cold and ruthless. Yet she felt warm and content, as if she belonged here and would never want to leave. Brand had reminded her that she hadn't suffered through an Alaskan winter. But the thought didn't frighten her. She was ready for that challenge.

Brand joined her. "I want to tell you about Sandra."

Carly didn't want to hear about the wife he'd loved and lost, but she recognized that Brand needed to tell her. If he talked things out with her, a virtual stranger, maybe then he could bury the past.

"We met in college. I guess I told you that, didn't I?"

Carly's hands formed fists deep inside her pockets. "Yes . . . yes, you did."

"She was probably one of the most beautiful women I've ever seen. Blond and petite. And so full of life. You couldn't walk into a room full of people and not find Sandra. Funny thing, though—she was the quiet sort. She didn't like a lot of attention." His face sharpened. "We were married almost eight years."

Carly's heart was pounding frantically. Each pain-filled word seemed to come at her like an assault. He didn't need to say how difficult it was for him to speak of his wife. It was evident in his voice, in the way he looked straight ahead, in the way he walked.

"She had myelocytic leukemia. The most difficult type to treat and cure. We knew in the beginning her chances of beating it were only one in five. Watching her die was agony." He paused, waiting several moments before he continued speaking. "But death was her victory. She was at peace. She had every right to be bitter and angry, but that wasn't her way. I struggled to hold on to her, but in the end she asked me to let her go and I did. She closed her eyes and within the hour she was gone."

Carly felt tears form, which she quickly blinked away, embarrassed that he would see the emotion his story caused in her.

They continued walking for a long time, neither speaking. Carly didn't know what to say. Any words of comfort wouldn't have made it past the huge lump in her throat.

"I loved her," he said in a low, tortured voice. "A part of me will go to the grave grieving for Sandra."

Carly's heart swelled with emotion as she searched desperately for some way to communicate her regret. But no words would come. She wanted to tell him she understood how hard it must have been to release the one he loved. But she couldn't pretend to know how much it had cost him to watch his wife die. Gently, she laid her hand on his forearm, wanting to let him know her feelings.

Brand's fingers gripped hers as he paused and turned toward her. Tenderly, he brushed the hair from her face and kissed her forehead. "Thank you," he said simply.

"I didn't do anything." Her voice sounded weak and wobbly.

"Just by listening, you've done more than you know," he whispered, and took her hand in his. Silently, their hands linked, they strolled down the moonlit sidewalk.

Carly had a difficult time sleeping that night. Brand hadn't attempted to hold or kiss her, and for that she was grateful. She didn't know if she had the strength to refuse him anything. The thought was scary. Everything about Brand confused her. If she had a rational head on her shoulders she wouldn't have anything more to do with him. But he was a rare kind of man, more rare than the gold that had prompted so many into Alaska's fertile land a hundred years before.

For a long while she lay awake, watching shadows dancing on the walls taunting her. She shouldn't see him again, she told herself. Yet she could hardly wait for to-morrow afternoon, when they had planned to meet again.

Carly awoke the next morning with renewed determina-tion. Brand needed her . . . for now. She didn't walk away from anything. Her independence, her ability to meet challenges, had become her trademark. Friends didn't desert each other in times of need. And this was a crucial time in Brand's life. A time of transition. She would help him through that, be his friend. Perhaps she would even have the opportunity to introduce him to a few women.

Falling back against her pillow, Carly released a long, tortured sigh. Who did she think she was kidding? Intro-duce Brand to another woman? She nearly laughed out loud.

The phone rang just as she stepped into the shower. Wrapping a towel around herself, she hobbled into the living room, leaving a trail of water behind her.

"Yes," she breathed irritably into the receiver.

"Carly?" It was Brand. "You sound angry. What's wrong?"

"Some idiot phoned and got me out of the shower."

"Don't tell me you're standing there naked." His voice became low and slightly husky.

"I am standing in a puddle of water, catching a chill."

His warm chuckle quickened her heartbeat. "I won't keep you. I just wanted to make sure you hadn't changed your mind about this afternoon."

"I probably should. But no, I'll be ready when you get here."

Carly dressed in designer jeans, cowboy boots, and a Western-style plaid shirt. She was putting the finishing touches on her makeup when the doorbell rang. A hurried glance in the mirror assured her that she looked fine.

"Good afternoon," she said, and smiled a greeting. Her heart warmed at the sight Brand presented in gray slacks and a loose-fitting blue V-neck sweater. The long sleeves were pushed up past his elbows.

"I'm not dressed too casually, am I?" They were attending an art show. Diana thought Carly's generally informal dress outrageous. But Carly was herself and wore what she wanted, where she wanted. Cowboy boots and jeans sounded fine for an art show to her.

"Not at all." He smiled, holding her gaze for several seconds. He wrinkled his nose appreciatively and sniffed the air. "What smells so good?"

"Probably my perfume," she said, and playfully exposed her neck to him.

"It smells like clams."

Carly released a heavy sigh. "I hope you realize that you're going to have to learn to be a little more romantic than that. I had a bowl of clam chowder for lunch."

"I'll try thinking romantic thoughts, then. That's good advice." He helped her into her three-quarter-length leather jacket.

"Tell me about the art show. I'm not much into the abstract stuff, but I like the Impressionists."

His hand snaked out across her shoulder. "You'll like this show," he promised. "I don't want to tell you too much. I want your opinion to be unbiased."

"I know what I like."

"Spoken like a true expert."

The Anchorage Civic Center was crowded when they arrived, and they were forced to park several blocks down the street. Inside, people were clustered around a variety of paintings and sculptures.

With Brand at her side, Carly wandered from one exhibit to another. Not until she was halfway through the show did she see the painting of the child. Abruptly, she stopped, causing Brand to bump against her. He murmured something, but she didn't hear him as she walked to the lifelike oil painting.

The child was no more than five. Vulnerable, lost, hurting. Her pale pink dress was torn, the hem unraveled. Her scuffed shoes had holes, and one foot was dejectedly turned inward. The tousled hair needed to be combed. But it was the eyes that captured Carly's attention. Round, blue, and proud. So proud they defied her circumstances.

Carly stared at the painting for a long time before she noted that, in the far corner of one of the child's eyes, a tear had formed. Emotion rose within her. This was Carly as a child; this was the little girl in the nightmare.

Chapter Three

The dream was always the same. It ran through her mind like flickering scenes from a silent movie. She was small, not more than five, and hungry. So hungry that her stomach was empty and hurting. It was morning and she couldn't wake her mother. Several times she'd gone into the other bedroom and pulled at her mother's arm, but to no avail. At first Carly crawled back into her bed and cried, whimpering until she fell asleep. When she woke a second time, her stomach rumbled and gnawed at her. Sitting up, she decided she would cook her own breakfast.

The refrigerator was almost empty, but she found an egg. Mother always cooked those, and Carly thought she knew how. Filling the pan with water, she placed it on the stove and turned the knob. Then, afraid of a spanking, she ran into her mother's room and tried to shake her awake. But the dark-haired woman growled angrily at Carly and said to leave her alone.

Standing on a kitchen chair, Carly watched the egg tumble in the angry, boiling water. She didn't know how long Mother cooked things. Her mistake came when she pulled the pan from the stove. The bubbling water sloshed over the side and burned her small fingers. When she cried out and jerked her hand away, the pan of boiling water slid to the edge of the stove and toppled down her front.

This was the point where Carly always woke, usually in a cold sweat, her body rigid with terror. The dream had always been vivid, so very real. She didn't know if she had been burned as a child. No scars marred her body. There was only the dream that returned to haunt her at the oddest times.

"Carly." Brand's large hand rested on her shoulder. "Are you all right? You've gone pale."

"I want to buy this picture."

"Buy it?" Brand repeated. "It could run in the thousands of dollars."

Carly shook her head and shrugged his hand from her shoulder. She didn't want him near. Not now. She raised her fingertips to her forehead and ran them down the side of her face as she continued to study the portrait.

Of course, the child wasn't really her; she recognized that. The eyes were the wrong color, the hair too straight and dark. But the pain that showed so clearly through those intense eyes was as close to Carly's own as she had ever seen.

"The program states that this painting isn't for sale," Brand said from behind her.

Frustration washed through Carly. "I'll talk to the artist and change his mind."

"Her," Brand corrected softly. "Carly?" His voice contained an uncharacteristic appeal. "Look at your program."

Forcefully, she moved her gaze from the painting that had mesmerized her and glanced down at the sheet she'd been handed as she walked in the center door. For a moment her gaze refused to focus on the printed description. The painting was titled simply *Girl. A Self-Portrait* by Jutta Hoverson.

"Is she here?" Carly was surprised at how weak her voice was. "I'd like to meet her."

Brand placed his hand on her shoulder, as if to protect her from any unpleasantness, a gesture Carly found almost amusing. "I think you should read the front of your program," he said gently.

He was so insistent that Carly turned it over to examine what it was Brand found so important. The instant she read the heading she sighed and sadly shook her head. The art show was a collection of works done by prisoners: murderers, thieves, rapists, and only God knew what else.

Carly lifted her gaze from the program to the oil painting. "I wonder what crime she committed."

"I thought you knew."

"It doesn't matter. I still want this picture," she murmured, noting the way Brand was studying her. She didn't want to explain why this was so important to her. She couldn't.

"You feel more than just art appreciation," he said, as his gaze skimmed her face thoroughly.

"Yes, I do." Levelly, she met his look, which seemed to pierce her protective shield. She opened her mouth to explain, but nothing came out. "I . . . I was poor as a child." She couldn't say it. Something deep and dark was restraining the words. Being raised in foster homes wasn't a terrible tragedy. She'd been properly cared for, without the stigma that often accompanied girls in her circumstances. Having never known her mother might have been the best thing. The woman was a stranger, an alcoholic. For reasons of her own, her mother had never put Carly up for adoption. Carly resented that; the right to a normal family life had been denied her because her mother had refused to sign the relinquishment papers. As an adult, Carly thought that it wasn't love that had prompted her mother to hold on to her rights but guilt.

"You might write"—Brand hesitated as he turned the program over, seeking the artist's name—"Jutta Hoverson and ask her to change her mind. It says here that she's at the Purdy Women's Correctional Facility. If I remember correctly, that's somewhere near Tacoma."

"I will," Carly confirmed. Jutta Hoverson might be a stranger, but already Carly felt a certain kinship with her. She continued to stare at the painting, having trouble taking her eyes from something that so clearly represented a part of her past. "There, but for the grace of God, go I." She hadn't meant to speak the words aloud.

"What makes you say that?" Brand questioned.

Carly's momentary glance of surprise gave way to a dry smile. "Several things." She didn't elaborate.

Although they spent another hour at the show, Carly's gaze continued to drift back to the painting of the child. Each time she examined it she saw more of herself:

It was all there, in the dejected stance, the way one small foot was turned inward . . . in the hurt so clearly revealed in the eyes, the solitary tear that spoke of so much pain. So often in her life Carly had resisted crying, holding herself back until her stomach ached with the need to vent her emotion. Tears were considered a sign of weakness, and she wouldn't grant herself permission for such a display of helplessness.

The apartment looked bleak and dingy when they returned. Carly paused just inside the door, unable to decide if it was the apartment itself or her mood. Brand had followed her inside, although she hadn't issued an invitation.

"Carly." Just the way Brand said her name caused a warmth to spread through her. One large hand rested on each of her shoulders from behind. "Won't you tell me what's troubling you? You've been pensive and brooding all afternoon. Ever since you saw the painting."

"It's nothing," she said, as she unbuttoned her coat, forcing his hands from her shoulders as she slipped it from her arms and hung it in the closet. She couldn't very well ask him to leave without being rude, but she wanted to be alone for now.

"I'm sorry the show brought back memories you'd rather forget. But I think this is just the kind of thing friends are for. I spilled my guts last night. Now it's your turn." He lowered his long frame onto her sofa and leaned forward, his elbows resting on his knees, lacing his fingers together. "Talk. I'll try to be as good a listener as you were last night."

"I . . ." Carly's arms folded around her middle. "I . . . can't." She bit her lip. Brand's frustration was in his eyes for her to read. Her own feelings were ambivalent. She wanted to be alone, yet in an inexplicable way she wanted him there. The intense longing she felt for him to hold her was almost frightening. "What I need is time. Alone, if you don't mind."

"No problem." He jerked himself to his feet and was gone before she could say another word.

"Damn." She was being stupid and she knew it. But that didn't change the intensity of her feelings. Nor did it alter her black mood.

That night, Carly sat in the kitchen as she wrote a letter to Jutta Hoverson. Page after page of discarded attempts littered the table. There were so many things she wanted to say and no way she knew of putting them into words. After midnight, she settled on a few short sentences that simply asked Jutta if she would be willing to reconsider and sell the portrait.

Even after the letter was completed, Carly couldn't sleep. She hadn't meant to offend Brand, but she clearly had. He had revealed a deep and painful part of his own past, and she had shunned him this afternoon when it would have been natural to tell him why the painting had made such an impression on her.

She'd hesitated to open herself to him. The words had danced in her mind, but she'd been unable to say them. True, she didn't make a point of telling people her circumstances, but she didn't hide them, either. Something about the afternoon—and Brand—had made her reluctant to reveal her past.

———

No more sure of the answers when she awoke the next morning, Carly dressed and put on a pot of coffee. On impulse, she decided to phone Diana. Sometimes her friend could understand Carly better than she did herself. After ten long rings, she replaced the receiver. Diana had probably spent the night with Barney. She wished those two would marry. As far as Carly could tell, they were perfect for each other. Barney was the first man Diana had ever loved who didn't need to be rescued from himself. Invariably, Diana fell for the world's losers; she apparently felt her undying love would redeem them. After two disastrous marriages, Diana was in no hurry to rush to the altar a third time. But Barney was different. Surely Diana could see that. He loved Diana. Barney might not be Burt Reynolds, but he was wonderful to Diana, and Carly's friend deserved the best.

Carly spent the morning writing Diana a long letter, telling her about the painting and Jutta Hoverson. Almost as an afterthought, she decided to add a few lines about Brand and their . . . *friendship*. She'd meant to say only a few things, but writing about her reactions to him helped her understand what was happening. A couple lines quickly became two long pages.

Both letters went in Monday's mail.

By Wednesday, Carly still hadn't heard from Brand. Apparently, he'd come into the office one afternoon while she was out, but had spoken with George and hadn't left a message for her. That evening, Carly decided she couldn't bear another night of television. Shopping was sure to cure even the heaviest of moods.

Before Carly knew where she was headed, she found herself on the sidewalk outside of Brand's apartment house. His late-model car was parked against the curb. She didn't know which apartment was his, but all she'd need to do was look at the mailboxes.

Her first knock was tentative. Coming to see him was a *friendly* gesture, she assured herself. And she did feel bad about the way she'd behaved Saturday.

"Yes?" The door was jerked open impatiently. Brand stopped abruptly as surprise worked its way across his handsome features. "Carly." He whispered her name.

"Hi." Cheerfully, she waved her hand. "I was in the neighborhood and thought I'd stop in and see how you were doing. But if this is a bad time, I can come back later."

"No, of course not. It's a great time. Come on in." He stepped aside and ran his hand along the back of his neck.

Carly had to smile at the stunned look on his face. As she stepped inside, she noted that the interior of the apartment was stark. Carpet, furniture, draperies—nothing held the stamp of Brand's personality or made this home distinctly his. Strangely, Carly understood this. Since Sandra's death, Brand's life had been in limbo. He carried on because time had pushed him forcefully into doing so. She imagined that he didn't even realize how stark his home and his existence had become.

"Actually, your timing couldn't be better," he said, as he led the way into the kitchen. The apartment wasn't as spacious as her own. The living room blended into the kitchen, and the round table was covered with a variety of slips of paper. "I was trying to make heads or tails out of this bookkeeping nonsense. It might as well be Greek to me."

"I don't suppose you'd like some help?" Carly volunteered, and laughed at the relief that flooded his face.

"Are you crazy? Does a starving man reject food?" Turning one scratched oak chair around, Brand straddled it, looking somewhat chagrined. "I insist on paying you."

Mockingly, Carly pushed a ledger aside. "No way. Isn't helping each other out what friends are for?" His eyes smiled into hers, and she noted the lines that fanned from their corners in deep grooves. The realization that those lines weren't from laughter was reinforced as she caught sight of a framed picture on the television. *Sandra.* Carly's heart leaped into her throat.

Brand's gaze followed hers. "I told you she was beautiful."

Beautiful. The word exploded in her mind. Sandra had been far more than that. She was exquisite. Perfect. Carly scooted out of her chair and walked across the room, lifting the picture to examine it more closely. Blond and petite, just as Brand had described. But vibrant. Her blue eyes sparkled with laughter and love. This woman had been cherished and adored, and it was evident in everything about her that she'd returned that love in full measure.

"She was an only child," Brand explained. "Her father died of a heart attack shortly after we learned that Sandra had leukemia. Her mother went a year after Sandra. I think grief killed her. She simply lost the will to live."

Carly couldn't do anything more than nod. She was gripping the picture frame so hard that her fingers ached. She forced herself to relax, replacing the photograph on top of the television.

"There's another in the bedroom with Shawn and Sara, if you'd like to see that one."

Carly shook her head emphatically. The way she had reacted to that one picture was enough. Shawn and Sara? Did Brand have children? Certainly he would have explained if the two were his children. He would have mentioned them long before now. No, they were probably a nephew and niece. They had to be. Knowing that Brand had been married had been enough of a blow. Adding children to that would be her undoing.

Carly gave herself a vigorous mental shake. Brand could have ten children and it shouldn't bother her. She was his friend. They weren't dating. Saturday had been just another of their "this is not a date" outings. Even her coming to his place today hadn't been anything more than a friendly gesture.

Coming to stand beside her, Brand lifted the photo from the television. Carly heard him inhale deeply. "I think the time has come to put this away."

"No." The word came out sounding as if she'd attempted to swallow and speak at the same time. Carly wanted him to keep the picture out to serve as a reminder that she couldn't allow her feelings for him to shift beyond the friendship stage.

He ignored her protest, staring at the photo as if he were saying goodbye. A deep frown marred his brow. "I can't very well bring a woman to my apartment and have a picture of my wife sitting out," he explained reasonably.

Carly had difficulty swallowing. "I guess you're right."

He carried the picture into another room and returned a moment later. Carly was at the table, looking over the accounting books, pretending she knew what she was doing. Her bookkeeping classes had been years ago.

"Is what happened last weekend still bothering you?"

Carly shrugged. "I suppose you've guessed that I had a troubled childhood." Her fingers rotated the pencil in nervous reaction, and she didn't meet his eyes; instead, she focused her gaze on the light green sheets of the ledger. "The state took me away from my mother when I was five. I don't remember much about her. I got a letter from her once when I was ten. She was drying out in an alcoholic treatment center and wrote to say that she'd be coming for me soon and that we'd be a real family again. She sent her picture. She wasn't very pretty." Carly paused, thinking that the family resemblance between them was strong. Carly wasn't pretty, either. Not like Sandra.

"What happened?" Brand prompted.

Carly set the pencil on the table and interlaced her fingers. "Nothing. She never came."

"You must have been devastated." Brand resumed his position in the chair beside her, his voice gentle, almost tender.

"I suppose I was, but to be truthful, I don't remember. At age twelve I was sent to the Ruth School for Girls for a time, until another foster home could be found. That was where I met my friend Diana. Since then we've been family to each other—the only family either of us needs." Her voice was slightly defensive.

"But who raised you?"

"A variety of people. Mostly good folks. With all the horror stories I've heard in recent years, I realize how fortunate I was in that respect."

"The art show upset you because you saw yourself in that portrait." His observation was half question, half statement.

"That picture was me at five. Seeing it was like looking at myself and reliving all that unhappiness."

Brand reached out and tenderly cupped the underside of her face. Carly's hands covered his as she closed her eyes and surrendered to the surging tide of emotion.

Brand didn't say a word. He didn't need to. His comfort was there in his healing touch as he caressed the delicate slope of her neck. His fingertips paused at the hammering pulse at the hollow of her throat before lightly tracing the proud lift of her chin.

"You're a rare woman, Carly Grieves," he whispered huskily.

Their eyes met and held. They were two rare souls. The wounded arctic wolf and the emotionally crippled little girl.

Slowly, ever so slowly, his hands roamed from the curve of her neck to her shoulders, cupping them and deliberately, tantalizingly, drawing her mouth to his.

Her lips trembled at the featherlight pressure as his mouth softly caressed hers. This wasn't a kiss of passion, but one of compassion.

Confused emotions assaulted her. She knew what he was trying to convey, but she didn't need or want his sympathy. Her hand curved around the side of his face, her fingers curling into the thick hair at his nape. "Brand," she whispered urgently, the moist tip of her tongue outlining his mouth.

He moaned as he hungrily increased the pressure, his arms half lifting her from the chair as he claimed her lips with a fierceness that stole her breath—and melted her resistance.

Simultaneously, they stood, their bodies straining against each other as their mouths clung. His tongue probed the hollow of her mouth, meeting hers in dancing movements that sent wave after wave of rapture cascading through her. His hands found her hips and buttocks as he molded her against his unyielding strength. Her senses exploded at the tantalizing scent of tobacco and musk and the taste of his tongue.

The profound need building within Carly was quickly becoming a physical ache. Her hard-won control vanished under the onslaught of his touch. Her cool, calm head—the one that before this had reacted appropriately to every situation—deserted her. Raw desire quivered through her, warming her heart and exposing her soul.

Breaking the contact, Brand's eyes locked with hers. He seemed to be searching for some answer. Carly could give him none, not understanding the question. Together, their breaths came ragged and sharp as they struggled to regain their composure. Carly fought desperately for her equilibrium and pressed her forehead against the broad expanse of his chest.

"Are friends supposed to kiss like that?" Her voice was barely above a whisper.

Brand's arms went around her as he rested his chin against the crown of her head. "Some friends do." He didn't sound any more in control of himself than she did.

"I'm . . . I'm not sure I'm ready for you to be this type of friend." A rush of cool air caressed her heated flesh, bringing her gradually back to reality. Gently but firmly, she pulled free from his embrace. Suddenly she felt naked and confused. Kissing Brand was like striking the head of a match; their desire for each other overpowered common sense. They'd known each other only a short time and yet she was weak and without will after just a few kisses. Diana wouldn't believe she was capable of such overwhelming emotion. Carly had trouble believing it herself.

"I've frightened you, haven't I?"

Her arms were folded across her stomach. "Brand, I'm twenty-five years old. I know what to expect when a man kisses me." Carly knew she sounded angry, but that anger was directed more at herself than at him.

His low laugh surprised her. "I'm glad *you* know about these things, because I feel as shaky as I did the first time I kissed a woman. It's been over two years since I've made love."

Carly's hands flew to her ears. She didn't want to hear this. Not any of it. With brisk strides, she walked to the other side of the room. Coming here today had been a colossal mistake. One she wouldn't repeat—ever.

"Gee, look at the time." She glanced at her gold wristwatch and slapped her hands against her sides.

"Time passes quickly when you're having fun, or so they say."

"Carly?" he ground out impatiently.

She took a couple steps in retreat until she found herself backed against the front door. She turned, her hands locking around the doorknob in a death grip.

"I'll talk to you later in the week," Brand murmured, and just the way he said it told her that their next meeting wouldn't end with her running out the door like a frightened rabbit.

The phone was ringing when Carly stepped through the door of her apartment. Thinking it might be Brand, she stared at it for several long seconds while she shrugged off her jacket. No, he wouldn't phone. Not so soon.

"Hello," she answered, a guarded note in her voice.

"Carly, it's Diana."

"Diana!" Carly burst out happily. Rarely had there been a time she'd needed her friend more. "You can't afford these calls, but thank God you phoned."

"What's up? You sound terrible, and it's not this crummy long-distance echo, either."

"It's a long story." It wasn't necessary to explain everything to Diana; just hearing her voice had a soothing effect. "Tell me what prompted this sudden urge to hear my voice."

"I couldn't stand it another minute." Diana laughed lightly. "Your letter arrived and I didn't want to have to write and wait for your reply. Tell me about him."

Carly's heart sank. "Do you mean Brand?"

"Is there someone else I don't know about?"

Stepping over the arm of her sofa, Carly walked across the couch, dragging the telephone line with her as she went. "There's nothing to tell. We're only friends."

"When you show this much enthusiasm for any male, I get excited. Now, what's this bull about the two of you just being friends? Who are you kidding?"

"Diana . . ." She exhaled a trembling breath as she sat down. "I don't know what to think. Brand's been married."

"So? If you remember correctly, I've left two husbands in my wake."

"But this is different. She died of leukemia and it nearly killed him, he loved her so much."

"Well, sweetie, I hate to say it, but this guy sounds perfect for you. You're two of a kind. Both of you are walking through life wounded. Has he gotten you into bed yet?"

"Diana!" Carly was outraged. Hot color seeped slowly up her neck.

"I swear, you must be the only twenty-five-year-old virgin left in America."

"If you don't stop talking like that, I'm going to hang up," Carly threatened.

"All right, all right."

Carly could hear Diana's restrained laughter. The woman loved to say the most outrageous things just to get a rise out of Carly.

"Take my advice." Diana's tone was more serious now. "You can hunt all your life for the perfect male and never find him. He doesn't exist. And even if by some fluke of nature you find someone who suits you, he's liable to expect the perfect female. And neither one of us is going to fill those shoes."

Crossing her legs beneath her, Carly managed a weak sigh. "I suppose you're right."

"I'm always right, you know that," Diana responded, with a small laugh. "Now listen, because I've got some serious-type news."

"What?" Carly straightened at the unusually deep intonation in Diana's voice.

"Against my better judgment and two miserable failures, Barney has convinced me that we should get married."

"Diana, that's wonderful. *You* two are the ones who belong together. This is fantastic."

"To be honest, I'm rather pleased about it myself. I'm not getting any younger, you know, and I'm ready to face the mommy scene. Barney and I've decided to have a family right away. Can you picture me changing diapers and the whole bit?"

"Yes," Carly returned emphatically. "Yes, I can. You'll make a wonderful mother."

"Time will tell," Diana chuckled. "At least I know what *not* to do."

"We both do," Carly agreed. "Have you set the date?"

"Next month, on the fifteenth."

"But that's only a little over three weeks away." Mentally, Carly was chastising Diana and Barney for not getting their act together sooner. This was one wedding she didn't want to miss. But she could hardly ask for time off now.

"Believe me, I know. But the wedding won't be anything fancy. It'd be ridiculous for me to march down the aisle at this point. Barney and I want you here. It's important to both of us."

Disappointment made Carly's hand tighten around the receiver. "I can't, Diana," she said, with an exaggerated sigh. "Why couldn't you have made up your mind before I left Seattle?"

"Barney insists on paying your airfare. Now, before you say a word, I know about that pride of yours. But let me tell you from experience, it's better not to argue with Barney and all his money. So plan right now on being here."

Carly would have enjoyed nothing more. "But I can't ask for time off from work. Hamlyn would have my head."

"Threaten to quit," Diana returned smoothly. "If Hamlyn gives you any guff, tell him where to get off. By this time he's bound to recognize what a jewel you are."

"Diana, I don't know."

Some of the teasing quality left Diana's voice. "You're the closest thing I've got to family, Carly. I've been married twice, and both times I've stood before a justice of the peace and mumbled a few words that were as meaningless as the marriage. I want this time to be right—all the way."

Carly understood what Diana was saying. She hadn't been present at either of her friend's other weddings. "I don't care what it takes," Carly replied staunchly, "wild horses couldn't keep me away."

"Great. I'll let you know the details later. We're seeing a minister tonight. Imagine me in a church!" She laughed. "That should set a few tongues wagging!"

"I'll phone sometime next week," Carly promised, as

she replaced the receiver. A smile softened the tense line of her mouth. Diana a mother! The mental picture of her friend burping a baby was comical enough to lighten anyone's mood. But she'd be a good one. Of that Carly had no doubt.

The days flew past. Carly dreaded seeing Brand, but she didn't doubt that he'd be true to his word. The next time they were together could prove to be uncomfortable for them both. He wouldn't avoid a confrontation—that she recognized.

Friday afternoon, George casually mentioned that Brand was on a flying assignment and wouldn't be back until the following day. Carly breathed easier at the short reprieve. At least she would have more time to think about what she wanted to say to him. One thing was sure: It would be better if they didn't continue to see each other. Even for *non*-dates. She didn't know what unseen forces were at work within her, but Brand St. Clair was far too appealing for her to remain emotionally untouched. He needed a woman. But not her. She'd make that clear when she saw him. Once it was stated, she could go back to living a normal, peaceful life. She might even investigate learning to knit. By the time Diana was pregnant, Carly might have the skill down pat enough to knit booties, or whatever it was babies wore.

Carly was sorting through her mail late Friday afternoon, still thinking about motherhood and how pleased she was for her friend. As she shuffled through several pieces of junk mail, a handwritten envelope took her by surprise. Glancing at the return address, she noted it was from the Purdy Women's Correctional Facility. The name on the left-hand corner was Jutta Hoverson.

Chapter Four

Memories of the proud child in the oil painting ruled Carly's thoughts as she clutched Jutta Hoverson's reply. Disappointment washed through her. The letter had been direct and curt. Jutta hadn't bothered with a salutation. I TOLD THE PEOPLE TO SAY THAT THE PAINTING IS NOT FOR SALE. I DON'T WANT TO SELL THIS ONE. Her large signature was scrawled across the bottom of the lined paper. And then, as if in afterthought, Jutta had added: I HAVE OTHER PAINTINGS. She'd provided no information. No prices. Not that it mattered; Carly wanted only the one.

She must have read Jutta's brusque words a dozen times, seeking a hidden meaning, desperately wanting to find some clue that the woman was willing to sell the self-portrait. There hadn't been many things in her life that Carly had wanted more than that painting. A week after the art show, the small child remained vivid in her memory; she could still envision the proud tilt of her chin and the hidden tear in the corner of one eye. So many times in her life Carly had joked about her past. If someone had questioned her about being raised as she was, Carly's flippant reply was always the same: Superman had foster parents. Even in the bleakest moments of her life, Carly had forced herself to be optimistic. Her childhood had made her emotionally strong and fortified her fearless personality. But tonight, with the letter from Jutta in her hand, Carly didn't feel like playing a Pollyanna game. She felt like eating twenty-seven chocolates, soaking in the bathtub, reading a book, and downing an aspirin . . . all at the same time. Diana would get a kick out of that.

As it turned out, Carly didn't do any of those things. She went to a theater and paid to see a movie she couldn't remember. She sat in the back row and slouched so far down that she had trouble seeing the screen. After devouring a bag of popcorn, she returned home and downed half a jar of green olives and considered the popcorn and olives her dinner.

Carly woke the next morning depressed and slightly sick to her stomach. Her mood swings weren't usually this extreme. She liked to think of herself as an even-keeled sort of person, although Diana claimed Carly was eccentric. Admittedly, she didn't know anyone else who kept earplugs on her nightstand in case of a storm so she wouldn't hear the thunder.

What an ironic sort of person she was. Unafraid of change or danger, Carly often leaped into madcap schemes without thought.

She knew Diana had worried herself sick the weekend Carly had climbed Mount Rainier. The only mountain climbing she'd ever done had been that one weekend on Washington State's highest peak. And yet Carly was frightened of a tempest.

A long walk that morning released some of the coiled tension. Her fingers pressed deep within the side pockets of her jeans, she kicked at rocks and pieces of broken glass along the side of the road. Something green flittered up at her. The reflection of the lazy rays of the sun flashed on a discarded and broken wine bottle. Carly stooped to pick it up. Its edges were worn smooth by time. Feeling a little like a lost child, Carly tucked the fragment into her pocket. A rush of emotion raced through her. *She* was like that glass. Discarded and forgotten by her mother, scoured by time.

Carly had followed her feet with no clear destination in mind, and soon found herself in a park. The happy sound of children's laughter drifted toward her. She stood on the outskirts of the playground, watching. That was the problem with her life, she mused seriously. She was always on the outside looking in.

Well, not anymore, her mind cried. *Not anymore.* With a determination born of self-pity, she ran to the slowly whirling merry-go-round.

"Hi." A boy of about seven jumped off a swing and climbed onto the moving merry-go-round. "Are you going to push?"

"I might." Carly started to trot around. The boy looked at her as if she were a wizard who had magically appeared for his entertainment.

"Didn't your mother ever tell you not to talk to

strangers?" Carly asked him as she ran, quickly losing her wind. She climbed onto the ride and took several deep breaths.

"You got kids?" the boy countered. "I think it would be all right if you had kids."

"Nope. There's only me." But Carly wasn't trying to discourage his company. She had no desire to be alone.

The boy's brows knit in concentration before he gave Carly a friendly grin. "You're not a real stranger. I've seen you in the grocery store before."

Carly laughed and jumped off the merry-go-round to head toward the swing set.

"I saw you buy Captain Crunch cereal." He said it as if that put her in the same class as Santa Claus and the Tooth Fairy. He ambled to the swing set and took the swing next to hers, pumping his legs and aiming his toes for the distant sky until he swung dangerously high. Carly tried to match him but couldn't.

"I saw you pick up something on the path. What was it?"

"An old piece of glass," Carly answered, still slightly out of breath.

"Then why'd you take it?" He was beginning to slow down.

"I'm not sure."

"Can I see it?"

"Sure." Using the heels of her shoes to stop the swing, she came to a halt and stood to dig the piece of glass from her pocket.

The young boy's eyes rounded eagerly as she placed it in the palm of his hand. "Wow. It's neat."

It was only a broken, worn piece of a discarded wine

bottle to Carly. Tossed aside and forgotten, just as she had been by a mother she couldn't remember.

"See how the sun comes through?" He held it up to the sky, pinching one eye closed as he examined it in the sunlight. "It's as green as an emerald."

"Feel how smooth it is," Carly said, playing his game.

The boy rubbed it with the closed palms of his hands and nodded. "Warm like fire," he declared. "And mysterious, too." He handed it back to her. "Look at it in the light. There's all kinds of funny little lines hidden in it, like a treasure map."

Following his example, Carly took the green glass and held it up to the sun. Indeed, it was just as the young boy had said.

The muffled voice came from the other side of the park.

"I gotta go," the boy said regretfully. "Thanks for letting me see your glass." Taking giant steps backward, he paused to glance apprehensively over his shoulder.

"Would you like to keep it?" Carly held it out for him to take.

His eyes grew round with instant approval, and just as quickly they darkened. "I can't. My mom will get mad if I bring home any more treasures."

"I understand," Carly said seriously. "Now, get going before you worry your mother." She waved to him as he turned and kicked up his short legs in a burst of energy.

Carly's hand closed around the time-scoured glass. It wasn't as worthless as she'd thought, but a magical, special piece. What else was there that was as green as an emerald, as warm as a fire, and as intriguing as a treasure map? Tucking it back into her pocket, she strolled toward her apartment, content once again.

Stopping off at the supermarket, Carly returned home with a bag full of assorted groceries. The flick of a switch brought the radio to life. The strains of a classic Carole King song filled the small room with "You've Got a Friend." Carly hummed as she unloaded the sack. Unbidden, the image of Brand fluttered into her mind. She straightened, her hand resting on her hip. Brand was her friend. The only real friend she'd made in Anchorage.

The soft beat of the music continued, causing Carly to stop and ponder. The song said all she had to do was call his name and he'd be there, because he was her friend.

But Brand was flying today. At least, George had said he wouldn't be back until late afternoon.

Maybe she should phone him just to prove how wrong that premise was. Carly reached for her cell and punched out Brand's number. Her body swayed to the gentle rhythm of the song and she closed her eyes, lost in the melody.

"Hello," Brand answered gruffly.

The song faded abruptly. "Brand? I didn't think you'd be back." Her heart did a nonsensical flip-flop. "I . . . ah . . . how was your trip?" She brushed the bangs from her forehead, holding them back with her hand as she leaned her hip against the counter.

"Tiring. How are you?"

"Fine," she answered lightly, disliking the way her pulse reacted to the mere sound of his voice. As much as she hated to admit it, Carly had missed Brand's company. Then, to fill an awkward pause: "The radio's playing 'You've Got A Friend.'"

"I can hear it in the background."

Carly could visualize Brand's faint smile.

"I heard from Jutta Hoverson." Her fingers tightened around the receiver.

"Jutta . . . oh, the artist. What did she say?"

Carly exhaled a pain-filled sigh. "She's not interested in selling."

"Carly, I'm sorry." Brand's voice had softened. "I know how much you wanted that painting."

She appreciated his sympathy but didn't want to dwell on the loss of the artwork. "I'll bet you're hungry," she surprised herself by saying. "Why don't you come over and I'll fix you something? Friends do that, you know."

He didn't hesitate. "I'll be there in ten minutes."

Brand sounded as surprised by the invitation as she was at making it. But it *was* understandable, Carly mused; she wanted to be around people. If she'd been in Seattle, she'd have wandered around the waterfront or Seattle Center. Setting up a tray of deli meats and a jar of olives, Carly realized that her mood required more than casual contact with the outside world. She wanted Brand. The comfort his presence offered would help her deal with Jutta's refusal to sell the painting. Wanting Brand with her was a chilling sensation, one that caused Carly to bite her bottom lip. She didn't want Brand to become a habit, and she feared being with him could easily become addictive.

The doorbell chimed. She glared at the offending portal, angry with herself for allowing Brand to become a weakness in her well-ordered life.

"Hi." She let him in, welcoming him with a faint smile.

"Here—I thought these might brighten your day." Brand handed her a small bouquet of pink and white carnations and sprigs of tiny white flowers. The bouquet wasn't the expensive florist variety but the cheaper type from the supermarket.

Without a word, Carly accepted the carnations, her fingers closing over the light green paper that held them together. Brand's gesture made her uneasy. Flowers were what he might bring a *date*. And George had mentioned something about the heavy medical bills Brand was paying off. His *wife's* bills. She didn't want him spending his hard-earned dollars on her. She frowned as she took the bouquet from him.

"What's the matter?" Brand asked, and she was reminded anew how easily he read her.

Carly lowered her chin, not wanting to explain. "Nothing."

"Are we back to that?" Irritation marked his words. "Have we regressed so far in such a short time?"

"What do you mean?" She raised her head, barely managing to keep her voice even and smooth. Moistening her lips was an involuntary action that drew Brand's attention. He wanted to take her in his arms and hold her; it was written in his eyes. He knotted his hands, and Carly recognized the strength of the attraction that pulsed between them. The knowledge should have given her a feeling of power, but instead it upset her. As much as possible she hoped to ignore the attraction between them.

"We went to the art show and it was obvious something was troubling you," Brand said, studying her closely. "I wanted you to tell me what it was, but you made me ask. I don't remember your exact words, but the message was clear. There was nothing wrong." His voice became heavy with sarcasm. "Well, Carly, that was a lie. There *was* something wrong then, just as there's something the matter now. I have a right to know."

Carly pressed her lips firmly together. She tried to hide her feelings but found it impossible. In the past she'd gone out of her way to anger him whenever he got too close. Brand inhaled a steadying breath as his hands settled to either side of her neck and he pulled her toward him. "I won't let you do it, Carly. I'm not going to fight with you. Not when you've wiggled your way into my every waking thought for the past week."

Pride demanded that she turn away, but Brand's hold tightened, his fingers bringing her so close she could feel his warm breath against her face. A battle warred in her thoughts. She cursed herself for craving the comfort of his arms, and in the same breath, she reached for him. Not smiling. Not speaking.

Needing was something new to her, and Carly didn't like to admit to any weakness.

Brand's arms slipped around her waist as he drew her into his embrace. The only sound in the room was the radio, playing a low and seductive melody from the far corner.

He didn't try to kiss her, although she was sure that had been his original intention. Apparently he realized she needed emotional comfort at that moment. While he might want to kiss her, he restrained himself. Carly was grateful. Her defenses were low. His hand cupped the side of her face, pinning her ear against his heart. She could hear the uneven thud of his pulse. It felt so incredibly good to be in his arms and comforted. She felt secure and at peace. Good to be with him . . . bad for her emotionally, for fear she might come to depend on him . . .

Confused, Carly didn't know what to think anymore. All she knew was that she was too weak to break away.

"I thought you offered to feed me," Brand said after a long, drawn-out moment, his voice husky.

"Are sandwiches all right?" She turned and brought out the tray of deli meats and the jar of green olives, setting them on the counter. A loaf of bread followed, along with a jar of mayonnaise and another of mustard.

"Fine. I could eat a"—he paused as he surveyed the contents of the plate—"pastrami, turkey, beef, and green olive sandwich any day."

"There are store-bought cupcakes for dessert."

"Fine by me," Brand replied absently, as he built a sandwich so thick Carly doubted that it would fit into his mouth.

After constructing her own, she joined Brand at the kitchen table. "I guess I should have warned you that my cooking skills are somewhat limited." She popped an olive into her mouth.

"Don't apologize."

"I'm not. I'm just explaining that you'll have to take me as I am. Fixing a meal that requires a fork is almost beyond my capabilities."

Chuckling, he lifted his napkin and dabbed a spot of

mustard from the corner of his mouth. "Do you think there's any chance that Jutta will change her mind and sell the painting?"

The letter was on the table and Brand couldn't help but notice it. Carly took it out of the envelope and handed it to him to read. "I don't think she'll sell, but I don't blame her. She'd like me to ask her about some of her other work."

"What do you plan to do?" Brand pushed his empty plate aside and reached over and took an olive from hers.

She slapped the back of his hand lightly and twisted to reach for the jar on the counter. "Take your own, bub," she rebuked him with a teasing grin.

Brand emptied several more onto his plate and replaced the one he'd taken of hers. "Well?" He raised questioning eyes to hers.

"I think I'll write her again. Even if she won't sell the portrait, I'd like to get to know her. Whoever Jutta Hoverson is or whatever she's done doesn't bother me. It's obvious the two of us have a lot in common."

Brand didn't respond directly; instead, his gaze slid to the bouquet of carnations she'd flippantly tossed on the countertop. His expression was gentle, almost tender. "You'd better put those in water."

Carly's gaze rested on the pink and white carnations, and she released her breath. "You should take the flowers home with you."

"Why?" He regarded her closely, his expression grim.

"I thought you were paying off Sandra's medical bills."

"What's that got to do with anything?"

"We're friends, remember?" Her voice was low.

"Flowers are something you'd bring to impress a date. You don't need to impress me, St. Clair. I'm a friend. I don't ever plan to be anything more."

Brand sat still and quiet, and although he didn't speak, Carly could feel his irritation. "I wasn't trying to impress you." His voice was deep. "My intention was more to cheer you up, but I can see that I failed." Silence filled the room as Brand stood, carried his empty plate to the sink, and, without a word, opened the cupboard beneath her sink and tossed the flowers into the garbage. His expression was weary as he turned back to face her.

"Brand," Carly tried. She hadn't expected him to react in such a disgruntled way.

He ignored her as he headed toward the front door. "Thanks for the sandwich," he said before the door closed behind him. The sound vibrated off the walls and wrapped its way around Carly's throat.

An hour later, Carly had written a reply to Jutta Hoverson. The second letter was easier to write than the first. Again she mentioned how much she'd enjoyed Jutta's work, and she recounted the time she'd visited the Seattle Art Museum in Volunteer Park. She told Jutta that she didn't appreciate the abstract creations, but a friend told her that they supposedly had a lot more meaning than met the eye. Rereading that part of the letter caused Carly to smile. Of course, the friend had been Diana, and the comment was typical of Diana's sense of humor.

Carly closed the letter by asking Jutta to send more information about her other paintings. As she took a stamp from the kitchen drawer, she caught sight of a single carnation that had remained on top of the counter next to the sink. She paused with the stamp raised halfway to her tongue. The carnation looked forlorn and dejected. Feeling bad about the way she'd treated Brand, she opened the cupboard beneath the sink and pulled the bouquet from the trash. She gently brushed the coffee grounds from the pink and white petals. Having no vase, Carly placed them in the center of the table in the empty olive jar, which served admirably as a holder.

She regretted what she'd said to him. There were better ways of expressing her feelings. But hindsight was twenty-twenty. That was another of Diana's favorite witticisms. Dear heaven, how she missed her friend.

After a restless evening in which her mind refused to concentrate on any project, Carly realized that she wouldn't feel right about anything until she'd apologized. Humble pie had never been her specialty, but, as she recalled, though the initial bite was bitter, the aftertaste was generally sweet. At least she'd be able to go on with the rest of her day. And the sooner the apology was made, the better. To take the easy way out and phone him tempted her, but Carly resisted. Instead, she donned a thick cable-knit sweater and drove the distance to Brand's apartment.

Her knock on his door was loud and hard. She waited long enough to wonder if he was home. His truck was outside, but that didn't mean much. She finally heard movement inside the apartment and placed a pink carnation between her teeth before the door was opened. "Peace?" she offered.

"Carly." He frowned, as if she was the last person he expected to see. His expression clouded before he said, "Come in."

Carly removed the flower and attempted to spit out the taste of the stem and leaves as she moved inside. "Well?" she questioned.

Brand moved a hand over his face, as if he thought she might be an apparition. "Well, what?"

"Am I forgiven for my cavalier attitude?"

He looked at her blankly, as if he still didn't understand what she was asking. "You mean about the flowers?"

Carly tipped her head to one side. Brand had obviously been asleep and she'd woken him. Things were quickly going from bad to worse. "I'm sorry, I . . . I didn't know you were in bed."

"Care to join me?" Brand teased softly, and pulled her into his arms. He inhaled, as if to take in the fresh scent of her. "It's been a long time since I had someone warm to cuddle."

Carly tried to remain stiff, but the instant she was in his arms, she melted against him. He smiled down on her, and his finger traced the smooth line of her jaw. His touch had the power to weaken her resolve. This was bad, and it was getting worse. To complicate matters even more, Brand could see exactly how she felt.

He chuckled softly, and his breath tingled the side of her neck as he leaned forward to nuzzle the curve between her neck and shoulder. "Why don't you put on some coffee while I grab a shirt and shoes?" He reluctantly moved away.

Carly released a sigh of relief when he left her. Not

knowing what to do with herself, she wandered into his kitchen. Her back was to Brand when he entered the room a few moments later. "My coming today was a gesture of friendship," she began, and smiled tightly as she turned to face him. "I felt bad about what happened at my place. My attitude was all wrong. You were being kind and I . . ."

"Friendship." Brand repeated the word as if he found it distasteful. "I think it's time you woke up to the fact that what I feel for you goes far beyond being pals."

"But you agreed . . ." Carly was having difficulty finding her tongue. "We aren't even dating."

The coffee was perking furiously behind her, and Brand brought down two mugs and filled them before carrying both to the table. "We aren't going to argue about it. If you want to ignore the plain and simple truth, that's up to you."

The arrogance of the man was too much. "You think I'm going to fall in love with you?" she asked incredulously.

Brand blew into the side of the ceramic cup before taking a tentative sip. "If you're honest with yourself, you'll admit you're halfway there already."

Carly slapped one thigh and snickered softly. "I don't think you're fully awake. You're living in a dream world, fellow."

Brand shrugged. "If you say so."

"I know so." Carly sat across from him and cupped the mug with both hands, letting the warmth chase the chill from her blood. "In fact, if that's your attitude, maybe it'd be better if we didn't see each other again. Not at all."

Brand shrugged, giving the impression that either way was fine with him. "Maybe."

Carly laid the palms of both hands on top of the table and half raised herself out of her chair. "Would you please stop it?"

Brand tossed her a look of innocence. "I told you I wasn't going to argue with you, Carly. That's exactly what you want, and I refuse to play that game. Anytime you feel someone getting too close, you do whatever it takes to push them away. It took me a while to realize it, but now that I do, I'm not going to let you do it with me."

"You're so wrong," she insisted.

"Am I?" he challenged.

"Okay, whatever. I don't want to fight." She could see it would be a losing battle, and she was a poor loser.

"But fighting is what you do best, isn't it?" he asked. Closing her eyes, Carly clenched her teeth and groaned. "You know, I'm beginning to think that the rocks in my head would fill the holes in yours."

Brand laughed and reached across the table to take her hand and raise it to his lips, but Carly pulled it free.

Undeterred, Brand continued, "Why don't you come over here and put your arms around my neck and kiss me the way you've wanted to do from the moment you walked in the door?"

Stunned, Carly nearly dropped her mug. It thumped against the table, and hot coffee sloshed over the sides. She jumped up to get a rag to catch the liquid before it flowed onto the floor. The color drained from her face as she sopped up the mess. She *had* wanted to kiss him. In the back of her mind, she had formed a picture of her apology being followed by Brand kissing her senseless. Carly closed her eyes and exhaled sharply.

The sound of Brand pushing back his chair filled her with dread. She nearly panicked with the need to escape.

"Oh, no, you don't." He spoke softly as his hand caught her shoulder and turned her into his arms.

"Brand, I don't think this is a good idea," she pleaded, and then swallowed to control the husky tremor in her voice. "I have to go . . . there's something—"

She wasn't allowed to finish as his mouth swooped down on hers. Her lips parted, whether to protest or welcome him she couldn't tell. Her response had an immediate effect on him. All gentleness left him and his hold tightened as he hungrily devoured her mouth. His hand at the back of her neck increased its pressure, lifting Carly onto the tips of her toes.

If she'd been confused before, it was nothing compared to the deluge of sensations that rocked her now. Her knees went weak. Nothing made sense as she surrendered to her swirling desire. Her tongue outlined Brand's mouth and he groaned. He broke off the kiss long enough to move with her to the chair and pull her into a sitting position on his lap.

Their eyes locked, and words became unnecessary as he wrapped his hands in her dark hair, directing her mouth back to his. She felt his hunger as his mouth reclaimed hers. Together they strained to satisfy each other. When she felt she could endure no more, she broke away and buried her face in the curve of his neck.

Brand's hands explored her back beneath the sweater. "Don't fight me so hard," he murmured.

Carly sighed thoughtfully. "The way I see it, I'm not

fighting near hard enough." She could feel his smile against her temple. "The things you make me feel frighten me," she whispered, after a long moment.

"I know."

"I don't want to fall in love with you," she whispered.

"I know that, too."

Carly's eyes rested on the clean top of the television. "What did you do with Sandra's picture?" He'd put it away, she knew, but she needed to know where.

"It's in a drawer."

Somehow she'd expected him to wince when she mentioned the wife he'd lost, but he didn't. "Top or bottom?"

A hand on each shoulder turned her so that she could look him in the eye. "Bottom."

She lowered her gaze, embarrassed at revealing the depth of her insecurity.

"Now," he said, and a hint of firmness stole into his voice. "When are you going to stop running from me?"

"I don't—"

Narrowed, disbelieving eyes forbade her from finishing. "Carly, look at me. I'm through with this 'we're not dating' business. We are *seriously* dating, and I won't take no for an answer. Understand?"

She nodded numbly. All the old insecurities bobbed to the surface of her mind, but when Brand put his arms around her those doubts seemed inconsequential. Only when she was alone did they grow ominous and forbidding.

Brand patted the lump of discarded glass in her jeans pocket. "Either you've got a serious problem with your bones or you're sprouting something in your pocket."

Carly smiled and arched her back so she could withdraw the glass. "Here." She gave it to Brand. "I found a treasure."

"Treasure?" He eyed her warily.

"It's as green as an emerald."

"Yes," Brand agreed.

She took it back, rubbed it between the palms of her hands, and held it to his face. "And warm as fire."

"Not quite that hot."

"We're imagining here," she chastised playfully. "Now hold it up to the light."

Brand did as she requested. "Yes?"

"See the cracks and lines?"

"So?"

"It's as intriguing as a map. A treasure map," she added, repeating the youngster's assessment. "And I bet you thought this was just a plain old piece of broken glass that time had smoothed."

Brand closed his fingers over the green glass and a sadness suddenly stole over him. "That's the kind of wonder Shawn would discover in this."

"Shawn?" A chill settled over her even before Brand could explain.

"My son."

"You have children?" The question came out breathlessly, her voice low and wobbly.

"Yes. Shawn and Sara."

Suddenly Carly knew what it must feel like to die.

Chapter Five

Several hours later the knot in her stomach still hadn't relaxed. Even now her breath came in short, painful wisps. Brand had children. Beautiful children. He'd taken a family photo from his wallet and Carly had been forced to stare at two blond youngsters. Both Shawn and Sara had been gifted with Sandra's beautiful eyes and hair color.

For every second that Carly had studied the picture she'd died a little more. Brand had explained that his children were living with his mother in Oregon, but they'd be joining him in a couple months, once school was out for the summer.

"How old are they?" Somehow Carly managed to ask the question.

Brand's eyes were proud. That he loved and missed his family was obvious. "Shawn's seven and Sara's five."

Carly nodded and returned the photo.

"You'll like them, Carly."

Brand sounded so confident, unaware of the turmoil that attacked her.

A few minutes after that, Brand walked her to his front door. "I'll see you tomorrow," he said, and gently kissed her brow. "We can talk more about us."

Carly wanted to scream that there wasn't anything to discuss, but she held her tongue, realizing an argument would solve nothing.

On the way out the door, her shoe caught on the rug and she stumbled forward. She would have fallen if Brand hadn't caught her.

"Are you okay?"

"Fine," she mumbled. "I'm fine."

Brand knelt at her side and retrieved her shoe. "The heel's broken. I can probably fix it, if you like."

"No, no, it's fine. Don't worry."

The instant Carly was back in her apartment, she took off the shoes and threw them both in the garbage. For the first time in recent memory, she was pleased that Diana wasn't around to witness this latest attack of wastefulness. Yes, the shoes could be repaired. But not for her. All too often in her life she'd been forced to wear repaired shoes. But not anymore.

Diana saw her attitude as ridiculous, but Carly considered the cost of new shoes a small price to pay.

Moon shadows danced across the walls as Carly lay in bed, unable to sleep. It was hours later. Already she was dreading seeing Brand again and what she had to tell him. Every condition she'd set for their relationship had been broken. He had come right out and told her he wanted more from her than friendship.

The most disturbing thing had been that Brand had known how badly she'd wanted to kiss him. He had been able to see it when she hadn't even admitted it to herself. If she was that easy to read, Carly doubted that she could disguise any of her feelings. And she was dangerously close to falling in love with Brand St. Clair. Placing Sandra, Shawn, and Sara out of the picture, Brand could make her feel more of a woman than she had at any other time in her life. The attraction between them was so strong she didn't know if she could fight against the swift current that seemed to be drawing them together.

In the morning, Carly dressed for work. Standing in the kitchen, she was buttering a piece of toast when the discarded loafers caught her eye. Throwing them out was a wasteful, childish action. Having them repaired would be such a little thing. This quirk, this penchant for perfection, was ruining her life. Carly turned her back and ignored the shoes. They were old, worn, and she'd have thrown them out in a few weeks, anyway. *But they were comfortable,* her mind returned quickly.

At the front door on her way out, Carly suddenly turned around and went back into the kitchen. She lifted the shoes out of the garbage and set them on the floor. Time. All she needed was time to think things over.

———

"Morning, George." Carly set her purse on top of her desk and walked across the room to pour herself a cup of coffee.

George had a clipboard in his hand. A deep scowl darkened his face. "Do you remember the Longmeir shipment to Palmer?"

Leaning her hip against her desk, Carly cupped the coffee mug with both hands. "Sure, we trucked that out last week."

George set the clipboard aside. "It didn't arrive."

"What?" Carly straightened. Two days after arriving at Alaska Freight Forwarding, she'd learned that Longmeir was their best and most demanding customer. The mining company had bases throughout the state and depended on Alaska Freight to ship the needed supplies to each site in the most expeditious, most dependable, and most economic way. Carly had been the one to decide to truck this latest shipment rather than use rail cars. George had concurred with her suggestion, but the decision had been hers.

"Needless to say, that freight's got to be found. And fast."

Brushing the hair from her forehead, Carly pulled out a desk chair. "I'll get on it right away."

"Do that," George ordered crisply.

By late afternoon Carly had gone through fifteen cups of coffee. Near closing time she tracked down the lost shipment. The truck driver had delivered it to the wrong camp, but that site had no record of accepting the shipment. There had been foul-ups at both ends—and Charles Longmeir wasn't a man to accept excuses. Carly stayed until everyone else had left for home. She had an idea that once the handler at the other camp inventoried his supplies, they'd be able to verify the location and make the necessary adjustments. However, that couldn't be done until morning. Rotating her neck to ease the tense muscles, Carly couldn't recall a worse Monday.

Letting herself into her apartment, she felt mentally and physically exhausted. George had voiced his displeasure all day. If they lost the Longmeir account, she might as well kiss her job goodbye. George hadn't actually said as much, but the implication was there. To complicate matters, she was due to investigate a large claim on another order that had arrived damaged. Her stomach felt acidic, and she could feel the beginnings of a headache prickling at her temples. Little wonder. She hadn't eaten anything since her toast that morning.

The phone rang at seven-thirty, and Carly didn't answer it, certain Brand was at the other end of the line. She didn't feel up to seeing him that night. All she wanted was a glass of wine, a hot bath, and bed. In that order.

She hadn't finished the wine when someone knocked on her door. Carly didn't need to be told it was Brand.

"Hi." He greeted her with a light brush of his mouth against hers.

Carly was astonished that such a little thing as this brief kiss could affect her, but it did. "Brand, I've had a rotten day. I'm not in the mood for company."

"I know. George told me about the Longmeir shipment." He ignored her lack of welcome and walked past her into the kitchen, carrying a grocery bag. "I'll only stay a few minutes," he promised. "Now, sit down, put your feet up, and relax."

"Brand," Carly moaned, half pleading, half amused.

She was still holding the front door open, but he was in her kitchen, humming merrily. "Just what do you think you're doing?" she challenged.

"Taking care of you."

Carly closed the door and marched into the kitchen. "I don't need anyone."

Brand was at her stove, a dish towel draped over his arm as he cracked fresh eggs against the side of a bowl. "I know that." Again he pretended not to notice her lack of welcome "You've been on your own for a long time. But I'm here now."

"Brand, please . . ."

He turned and planted his hands on both of her shoulders, his eyes holding hers with such warmth that she couldn't resist when he lowered his mouth to hers. His kiss brought her into quick submission.

He smiled down on her. "Now, go relax. I'll call you when dinner is ready."

Carly complied, wondering why she allowed him this amount of control over her. Leaning her head against the back of the love seat, her eyes drooped closed. The sound of Brand's humming as he worked lulled her into a light, pleasant sleep. Eyes shut, Carly's mind followed Brand's movements about her apartment. She heard him whipping the eggs and chopping something on the cutting board; she heard the sizzle of the butter when he added it to the hot skillet. That sound was followed by another she couldn't identify, then finally she heard the eggs being stirred in the pan and bread being lowered in the toaster. Delicious smells drifted toward her, and Carly realized how hungry she was.

"Dinner's ready," Brand called, and he stood behind her chair, waiting to pull it out as she approached.

Her eyes widened at the sight of the appealing omelet. Melted cheese and pieces of onion and green pepper oozed from the sides of his tantalizing masterpiece. "Wow," she said, as she sat down. "You never told me you could cook like this."

"There wasn't any reason to mention it before now. I've been on my own long enough to learn the fundamentals."

Carly took the first bite and shook her head in wonder. "This is fantastic."

"I didn't think you'd want dinner out."

"After a day like today, all I want is a hot bath and bed."

A mischievous grin curved the edges of Brand's mouth. "If that's an invitation, I accept."

The sexual banter between them seemed to grow more pointed with every meeting. Carly shook her head forcefully. "No, it wasn't," she announced primly.

She finished her meal and carried the plate to the sink. "How did you know I hadn't eaten?" Carly asked, not turning around. Most people would have had their dinner before now. A glance at her wristwatch told her it was nearly nine.

His eyes grew warm. "Because I'm beginning to know you, Carly Grieves. You don't eat when you're upset."

"I drink coffee."

"Yes, you drink a ton of coffee. It's a wonder you haven't gotten an ulcer."

Making busywork at the sink, Carly was torn between needing him to stay and wishing he'd leave her alone. The feelings she'd battled over the weekend returned a hundredfold. "Aren't you going to thank me for dinner?" he asked softly, coming to her side. He slipped his arms around her waist from behind and kissed the gentle slope of her neck.

Carly went still as she breathed in the clean male scent of him. "Thank you, Brand." Her voice was barely above a whisper.

"I was hoping you'd have other ways of expressing your appreciation," he whispered, and gently nibbled on the lobe of her ear.

"I don't." She prayed he couldn't detect the thread of breathlessness in her voice.

His hand stole beneath her sweater and slid across her ribs as his mouth sought and found the sensitive areas on her neck. Carly tilted her head to one side, loving the delicious sensations he brought to life within her. A trembling weakness shook her and she melted against him, her softness reveling in the touch of his hard length. Brand turned her into his arms, and she linked her hands at the base of his neck.

"Kiss me, Carly," he ordered huskily.

She defied him with her eyes, not wanting to give in to him. Not so easily. Her pride—and so much more—was at stake. She couldn't allow herself to become involved with this man.

Their gazes locked in a silent battle of wills. His dark eyes were narrowed with demand. Unable to meet his look, Carly's gaze slid to his mouth. His lips were slightly parted, eager. And Carly couldn't deny him . . . couldn't deny herself.

Finally she obliged, her mouth slanting over his, kissing him with a thoroughness that left them both weak and breathless. He clung to her as if he was afraid to let her go.

"Are you happy now?" she asked, rubbing her cheek along the side of his jaw in a feline caress. The abrasive feel of his unshaven beard against her skin's smoothness was strangely welcome.

"No." He kissed the corner of her mouth, seeking more, but Carly successfully forestalled him. "Brand, I want you to teach me to fly."

"What?" He stiffened and pulled his head back to study her.

"You heard me."

"But why?"

"Why not?" she quizzed.

"I can think of a hundred reasons."

"I thought you said you wanted me to look at your accounting books."

"You know I do." He broke away from her and strode to the other side of the kitchen, his face tight and troubled. The mute suggestion that he couldn't think with her so close pleased her. He paused and folded his arms over his chest.

"I suggest we trade labor," Carly continued.

Brand didn't look pleased, although he appeared to be mulling the suggestion over. "You'll have to read several books."

"I'm not illiterate," Carly challenged with a light laugh. "I'll have you know I read books all the time."

Brand's glance was wry, and he returned evenly, "Yes, I imagine you do."

"Well?" The idea made perfect sense to her.

Brand shrugged and walked into the living room to pick up the remote. "I suppose," he said, and turned on the television.

Carly wasn't fooled. Brand didn't like her idea, but she'd show him how much sense it made. The afternoon they'd spent in the air had only whetted her appetite for more. Soaring through the air, viewing the world from the clouds, would be a magical experience. And having Brand teach her would be the most feasible way.

"Come and watch this movie with me," Brand said. A trace of amusement sparkled from his eyes, an invitation.

"What's so funny?"

"Nothing." He returned his attention to the television. His hand moved to cup her shoulder when she sat down beside him.

The movie was one Carly had seen, but she didn't say anything. It felt warm and pleasant to be held by Brand. His touch was gentle, yet almost impersonal.

He didn't leave until after the eleven o'clock news, kissing her lightly at the front door. "Are you sure you don't want to thank me for dinner again?" he whispered against the soft wisps of hair that grew at her temple. "I could easily be persuaded to accept your gratitude."

His voice was only half teasing, and Carly knew it. "Next time I'll throw you out the door," she declared with mock severity.

"I'll see you tomorrow night—it's your turn to cook," he said, with a self-assured chuckle.

"My turn . . ." She had no intention of seeing him the following day.

"Yes. I'll bring the ledgers over after work."

"Brand, I told you before I'm not much of a cook. I eat a lot of green olives and chocolate." Carly crossed her arms to chase away a sudden chill.

"Don't worry about it. Until tomorrow," he said, and gave her a lingering kiss to seal the promise.

Carly's spirits lifted the next morning when she got a call confirming that the lost shipment was indeed at the wrong warehouse, as she'd pinpointed. The handler promised to have the equipment en route to the proper camp that afternoon, by company truck.

George looked as relieved as Carly felt. "None of this trouble was your doing," he said by way of apologizing. "And, listen, I've been thinking about that wedding you said you wanted to attend."

Carly's hand tightened around her pencil. When she'd approached George about Diana's wedding, he'd been less than enthusiastic about giving her days off. He hadn't answered her but had mumbled something under his breath about no vacation time being due her until next summer. His expression had been so forbidding that she'd let the matter drop.

"Yes," she said, holding her breath.

"Go ahead. Just be sure your assignments are complete and all the claims have been taken care of."

"I will," Carly responded evenly, then grinned up at the white-haired man. Over the weeks she'd come to overlook his gruff exterior. "Thanks, George."

"Just make sure your friends understand that I won't have you gallivanting to Seattle every time one of them decides to get married."

"I wouldn't dream of asking." Lowering her head, Carly tried unsuccessfully to disguise a smile.

"When will you be leaving?" George flipped open the appointment book on the top of his desk.

"I'd like to leave a week from Thursday." She waited for a flurry of complaints, but none came.

"Fine. When can I expect you back?"

"The following Tuesday—Wednesday at the latest."

George didn't blink. Carly could hardly believe it. She would phone Diana the minute she got home . . . Oh, darn, Brand was coming over for dinner. And she couldn't cook. He *knew* that. Well, a couple frozen dinners would discourage him. Brand seemed to be under the impression that just because they were trading skills, they would be seeing each other every night. She hadn't made this proposition as an excuse to see more of him— but he'd learn that soon enough.

During the drive from work to her apartment, Carly felt the faint stirrings of guilt. After a hard day, Brand would need something more than a frozen dinner, and she wasn't capable of putting together anything more than soup and a sandwich. Frustrated with herself because she cared, she took a short side trip to the local fried-chicken outlet.

Brand was at the door only minutes after she arrived home. His arms were loaded with books. "Whatever you're cooking smells good."

"I didn't cook anything," she announced coolly, as she set two plates out on the table.

"You don't sound very relaxed. Did you find the freight?"

"I located it. And it was exactly where I'd assumed it

had to be," she answered absently, neatly folding two paper napkins and placing them beside the plastic forks.

"Are you going to kiss me hello or will I be forced to take you in my arms and—"

Carly leaned over and brushed her lips against his cheek in a sisterly manner. "Go ahead and put that stuff on the coffee table."

For a second it looked as if Brand was going to argue with her. He hadn't appreciated her miserly kiss, and his look said as much.

"Go on," she urged, struggling to hide her satisfied smile. "Everything here's ready." She surveyed the table. Fried chicken, mashed potatoes, giblet gravy, coleslaw, and fresh biscuits. She hadn't eaten a meal like this since Diana and Barney had taken her out for a going-away celebration.

"I'll be back in a minute." Brand set the books aside and returned a moment later with a large box.

"Good grief, what's that?"

He glanced sheepishly at the department-store box under his arm. "Receipts, canceled checks, and the like."

"A whole box?"

Brand nodded, slightly abashed. "I'll help if you want."

She'd been party to his kind of assistance in the past. "No, thanks." She raised one hand in defense. "You'd only mess up my system." *And my mind,* she added silently.

They talked as they ate. Brand explained that he would be around town most of that week, but he had some distance flying coming up in the early part of the next. Carly listened, thinking that he was talking to her as he would a wife. The idea terrorized her. She'd hoped to pull away from Brand, but her life became more entwined with his every day. The crazy thing was that it was her own doing. She was the one who'd suggested they trade skills.

"Speaking of traveling," she said, wiping her fingers clean on a yellow napkin. "I'm going to be doing some of my own. I'll be leaving next week for Seattle."

"Any special reason?" His smile seemed an effort.

"Diana's getting married." Her eyes brightened with an inner glow of happiness for her friend. "I'm booking my flight for a week from Thursday morning." The wedding was scheduled for Friday night, but Carly wanted to be there early enough to soothe any attacks of nerves Diana might have.

"And you'll be back . . ."

"The following Tuesday. Brand . . ." She took a deep breath. "What do you think of the idea of me stopping in Purdy and meeting Jutta Hoverson? It wouldn't be out of my way. Diana would let me use her car. I'd really like to meet her."

"Why?"

She glanced away, not wanting him to see how much the idea excited her. "Several reasons."

"Are you hoping that she'll sell you the painting?"

The question unaccountably provoked her. "No, of course not. That's not it at all. I . . . I just want to see what she looks like, that's all. I'm sorry I mentioned it." Carly frowned. "Not everyone has ulterior motives, you know."

Brand laughed. "Now, don't get all shook up. I was only curious."

Carly removed a piece of lint from her skirt. "I think you should remember something, St. Clair." Her words were clipped and impatient. "I have more in common with Jutta Hoverson than I'll ever have with you."

He frowned. "You're doing it again. I'm getting too close and you'd rather fight and I won't do it."

"Is this what you did every time Sandra had a complaint? Did you refuse to fight with her, too?"

"Leave Sandra out of this."

"No," she snapped.

Silence hung between them like a dark gray thundercloud. Electricity filled the room, ready to arc at the slightest provocation.

Rising, Brand rammed his hands deep within his jeans pockets. "Sandra and I fought just like every couple does, but I won't fight with you, Carly."

"Why?" She felt like shouting at him, but when she spoke her voice was low and filled with frustration.

"Because it's exactly the excuse you're looking for to shove me out of your life. I've been chipping away for too long at the wall you've built around yourself to blow it over a stupid argument." He paused and rubbed his eyes. "I was in Oregon last week."

Brand had been gone almost the entire week and she'd assumed it was on business. He didn't need to tell her what had drawn him to his home. His children were there.

"For the first time since Sandra died, I found I could look at my son and daughter and not feel the gutwrenching pain of having lost their mother. You've done that for me, Carly."

"No," she mumbled, and shook her head from side to side.

"Yes. Now, listen to me. If you weren't running so hard from me you'd see what's right in front of your nose."

Coming to her feet, Carly took Brand's plate from the table and carried it to the sink. She didn't want to look at him, she didn't want to hear him. Filling the sink with water, she hoped to drown out his words.

"I took Shawn and Sara to Cannon Beach with me. Sandra loved the beach," he continued, ignoring Carly's frenzied movements. "I hadn't been there since she died."

Carly's fingers gripped the edge of the sink as she closed her eyes, silently screaming for him to stop. She wasn't a part of his life. He had no reason to tell her these things. She shouldn't be that important to him.

"I'd always thought, whenever I went back, that I wouldn't be able to stand looking at the ocean again. Sandra had loved it so much. But nothing had changed . . . even though I guess maybe I thought it would. But the wind blew and the sea rumbled and the shorebirds soared as they always have."

"Please," Carly pleaded. "I don't want to hear this."

"But you're going to, even if it means I have to force you to listen."

Without turning around, Carly knew that Brand's mouth had tightened into a grim line. Arguing would be useless.

Brand began again. "One afternoon, while Shawn and Sara were playing in the sand, I stood with the wind blowing against me and closed my eyes. A picture of Sandra filled my mind. But not in the ordinary sense of remembering. She was there, smiling, happy, as she'd always been at the beach, smelling of wildflowers and sunshine. As long as I kept my eyes closed she was there with me and the children. The only sounds were those of the children and the whisper of the wind. But when I strained I thought for an instant I could hear the faint call of Sandra's laughter."

Tears filled Carly's eyes, and she blinked in a desperate effort to forestall their flow. "Don't," she murmured. "Please don't do this to me." Her mind was filled with the image of this proud man standing on the beach with the wind buffeting against him, communicating with his dead wife.

"You don't understand," Brand said softly. "For the first time since she died, I felt her presence instead of her absence. For two years my memories of her have been tied up with the agony of her death. I looked out at the ocean and felt a sense of life again. That desolate darkness I'd wrapped myself in was gone. The time had come to go back. Back to the world. Back to people. Back to my children. But mostly back to you."

Carly wiped the tears from her face with both hands.

"It was you who brought back to life feelings I had assumed were long dead. You, Carly." He moved so that he was standing directly behind her. "I'm falling in love with you. From the moment I walked into your office I knew there was something special about you. You've hidden from me, dodged me, fought me. But the time's come, my sweet Carly, for you to look out over the ocean and choose life."

Her lips went dry, and she moistened them. Fresh tears burned for release, but she held them back as she'd always done, her throat aching with the effort. Turning, she slipped her arms around his waist and buried her face against his broad chest. Brand wrapped his arms around her so tightly that for a moment she couldn't breathe. He needed her; Carly could feel it. His breathing was slow and ragged, as though it was an effort for him to hold back the emotion.

"I guess this means we're dating," she said after a long pause.

Her words were followed by the low rumble of Brand's laughter. "Yes, I guess you could say that."

"Brand . . ." She hesitated. "All this frightens me."

"I know. I was afraid, too."

"But you're not anymore?"

"No." His hand traced the outline of her face, tilting her chin so that he could meet her troubled gaze. "Not anymore."

"Why . . ." She swallowed at the painful knot blocking her larynx. "Why didn't you tell me about your children?"

"I had trouble even talking about them. They were part of the life I'd left behind."

"But you said they're coming to Alaska soon."

"As soon as school's out. I told them about you."

Carly stiffened. "What did you say?"

He kissed the tip of her nose. "I told them I had a special friend that I was beginning to love just as I loved their mother."

"Oh, Brand, I wish you hadn't," she whispered, her voice trembling.

He ignored her, but his grip tightened, as if he was afraid she'd bolt and run as she'd done so many times in the past. "A funny little friend who climbed mountains and jumped out of airplanes and liked to eat green olives and chocolate."

"And . . . and what did they say?"

Brand laughed and mussed the top of her head with his chin. "Shawn wanted to know if you'd take him with you the next time you decide to climb Mount Rainier. And Sara was more concerned about whether or not you liked video games."

Carly's smile was shaky.

Sandra's children would be joining him soon. A sense of unrest attacked her. True, she could climb mountains and jump out of airplanes, but the thought of meeting these two children filled her with indescribable terror.

Chapter Six

Brand came into Carly's office yawning on Thursday afternoon. "I'm bushed," he declared, as he sat down in George's desk chair. "I don't know, Carly. Someone's changed the rules in the last ten years."

Rising, she poured him a cup of steaming coffee. "What do you mean?"

"I'm too old for these late nights. I used to be able to get by on four or five hours' sleep. But no longer. I'm too old for this."

They'd been together every day. They talked, watched television, went for long walks, and discussed flying. Not once had Brand left Carly's apartment before midnight.

Responding to his tiredness, she put her hand over her own mouth and yawned loudly.

"I'll be late tonight," Brand said, after taking the first sip from the coffee cup.

"Good," Carly returned with a lazy smile. "That'll

give me a chance to go over those flying theory books you brought me."

Brand lowered his gaze, but not before Carly saw his frown. Although he hadn't said anything to discourage her, it was obvious he didn't want her to learn to fly. He'd know soon enough, Carly mused now, that she was her own woman. Diana had often reacted with the same show of reluctance at Carly's adventurous inclinations. She could almost hear her friend protesting her sudden interest in gaining a private pilot's license.

"Do you want me to have dinner ready for you?" The offer was more selfish than generous; Carly realized how much she looked forward to their time together in the evenings. Not that they did a lot of social things. Brand's finances wouldn't allow for much of that. Maybe once a week they could dine out or take in a movie, but certainly not every night.

Brand wanted to take her to dinner Friday night, and Carly had agreed, although she'd felt less nervous when the captain of the football team had asked her for a date in high school!

"I may not be back until after ten," Brand warned.

"No problem. And you know better than to expect a three-course meal."

Setting his empty mug aside, Brand stood and kissed her on the cheek. "I'll see you later," he promised, his voice low and husky.

George returned to the office just as Brand was leaving. Carly stood at the window until Brand had climbed into his car and was gone.

"You two have been seeing a lot of each other, haven't you?"

Carly's answer was a nod. Her private life had nothing to do with the office, and she wasn't going to elaborate on her relationship with Brand to satisfy George's curiosity.

"He's a rare man, Brand St. Clair."

She could feel George studying her. Carly's boss had seen the look on her face—and knew the cause. "Yes, he is," Carly agreed, and turned back to her desk.

"He's driven himself hard. But he looks more relaxed now than I can ever remember," George continued.

Carly said nothing, not wanting to encourage him.

"I don't suppose you could say anything to him about becoming a full-time pilot for Alaska Freight Forwarding, could you?"

Mercifully, the phone rang, so Carly didn't have to answer George. By the time she'd replaced the receiver, her employer had left the office.

When Carly returned to the empty apartment that evening, she felt restless. Usually Brand arrived shortly after she did. Now, for the first time in days, the evening stretched out ahead of her, devoid and lonely. The thought shocked Carly. A couple times she found herself glancing at her watch and mentally calculating how long it would be until Brand arrived. This was exactly what she hadn't wanted.

Bit by bit, Brand had wiggled his way into her life. She did his bookkeeping, and in return he was teaching her how to fly an airplane. That had been their original plan. Instead, their evenings had been spent simply enjoying each other's company. Sometimes Brand dropped by the office unexpectedly, for no more reason than to have a cup of coffee and chat for a few minutes. Now a day without spending time with Brand seemed unnatural. She had tried to tell Diana about these fears concerning her relationship, but never quite did. What she was feeling about him came from the heart and not from the mind. These emotions were foreign to her, and she wasn't sure she could explain what was happening to her dearest friend when she wasn't entirely sure herself. And although she loved her friend, there were certain things even Diana couldn't be expected to understand.

There was so much Carly didn't know about Brand, and yet she felt she knew everything she would ever need to know. Nothing in his life had ever been done half-heartedly. Only a man who loved with such intensity could grieve the way he had for Sandra. Only a man with as much insight into and understanding of her personality could be as patient as Brand had been with her.

With all that she was, she loved him. The realization came to her gently, warm and secure, kindling a fire that glowed. She did love Brand. What she didn't know was whether or not her love for him was strong enough to overcome the fears and anxieties ingrained in her conscience since childhood.

The FCC flight manual was balanced on her bent knee and the television was on with the volume turned down when Brand knocked lightly against her door.

"Hi." She greeted him with a hug. "Are you hungry?"

"Starved." He groaned and pulled her into his arms. "But before you go into the kitchen I expect a proper greeting. None of those miserly kisses you seem to be so fond of giving me."

Smiling seductively, Carly slid her hands up his chest and allowed them to rest on the curve of his shoulders. "Remember," she whispered huskily, as she fit her body intimately to his, "you asked for this." She kissed one corner of his mouth and then the other. Then she outlined the contour of his lips with her tongue, darting it in and out of his mouth with a teasing action that affected her as much as it did Brand.

His hands began to caress her back in an unhurried exploration as his mouth opened to hers, taking the role of aggressor. His lips parted hers. Carly clung to him, drained of strength.

They broke apart, each gasping for air.

"A few more of those and I won't be responsible for what happens," he murmured breathlessly.

All the blood flowed from her face. The point in their relationship was fast approaching when kissing would satisfy neither of them. Carly knew that Brand yearned to make love to her, and frankly she wanted him, too, but this was a serious step in their relationship and she wasn't sure either of them were ready.

"Let me get your dinner," Carly said, as she turned away. She could feel Brand's smile hit her straight between the shoulder blades. He was assuming she was running again, and he was right.

Happy—perhaps happier than she'd ever been at any time in her life—Carly worked in her small kitchen as Brand leafed through the newspaper. She built him a three-tiered sandwich, piling each piece of bread high with meat from the local deli, adding sliced tomatoes and cut pickles. She topped her creation with a giant green olive that was speared with a toothpick. Then she adorned the plate with potato chips and proudly carried her masterpiece in—only to discover that Brand was asleep on her sofa.

Carly toyed with the idea of waking him, but he looked relaxed and so peaceful that she couldn't make herself do it.

Returning to the kitchen, Carly bit into a crunchy potato chip and covered the sandwich with plastic wrap. He could eat it tomorrow. Leaning against the counter, Carly yawned.

She tucked an extra pillow under Brand's head and covered him with a spare blanket. The temptation was strong to linger at his side, to make an excuse to touch him. Her fingers flexed with the desire to brush the thick, dark hair from his forehead. But such an action might wake him, and she didn't want to risk that.

An hour later the flight manual could no longer hold her wandering attention. Time and again her gaze slid from the fine print on the page to the sleeping figure across from her. If Brand hoped to bore her with dull reading, he was succeeding, but she wouldn't let him know that. A lot of what she'd gone over tonight might as well have been in a foreign language. What she needed was a *pre*-preflight instruction manual. But she wouldn't give up. Now she was more determined than ever to get her pilot's license.

She hesitated in the lighted doorway of her room, watching the moon shadows surround Brand. Realizing that she loved Brand was one thing; what she was going to do about it was something else entirely. So many questions remained unanswered. Most important were the ones neither of them had voiced.

When Carly woke the next morning, Brand was gone. A note was propped on the table apologizing for his lack of manners. He assured her that his falling asleep didn't have anything to do with her company, but only the fact that thirty-three years were taking their toll. He reminded her of their dinner date that evening and asked her to wear her best dress because they were going to do the town. His hurried postscript mentioned that the sandwich had been fantastic.

Carly sat with a glass of orange juice and a plate of toast as she reread every word of his note. The happiness she'd felt finding it washed over her. It was as if Brand had written her a poetic love letter. Perhaps she was suffering a second adolescence. Good grief, she hoped not. The first one had been difficult enough.

That afternoon, at the stroke of five, Carly was out the office door. She wanted to luxuriate in a scented bath and be as beautiful and alluring as possible when Brand arrived.

The phone was ringing when she walked through the apartment door.

"Hello." Her voice was singsongy with happiness.

"Carly, I'm going to be late."

"Brand, where are you?" The line sounded as if it were long distance.

"Lake Iliamna."

"*Where?*" He might as well have said Timbuktu.

"The largest lake in Alaska. There's a lodge here."

"Oh." That didn't mean anything to her. "I take it you're using the float plane."

Brand's low chuckle warmed her blood. "The woman's a genius."

"When should I expect you?"

"Honey, I don't know. It could be hours yet."

The endearment rolled off his tongue seemingly without thought, and Carly wondered if that was a name he'd called Sandra. She pushed the thought from her mind forcefully. She couldn't, she *wouldn't,* allow Brand's first wife to haunt their relationship. Not any more than she already did.

"Carly, you're terribly quiet all of a sudden. Are you angry?"

She jerked herself from her musings. "Of course not. Listen, Brand, would you rather cancel the whole thing? I don't mind. We can go out to dinner another time."

"No," he returned. "I want to see you. I *need* to see you. That is, if you don't mind waiting."

"No," she whispered softly. "I don't mind."

By eleven, Carly was yawning and rubbing her eyes to keep from going to sleep. An old rerun of *Law & Order* was the only thing that kept her from drifting into a welcome slumber.

Brand arrived at midnight. "Carly, I'm sorry," he said the moment she opened the door. "I came right from the airport. Give me another half hour to go home and change. I'll be back as soon as I can."

"We can't go out now." Carly could only guess what it had taken for him to offer. One look at the fatigue in his eyes was all she needed to see that he was exhausted.

"Nothing's open at this time of night," she reasoned in a soft voice.

"We'll find something," he assured her, but not too strenuously.

"Nonsense. I'll let you do your magic with eggs, and we can eat here."

His arms brought her into his embrace even with his eyes closed. "I can't argue with you there. It's been a long day."

"What time did you leave my apartment?" He'd spent at least part of the night on her sofa.

"Three. Which was a good thing, since I was due to take off from the airport at four."

"Good heavens, Brand," she lamented. "You've been up nearly twenty-four hours."

His smile faltered. "Don't remind me. Tell me about your day."

"There's not much to tell. I got a letter from Jutta Hoverson. She wrote me the day my letter arrived, which makes me feel good."

"What did she have to say?"

"Not much. She's doing some charcoal sketches. The painting of the child was her first oil work. Unbelievable, isn't it?"

Brand sat down in the kitchen while she took food from the refrigerator. "And I phoned Diana to tell her what time my flight would be landing in Seattle. She's too calm about this wedding business. It won't surprise me if she tries to cancel the whole thing at the last minute."

Carly set a tall glass of milk in front of Brand. "Drink," she ordered. "I'll whip up something in a jiffy."

It surprised her that Brand didn't fall asleep in her kitchen chair. After he'd eaten, she led him to the front door. His good-night kiss was as gentle as it was sweet. "I'll phone you tomorrow," he promised. He was making several short flights on Saturday but couldn't invite her along because he was scheduled to fly crew into camps and there wouldn't be any space in the plane for her.

Carly spent Saturday morning shopping for a dress for Diana's wedding. Although she spent several hours browsing, she couldn't find what she wanted. Problem was, she wasn't sure what she was looking for. But she knew she'd recognize it when she saw it. Shopping had never been her forte, and she decided to leave it until she arrived in Seattle. Diana would know exactly where to go.

The rest of the afternoon was spent answering Jutta's short letter. The woman hadn't said much. Few personal details were given in the note. Carly had no idea of her age or background. In her reply, she explained that there was a possibility that she would be able to visit Jutta the following week. She mentioned that she'd like to look at the charcoals then.

With the letter finished, Carly glanced at her watch, surprised to see that it was dinnertime. Not having heard from Brand, Carly assumed that it would be another late night for him.

He showed up around nine, declined her offer for dinner, and promptly fell asleep on her sofa. This time Carly decided to wake him. Enough was enough.

"Brand." Her hand on his shoulder shook him lightly awake.

He bolted upright and blinked. "What happened? Did I fall asleep again?"

Arms crossed, Carly paced the floor in front of the sofa, unsure how to express her frustration.

"What's wrong?" He was awake enough to recognize that she was upset.

"Plenty, and—and don't tell me that you don't want to argue, because this time you're listening to me. Understand?"

Brand wiped a hand across his eyes and nodded. A wary look condensed his brow as his eyes followed her quick, pacing steps.

Without preamble, Carly began. "I won't be a pit stop in your life, Brand. Maybe some women can live like that, but I'm not one of them. I want to talk to you when you're not so tired that you're rummy. And when I leave the room I want to come back and find you awake."

"A pit stop?" Brand repeated blankly. "Carly, it's not that. Seeing you, being with you, is more important to me than anything."

"Then why am I stuck with the leftovers of your life?" The hurt was impossible to hide.

He rose with the intention of taking her in his arms, but Carly wasn't in any mood to be kissed. She sidestepped him easily. "Go home, Brand. Get a decent night's sleep, and maybe we can talk later."

Sitting back down on the couch, Brand rested his elbows on his knees. He folded his hands together with his index fingers forming a small triangle. "I don't want to leave. We need to talk this out." His eyes showed the strain of the past week.

"As far as I can see, there's nothing more to say. I understand why you work the hours you do." She took the chair opposite him. "You can't start a new life with me or anyone else while Sandra's medical expenses are hanging over your head . . ."

"I paid those off six months ago," he announced in a tight whisper.

"Then why are you pushing yourself like this?"

He didn't answer; instead, he stood and walked to the far side of the room. He paused with his back to her and smoothed the hair along the side of his head. "You're right, Carly. You deserve more than what I've been giving you." His look was sober as he turned, his eyes searching hers. "I love you, Carly. I thought those feelings within me had died with Sandra. But I was wrong." His voice was a hoarse whisper. "I love you, my sweet Carly."

Brand didn't need to tell her that he'd said those words to only one other woman in his life. Carly's fingers were trembling so badly that she clenched them into fists at her sides. Everything that she wanted and everything that she feared was staring her in the face.

"Well?" Brand was waiting for some kind of reaction.

"Thank you," she whispered, her voice so tight it was hardly recognizable. "I'll always treasure that."

"You don't know how you feel about me?" Brand asked.

"I . . . know what I feel." Swallowing was difficult.

"And?"

"You're waiting for me to declare my love. That's

what you want, isn't it?" She was speaking loudly and being obtuse because she was afraid.

"Only if that's what you feel." Everything about Brand softened, as if he recognized the turmoil taking place within her.

"All right, I love you! Are you happy?" she cried out on a sob. Her whole body was shaking.

"I'm not, if it makes you so miserable."

"It's not that." Oh no, she was going to cry. Her throat ached with the effort to suppress the tears.

"Carly, I want to marry you."

"No." The denial was torn from her in shocked dismay. This was the one thing she'd feared the most. Tears slid down her face and scalded her cheeks. A hand covered her mouth as she shook her head violently from side to side. "I can't, Brand. I won't marry you."

"Why not?"

There wasn't any explanation that made sense, even to herself. How could she possibly hope to make him understand? "You . . . you had Sandra. You have children." Her voice wobbled, and she tried desperately to control its quivering but failed.

"What's that got to do with anything?"

Carly moved into the kitchen and picked up the low-heeled loafer from beside the garbage pail. "I'm throwing these away because . . . because there was never enough money for me as a child and everything had to be fixed and repaired until it was beyond rescuing. I don't want that anymore."

"Carly, you're not making any sense."

"I don't expect you to understand. But I am what I am. You've been married and you've loved." She swallowed down the hurt. "I want to be a man's first love. I want a man to feel for me what you did for Sandra."

"Carly, I do."

"But I want to be your first love," Carly cried. "Don't you understand? All my life I've been forced to take someone else's leftovers. I've always been second and I won't be again, not with a husband. Not with a man." Brand looked as if he might come closer to her, and she held out a hand to warn him to stay away. "You have beautiful children, Brand. A boy and a girl. Don't you see? I can't give you anything you don't already have. You've had a wife. You have children."

The grimness of pain returned to his eyes. "Then what do you suggest we do?"

"Must we do anything?"

"Yes," he said, and then repeated softly, "yes. When two people love as strongly as we do, they must."

Carly lowered her eyes under the intensity of his. "I don't know what to do, Brand," she said, her voice low and throbbing. "Maybe we could be"—the word stuck in her throat—"be lovers."

A sad, wry smile slanted Brand's mouth as he shook his head. "Maybe that kind of relationship would satisfy some men. But not me. I've never done anything halfway in my life." His pause demanded that she meet his gaze. "There's so much more that I want from you than a few stolen hours in bed. What I feel goes beyond the physical satisfaction your body will give mine. I want you by my side to build a new life here in Alaska."

"Please," Carly pleaded, struggling to speak, "don't say any more."

Brand ignored her. "Together we can give Shawn and

Sara the family life they crave. And, God willing, we'll have more children."

Her pain was real and felt like a knife blade slicing through her. "No. I'm sorry . . . so sorry. I can't."

He took a step toward her, and Carly backed up against the kitchen counter, unable to retreat farther.

"You're reacting with your emotions."

She glared at him, wanting him to give her some insight she didn't already have. "None of this makes sense to you. I realize that. I'm not sure I can even fully understand it myself. All I know is what I feel. I won't be a secondhand wife and a secondhand mother."

"Carly . . ."

"No." She shook her head forcefully. "We've said everything that's important. Rehashing the same arguments won't solve a thing."

He clenched and unclenched his hands with frustration and anger.

"Please," she whispered in soft entreaty. "We're both tired."

Wordlessly, Brand turned, grabbed his jacket from the back of the sofa, and left. When the door closed behind him, Carly began to shake with reaction. If it wasn't so tragic, she'd laugh. Brand was so far ahead of her in this relationship. He wanted to marry her—and she had gone only as far as admitting they were dating.

It was nearly two a.m. before Carly went to bed. She knew she wouldn't sleep, and she lay waiting until exhaustion overtook her troubled thoughts. Tomorrow was soon enough. Maybe tomorrow some clear solution would present itself. Tomorrow . . .

But the morning produced more doubts than reassurances. Loving someone didn't automatically make everything right. And yes, she loved Brand. But Diana was right, as her friend almost always was when it came to understanding Carly. Brand and Carly were two wounded people who had found each other. The immediate attraction that had sparked between them wasn't physical but spiritual.

When Carly hadn't heard from Brand by Monday afternoon, she realized that he was giving her the room she needed to think things through. His actions proved more than words the depth of his love. Arguing with her would do nothing but frustrate them both.

At any rate, on Thursday morning she would be leaving for Seattle and Diana's wedding. With all the stress Diana was under, Carly couldn't unload her problems on her friend, but at least she would have some time away, close to the only people she had ever considered real family. And Carly needed that.

Tuesday morning, at about ten, Carly heard the familiar sound of Brand's car pulling up outside the office building. Her hand clenched the pencil she was holding, but a smile was frozen on her face when he walked through the door.

"Hello, Carly." He was treating her politely, like a stranger.

"Hi." Her lips felt so stiff she could barely speak.

"You're leaving this week, aren't you?"

He knew exactly when she was going, but Carly played his game. "Thursday morning."

He sauntered over to the coffeepot and poured himself a cup. Without looking at her, seemingly intent on his task, he spoke. "Will you go out to dinner with me Wednesday night?"

"Yes." There was no question of refusing. The breathing space he'd given her hadn't resolved her dilemma. If anything, she felt more troubled than before. "I'd enjoy that."

He nodded, and for the first time since entering her office, he smiled. "I've missed you."

"I've missed you, too," she whispered.

Brand took a sip of his coffee. "Where's George?" he asked, suddenly all business.

"In the warehouse." She cocked her head to one side, indicating the area to her right.

"I'll pick you up at seven," he announced, his hand on the doorknob.

"Okay." He was gone and Carly relaxed.

Wednesday evening, with her suitcases packed and ready for the morning flight, Carly dabbed perfume at the pulse points behind her ears and at her wrists. The dress she wore was the most feminine one she owned, a frothy pink thing that wasn't really her. Diana had insisted she buy it, and in a moment of whimsy Carly had done just that. She wasn't sure why she'd chosen to wear it for her dinner date with Brand tonight. But she'd given up analyzing her actions.

Promptly at seven, Brand was at her door. He looked uncomfortable in the dark suit he wore. His hair was cut shorter than she could remember seeing it, and he smelled faintly of musk and spice.

They took one look at each other and broke into wide smiles that hovered on the edge of outright laughter.

"Are we going to act like polite strangers or are we going to be ourselves?" Brand arched one dark brow with his query.

Carly toyed with her answer. If they remained in the roles for which they'd dressed, there was a certain safety. "I don't know," she answered honestly. "If I return to Carly, the confused woman in love, then the evening could be a disaster."

"I, for one, have always courted disaster." He ran his finger down her cheek and cupped the underside of her face before kissing her lightly. "And so have you," he added.

Warm, swirling sensations came at her from all sides, and Carly had to restrain herself from wrapping her arms around his neck and kissing Brand the way they both wanted to.

He took her to the most expensive restaurant in town and ordered a bottle of vintage Chablis.

"Brand," Carly giggled, leaning across the table. "You can't afford this."

His mouth tightened, but Carly could see that he was amused and hadn't taken offense. What was the problem, then? She put her niggling worry aside as Brand spoke. "Don't tell me what I can and can't afford."

"I do your books, remember?"

"Sometimes I forget how much you know. Now, sit back and relax, will you?"

"Why are you doing this?"

"Can't a man treat the woman he loves to something special without her getting suspicious?"

"Yes, but—"

"Then enjoy!" His humor was infectious.

They toasted her trip and Carly talked about Diana and Barney, recalling some anecdotes from her friends' courtship.

Midway through dinner, Carly knew what was troubling Brand. It came to her in a flash of unexpected insight. She set her fork aside and lazily watched Brand for several moments.

"What's the matter?" He stopped eating. "Is something wrong with your steak?"

Carly shook her head. "No, everything's fine."

"Then why are you looking at me like that?" Brand watched her curiously as she stretched her hand across the table and took his.

"Running has been a problem ever since I met you, hasn't it?" she asked softly. "But, Brand, this time I'm coming back."

Brand nodded, still showing only a façade of unconcern. "I know that."

"But you were worried?" She released his hand.

He concentrated on slicing his rare steak, revealing little of his thoughts. "Perhaps a little."

"You don't need to worry. If I ever walk away, you'll know when and the reason why."

He answered her with a brief shake of his head, but

Carly noticed that he was more relaxed now. "Do you want to go dancing after dinner?" he surprised her by asking.

"Dancing?" She eyed him suspiciously. He'd told her he didn't dance the first time they'd gone out for a meal. "I thought you said you didn't."

"That was before."

"Before what? Have you secretly been taking lessons?" she teased.

The humor drained from his eyes, and he sought and found her gaze. "No, that was before I ever thought I'd find anyone who'd make me want to dance again."

Chapter Seven

~⌒~

Carly eased the strap of her carry-on bag over her shoulder as she made the trek through the long jetway from the airplane into the main terminal at Sea-Tac Airport.

Her eyes scanned the crowd at baggage claim until she caught a glimpse of Diana, who was nervously pacing the area. Her friend hadn't changed. Not that Carly had expected her to. Somehow she never got used to the fact that Diana was only five feet, four inches. Their hair color was the same ordinary shade of dark brown. But there the resemblance stopped. Carly was a natural sort of person who didn't bother much with fashionable hairstyles or trendy clothes. She was too proud of her individuality to be swayed by the choices of others. But it was not so with Diana, who often dressed in the most outrageous styles and clothes. *Flamboyant* was an apt one-word description of her best friend.

"Diana."

Carly watched as her friend whirled around and quickly made her way through the crowd.

"Darling, you're gorgeous." Diana threw her arms around Carly. Such an open display of affection was typical of Diana, who acted as though she hadn't seen Carly in years instead of only a few weeks. "But too thin. You're not eating enough. I knew this would happen. I read an article that said how hard it is to get supplies into Alaska. You're starving and too proud to admit I was right. I hope to high heaven you're ready to move back where you belong."

Carly laughed. "If you think getting supplies is difficult, you should try heating an igloo."

They teased and joked as they waited for Carly's suitcase to come around the conveyor belt in baggage claims.

"Where's Barney?"

"Working. He sends his love, by the way." Each carrying a suitcase, they crossed the sky bridge to the parking garage. "Wait until you see his wedding gift to me."

"Diamonds? Furs?"

"No." Diana shook her head solemnly. "I told him not to bother. Neither one of my other husbands did."

When Diana paused in front of a red convertible, Carly's mouth dropped open. "The car. Barney got you a red convertible?" This was the kind of car Diana had always dreamed of owning.

Diana shook her head in feigned dismay. "That's only half of it."

"You mean he got you two cars?"

One delicately outlined brow arched. "Better."

"Better?" Carly gasped playfully.

A few minutes later, Carly understood. Diana exited

off the freeway and took a long, winding road that led to an exclusive row of homes built along the shores of Lake Washington.

"Barney bought you a house!"

"He said I'd need some place to park the car," Diana explained excitedly, as she pulled into the driveway and turned off the ignition. "I still get a lump in my throat every time I see it." She bit her bottom lip. "I remember not long after we met, Barney was telling me that someday he was going to build a house. I told him about the one I had pictured in my mind from the time I was a little girl. A house full of love."

"And Barney built you that house." Carly shook her head in wonder. "Tell me again where you found this man!" she begged.

"The crazy part of it is how much Barney loves me!" Diana sounded shocked that anyone could care for her with such fervor. "And it isn't like I'm a vestal virgin who's coming to him spotless. With my track record, any sane man wouldn't touch me with a ten-foot pole." Tears filled the dark brown eyes. "You know, Carly, for the first time in my life I'm doing something right."

Carly's hand squeezed her friend's as tears of shared happiness clouded her own vision. "Look at us," she said, half laughing, half sobbing. "You'd think we were going to a funeral. Now, are we going to sit out here all day or are you going to show me the castle?"

With a burst of energy, Diana led Carly from room to room, pointing out details that a casual inspector might have overlooked. Every aspect of the house was impressive, with high ceilings and the liberal use of polished oak.

"It's beautiful," Carly said with a sense of awe. "I counted four bedrooms."

"Two boys and a girl," Diana announced thoughtfully. "As quickly as we can have them."

Shaking her head, Carly eyed her friend suspiciously. "And you used to tell me diaper rash was catching."

Laughing, Diana led the way into the kitchen and opened the refrigerator. "Barney and I can hardly wait for me to get pregnant." She handed Carly a cold soda. "Here, let me show you what I got him for a wedding gift." She led Carly into the family room off the kitchen and pointed to the leather recliner. "They delivered it a couple of days ago. For a while I was afraid it wouldn't arrive before the wedding."

"I'll bet Barney loves it."

"He hasn't seen it yet," Diana explained. "He won't be moving in until after the wedding."

"Oh." The surprise must have shown in Carly's eyes. The couple had been sleeping together for months.

"I suppose it sounds hypocritical at this point, but Barney and I haven't lived together since we talked to the pastor."

"Diana," Carly said softly. "I'm the last person in the world to judge you. Whatever you and Barney do is your business."

"I know. It's just that things are different now. We're different. We even started attending church. Every Sunday. Can you believe it? At first I thought the congregation would snicker to see someone like me in church. But they didn't. Everyone was so warm and welcoming. In fact, a few ladies from the women's group volunteered to have a small reception for us after the wedding."

"That's wonderful."

"Barney and I thought so, too." Diana's eyes lit up
with a glow of happiness. "For a long time I expected
something to happen that would ruin all of this. It's been
like a dream, and for a time I felt I didn't deserve Barney
or you or the people from the church."

"But, Diana—"

Diana interrupted by putting her hand over Carly's.
"My thinking was all wrong. Pastor Wright pointed that
out to me. And he's right, no pun intended. We did a lot
of talking about my background, and now I see how
everything in my life has led to this point."

Carly wondered if she'd ever find this kind of serenity
or that special glow of inner happiness Diana had.

"I hope you're hungry," Diana said. "We're supposed
to meet Barney in a half hour for lunch."

"I'm starved." Carly sighed dramatically. "As you've
guessed, I haven't eaten a decent meal in weeks. Food's
so hard to come by in the Alaskan wilderness. And I just
haven't acquired a taste for moose and mountain goat."

Dressed in her pajamas, Carly sat cross-legged on top of
Diana's huge king-size bed. "One thing I've got to do
tomorrow is buy a dress. I couldn't find anything I liked
in Anchorage, but then, I wasn't in much of a mood to
shop."

"I already beat you to it. Knowing you'd put it off to
the last minute, I scheduled time for us to go shopping
tomorrow." Diana sat at the vanity, applying a thick layer
of white moisturizing cream to her face. "Are you going

to tell me about him or do I have to pry every detail out of you?"

Carly dodged her request. "It may take months for you to get pregnant if Barney sees you smear that gook on your face every night."

"Quit trying to avoid the subject." Some of the teasing humor left Diana's eyes.

"All right, all right. I'm in love with Brand." The burst of happy surprise Carly had expected didn't follow.

"I already knew that. I've known from the moment you started telling me about him. Obviously, he's in love with you, too."

Carly answered with a curt nod. "He asked me to marry him before I left for Seattle."

"And?"

"I told him no," Carly said sadly. "I can't, Diana. He's everything I want and everything I fear all rolled into one."

"Is it because of his wife and the two kids?"

"Aren't you nervous about the wedding?" Carly asked hastily, wanting to change the subject.

"This is my third wedding. I'm over the jitters. Now, let's get back to you and Brand."

"I don't want to talk about me," Carly said stubbornly. "Brand and I have gone over every detail until we're blue in the face. I can't change the way I feel."

"Sweetie." Diana only called her that when she was either very sad or very serious. "It's time you grew up."

Somehow she'd hoped that Diana, of all people, would understand. "All right, I admit that there will probably never be anyone I'll feel this strongly about again."

"But you're afraid?" Diana prompted.

"Out of my wits."

Diana's soft laugh filled the bedroom. "I never thought you'd admit it."

"This is the exception." Carly fiddled with the nylon strings of her pajama top. "In a lot of ways you and I are alike. For one thing, I have trouble believing Brand could honestly love me. I'm terribly insecure, often irrational, and a card-carrying emotional cripple."

"Do you remember how long it took Barney to convince me to marry him? Months."

"Brand's not as patient as Barney. He thinks that because we're in love everything will work itself out."

"He *sounds* like Barney," Diana murmured, more to herself than for Carly's benefit.

"His children are coming to Alaska the middle of next month." Carly's voice was unsteady. Shawn and Sara were the focus of her anxieties.

"Sandra's children." Diana had a way of hitting the nail on the head.

Carly winced and nodded.

"And nothing's ever frightened you more."

"Nothing." Her whisper was raw with fear.

"All our lives I thought you were the fearless one," Diana whispered, "but deep down you've been as anxious as I have. Be happy, Carly." She wiped the moisturizer from her face with tissues as she spoke. "As much as I'd like to, I can't tell you what to do. But I urge you to stop being so afraid of finding contentment. Believe that Brand loves you. Count yourself blessed that he does."

Carly laughed, but the soft sound came out more like

a sob. "For not wanting to tell me what to do, you sound like you're doing just that."

Diana's eyes locked with Carly's in the vanity mirror. "Go for it, kid."

Carly couldn't remember a more beautiful wedding. Tall white baskets filled with huge floral arrangements adorned the sanctuary. A white satin ribbon ran the length of the railing in front of the altar.

Barney, the short jeweler Diana had met at a Seahawks football game, stood proudly with his bride at his side. His dark hair had thinned to a bald spot at the top of his head, and his nose was too thin for his round face. Barney definitely wasn't the type of man to stop female hearts. Carly recalled the first time she'd met him, and her surprise that Diana would be dating such a nondescript man. But her attitude had soon changed. From the first date, Barney had treated Diana like the most precious woman in the world. Carly loved him for that. Barney's love and acceptance had changed Diana until she glowed and blossomed under them.

Diana had never looked happier or more beautiful. She stood beside Barney, their hands entwined, linking them for life. As the maid of honor, Carly held the small bouquet Diana had carried to the altar.

Both Diana's and Barney's voices rang strong and true as they repeated their vows. A tear of joy slipped from the corner of Carly's eye as Barney turned and slipped the diamond wedding band onto Diana's slim finger.

Diana followed, slipping a simple gold band onto

Barney's thick finger, her eyes shining into his as she did so. This time Diana was confident she was marrying the right man. And Carly was convinced Diana was the right woman for him.

"I now pronounce you husband and wife." The pastor's strong voice echoed through the church.

Diana looked at Barney with eyes so full of love that Carly felt a lump in her throat. Whatever the future held, these two were determined to nurture their love and faith in each other. The commitment was on their faces and in their eyes for everyone to read. And it didn't go unnoticed.

The reception was held in the fellowship hall connected to the church. The wedding party was small. Diana had invited only a few friends, while Barney had asked his two brothers and their families. Three or four other couples who had met Diana and Barney through the church also attended.

Carly stood to the side of the reception hall and sipped her punch. Her eyes followed the newly married couple. Suddenly an intense longing she couldn't name filled her.

She wanted Brand with her. She wanted to turn and smile at him the same way that Diana was smiling at Barney. And more than that, she needed to see again the love that had shone from his eyes as he had waved goodbye to her at the airport. Her chance for happiness was waiting for her in Anchorage; the question was whether or not she had enough courage to look past the fact that Brand had known this kind of love and happiness before meeting her.

Carly paused and took another sip of the sweet

punch. With all her hang-ups, she wondered what kind of mother she would be to Shawn and Sara. Only a minute ago she'd begun to feel a little confident; now she was filled with as many insecurities as ever. As much as she wanted to find parallels in her relationship with Brand with what had happened between Diana and Barney's, she couldn't. The two couples faced entirely different circumstances.

Following the reception, Diana, Barney, Barney's relatives, and Carly went to dinner at Canlis, a plush downtown Seattle restaurant. From the restaurant, the newlyweds were leaving for a hotel, then for a two-week honeymoon in Hawaii Sunday evening. Diana insisted that Carly stay at the house, and also gave her the keys to the car so that she could drive it home.

It was some time later when, yawning, Carly walked into the guest bedroom and kicked off her tight heels. The thick carpet was like a soft cushion under her bare feet. The day had been full and she was tired, but the thought of bed was dominated by her need to hear Brand's voice.

He answered on the first ring, and even a distance echo couldn't disguise how glad he was to hear from her.

"How was the wedding?"

"Wonderful. Oh, Brand, I can't even describe how beautiful everything was."

"Well, I certainly hope it had the desired effect. There's only one wedding I want to attend, and that's *ours*." The teasing inflection in his voice didn't mask his sincerity.

"Oh Brand, please don't go there. I couldn't bear to argue."

"Arguing is the last thing I have on my mind." His voice became low and sensual. "In fact, if you knew what I was thinking, you'd probably blush."

"I do not blush." She might be a virgin, but she wasn't a shrinking violet.

Brand chuckled. "This time you would."

"I take it you miss me."

He laughed. "You have no idea."

"But I've only been gone a day."

"Almost two days. Not that I've noticed."

"I can tell."

"Well, come on. Say it," Brand prompted.

"Say what?"

"How much you've missed me. I'm especially interested about what went on in that beautiful mind of yours when you heard your friend repeat her vows. Did you think of me and wish that I was at your side so we could say them to each other?"

"Obviously you crept into my thoughts or I wouldn't have phoned." Carly would admit to nothing. She wrapped a strand of hair around her ear. Sometimes Brand knew her as well as she knew herself.

"But you won't admit to thinking about me during the wedding ceremony."

"You're right," Carly said in a low, sensual tone. "I won't admit to anything until I see you."

She heard Brand's swift intake of oxygen. "You'd better not have changed your mind about flying home Monday."

"No, I'll be there. But don't say anything to George—he thinks I'm arriving later in the week."

"Don't worry. My lips are sealed."

"Darn. I have a thing about sealed lips."

"What's that?"

"I never kiss them," she announced, and the sound of Brand's laughter mingled with the sound of her own.

They talked for almost an hour, and could have gone on for another. Even after she hung up, Carly itched to phone him back and say all the things she hadn't had the courage to mention the first time. Only the knowledge that she would be back home Monday evening deterred her.

After talking to Brand, Carly took a hot bath, soaking up the warmth of the water. A chill had found its way into her blood. Tomorrow she would be driving to Purdy and the Purdy Women's Correctional Facility. Jutta Hoverson hadn't replied to Carly's latest correspondence, but one thing was certain. It wasn't the charcoal sketches Carly was interested in seeing. It was Jutta Hoverson.

Visiting hours were scheduled for the afternoon, so Carly had a late breakfast and lingered over the morning paper. She dressed carefully, wanting to appear neither too casual nor too formal. Finally, she chose a three-piece slacks suit that was just right. Fleetingly, she wondered if Jutta had any apprehensions about the meeting. Probably not.

Once at the center, Carly signed in at the desk and was asked to place her valuables in a rented locker. Carly had seen identical ones at airports and bus depots. She placed her purse inside, inserted the quarter, and stuck the key into her jacket pocket.

The waiting area was soon filled to capacity. An uncomfortable sensation came over Carly as she studied the others in the room. Not in the habit of making snap judgments about people, she was amazed at her immediate distrust of the few men who regarded her steadily. Carly admitted that she did stick out like a little green Martian. Compared to the others, she was decidedly overdressed. Her uneasy feeling intensified as the waiting area emptied. The visitors were led away in small groups to another room, where they walked through a metal detector and were briefly questioned. From there, each group was directed into a large room with several chairs against the walls.

There Carly took a seat close to the window and tried to ignore the iron bars that obstructed the view. The stark silence of the room was interrupted by a crying child who was pitifully asking to see his mommy.

An iron door slid open and the women prisoners filed into the room one by one. Carly had filled out a card when she entered the building, requesting to see Jutta Hoverson, but she had no way of identifying her.

The little boy broke loose and ran into the arms of one woman, who swooped him into her embrace. The scene was a touching one, and Carly wondered what the young woman had done in her life to be thus separated from her child.

"Are you Carly?"

Carly's attention skidded from the youngster to the tall, thin woman standing before her. "Yes." She rose. "Are you Jutta?" Never would Carly have envisioned Jutta this way. Her hair was long and hung in straight braids the same shade of brownish-red, except that it was mostly gray now. The glasses she wore slipped down the bridge of her nose, and Carly doubted that they had ever fit her properly. Her clothes were regular street clothes, but drab and unstylish. Jutta looked as nervous as Carly felt.

"It's good to meet you," Carly began stiffly.

"They wouldn't let me bring out the sketches without some kind of approval beforehand."

"That's all right." The stilted, uncomfortable feeling intensified. "Can we sit down and visit for a while?"

Jutta shrugged one shoulder and sat. "I don't suppose you've got a cigarette?"

"Sorry, no . . ."

"I forgot, they don't let you bring anything in here, do they? I suppose you're curious to know what I did to end up here," Jutta challenged, clearly on the defensive.

The one thing Carly didn't want to do was make the woman uncomfortable. "Not unless you want to tell me."

"I don't see why not. It's a matter of public record. I forged checks, and it wasn't the first time, either."

"How long is your sentence?"

"Long enough. I've been in Purdy two years now and I don't expect to get approval from the parole board for another two."

"Did you start painting in . . . here?"

"Yes."

"I thought the painting of the child was excellent."

"I won't sell that one."

"Yes, I realize that," Carly assured her quickly. "Since it obviously means so much to you, I don't think you should."

"What I can't understand is why someone like you

would want it." Jutta's deep blue eyes narrowed as they studied Carly. "You're a regular uptown girl."

That was probably the closest thing to a compliment that Jutta would give. "The picture reminded me of myself when I was five."

"You were poor?"

Carly answered by nodding.

"You seem to be doing all right now."

"Yes. I'm fine."

"You haven't mentioned a man. Are you married?"

"No." Carly shook her head automatically. "But . . . I've been thinking about getting married," she said stiffly.

"It seems to me if you have to think about it, then you probably . . ."

"No," Carly interrupted. "It isn't that. I love him very much. But . . . well, he's got children."

"I'd have thought you'd be the type to like children."

"I do." Carly was uncomfortable with this line of conversation and sought a means of changing it. "Do . . . do you have children?"

"I've got a kid, but I never married," Jutta stated defensively. "He's grown now. I haven't seen him in ten, maybe fifteen years. Last I heard he was in prison. Like mother, like son, I guess. Don't keep in contact with him much."

Carly hadn't expected Jutta to be so honest. If anything, she'd thought the artist would rather not answer personal questions. "I don't remember my mother," Carly admitted softly, her gaze falling to her hands. "The state took me away from her and put me in a foster home when I was young."

"Have you seen her since?"

"No. I did try to find her when I was twenty. But I didn't have any luck. To be honest, I think her drugs and alcohol must have killed her."

"A lot of women get hooked on that stuff. And worse."

"I don't feel any bitterness or anything. I can hardly remember her."

"She beat you?" Jutta asked.

"No. At least I don't think so."

"Then you were lucky."

"Yes," Carly agreed. "I was lucky."

Carly thought about their conversation as she drove back toward Seattle over the Narrows Bridge. Jutta wasn't at all what she'd expected. The woman was forthright and sincere. She was brusque and a little abrasive, but her life had been hard, her experiences bitter. In some ways Carly saw the mother she had never known in Jutta. And in other ways she saw reflections of the proud child of the painting.

Their conversation had been stilted in the beginning, but by the end of the hour they were slightly more comfortable in each other's company. Jutta had explained far more about herself than Carly had expected. She said that there was a letter waiting for Carly in Anchorage and admitted, almost shyly, that she enjoyed getting mail.

Diana and Barney returned home early Sunday afternoon from their two-night honeymoon before their flight to Hawaii. They were both radiant.

"Welcome home," Carly said, and embraced Diana warmly. "I didn't expect you back so soon."

"Barney's got a business meeting this afternoon. And I wanted to get back early enough to pack and get ready for our trip."

"I've already called for a taxi." Carly glanced at her watch. "My flight leaves in another two hours."

"But I thought we'd have time to visit."

"Are you nuts?" Carly said, and kissed her friend on the cheek. "I'm leaving so you and Barney can begin your life together in peace."

"We're going to be so happy," Diana said with confidence.

"I know you are. And I can't think of anyone who deserves it more than the two of you."

"I can." Diana's happy gaze clouded with concern. "I want you to know this kind of happiness, Carly. You're the closest thing I have to family. If you walk away from Brand, it's something you'll regret all your life."

Unable to break the tension in the air, Carly hugged her friend again. "I'm not going to lose Brand," she whispered the promise.

The taxi arrived ten minutes later. Amid protests from both bride and groom, Carly left. Diana and Barney, arms entwined, stood on the sidewalk waving as the driver pulled away. From her position in the backseat, Carly turned and blew them both a kiss. Leaning the back of her head against the seat, Carly closed her eyes for the remainder of the ride to the airport.

Although he hadn't mentioned it, Carly was certain Brand would meet her plane. And when she saw him she knew that look would be in his eyes again—the look that demanded an answer to his wedding proposal. She wanted to marry him, but pushing all her doubts and insecurities aside wouldn't banish them.

Jutta had assumed that Carly couldn't love Brand if she hesitated before marrying him. Yet just the opposite was true; every minute she was away she discovered she loved him more. Little by little, bit by bit, he had worked his way into her life, until she realized now how lost she would be without him.

Diana had said the time had come for her to grow up, to set aside the hurts of her childhood and deal with the realities that faced her. How simple it sounded. But she was dealing with emotions now. Not reason. So many times in the last few days Carly had caught herself wondering about Brand and Sandra. Such thinking was dangerous. And unreasonable. Sandra was gone. *She* was here now, and crazy in love with the leftovers of Sandra's life.

With the approach of summer the days were growing longer. It would be dark in Seattle now, but when the plane touched down at the Anchorage airport the sun was still shining.

As she'd hoped and as she'd feared, Brand was there. She paused midstride when she saw him standing to the side, waiting for her. He seemed tired, and his eyes were sad. She hadn't seen him like that since the night he'd first told her about Sandra.

When he smiled the look vanished, and her heart melted with the potency of it. Quickening her pace, she walked to his side. "Hi," she whispered, her eyes not leaving his.

"How was the flight?"

"Uneventful."

He took the carry-on bag from her grasp, his eyes not quite meeting hers. "All day I had the fear you'd stay in Seattle."

"I told you I was coming back."

He nodded as if he didn't quite believe her. "I don't know, Carly." He ran a hand through his thick hair in an agitated action. "I've told myself a thousand times I was making a fool of myself. It's not a comfortable feeling to think the woman you love is going to walk out on you without a minute's hesitation."

"Brand," she argued, "I'm not going to do anything of the sort."

Long strides took him to the area where they were to wait for her luggage. "I don't like what I'm becoming . . ."

A chill came over her at the fear in his voice. Carly's hand gripped his forearm. "Do I get a chance to say something or do I have to listen to your tirade first?"

"Go ahead," he answered, without looking at her.

She swallowed. "I guess the simplest way of saying it is yes."

"Yes what?"

"Yes, I want to be your wife."

Chapter Eight

Brand blinked twice and then straightened. Carly watched as his face mirrored his confusion. "What did you say?"

"You did ask me to marry you, didn't you?" For a fearful instant, she feared she'd been wrong. "And, by heavens, you'd better not have changed your mind. Not after all the soul-searching I went through to reach a decision."

"I haven't changed my mind." An intense look darkened his eyes, and a muscle worked along the side of his jaw as he stared at her as though seeing her for the first time. He looked as if he couldn't quite believe her. "Let's get out of here." He jerked her suitcase from the carousel at the baggage-claim area and ushered her out of the airport terminal.

Brand didn't say another word until they were inside her apartment. "Now, would you care to repeat yourself?"

"I said I'd marry you."

An incredulous light brightened his eyes as the beginnings of a smile spread across his mouth. "You mean it?"

"Of course I do." Carly smiled softly as she reached out and traced the outline of his lips with the tip of her index finger.

Brand pulled her into his arms. Crushed against him, Carly opened her mouth to his probing kiss, reveling in the passion she felt in him. Again and again his lips ravaged hers as if he couldn't get enough of her.

"I won't let you change your mind," he whispered against her temple. "Not now. Not ever."

Weak with longing, Carly pressed light kisses on his eyelids, his cheek, and his jaw. "I'm not going to back out. I only pray that we're doing the right thing."

"We are." His arms tightened around her waist. "I know it in my heart."

He kissed her again with a gentleness that stirred her. She *was* doing the right thing. Yes, she was afraid, and there were many fears yet to face, but Diana was right. If Carly walked away from Brand and his children she would be turning away from the best thing that had ever happened to her. The choice was clear—either marry Brand or lose him forever.

Brand inhaled deeply and took a step back. His hands settled on either side of her face as his eyes met hers. "We'll get the blood test tomorrow."

Carly nodded.

"And be married by Friday."

Her lashes fluttered down. Everything was happening so fast. Clearly, Brand feared she'd have second thoughts. "Okay," she agreed, but her voice wobbled.

His warm breath fanned her face an instant before he covered her mouth with his. Carly dug her fingers into his shoulders, unaccustomed to the sensations that he was arousing within her. Her lovemaking experience was limited, but Brand wasn't aware of that. He would learn of her inexperience soon enough.

She wound her arms around his neck and buried her face in his throat, kissing him with a compulsion she couldn't define. All she knew was that she wanted to be closer to him.

"Carly," he said, and groaned.

He kissed her with driving urgency, setting her down on the sofa and pressing her back so that she was lying flat.

"Carly . . . dear God." He brushed the hair from her face, his eyes finding hers. His fingers were shaking as he framed her face with his hands. "If we don't stop now, we'll end up making love right here."

Something in his eyes gave him away. "Are you afraid?" she whispered. He'd told her once that he hadn't made love to a woman since Sandra.

He released her and the silence stretched until Carly raised herself up on one elbow to study him. He regarded her steadily and nodded. "It's been a long time."

His honesty had been painful for him, but Carly offered him a trembling smile and lovingly kissed his brow. "We've waited this long. We can wait until after we're married."

His mouth teased the corner of hers as their breaths mingled. "I don't deserve you," he murmured, holding her close. "I'm no bargain."

Her soft laugh followed. "For that matter, neither am I."

Later, as Carly dressed for bed, she examined herself in the mirror and was shocked at how pale and waxen her features were. She prayed she was doing the right thing in agreeing to marry Brand. She was afraid, too, far more than he realized. His honesty had been a measure of his love. He wouldn't lie to her, and Carly admired him all the more for that.

The following morning, Brand picked her up and they went together for their blood tests.

"I'd like to have a minister marry us," Carly announced after they'd climbed into the car once more. They hadn't discussed who would perform the ceremony. From the way Brand was rushing things, Carly had the impression that he wanted a justice of the peace to do the honors.

Brand's fingers captured hers as he smiled faintly. "I'd prefer that, too."

An inner glow of happiness touched her eyes. "Where to next?" she asked cheerfully.

Brand reached for the folded newspaper on the seat between them. "I thought we'd look for a house to rent."

The mention of a house was a forceful reminder that Shawn and Sara would be joining them in less than a month.

"Yes," she said, and swallowed back the surge of panic that filled her. "We should do that."

Brand handed her the newspaper. "We'll need at least three bedrooms."

Carly nodded stiffly and read off a couple of the listings. "Do you want to check them out now?"

His eyes sought hers. "Sure. We have all day."

They found a rental through a real estate broker that sounded perfect. The picture showed a modern home with three bedrooms and a large yard. Another room off the kitchen could be used as an office for Brand.

"It's perfect, I know it. We don't even have to go see it." Carly watched Brand's eyes agree as he read over the details.

"There's a problem." The broker went on to explain that the house was badly in need of a thorough cleaning and paint job.

"It'll work out fine," Carly assured Brand later, when they were back in the car. "We can do the painting at night after work. If we work hard enough, everything will be ready by the time Shawn and Sara arrive."

"Carly." One corner of his mouth lifted. "The first weeks after we're married, we're going to have enough to do without fixing up a house."

She snuggled closer to his side and playfully nibbled at his earlobe. "I thought soon-to-be-husbands were supposed to humor their soon-to-be-wives."

"I have a lot more in mind than humoring." His voice was husky with longing as he turned her into his arms.

Carly surrendered to his kiss, wondering if she would always feel this rush of excitement at Brand's touch. She couldn't imagine it ever being any different.

After lunch they stopped in and talked to George, who pumped Brand's hand in congratulation but frowned when he heard Carly would need Friday off, in addition to a few extra days later on when they moved.

Later, when Brand dropped her off at her apartment and left to do errands, Carly had to pinch herself. She could scarcely believe that in a matter of days she was going to be both a wife and a mother.

A hot cup of coffee helped soothe her nerves. She was taking on a lot in a short amount of time. She had yet to met Brand's children. The responsibility of taking over the role as their mother overwhelmed her. But she'd do it. She'd be the best stepmother she could be and love them in a way that honored their mother. "Do you want to call Diana and Barney?" Brand asked later that night.

"No. Not until after we're married. Otherwise Diana will insist on leaving Hawaii and flying here to check you out before the wedding." She was only half teasing.

"I want to meet this friend of yours," Brand said.

"And you shall but all in due course," she promised.

He frowned a bit. "Don't you want Diana here for our wedding?"

Her husband seemed to forget Diana and Barney were on their honeymoon. "Brand, Diana's barely been married a week. I'd love to have her at our wedding, and she'd be here, too, but not if we're married this Friday. Do you want to wait?"

He looked at her as if she were joking. "No way."

"That's what I thought." The truth was, Carly didn't want to wait, either. "There will be plenty of time for you to meet Diana and Barney. I'll keep our wedding a secret until after the ceremony, and then tell her." Carly couldn't see interrupting her friend's honeymoon.

"Will she be surprised?"

Carly knew Diana's reaction would be closer to shock. "Yes." She laid her head on Brand's shoulder. "But there are advantages to being married only a week after my best friend," she said lightly. "We'll be able to celebrate our anniversaries together."

Brand's arm came up around her shoulders. "We'll have lots of those, Carly." His warm breath mussed her hair. "You've given me so much. Now it's time for me to return some of that. We'll be happy, won't we?"

She closed her eyes at the tenderness in his voice and responded with a gentle nod of her head because her throat felt thick with emotion.

No week had ever passed so quickly. Friday evening, with only a handful of people present, Carly Grieves became Brandon St. Clair's wife. A simple gold band adorned her ring finger. With so many expenses coming their way in the near future, Carly had decided against diamonds. Brand wore a gold band identical to hers.

Following the ceremony, Brand's eyes smiled into hers. His arm wrapped around her waist and held her close to his side. "Hello, Mrs. St. Clair."

"Hello, Mr. St. Clair."

George, looking uncomfortable in a suit and tie, shook Brand's hand and slipped him an envelope. "Just to give you two a start on a few things you're going to need," he said gruffly.

"Aren't you going to kiss the bride?" Carly asked her boss, with familiar affection.

George cleared his throat and looked to Brand for permission.

"Go ahead," Brand urged, and squeezed Carly's waist.

Standing on the tips of her toes, she lightly brushed her lips against George's cheek.

The older man flushed with pleasure. "I suppose this means you're going to be wanting extra time off every week."

"No. Things should settle back to normal once we return from Oregon," Carly said, lowering her gaze. They would be making a trip to Portland next week. She didn't mention that Brand's children would be coming in less than a month. The changes that would mean in her schedule hadn't been discussed.

"Are you ready to leave?" Brand asked.

"For our pre-honeymoon?" Carly questioned eagerly. Brand had been busy all week on what he termed "their surprise weekend plans." Carly suspected they wouldn't be leaving Anchorage, since they both were due back at work on Monday morning. Brand was scheduled to fly into Dutch Harbor on the Aleutian Islands in the first week of the month; he wanted Carly to fly with him, and on the return trip they'd stay at the lodge at Lake Iliamna. That was to be their official honeymoon. But this first weekend was a surprise Brand had planned especially for her.

His late-model Chevy was waiting for them in front of the church. Brand helped her inside and ran around to the front of the vehicle. "Are you ready for this?" he asked as he inserted the key in the ignition.

Carly tucked her arm in his and leaned her head quietly against his shoulder. "I've been ready for this all my life, Brandon St. Clair."

"Do you want to guess where we're going?"

"I haven't the foggiest idea. But it must be special, after all the time you've dedicated to it this week." She had only seen him one night that week after work.

Brand pulled up to the curb and parked the car. "Recognize this?"

"The rental house?" Wide brown eyes turned to Brand. "We got it?" Brand hadn't mentioned the house since that first day.

"Come and see." He jumped out of the car and walked around to the passenger side, lifting her into his arms. He closed the car door with his foot.

One step inside the house and Carly saw that the real estate agent hadn't underestimated the extent of the repairs that it required. The walls were badly in need of paint, and the entire place required a thorough cleaning.

"Close your eyes," Brand instructed. "All this is to be blocked from your mind." He carried her through the living room and down a long hallway.

"Brand, for heaven's sake, let me down," Carly objected. "You'll hurt your back."

"Don't tell me you're going to be one of those wives who complains all the time."

Carly laughed, her mood happy. "All right, I won't tell you." Playfully, she nibbled on the lobe of his ear.

Brand's hold tightened as he leaned forward and opened the door that led to the master bedroom.

The teasing laughter faded as Carly looked at the room for the first time. The walls were freshly painted in a light shade of blue. The navy blue bedspread and draperies were made from identical floral patterns.

"Oh, Brand." Carly breathed with a sense of awe. No wonder she hadn't seen him all week. He'd obviously been working here every night.

"The bedroom set is my wedding gift to you," Brand said tenderly as he lowered her feet to the plush carpet.

Running her hand along the polished surface of the oak dresser, Carly felt a surge of love that ran so deep it stole her breath. Finding the words to say what was in her heart would be impossible. Letting the spark of appreciation in her eyes speak for her, Carly looped her hands around Brand's neck and kissed him. "Thank you," she whispered. "You must have worked every night."

Brand arched her closer by pressing his hands into the small of her back. She could feel his smile against the crown of her head. "At least I was able to keep my hands off you. Maybe it's old-fashioned, but I wanted you to be my wife before we made love."

A sigh escaped her and Carly laid her head on his chest, closing her eyes. She'd thought a lot about their wedding night, and her feelings were mixed. She was eager and excited but at the same time apprehensive. In some ways she wished their lovemaking had been spontaneous and in others she was pleased that they'd waited until after the ceremony.

A finger under her chin raised her mouth to Brand's. When he kissed her, all of her pent-up longings for him exploded in a series of deep, hungry explorations. His hand manipulated the zipper at the back of her dress and artfully slipped the garment down her arms until it fell at her feet. Carly stood before her husband wearing only her creamy silk camisole, panties, and nylons. His hands at her breasts were tantalizingly intimate through the flimsy material, and her nipples became pebble hard, straining against his palm.

"Brand," she murmured breathlessly. "My suitcase is in the car. My silky nightgown's in there." She became lost again in one of his kisses.

"I want to get these things off you," Brand groaned, "not add another set."

"But I bought it especially for tonight."

Immediately, his mouth hardened in possession, claiming the trembling softness of hers. "Does it mean that much to you?"

Her hands crept upward, fingers sliding into the thick hair that grew at the base of his neck. "No. All I need is you."

The silk camisole had ridden up, and she could feel the roughness of his suit against her bare midriff. The buttons of his shirt left an imprint on her soft skin.

Brand's mouth worked sensuously over hers as Carly moved away just far enough to unfasten his buttons and slide his suit jacket and shirt from him. He helped as much as he could, his warm breath igniting her desire. Once free of the restricting clothing, Brand lifted the camisole over her outstretched arms so that her bare breasts nuzzled his chest. Wave after wave of pleasure lapped against her as her fingers sought his face, marveling at the strength of his features, sharpened now in his excitement.

"Carly." He ground out her name as he shifted his attention to the creamy curve of her neck and shoulder.

Wordlessly he took a step in retreat and, jerking aside his belt, removed the remainder of his clothes. Carly slipped out of her things and walked into his loving embrace. Brand lifted her into his arms and carried her to the bed.

"I love you, Carly," he whispered.

"And I love you," she returned. Her eyes misted with the intensity of her feelings. "I'll make you a good wife, Brand," she vowed. "And I'll be a good mother."

Tenderly, he laid her on top of the bed and placed a hand on either side of her face, his eyes boring into hers. "I already know that," he said, and pressed the full weight of his lean body onto hers. Carly's pulse raced hot and wild, and she knew he was just as aroused as she. His skin was fiery to the touch as she ran her hands down his back and hips. The heat fused them together.

"Carly?" Brand's voice was filled with wonder and surprise after their lovemaking. "Did I hurt you?"

"No," she said with a heartfelt sigh. "It was wonderful."

He smoothed the hair from her face. "It gets better," he promised each time.

He held her tightly, kissing her cheeks and eyes until his breathing had returned to normal. "Why didn't you tell me you were a virgin?"

"I didn't know how," she whispered, relaxing in the crook of his arm. "It was beautiful. I had no idea it would be this good."

"You're not disappointed?"

Carly raised herself up on one elbow and kissed the corner of his mouth. "You're joking."

Chuckling, he brought her back into his arms, his hand pressing her head to his chest. "It was wonderful for me, too, Carly."

"Can we do it again?"

"Again?" he asked. "You shameless hussy, I've barely recovered from the first time. Give me five minutes."

"That long?" Her mouth made a languorous foray over his chest and up past his shoulder until she located his mouth, teasing him with short, biting kisses. She centered her attention on one side of his mouth and worked across to the other.

Brand's fingers tightened as he rolled with her in his arms so that their positions were reversed. He kissed her deeply, urgently. They made love quickly; the explosive chemistry between them demanded as much.

Carly clung to him afterward, not wanting ever to let him go.

"Satisfied now?" he whispered against her ear.

She shook her head. "I don't think I'll ever be satisfied."

"Me, either," he said, holding her tightly at his side.

The next thing Carly knew, Brand was kissing her awake. "Are you hungry?"

"No, sleepy," she said with a yawn. "What time is it?"

"Ten. We haven't eaten dinner yet and I'm starved."

Carly sat up and pulled the sheet over her bare breasts. She'd hardly eaten all day and recognized the ache in the pit of her stomach as hunger pangs.

Brand slipped out of bed and reached for his pants. "I packed us a picnic basket. Wait here and I'll get it."

A couple minutes later, Brand returned, carrying Carly's suitcase and a basket with a bottle of champagne and two glasses resting on the top.

Carly slipped her white lace and silk gown over her head while Brand opened the champagne and poured them each a glass.

"To many years of happiness," Brand said, as he touched his glass to hers.

"To us," Carly added, and she took a sip of the sparkling liquid. The champagne tickled her throat. Laughing, she held her glass out for more. "What's there to eat?"

After refilling her glass, Brand opened the basket and brought out a large jar of green olives, a thick bar of chocolate, and some fried chicken.

Carly was so pleased she wanted to cry. "Oh, Brand, you're marvelous."

"I know what you like."

"You do?" she asked him seductively, locking her arms around his neck. "You may have to revise your list."

He pulled her into his embrace and nuzzled her neck. "Gladly," he whispered, just before his mouth claimed hers.

The only time they left the bedroom over the next two days was to make a quick run to Carly's apartment for more food.

Sunday morning Carly phoned Diana and Barney.

Diana answered her cell. "Carly!" she exclaimed. "This is a surprise. How's everything?"

"Great. But I thought you should know that I took your advice."

"My advice?"

"Yup. Would you like to talk to my husband?"

"Carly, you did it? You actually married Brand. My goodness, you're right, he is a fast worker! Why didn't you let me know? Yes, yes, let me talk to Brand."

Carly handed the phone to Brand and let him introduce himself to her friend. Wrapping her arms around his waist, she laid her head on his chest and was able to listen in on their conversation.

"No fair giving away all my childhood secrets." Carly's voice was playfully indignant when she took back the receiver.

"I wasn't," Diana denied, with a telltale laugh. "Well, not *everything*."

"I like being married," Carly admitted, with a catch in her voice. "Why didn't you tell me how great it is?"

"That's the problem," Diana said quickly. "You've got to be married to the right man."

Carly couldn't imagine sharing her life with anyone but Brand. "I've found him."

"So have I," Diana murmured. "Be happy, Carly."

Diana sounded as though she was close to tears. "I will. You, too."

When she replaced the receiver, Brand took her in his arms. "Shall we name our first daughter Diana?"

"Diana?" Carly feigned shock, and teased him lovingly. "I was thinking more along the lines of Brandy—after her father."

Groaning, Brand shook his head. "I think I'll pray for sons."

"Brand." She took his hand and batted her long lashes. "You want to try it in the shower here?"

"Are you crazy? You nearly drowned me the last time."

"Yes, but it was fun, wasn't it?"

"Carly." Brand brushed the hair from his forehead and sighed, attempting to hide a smile. "I'm too old for those kinds of tricks. I prefer a nice, soft mattress."

"But I'm sure we must have done something wrong. Everyone makes love in the shower. At least they always do in the books I read."

Brand rolled his eyes mockingly. "All right, if you insist." He pulled her into his embrace and kissed her until she was breathless and clinging. "This is my punishment for marrying a younger woman," he complained.

"No . . ." She giggled. "This is your punishment for marrying a virgin."

Monday arrived all too quickly. Brand dropped her off at the apartment so she could drive her car to work.

"Do you want to meet back here this evening or at the house?"

Brand appeared to mull the question over. "The house. I'll pick up something for dinner and we can start painting after we eat."

Carly dreaded the job. Every room in the house needed a fresh coat. She wanted to do Shawn's and Sara's bedrooms herself. It seemed like a little thing, but it would help her to assimilate the fact that she was going to be a mother to those two. Having come into a similar situation, Carly was determined to make them feel loved and welcome from the beginning.

Brand met her at the house with hamburgers and two thick vanilla malts.

They sat at their hastily purchased kitchen table and Carly handed her malt back to Brand.

"I thought you liked vanilla."

"I do, but I'm watching my weight."

He arched one brow questioningly. "You're almost too thin as it is."

"That's because you nearly starved me to death this weekend," she tossed back.

He stood and came around to her side of the table. "Is that a fact?" he asked, as he took her in his arms.

Her hands slid over his chest as their eyes met and held. The look in his eyes trapped the oxygen in her lungs.

"Ever read anything in those novels you mentioned about making love on the top of a table?" he asked her in a low, husky tone, his eyes sparkling with mischief.

"Mr. St. Clair, you shock me."

Brand straightened and began undoing the buttons of his shirt.

Surprised, Carly watched him with her mouth hanging open. "I thought you were teasing."

"Nope." He unbuckled his belt.

"What about dinner?"

"It can wait." He reached over and unfastened the buttons of her blouse.

Holding her breath, Carly reached around and unzipped her skirt. "I thought you wanted to paint."

"What I want should be evident."

The skirt fell to the floor, leaving her standing in her teddy and stockings.

Brand was devouring her with his eyes. She undid his pants and dropped them to the floor.

Slowly, his hands shaking slightly, Brand removed the remainder of her clothes until they were both naked. Then he scooped her up and carried her down the hall.

Their lovemaking was urgent, explosive, and they clung to each other afterward.

"I thought you wanted to do it on top of the table."

"The bedroom wasn't that far away."

She smiled and kissed the side of his neck. "Almost too far, as I recall."

"I don't think you fully understand yet what you do to me," he whispered.

Carly rolled onto her stomach and hooked one bare leg over his. "If we keep this up we won't be finished painting the house till Christmas."

Brand wrapped his arms around her and breathed in deeply. "The thought of hiring painters is growing more appealing by the minute."

Chapter Nine

The clock radio clicked and immediately soft music floated into the sunlit bedroom.

"Morning." Brand pulled Carly close to his side and leisurely kissed her temple.

"Already?" she groaned. Her eyes refused to open as she snuggled deeper within Brand's embrace. He was warm and gentle, and she felt too comfortable to move.

"Do you want me to make coffee this morning?"

Dark brown eyes flew open and she struggled to a sitting position. "No, I'll do it." Pausing at the side of the bed, Carly raised her hands high above her head, stretched, and yawned.

"Aren't you ever going to let me get up first?" Brand teased with loving eyes.

"Nope." She leaned over and lightly brushed her mouth over his.

Brand's arms snaked around her waist, and he deepened the contact with hungry demand. "What time is it?" he growled in her ear.

"Late," she teased, and kissed him back spiritedly. "Much too late for what you have in mind." Giggling, she escaped from his embrace and grabbed her light cotton robe from the end of the bed before heading for the kitchen. Mornings were her favorite part of the day. Waking up with Brand was the culmination of every dream she'd ever hoped would come to pass.

When the coffee had finished perking, she carried a cup in to Brand. He generally left for work an hour earlier than she needed to be at Alaska Freight, but they woke together and Carly dutifully cooked his breakfast and got him out the door. Then she turned her efforts to preparing for her own day.

Brand strolled into the kitchen as she was laying strips of bacon into a hot skillet. The fat sizzled and filled the room with the aroma of cooking meat. Nuzzling the side of her neck, Brand wrapped his arms around her from behind. "You smell good."

"That's not me, silly. That's the bacon."

His hand slid from her waist to press against her smooth, flat abdomen. "We haven't talked about this much, but I'd like it if you got pregnant soon." He was so pensive and serious, a mood neither of them had had time for during these past few days.

Carly set down her fork and turned in his arms. "There's no rush, is there? I'd like to adjust to one family before starting another."

Brand pulled out a kitchen chair and sat down. His hands hugged the coffee mug. "There won't be two families, Carly, only one."

Sighing, she came up behind him and slipped her arms around his neck. "That's not what I meant. Even if I was to get pregnant tomorrow, there'd still be six years between the baby and Sara. It would be almost like raising two families."

Brand nodded and placed his hand on hers. "I know. It's just that I've been separated from Shawn and Sara for so long that I don't want to put any more distance between us. I want us all to be one family, no matter how many children you and I may have."

"We will be a family," she promised, and returned to the stove. This weekend was the time they'd arranged to fly to Portland so Carly could meet the children and Brand's mother.

The two eggs were overcooked when she set the plate in front of Brand. He didn't say anything, but she knew he preferred his eggs sunny-side up. "Sorry about that," she said.

"Don't worry, the eggs are fine."

Carly took a long swallow of her orange juice.

"Are you worried about this weekend?" Brand wanted to know.

She was terrified, but didn't want Brand to guess. "I'm looking forward to meeting your family . . . *our* family," she corrected.

Brand kissed her tenderly before heading out the door. "Have a good day, honey."

The endearment rolled easily off his tongue, and again Carly had the feeling it was the same affectionate term he'd used with Sandra. She cringed. The pain was quick and sharp. She bit the inside of her cheek as she pulled open a kitchen drawer and brought out a cookbook. For the sixth time in as many days, she read the recipe for chicken and dumplings. The meal was to be a surprise for Brand. This would be her first home-cooked dinner for her husband.

Before very long, cooking would be a part of her everyday life, and the sooner she mastered the skill, the better. Shawn and Sara wouldn't be satisfied with green olives and chocolate. At least not after the first week.

The chicken was simmering on the stove as Carly dressed for work. The aroma of the bacon had made her feel weak with hunger. The small glass of orange juice had constituted her entire breakfast, and dumplings were out. To be on the safe side, she stepped on the scale. Two pounds. She'd been starving herself for ten miserable days and was only down two pounds. *Some* women were naturally svelte and others had to work at it. There wasn't any justice left in the world anymore, she grumbled on her way out the front door.

On her lunch break, Carly savored an apple, cutting it into thirty pieces in an effort to take her mind off how hungry she was. As part of her lunch break, Carly drove into town and bought Sara a doll, and Shawn a book on Mount McKinley. She knew so little about these two who were destined to be a major part of her life. Her nerves were crying out with vague apprehension at the coming meeting. Fleetingly, she wondered how they felt about meeting *her*.

Before returning to the office, Carly stopped off at the apartment and checked on the dinner. She reread the cookbook instructions, confident that she had done everything properly.

On the way out she stopped at the mailbox and collected the mail. Another letter from Jutta had arrived, and she ripped it open eagerly. Jutta sent her congratulations and claimed to be working on another oil painting that she thought Carly would like. She said she'd sell this one cheap.

Carly smiled, folded the letter, and placed it back inside the envelope. Jutta seemed to think the only interest Carly had in her was because of her artwork. As their friendship grew, she was certain that Jutta would feel differently.

Because she wanted Brand to be pleasantly surprised with her dinner, Carly left the office early. George was being a dear about everything, including the extra days off she needed. Carly felt like giving him a peck on the cheek as she rushed out the door, but hesitated, knowing he wouldn't know how to react to her display of affection.

Brand got home a half hour after she did. "I'm home," he called cheerfully.

"Hi." She stepped from the kitchen. The corners of her mouth trembled with the effort to hold back her tears.

He stopped in the middle of the living room and sniffed the air. "Something smells bad."

"I know." She swallowed tightly. "I tried to cook you a special dinner. It . . . it didn't work out." She gestured with one hand in angry bewilderment. "I . . . I don't know what I did wrong."

"Let me see," Brand offered as he headed for the kitchen.

"No!" she cried theatrically. "Don't go in there!"

"Carly." He gave her a look she felt he must reserve for misbehaving children.

Bristling, she cradled her stomach with her arms and shouted at him, "Go ahead, then, have a good laugh."

Brand's eyes softened. "I'm not going to laugh at you."

"Why not? It's hilarious. How many husbands do you know who come home to be greeted with the news that their dinner's on the ceiling?"

Brand did a poor job of disguising his amusement.

Anger swelled like a flood tide in Carly until she wanted to scream. "I'm sorry I can't be as perfect as Sandra. I tried." Sobs took control of her voice. "I really tried."

"Carly." He went pale and reached for her.

She broke from his grasp and gave way to huge hiccupping sobs, warding him off with her arm. "Don't you dare touch me." Each word was enunciated clearly.

Brand looked as if she'd struck him physically. He moved to the sofa and sat down. "I wondered." His voice was husky and raw. "But I didn't want to believe what was right in front of me."

The tears welled up and spilled down her face as she held her breath in an effort to stop crying.

"You did all this because of Sandra?" Brand asked flatly.

Carly nodded.

"And this insane dieting is because of her as well." It was a hard statement of fact and not a question.

"She was svelte."

"She was *gaunt*. Cancer does that to people." He rubbed his hand over his face. He was upset and didn't bother to conceal it. His mouth was pinched and his eyes narrow. "What do I have to do to make you understand that I don't want another Sandra?"

"I thought . . ."

"I know what you thought." He paced the floor. "For two years I grieved for Sandra. The ache inside me was so bad I ran from my children and separated myself from the world."

She kept her face averted, burying her chin in her shoulder. A dark curtain of hair fell forward.

"I love you, Carly. Your love has given me back my children and a reason to go on with my life. I don't want to bury myself in the past again. With you at my side, I want to look ahead at the good life we can share." He turned and walked over to her. "I want you. None other." Holding her, he wove his fingers in her hair and forced her to look up at him. She couldn't bear it and closed her eyes. Fresh tears squeezed through her lashes. Every breath was a sob.

"What I feel for you is entirely different from my love for Sandra," he continued. "She was an only child, pampered and loved all her life. Even as a little girl she was sickly. Her family protected her, and when we married I took over that role."

Carly made an effort to strain away from his hands, but her attempt did little good She didn't want to hear any more about Brand's first wife. Every word was like a knife wound.

"With Sandra, I felt protective and gentle," he said in

a low, soothing voice. "But with you I'm challenged and inspired. My love for you is deeper than anything I'd ever hoped to find on this earth. Don't compete with a dead woman, Carly."

She groaned with the knowledge that he was right. There was no winning if she set herself up as a replacement for Sandra. Trying desperately to stop crying, she put her arms around his neck. "I'm sorry," she wept. "So sorry."

"I am, too, love," he breathed against her hair. "I should have recognized what was happening."

"I wanted to be perfect for you and the children."

"You are," he whispered tenderly. "Now, let's see what can be salvaged from your dinner."

"Not much, I'm afraid." She inhaled a steadying breath. "It may be far worse than you realize," she said, avoiding his eyes. "I think my dumplings may have dented the ceiling and we'll be out the damage deposit."

He started laughing then, uncontrollably, and soon she was laughing with him, free and content with the knowledge that she was loved for herself.

Chapter Ten

Carly's fingers tightened around Brand's arm. "Are you sure I look okay?"

"You're beautiful." He squeezed her hand. "You're perfect. They're going to love you."

Carly wished she had the same unfailing optimism. Shawn and Sara would be meeting them at the Portland Airport and the FASTEN YOUR SEAT BELT sign was already flashing in preparation for landing.

A thin film of nervous perspiration broke out across her upper lip and forehead, and she wiped it away with her free hand. A thousand nagging apprehensions crowded their way into her mind. The tightening sensation that attacked the pit of her stomach was identical to the one she'd experienced as a child whenever she'd been transferred into a new foster home. If she couldn't fit in with this new family, her life would be a constant battle. The identical situation was facing her with Shawn and

Sara. So much of her happiness with Brand depended on what happened this weekend.

"Carly." Brand squeezed her hand again. "Relax. You're as stiff as new cardboard."

"I can't help it." Even her whisper was tortured. "What will we do if Shawn and Sara don't like me?"

"But they're going to love you," Brand argued.

"How can you be so sure?" She knew she sounded like a frightened little girl. How could anyone who'd leaped headlong into as many adventures as she had be so terrified of two small children?

Brand tightened his hold on her fingers and raised them to his mouth to tenderly kiss the inside of her palm. "They're going to love you because I do."

A flood of emotion clouded her eyes. "I want to make this work, Brand," she said, and she lowered her eyes so he couldn't see how overemotional she was becoming. "I really do."

"I know, love."

Carly's heart fell to her ankles when the plane touched down. A few minutes later, they were walking down the jetway that led to the cavernous terminal and the baggage claim area.

"Daddy, Daddy!" The high, squeaky voice of a young girl came at them the moment they cleared the secure area.

Brand fell to one knee as blond-haired Sara threw herself into his arms. Shawn followed, and squeezed his father's neck so tightly Carly was amazed that Brand was still breathing. With a child on each hip, Brand stood.

"Shawn and Sara, this is Carly."

"Hi, Carly." They spoke together and lowered their eyes shyly.

"Hello."

"Daddy told us all about you," Sara said eagerly.

"Did you really climb a whole mountain?" Shawn queried, with a hint of disbelief.

"It was the hardest thing I ever did in my life," Carly confirmed. "By the time I made it down, my nose was redder than Rudolf the Red-Nosed Reindeer's and my lips had blisters all over them."

"Wow." Shawn's big blue eyes were filled with awe. "I'd like to climb a mountain, too."

"Someday, son," Brand promised.

"Welcome home, Brand." A crisp, clear voice spoke from behind them.

Carly's attention was diverted to the older woman who stood apart from the small group. Her hair was completely gray, but her eyes were like Brand's—only faded and with a tired, faraway look.

Brand lowered the children to the floor. "Mom, this is my wife, Carly."

"Hello, Mrs. St. Clair." Carly stepped forward and extended her hand.

Brand's mother shook it politely and offered her an uncertain smile. "Please, call me Kay. With two Mrs. St. Clairs around, there's bound to be some confusion."

Carly's spirits plummeted. Brand's mother didn't bother to disguise her lack of welcome. "Thank you," she said stiffly.

The older woman's eyes centered on the children and softened. "Say hello to your new mother, children."

"Hello," they cried in unison, with eager smiles.

"I imagine you're tired," Kay St. Clair said conversationally on the way to pick up their luggage. "How was the flight?"

"Fine." Carly's mind searched frantically for something to say. "The weather certainly is nice." Bright, sunny skies had welcomed them to Oregon.

"But then this must be paradise compared to Alaska," Kay returned in the same bland tone she'd used earlier.

The sky had been just as blue and beautiful in Anchorage, but Carly let the subject drop. There wasn't any reason to start off this relationship with a disagreement by comparing the two states. Indeed, Oregon was beautiful, but Alaska was equally so, only in a different way. But Carly doubted that she could explain that to Brand's mother.

Lunch was waiting for them back at a stylish two-story brick house with a meticulously kept yard and spotless interior. The entire house was so clean that Carly thought it had probably been sterilized. Framed pictures lined the fireplace mantel in the living room. There were photographs of Brand's two younger brothers and their families—and a picture of Brand with Sandra on their wedding day. Carly's gaze was riveted to the picture, and the color washed from her face. Abruptly, she turned away, unable to bear the sight. By keeping the photo on the mantel, Brand's mother had made her statement regarding Carly.

If Brand noticed how little she ate, he said nothing. Shawn and Sara carried the conversation beautifully. Their joy at seeing their father again was unabashedly enthusiastic. Carly discovered that it would be easy to love those two, and she silently prayed that they could come to love and accept her.

Kay St. Clair cleared her throat before addressing Carly. "Tell me, what did your family think of this rushed marriage?"

"My family?" Carly knew just by looking at Kay St. Clair that she was a woman who put a lot of stock in one's background. "I'm afraid I don't have any, Mrs. St. Clair . . . Kay," she amended.

"Don't be silly, child, of course you do. Everyone has family."

"Carly was raised in foster homes, Mother," Brand explained for her.

"You were orphaned?" Kay St. Clair disregarded her son and centered her full attention on Carly.

"Not exactly. I . . . I was taken from my mother by the state when I was Sara's age."

"What about your father?" Shock had whitened the aging face. Lines of disapproval wrinkled her brow as Kay St. Clair set her fork aside.

"I never knew my father."

A soft snicker followed. "Are you sure your parents were married?"

"Mother," Brand barked. "You're insulting my wife."

Carly placed a hand on his forearm and shook her head. She didn't want to cause any discord between Brand and his mother. "As a matter of fact, I'm not completely sure that they were."

Shawn and Sara had lowered their heads at the sound of raised voices. They sat across from Carly looking so small and frightened that her heart ached with the need to reassure them.

"I hope you like surprises." Carly directed the comment to the children. "Because I brought you each one."

"You did?" Shawn's face brightened with excitement. "Can I see it?"

"Can I see mine, too?" Sara's eyes found her grandmother's, and some of her eagerness faded. "Please," she added politely.

"After we finish lunch," Carly promised, and winked.

"Both Shawn and Sara have to brush their teeth first," Kay St. Clair inserted with a heavy note of censure.

"We never brush our teeth after lunch. Why do we have to do it today?" Shawn asked, a puzzled look in his eyes.

Their grandmother bristled noticeably. "Because we were too busy this morning. And until you move in with your father and . . . Carly, you must do as I say."

"Yes, Grandma," Shawn and Sara returned, like finely trained puppets.

Carly watched as a frown worked its way across Brand's face. His mother's reaction to Carly seemed to be as much of a surprise to him as it was to her. Brand hadn't told her a lot about his mother, and she'd pictured her as the round, grandmotherly sort. Kay St. Clair certainly wasn't that. She obviously cared for Shawn and Sara, and they returned that love, but she wasn't the warm, open person Carly had expected. But then, *she* wasn't the bride Kay St. Clair had anticipated, either.

"You have a lovely home, Kay." Carly tried again, knowing how difficult this meeting was for the older woman.

"Thank you. I do my best." The words were polite.

Carly swallowed tightly and looked at Brand. He was

pensive, sad. He must have felt her gaze because he gave her a reassuring smile. But it didn't fool Carly. She knew what he was thinking.

"Are there parks in Anchorage?" Shawn wanted to know.

"Lots of them," Brand confirmed.

"Are there any close to where we're going to live?"

"Not real close," Carly answered. "Farther than walking distance. But there's a big backyard in the house we're renting and I think we can probably persuade your dad to put up a swing set."

"Really?" Sara's blue eyes became round as saucers. "Grandma doesn't like us to play on her lawn."

"Children ruin the grass," Kay announced in starched tones. "So I take Shawn and Sara to the park."

"Almost every day," Sara added.

"How nice of your grandma to do that for you." Brand's mother had obviously tried hard to give the children a good home.

"I'll be sending a list of instructions with Shawn and Sara," Kay said, her eyes avoiding Carly's. "It's quite extensive, but I feel the transition from Oregon to Alaska will be much smoother for them if you follow my advice."

"Mother, I don't think—"

"That was thoughtful of you," Carly said, interrupting her husband. "I'll be pleased to read them over. Mothering is new to me, and I'll admit I have lots to learn."

"I'm finished now, Grandma," Shawn said eagerly. "Can I go brush my teeth?"

"Say it properly," Kay St. Clair ordered.

"May I be excused, please?"

A small smile of pride cracked the tight lines of the older woman's face. "Yes, you may be excused. Very good, Shawn."

"May I be excused, too?" Sara requested.

"*Excused,*" Kay corrected. "Say it again."

"Excu . . . excused." Sara beamed proudly at having managed the difficult word.

"Yes. Both of you brush your teeth and then you can see what your father brought you."

"Carly brought the gifts." Brand corrected the intended slight.

Her meal was practically untouched when Carly set her fork aside. "If you'll excuse me, I'll get the gifts from my suitcase." She didn't wait for Kay's permission, although she had the suspicion that it was expected of her.

The edge of the mattress sank with her weight as Carly covered her face with her hands. This meeting with Kay St. Clair was so much worse than she'd anticipated.

"We brushed our teeth." Shawn and Sara stood in the open doorway, startling her.

Carly forced herself to smile. "Then I bet you're ready for your presents."

They both nodded with wide-eyed eagerness.

Carly took out the two decoratively wrapped packages from inside her suitcase and handed them to Shawn and Sara.

They sank to the floor and ripped off the ribbon and paper with a speed that was amazing.

"A doll," Sara cried, her young voice filled with happy delight. "I've always, always wanted one just like this."

Two young arms circled Carly's neck and hugged her close.

Carly squeezed her fondly in return. "I'm glad you like it."

"Wow." Shawn's eyes were wide as he leafed through the picture book about the Alaskan mountains. "Thank you."

"Can we show Grandma?" Sara wanted to know.

"Of course." Carly followed them into the living room and noted again the censure in Kay St. Clair's eyes as she examined the gifts.

"I never did approve of those dolls." She spoke to her son, but the slight was meant for Carly.

Indecision flared in Brand's eyes. He was as confused and unsure as Carly.

"Daddy said you were going to be our new mother. Can I call you Mom?" Sara asked, tugging at Carly's pants leg.

"If you like."

Kay St. Clair's mouth narrowed into a tight line.

"Maybe you should call me Carly," she added hurriedly.

Brand brought Sara onto his knee. "You do what's the most comfortable for you."

"But I thought we already had a mom."

"You did," Kay St. Clair inserted coolly. "But she died."

"I think I'll call you Carly," Shawn stated thoughtfully, after a long pause.

"If that's what makes you most comfortable." Carly responded as best she could under the circumstances. In one foster home where she'd lived, the parents had insisted she call them Mother and Father. Half the time the words had stuck in her throat. She wouldn't be offended if Shawn chose to call her by her first name.

"I think I'll call you Mom," Sara said from her father's knee. "I don't remember my other mommy."

"Sure you do, Sara," Kay St. Clair said sharply.

"All I can remember is that she smelled funny and she didn't have any hair."

A pained look flickered in Brand's eyes, one so fleeting that for a moment Carly thought she'd imagined it. But when he spoke, the pain in his voice confirmed the sadness in his eyes.

"That was the smell of the hospital and all her medicine," Brand explained carefully. "She lost her hair because the doctors were doing everything they could to make her well again. One of those treatments was called chemotherapy."

"And it made all her hair come out?" Two pairs of serious blue eyes studied Brand.

He nodded. "But your mother had real pretty hair. Just like yours, Sara."

The small face wrinkled in deep thought. "I wish I could remember her better."

"I do too, sweetheart," Brand murmured tenderly, holding his daughter in his arms.

Standing outside the circle of this poignant family group, Carly felt a brooding sense of distance, of separation. These three—four, if she included Brand's mother—were a family in themselves. The breath caught in her lungs as she watched them. All the emotional insecurities of her childhood reared up, haunting her, confronting her with the unpleasant realities of this marriage.

Again, just as she had been as a child, she was on the outside looking in. She belonged, and yet she didn't. She wasn't part of the family but separate. Any love and attention she'd received when growing up had always been what was left over from that given to the family's real children. She wasn't Brand's first wife but his second. And clearly a poor second, judging from his mother's reaction after meeting her.

"If you'll excuse me, I'd like to lie down." Her voice was barely above a whisper. She avoided Brand's eyes as she turned toward the bedroom.

Her heart was pounding so hard and fast that by the time she reached the bed she all but fell onto the soft mattress. Everything she'd dreaded and feared was happening. And the worst part of it was she could do nothing to change what was going on around her.

When she heard Brand's footsteps, Carly closed her eyes and pretended to be asleep. He hesitated in the doorway—before turning away.

Carly didn't know how long she stared at the ceiling. The muted sounds coming from the bedroom next to hers distracted her troubled thoughts. As much as she wanted to hide, Carly knew she couldn't stay in the bedroom for the entire weekend.

After combing her hair, she added blush to her cheeks. If she didn't, Brand was sure to comment on how pale she looked.

As she walked past Sara's room, Carly paused and glanced inside. The little girl was sitting on top of her mattress. A jewelry box was open in front of her, and whatever was inside commanded her attention.

"Hi."

"Hi . . . Mom." Sara looked up and spoke with a shy smile.

"What are you looking at?"

"Pictures of my other mommy."

Carly's heart plummeted. She was a fool to believe that Sandra wouldn't haunt her. Borrowed dreams were all the future held. Another woman's husband. Another woman's children.

"Would you like to see?"

Some perverse curiosity demanded that Carly look. Sitting on the bed beside the sweet, blond-haired child, she examined each color print.

"My hair is like hers, isn't it?"

"Yes." The strangled sound that came from Carly's throat made Sara turn and stare at her.

"She was real pretty, too," Shawn said from the hallway. "Sometimes she sprayed on perfume and smelled good." Shawn seemed to want to correct his sister's memory.

"Did she read to us?" Sara inquired softly. "Like Grandma does sometimes?"

"Yup. Don't you remember, Sara? Don't you remember anything?"

Carly couldn't stand much more of this. She was certain the children didn't often talk about their mother. Brand's presence had resurrected these curious memories. The pain it caused her to listen to them speak about Sandra was beyond description. She couldn't take their mother away from them, but she wasn't sure that she could live in the shadow of Sandra's memory.

"I think I'll go find your father," Carly said, hiding behind a cheerful façade.

"He's talking to Grandma on the patio," Shawn provided. "We're supposed to be resting." He added that second fact with a hint of indignation. "Second-graders shouldn't have to take naps," he mumbled under his breath just loud enough for Carly to hear. "When we come and live with you and Dad, I won't have to, will I?"

Carly ruffled the top of his blond head. "No," she whispered. "But don't say anything to your grandmother."

Shawn's wide eyes sparkled and they shared a conspiratorial smile.

"When are we moving to Anchor . . . Alaska?" Sara asked, tucking the pictures back inside the jewelry box.

"Three weeks." Hardly any time at all, Carly realized. Certainly not enough to settle the horrible doubts she was facing.

"Will you read to us and tell us stories?"

Carly stared blankly at the pair. "If you like."

"Goody." Sara clapped her hands gleefully.

"Shh," Shawn warned. "Grandma will hear."

Raised voices on the patio outside stopped Carly halfway through the kitchen. Brand and his mother were in the middle of a heated exchange. Their voices struggled to remain calm and composed. Carly doubted that Brand's mother ever shouted.

"But you hardly know her," Kay returned, with an uncharacteristic quiver that revealed how upset she was.

"I know everything that's necessary. Carly's given me back a life I thought I'd lost when Sandra died." There was an exasperated appeal in the way Brand spoke.

"There was no need to remarry so soon. Certainly you could have found someone more suitable," Kay St. Clair said, as she examined the rose bushes that grew in abundance around the patio.

Carly stood next to the sliding glass door, but neither was aware of her presence.

"I wish you'd give her a chance, Mother. Carly's the best thing that's ever happened to me. Don't I deserve a little happiness? Shawn and Sara . . ."

"That brings up another matter," his mother interrupted crisply. "How can you possibly think Carly is a proper replacement for the care I've given Shawn and Sara? When I told you I wanted to relax and travel for a time, I assumed you'd hire a housekeeper. I had no idea you'd marry the first woman to turn you on."

Brand's jaw went white and he seemed to struggle with his anger. The lines that were etched out from his eyes relayed the effort it took. There was a silent, dangerous glare in his eyes. "Carly is everything I've ever hoped to find in a woman."

Slowly, deliberately, Brand's mother shook her head with disapproval. "Can't you see that she's trying to bribe the children? Bringing them presents, telling them about a swing set. Really, Brand. And her family . . ."

"What does that have to do with anything?" Brand's tight expression grew grim.

"Honestly, son, sometimes you can be so blind." Kay cut a delicate rosebud from the flowering bush. "I don't mean to sound crass when I say that Carly is hardly the type of woman that men marry."

Shock waves tumbled through Carly. Her hand

reached for the kitchen counter to steady herself. Her knees felt so weak that she thought for a moment that she might collapse. In all her life no one had ever said anything that could hurt her more. With an attitude that bordered on the fanatical, she'd tried desperately not to be anything like her mother. Anger and outrage seared her mind.

Brand looked as if he was about to explode.

Stepping onto the patio, Carly tilted her head at a proud angle. "You will apologize for that comment, Mrs. St. Clair."

Carly didn't know who was more shocked: Brand or his mother.

Kay was obviously flustered, but to her credit recovered quickly and cleared her throat. "It's often been said that people who listen in on conversations don't hear good things about themselves."

Brand moved to Carly's side and slipped an arm around her waist, bringing her close to him. "You owe us both an apology, Mother."

Carly didn't want him to touch her but hadn't the strength to escape him. She felt stiff and brittle. Her heart was pounding so loud, she was convinced the whole city could hear it.

Kay St. Clair conceded. "Perhaps. Only time will prove what I say. Until then, I can only offer my regrets for any thoughtlessness on my part." Without a hint of remorse, she returned her attention to the rosebush.

Brand took Carly's hand and pulled her into the kitchen. "Let's get out of here," he insisted. "I won't have you subjected to this."

"No." Her throat worked convulsively. "We can't."

"Oh, yes we can." He raked a hand through his hair, his voice tight with impatience. "You don't have to take this from anyone. Least of all, my mother."

Gently, Carly shook her head. "She loves you, and she loves Shawn and Sara. I'm a stranger who's invaded her world. And I'm not carrying the proper credentials."

"Carly." Brand frowned, unsure.

"I understand her better than you think," Carly whispered. "If we leave now, the situation will be unbearable for Shawn and Sara."

"We could take them with us," Brand argued.

"And cause an even greater rift between you and your mother? Taking the children now would be heartless. She loves them, Brand."

"But she's hurt you, and I won't stand for that." His eyes roved over her face.

"Your mother's doubts and mistrusts are natural."

Brand's fingers bit into her upper arms. "Don't make excuses for her."

Carly closed her eyes and slowly shook her head. "The family I moved in with when I was fourteen had a natural daughter the same age. She hated me. It wasn't that I'd done anything. But I was there. I took away from the attention and love she felt was *her* due—not mine. I was a stranger with a murky past."

Brand brought her into his arms. "You're not a teenager anymore, Carly. You can't compare that to what's happening with my mother now."

Her smile was sad. She wouldn't argue with him, but in her heart, she knew. The situation was no different— and in many ways it was worse.

That night Carly lay awake. She could tell by the way Brand was breathing that he wasn't asleep either. The space between them seemed greater than just a few inches. In some ways whole universes stretched between them.

"You awake?" he whispered.

"Yes." She turned to cuddle him, nestling her head against his shoulder. The need to feel his arms around her was strong. "I'm cold."

Immediately, Brand's arms brought her more fully into his embrace. "Tell me what happened in that foster home you were talking about earlier."

"Why?"

"I need to know," he returned in a slow, uneven murmur.

"Her name was Joyce," Carly murmured softly. "She never did learn to like me. I was a threat to her. Not with just her family, but at school as well. When we were allowed to date, it didn't matter who asked me out, Joyce had to prove that she could take that boy away from me."

"Did she?"

Carly shrugged. "Sometimes. But it didn't matter." The only man Carly had ever really loved was Brand.

"Did you compete with her?"

"I tried hard not to," she admitted and smiled wryly. "But she was intimidated, simply by my being there."

"Her parents couldn't see what was happening?"

"I'm sure they could, but their hands were tied. If they'd intervened, then Joyce would have had all the more reason to hate me."

"So you were left to sink or swim," he said dryly.

As he spoke, Carly's fingers playfully tugged at the hairs on his chest.

"If you don't stop doing that, I won't be responsible for what happens," Brand ground out near her ear.

Carly giggled, releasing the tension that had stretched between them only seconds before. "That sounds promising."

"I can offer you a lot more than promises," Brand mumbled, and stopped her fingers, capturing one arm. Twisting, he repositioned himself so that he was holding her hands down at either side of her head. "Do you surrender?"

"Never," Carly said, and laughed softly. "I'd be crazy to give up when I'm winning."

"Winning?" he asked incredulously.

"You bet." She lifted her head just enough to press her mouth lightly to his. In a short, teasing action her tongue moistened his mouth. Brand released a short sigh and melted against her. His hands no longer pinned her to the bed as they sought softer, more feminine areas. Carly wasn't given the opportunity to move as his mouth ravaged hers. Pressing her into the mattress, he buried his face in the hollow of her throat, teasing her with his tongue.

"See?" she whispered happily. "What did I tell you? I'm winning."

"You're mighty brave in my mother's house." Brand knew how uncomfortable she'd be making love with only a thin wall separating them from Kay.

"Wait until you see how bold I can get!" Carly said, with a soft, subdued laugh.

"Daddy?"

The sound of the soft voice startled Carly. Brand rolled aside and Carly sat upright.

"I can't sleep." Sara stood in the doorway, tightly clutching her new doll under her arm.

"Did we wake you up?" Carly wanted to know, tossing Brand an accusing glare.

"No. I had to go potty and then I heard you giggle and I wanted to giggle, too."

Carly motioned with one finger for Sara to come to her. The little girl scooted eagerly across the floor to Carly's side of the bed. Leaning over, she whispered in Sara's ear and the child broke out in delighted laughter.

"What'd you say about me?" Brand demanded mockingly.

"How'd you know I said anything that had to do with you?"

"You had that look in your eye."

Carly threw back the sheets and Sara crawled under the covers with her. "You can't blame me if women often react to you with laughter. Isn't that right, Sara?"

The little girl agreed with an eager nod.

"What's all the noise about?" Shawn stood in the doorway, rubbing his eyes.

"Did your father wake you up, too?" Carly asked.

"No, Sara did. She was giggling."

"That was Carly," Brand corrected.

Shawn hesitated. "How come Sara gets to sleep with you?"

"That wasn't my idea," Brand said, and lifted the covers. "Might as well get the whole family in here."

Shawn climbed in beside his father. "I'm sleepy. Good night," he whispered.

Brand looked at Carly, with Sara snuggled close in her arms, and the tenderness in his eyes was enough to make her want to cry.

"Good night, family," Brand issued softly, and reached for Carly's hand.

Chapter Eleven

The float plane veered to the left after taking off from Dutch Harbor. The small settlement was in the long tail of the Aleutian Islands, which stretched like a graceful arc of stepping-stones between two continents. The Aleutians spanned hundreds of miles to the farthest western extension of North America. Carly gazed out of the window at Unalaska Island, which was wedged between the frigid North Pacific and the storm-tossed Bering Sea.

June had arrived, and Alaska had shed its cold winter coat, stretching and waking to explode in flowers and sunshine. To Carly, with Brand at her side, it was paradise.

She had only flown with him a handful of times, and usually on short trips that were accomplished in less than a day. Now, high above the dark waters, she was amazed by the harshness of the terrain below. The islands had few trees, all of stunted growth. Grass grew in abundance and covered the ground. The contrast with the magnificent cliffs and the forests thick with life on the Alaska mainland was striking.

Looking around her now, she was struck again by the serene mountains. Capped with snow, they stretched for miles in a land called "America's Siberia." Brand had explained that the Aleutian Islands contained the longest range of active volcanoes in the United States. Forty-six was the number he'd quoted her.

Brand turned his attention from the controls. "You're very quiet," he said, above the roar of the engine. Reaching for Carly's hand, he kissed her fingertips.

She offered him a dry smile.

"Are you tired?"

"Not at all. I'm overwhelmed by Alaska's diversity." What she was really thinking was how much she wanted Brand to teach her to fly. His reluctance was more obvious every time she brought up the subject. Carly didn't kid herself. She knew why.

"Dutch Harbor's got quite a history," Brand remarked. "During World War Two, when Japan was preparing for the battle of Midway, they bombed Dutch Harbor."

"Did their bombers fly off course?" Carly teased. "Midway's in the *South* Pacific."

"No, they'd hoped to draw the Pacific fleet north. The United States spent fourteen months and hundreds of lives in liberating the islands. Most of those men never saw the enemy. They died from the weather and disease."

Carly's mind filled with images of young men bloody, shaking, and freezing. She recalled having read something about the war in the Aleutians.

"How long before we arrive at Lake Iliamna?" She wanted to direct her thoughts from the unpleasant paths her mind was exploring.

"Not long. Are you anxious for our honeymoon?"

"What I want to know is what you had to promise George for me to get all this time off. I thought he'd explode because I wanted to attend Diana's wedding. Now he's given me time off two weeks running."

"What makes you think I promised him anything?"

"I know George." In some ways she knew him better than she did Brand.

His gaze roamed possessively over her face. "Don't ask so many questions."

Carly had faced a lot of unanswered questions this past week. Brand's children were beautiful, delightful. But she couldn't look at them without seeing Sandra. Brand knew that, and had tried in some illogical way to make it up to her all week. His mother had reminded Carly forcefully that she would never fit into Kay's image of a wife and mother. For a time Carly might be able to fool herself, but it wouldn't last long. She was an intruder in their lives, just as she had infringed on other lives as a child. There were no dreams for her. Only the borrowed ones of others.

Brand had sensed her qualms. All week he'd been watching, waiting. For what, Carly wasn't sure. He might have thought she was going to leave him, but she wasn't. At night, he'd reach for her. "I love you, Carly," was all he'd say. Their lovemaking was volcanic. With his arms wrapped securely around her, he fell asleep afterward. Carly wasn't so fortunate. She'd slept fitfully all week, waking in the darkest part of the night that precedes dawn. Often she was up and dressed when Brand awoke. They were both praying with a desperation born of silent torment that this time alone, this honeymoon, would set things right.

Lake Iliamna was as beautiful as Brand had described. The male proprietor of the log-cabin lodge welcomed them like family. He'd known Brand since childhood— which meant he'd known Sandra as well.

Carly tried not to think about that as they climbed the polished stairs that led to their suite. The honeymoon suite.

The moment the door closed, Brand reached for her and kissed her hungrily. His mouth lingered to tease the curve of her lips.

"Carly," he whispered, as he lifted the thick sweater over her head. "I need you." His fingers hurried with the buttons of her blouse, pushing it from her shoulders.

Carly's fingers were just as eagerly working at his clothing, and when they fell into the bed, she kissed him and whispered, "I do love you, Brand." Her voice was small and filled with emotion.

"I know." The desperate ring of his response spoke of his own fears. As if afraid he had admitted something he shouldn't have, Brand kissed her. The hard pressure of his mouth covered hers as he pushed her deep into the comfort of the mattress. It wasn't long before Carly lost herself in the golden sensations of his lovemaking.

Carly stood in her silk robe, gazing out of the window onto the serene, blue lake in the distance. Brand continued to sleep peacefully, undisturbed by her absence. She turned and studied him for an instant as she tried to swallow back the doubts that reared up to face her like a charging enemy. After they'd made love, Carly had lain in his arms and thought how much simpler life would be if she had become his lover instead of his wife. Shawn and Sara were due to arrive in Anchorage in less than two weeks and she wasn't ready. Not emotionally. Not in any way that mattered. These two wonderful children expected a mother . . . a family—not some emotionally insecure little girl who was struggling to reconcile her past. Shawn, Sara, and Brand deserved much more than what she could give them. At least, what she was capable of giving them now.

"Morning." Brand joined her at the window, slipping his hands around her slim waist. His mouth came down to lightly claim her lips and nibble on their softness.

"Why didn't you wake me?" His warm breath mingled with hers.

Carly wrapped her arms around his neck and tried to respond, but her body refused to relax.

"Honey, what's wrong?" His hands rubbed her back in a soothing, coaxing motion as his eyes lovingly caressed hers.

Whenever Brand called her by that affectionate term, she bristled and wanted to scream at him. "Don't call me that," she returned stiffly, hating herself for being so petty.

"'Honey'? Why not?"

Carly inhaled sharply. "Because that's what you used to call Sandra."

The morning light accentuated the frustrated, tired look in Brand's dark eyes. He released her and walked to the other side of the room. Jerking his hand through his hair, Brand expelled a hard breath. "Yes, sometimes I did. But that was then. You're now. Sandra has no part in our lives."

"But ultimately she affects us."

"Carly, please," he said, his fists clenched as he struggled to control his anger. "Sandra is *gone*. How long are you going to compete with a dead woman?"

Her arms cradled her stomach as she turned from him and stared sightlessly out the window. Arguing the matter was useless. Her heart was breaking. She couldn't let them continue as they had this week—stepping around each other, avoiding confrontations, pretending nothing was wrong. "I should never have married you, Brand. We would've been wonderful lovers." Her voice became a low, aching whisper. "But what we have now isn't going to work."

"I don't accept that. You're my wife and I won't let you go."

"You'll have to," she said gently, hating the emotion that moistened her eyes. "It isn't in me to let Shawn and Sara arrive feeling the way I do."

"They're coming, and there's nothing that can be done about it now." Frustration thinned his mouth. Her heart cried in anguish, but for a moment no sound came from the tight muscles of her throat.

"Do you think I enjoy feeling like this?" she cried. "I'd give anything to be different. Shawn and Sara are beautiful, warm children. But they're *Sandra's* children."

"They're our children," he returned.

"Then why do I see Sandra every time I look at them?"

"Because that's all your self-pity allows you to see. If

you'd look past your own insecurities, you'd recognize how much they want and need you. All three of us do, Carly." The desperate edge to his voice was painful to listen to. "Sandra has nothing to do with us," he said in a pleading voice.

"Then you can't recognize what's right in front of your eyes," she whispered, fighting back the emotion. "What makes you so uncomfortable about me learning to fly?"

Dark eyes narrowed harshly. "It's dangerous, and any one of a hundred things could happen—"

"And I could be killed," she finished for him. "Sandra died and you're afraid I will, too."

"All right," he shouted. "But what's wrong with being cautious? If I lost you, it'd kill me. If you blame Sandra for that, you're right."

"But where does it stop? Will you be afraid to let me climb or hike or anything else?" She didn't wait for him to respond. "I'm my own person and there will be lots of things I'm going to try."

"I just don't want you to do anything dangerous."

Carly fought to remain outwardly calm and controlled, but the battle was a losing one. "Because of Sandra," she said.

"Okay, you're right. I've already lost one wife."

"Brand," she murmured softly, "I can't take that kind of protective suffocation."

He began pacing the floor, clenching and unclenching his fists. Irritation and bewilderment produced a deep frown in him, but when he spoke his voice displayed no emotion. "I think I knew this was coming," he murmured, his voice thick with resignation. "You haven't been the same since we got back from Portland."

"Your mother is a very perceptive woman. She knew instantly that I wasn't the right kind of wife for you. And certainly not the kind of mother Shawn and Sara need."

"My mother knows nothing." Brand hurled the words at her. He turned and stormed across the room, dressing quickly. His hand was already on the doorknob when he paused and turned to Carly. "And you know nothing. Go ahead and run. See how far you get. I won't let go of you, Carly. You're my wife, and I intend to stay married to you the rest of my life." He left then, leaving Carly standing at the window feeling more wretched and miserable than she could ever remember.

The remainder of their honeymoon was a nightmare for Carly. They barely spoke to each other, and when they did, it was in stilted, abrupt sentences.

On the flight back to Anchorage, neither of them said a word. The lush green beauty of the world below was overshadowed by the heaviness in their hearts.

Brand carried their suitcases inside the door. Silently, he lugged Carly's luggage into the bedroom while she shuffled through the mail and noted that there was a long letter from Jutta. They corresponded often now. Carly felt she had gained a valued friend in the older woman. From that first stilted meeting at the correctional center, their relationship had flowered through the mail. Carly was often surprised at how articulate Jutta could be. She was often insightful and wise.

Brand hadn't said a word as they'd arrived home. She

tried to remain unaffected by his attitude, but she was having trouble succeeding. He'd been cold and distant since that first morning. Not that she blamed him.

Brand sat on the sofa, and when Carly chanced a glance at him, she noted the deeply grooved sadness in his eyes. Part of her yearned to go to him and erase the tension. She'd give anything to be different. Then he raised his gaze to hers and their dark eyes clashed. His narrowed and hardened, as if anticipating a battle. Rising, he moved to his luggage. "I'm going to the house. Until you've settled things within yourself, I'll be there."

"Maybe . . . maybe that would be for the best," she said evenly. "What about the children? They'll be arriving soon."

A thick brow quirked with mockery. "Why should you care?"

"Because it's only natural that I do. It wouldn't be fair for them—"

"Can't you accept them for who they are?" Brand demanded suddenly, cutting her off.

Carly went white. "Don't you realize how miserable I am over this whole situation?" she cried. "This horrible guilt is eating me alive." Somehow she realized that no amount of arguing would adequately explain her feelings. Nothing she could say would help him understand.

Brand bent down and picked up his suitcase. His face darkened. "I have two beautiful children. I'm tired of making excuses for them. And yes," he said, inhaling sharply, "they look exactly like Sandra."

Shock froze her for an instant at the deliberate pain he was inflicting. "You don't need to make excuses for

Shawn and Sara," she said, "you just don't understand what—"

"You're right," he interrupted. "I *don't* understand." He turned, and a moment later the front door slammed shut.

Stunned, Carly stood as she was for what seemed an eternity. The hand she ran over her face was shaking uncontrollably. Brand was right, so very right. He should never apologize for children like Shawn and Sara. She moved into the kitchen and put hot water on to boil for coffee. Standing at the counter, her fingers gripped the edge until she felt one long nail give way under the punishing pressure.

"Carly, what's wrong? You never phone this late unless it's important."

"Nothing," Carly lied on a falsely cheerful note. "I'm just calling to see if you're pregnant yet."

Diana laughed with the free-flowing happiness that had echoed in her voice from the moment she'd announced that she was going to marry Barney. "Not yet. But not from lack of trying. What about you and Brand?"

"No." The strangled sound was barely recognizable.

A short silence followed. "Are you going to tell me what's wrong?"

Carly choked on a sob. "It's not going to work with Brand and me."

"What do you mean it's not going to work?" Diana sounded incredulous.

"We aren't living together anymore. Brand moved into the house this weekend. I'm still here at my apartment." Holding the phone to her ear with her shoulder, Carly wiped the tears from her face with both hands. Tilting her head back, she stared blankly at the ceiling light. "I've gone over it a thousand times in my mind. I should never have married him. I can't be the right kind of mother for his children."

"Sweetie, hold on," Diana said softly in the motherly tone Carly alternately loved and hated. But she needed it now more than she ever had in her life. "You haven't been married a month. Even my first two marriages lasted longer than that. If you love him and Brand loves you, then things will work themselves out. Trust me."

Attempting a laugh that failed miserably, Carly sniffled. "I wish it was that easy."

"Listen, sweetie, it's plain to me that we aren't going to be able to settle this over the phone. I've been looking for an excuse to visit you . . ."

"Diana—no. You can't do that," Carly said urgently, and sniffled again.

"Wild moose won't keep me away. I'll let you know later when my plane's scheduled to arrive."

Carly tried to argue Diana out of a wasted trip. But her friend wasn't going to be able to do or say anything to change her determination. In the end Carly resigned herself to the fact that once Diana had made up her mind about something, it would take more than a few words to change it.

A half hour after talking to Diana, Carly parked her car in the driveway behind Brand's. Her fingers clenched unmercifully around the steering wheel as she gathered her resolve.

The first knock against the door was tentative.

"Come in."

Brand was painting the living room. Newspapers littered the carpet as he spread the antique-white latex color along the neglected walls. Carly recalled choosing this shade for its brightening effect. His roller hardly paused as Carly walked through the door.

"What do you want?"

She died a little at the unfriendly tone of his voice. "I thought I should help. It's . . . it's only right." Every day brought them closer to the time when Shawn and Sara would be arriving.

"What's right is having you live in this house with me as my wife," Brand returned. "If you want to do anything to help, then do that."

"I . . . I can't."

Brand didn't even hesitate. "Then go."

Shocked, Carly stood frozen, unable to move.

"Go," he repeated.

Hanging her head, Carly closed her eyes. "I know how irrational I seem," she said in a voice that was barely above a whisper. "And I realize you must be having a hard time believing this, but I love you."

Brand's grunt was filled with amusement. "Sure you do. If telling yourself that helps soothe your conscience, you keep right on believing it."

"Can't we talk without fighting anymore?" she asked in a tired voice.

Brand tipped his head to one side and arched his thick brows mockingly. "I don't know—can we?"

Carly bristled. She wouldn't be provoked into an argument, and that was clearly what Brand wanted. "Are you going to answer every one of my questions with one of your own?"

"Why not?" Brand was unhesitating. "I've been facing lots of questions lately."

The blood drained from her face so fast Carly thought she might faint. Every foster home, every family she'd ever known, had been the same. Just when it seemed that she had finally found a place where she belonged—where she could fit in with a family—it would happen. Something would come about and she'd be sent away. Then everything she had worked to build up would be washed out from under her and she'd be forced to start again. She didn't want it to happen this time. She desperately wanted things to work out. But already Brand was willing to send her out of his life.

With her hands folded primly in front of her, Carly watched him silently as he worked. Even strokes spread the paint across the flat surface. Finally, she gathered enough courage to begin again.

"Diana's coming."

Brand paused in the middle of a downward sweep of the roller and turned around. "Are you running back to Seattle?"

"No." The thought of leaving Brand and the children was intolerable. "She's coming because she wants to talk some sense into me."

Brand turned back to the wall. "I wish her luck. Heaven knows I've tried."

"Don't you think I know how unreasonable I sound?" Carly shot back angrily. "But it's not reason I *feel*. It's emotion. Is it so wrong to want to be a man's first wife? If that makes me sound selfish and childish, then I agree—that's exactly what I am. All my life I've accepted someone else's leftovers. It's the one thing—the only thing—I didn't want in a husband."

If she expected a reaction from Brand, he gave her none. With his back to her, he continued painting. Carly stood the grating silence as long as she could, then moved to the bedroom that was to be Sara's. Brand had already finished painting it a lovely shade of pink, but the windows were bare, as were those in the freshly painted blue bedroom across the hall. Everything was ready for Shawn and Sara. Everything except Carly.

Diana arrived two days later. Carly met her at the airport and hugged her tightly, holding back the tears.

"Good grief, you look terrible."

"That's what you said the last time you saw me," Carly admonished. Heaven knew she couldn't look any worse than she felt. "I don't suppose Barney was thrilled to have you come."

"Barney sends his love. Don't worry about him." Diana put her arm around Carly's waist. "Now, let's get out of here before you burst into tears in the airport."

Carly felt she was ready to do exactly that. She hadn't seen Brand in two days. If *she* wasn't running, he was. Twice she'd gone over to the house, and both times he was nowhere to be seen. No doubt he was in the air, working twice as many hours as any other pilot.

She doubted that he even knew or cared that she'd been to the house. On her first visit, she'd put up Priscilla curtains in Sara's room and made up her new bed with percale sheets printed with cartoon characters. The choice for Shawn's room hadn't been as easy, but she'd chosen drapes with *Star Wars* figures and a matching bedspread.

In her wanderings around the house, Carly had avoided the bedroom she'd once shared with Brand but had ventured into the kitchen. Neatly washed dishes were stacked on the counter to dry. Brand's efficiency reminded her that he didn't need her to keep his home. He would be fine without her.

"It really is lovely in this part of the world," Diana was saying, as Carly's thoughts turned from Brand.

"I told you it was." Her words sounded weak and emotionless, even to her own ears.

When they arrived at the apartment Carly put on water for coffee. Her shoulders drooped as she closed her eyes and pressed her lips together.

"Are you sure you're not pregnant?" Diana asked softly. "I can't remember you ever being so pale."

A cold feeling washed over her. For one crazy second she was completely torn. One part of her felt a rush of excitement, while another experienced a deep sense of dread. Adding a child to this situation would only complicate their problems.

"Carly?" Diana prompted her gently.

"No," she said, and swallowed. "There's no possibility of that." She brought down two ceramic mugs from the cupboard and added the dark coffee crystals. When the teapot whistled, she poured the liquid into the mugs. All of her movements were automatic.

As she delivered the steaming coffee to the kitchen table, Diana's eyes studied her carefully. "I've known you from the time you were an adolescent, Carly. I've witnessed these inner struggles of yours for years." Her hand reached across the table and patted Carly's. "Sweetie, isn't it time to bury the hurts of the past and move on?" Her wide-eyed gaze sought Carly's colorless face.

With her head bowed, Carly stared into the dark liquid. "He loved her so much." Her voice was trembling.

"But now Brand loves you."

"He still loves her, and she's standing between us like a steel wedge."

"Only because you see it that way. Won't you give Brand the right to have loved Sandra? He shared lots of years with her, and lots of memories. Are you trying to take that away from him, too?"

"Too?"

"He thinks that what you want is for him to give up his children," Diana declared with a faint note of censure.

"How could he think that?" she asked forcefully. "I'd never, never ask Brand to do anything of the sort—"

"But he doesn't know that."

Suspicions mounted within Carly. Diana seemed to know far too much about Brand's thoughts to be guessing. "How do you know all this? This has got to be more than speculation on your part."

Diana's gaze didn't flicker. "I talked to him a while ago."

"When?" Carly demanded in a shocked tone.

"Right after I talked to you. He phoned me, Carly. You've got him so twisted up inside he doesn't know what to do. He loves you, but he loves his children, too.

Brand seems to think that if he were to have one of his brothers raise Shawn and Sara, then you'd be satisfied."

Carly's widened gaze sought Diana's face as an icy chill attacked her heart. "That's not it."

"I tried to assure him it wasn't."

The palms of her hands cradled the hot mug until her flesh felt hot and uncomfortable. "What's wrong with me, Diana? Why am I like this?" Tears clouded her vision. "Why can't I thank God that someone as wonderful as Brand loves me?"

"I don't know, sweetie. I don't know." Carly's sadness was echoed in Diana's low voice.

Carly paced her bedroom floor that night, unable to sleep. She couldn't remember the last time she'd eaten a decent meal. Diana had been adamant. She seemed to think that a ready-made family was just the thing Carly needed. Carly had almost laughed. A family, *this* family, terrified her. She couldn't take Sandra away from the children, and she couldn't separate the children from Brand. There was no solution.

Diana was up before Carly the next morning. "How'd you sleep?" she asked.

"Fine," Carly lied. Exhaustion reduced her voice to a breathless whisper.

"Little liar," Diana murmured.

Carly went into the bathroom, avoiding her friend as she dressed for work. The sound of frying bacon filled the small apartment and Carly had no sooner vacated the bathroom when Diana came rushing in, looking pale and sickly.

Surprised, Carly watched as her friend lost her breakfast. When Diana was finished, Carly handed her a wet washcloth. "You okay?" she asked with a worried expression.

Diana took a couple deep breaths. "I'm wonderful."

"You are pregnant!"

"I guess so. I had my suspicions, but I wasn't sure." She laughed lightly. "But I am now."

"Congratulations." Carly's voice was softly disturbed. "You should be home with Barney, not in Alaska."

"It won't be any big surprise. Barney guessed last week."

"But you should see a doctor, or purchase one of those test kits."

"I will." Diana's soft laugh was filled with happiness. "As soon as I get back to Seattle."

"Which will be today, if I have anything to say about it. The last thing I need is a pregnant woman on my hands." Carly was teasing her friend. Diana's life was so perfect. Barney's love had made her friend complete. No one would recognize the Diana of only a year ago in the softly radiant woman she was now. Love had done that for her.

But in Carly's instance, love had created dark shadows under her eyes. It had left her restless and sleepless until exhaustion claimed her in the wee hours of the morning.

Carly held back the tears when she dropped Diana off at the airport later that day.

"I don't think I've done anything to help you, but this is something you've got to settle within yourself," Diana said, as she embraced her before boarding her flight.

"I know." Carly swallowed back the emotion building in her throat.

"Be happy," Diana murmured with tears glistening in her eyes. "Don't let the past rob you of the best thing to come along in your entire life."

Carly couldn't answer with anything but an abrupt nod of her head.

"Keep in contact now, you hear?"

Again Carly nodded. She waited until the plane had made its ascent into the welcoming blue sky before she wiped the moisture from her ashen cheeks and headed back to the office.

When she pulled up in front of Alaska Freight Forwarding, the first thing Carly noted was that Brand's car was parked outside. Her heart raced with a thousand apprehensions. Starved for the sight of him, Carly hurried inside, afraid she'd miss him if she didn't move quickly enough.

"Brand." She couldn't disguise the breathless quality in her voice.

He turned, and the intensity in his eyes stopped her.

"Carly." George stepped around from his desk. "Welcome the newest employee to our firm. You didn't think I'd give you all those days off without striking a deal with Brand, did you?"

Chapter Twelve

"You're working here?" The question managed to make it past the lump of shock that tightened Carly's throat. From the time she'd first started at Alaska Freight Forwarding, George had been trying to get Brand to become a full-time pilot for the company. But the money he made freelancing his services to the various businesses around town was far and above what he would make flying with one company. That Brand would agree to such an arrangement jolted Carly. And he'd done it so they could visit Portland and Lake Iliamna. She had no doubt that he now considered both those trips wasted in light of what had followed.

"Carly." Brand's greeting was polite and stiff.

"Hello." She didn't trust her voice beyond the simplest welcome.

A perplexed expression skirted its way across George's wrinkled face. "Yes, well, it seems you two have things to discuss." He glanced uneasily from Brand to Carly. "I'll be in the garage."

She waited until the door clicked shut. "Why didn't you tell me?" she asked.

Brand gave an aloof shrug, glancing at the clipboard that contained the flight schedule for the week. "It didn't seem important at the time."

She turned to him. "Diana and I had a long talk—"

"Obviously it didn't make a lot of difference," he cut in sharply. "Otherwise your things would be at the house where they belong."

Carly ignored the censure in his voice. The lines about his mouth were tight and grim. She remembered that the grooves had relaxed when he'd held her in his arms and they'd made love. She closed her eyes against an unexpected surge of guilt. Unwilling for Brand to see her pain, Carly lowered her eyes and pretended an interest in the correspondence on her desk.

"Diana said you phoned her." She spoke after a few moments.

His dark eyes blazed for just an instant, and Carly realized she'd said the wrong thing. He hadn't wanted her to know that he'd contacted her friend.

"I'm glad you did, because I want to clear away a few misunderstandings."

"Such as?" He set the clipboard aside and poured himself a cup of coffee. Lifting the glass pot up to her, he inquired if she wanted a cup.

Carly shook her head. The only thing she wanted was for them to come to some understanding about their marriage and the children.

Brand took a sip of hot coffee. "You said something about misunderstandings," he prompted.

"Yes." Carly swallowed and moistened her dry lips. "It's about Shawn and Sara."

Brand's dark features were unreadable as he leaned against the side of George's wooden desk. "The kids are my problem." Heavy emphasis was placed on the fact that he now considered the children his, when once he'd insisted that they were theirs. And really, how could she blame him? His attitude was the result of her insecurities and unreasonableness.

"But . . . I'm your wife and . . ."

Brand snickered. "My *wife?* Are you, Carly? Really?" he taunted, and turned abruptly toward the door. The knob clicked as he turned it. "My impression of husbands and wives was that they lived together. But then I've been known to be wrong."

Carly bit into her lip. Brand was lashing out at her in his anger, because he was hurting. Not knowing what else to do, Carly stood at the window to watch him leave. He was heading for the airport. A glance at the clipboard confirmed that he'd be flying to Fairbanks. If there was any consolation to Brand being on the payroll, it was that at least now she'd know where he was and when to expect him back. But the solace that offered was little.

Carly purposely stayed late that night, waiting until Brand had checked in with George. She wasn't looking for another confrontation, just the assurance that he'd returned safely. Immediately, it became apparent that having Brand work for the same company had as many drawbacks as advantages. In some ways she'd rather not know his schedule. Ignorance was bliss when she didn't realize he was overdue. Now it would be there for her to face every minute of every day.

The thought of returning to a lonely apartment held no appeal, so Carly decided to take a short drive. Almost without realizing it, she found herself turning the corner that led to the house. Her heart leaped to her throat when she noticed that Brand had installed a swing set in the side yard.

A chill raced up her spine as she parked alongside the curb and examined the polished metal toy. The swings were painted in a rainbow design, with racing stripes wrapped around the poles. Without much imagination, Carly could picture two pairs of blue eyes sparkling with happy surprise.

When her gaze slid away from the swing set, she saw that Brand was standing in front of the wrought-iron gate, studying her.

"Was there something you wanted?" he asked coolly.

A sad smile touched her mouth. "I see that you've risked bribing their affection with a swing set." She was reminding him of his mother's comment.

Their eyes met, and for a flickering moment amusement showed in his glance. "I saw the draperies. When did you bring those over?"

Looking away, Carly said, "A few days ago."

"Would you like to see what else I've done?"

Her nod was eager. If they talked, maybe Brand would come to understand her doubts. Maybe together they could find a solution.

If there was one.

He walked around the car and held open her door. When she climbed out, his hand cupped her elbow. The gesture of affection was an unconscious one; Carly was sure of that. But whatever his reason, or lack of it, she couldn't remain unaffected by his touch. A warmth spread its way up her arm. Brand had initiated her to the physical delights of married life, and after only a few days without him, she discovered that she missed his touch. She hungered for the need in his eyes when he reached for her and pulled her into his embrace. At night the bed seemed cold and lonely. She found that she tossed around in her sleep in an unconscious search for her husband.

Brand held open the screen door, allowing Carly to enter ahead of him. A small gasp of surprise escaped before she could control it. New furniture graced the family-size living room. The davenport and matching love seat were the ones they'd talked about purchasing from a local furniture store. Carly had liked the set immensely, but they'd decided to wait until they bought a house before purchasing furniture.

"You decided to go ahead and get the set," she stated unnecessarily. Another armchair was angled toward the fireplace. Carly had teased Brand about buying a chair that made up into a single bed. In discussing the purchase, she'd suggested that they try it out first by making love on it some night in front of a flickering fire.

The look in Brand's eyes confirmed that he remembered her idea. His hands moved to rest on either side of her neck. Carly closed her eyes at the pressure of his thumbs on her collarbones as he massaged her tender skin.

"Isn't the carpeting new, too?" She fought to keep her

voice level and so not betray what the gentle caress of his fingers was doing to her.

"Yes," he muttered, dropping his hands.

Carly relaxed and released an unconscious sigh. She couldn't understand why Brand was making so many expensive changes in a rental house. He must have read the question in her eyes.

He turned away from her and ran a hand through his hair, mussing the smooth surface. "When you liked the house so much, I made inquiries about buying it."

Carly nearly choked on a sob. He had done this for her. The irony of the situation produced a painful throb in the area of her heart. Brand was offering her the first home she'd ever known, and she was walking away from him. "You're buying the house? Why?"

He didn't answer her for several long moments. "Anchorage is my home now. Everything I want in life is here. Or soon will be," he amended. "I'm no longer running from the past."

The implication that she still was coated his voice. She wanted to beg him to give her more time to reconcile herself to the fact that she couldn't be his first love. That the children she'd be raising were those of another woman. And again . . . again, as she had all her life, she would be living on borrowed dreams. Her eyes begged him not to tell her how unreasonable she was being. She already knew. She couldn't hate herself any more than she did at that moment.

"The carpet's beautiful," she murmured. Her gaze drifted past Brand into the cheery kitchen. The room had been repainted a brilliant yellow. He didn't need to tell her that he'd done that for her, too. Once, a few weeks ago, she'd explained that she felt a kitchen should reflect sunshine. Brand had teased her at the time, commenting that they had enough painting to do. Maybe in a couple of months they'd get around to that. As it was, they'd barely have enough time to prepare the house before Shawn and Sara arrived.

A sob jammed her throat, making speech impossible. Tears blurred her vision. Brand must have seen her reaction to the house and all he'd done. When he reached for her, she went willingly into his arms. His broad chest muffled her sudden tears. Everything she'd ever wanted was here with Brand, but she couldn't accept it.

Home. Family. Love.

The ache in her heart was so profound that she felt like a wounded animal caught in a crippling trap. Only in her case, the trap was of her own making. She couldn't stay. She couldn't go.

"Carly," Brand whispered, and a disturbing tremor entered his voice. He paused to brush the wet strands of hair from her cheek. "Don't cry like that."

Her shoulders shook so hard that catching her breath was nearly impossible. She gasped and released long, shuddering sobs as she struggled to regain her composure. "Hold me," she pleaded, in a throbbing voice. "Please, hold me."

His arms came around her so tightly that her ribs ached. Carly didn't mind. For the first time in weeks, she felt secure again. His chin rested on the top of her head until her tears abated. Not until her breathing became controlled and even did she realize that, all the while she'd been weeping, Brand had been talking to her in soothing tones, reassuring her of his love.

"Are you okay?" he asked quietly.

"I'm sorry, so sorry," she murmured over and over. Her sorrow wasn't because of the tears, but because of what she was doing to them both.

In the momentary stillness that followed, Brand allowed a small space to come between them. Her gaze met his penetrating one as he reached out and wiped the moisture from her pale cheek with his index finger. Her lips trembled, anticipating his kiss, and he didn't disappoint her. His mouth captured hers. Warmth seeped into her cold blood at the urgent way in which his mouth rocked over hers.

"Brand." She said his name in a tortured whisper, asking for his love. She needed him. Just for tonight she hungered for the feel of his arms around her, and she longed to wake with him at her side in the morning. Just for tonight, tomorrow, with all its problems, could be pushed aside.

Hugging her more tightly, Brand lifted her into his arms and carried her down the hall and into their bedroom. The springs of the bed made a squeaking sound as he lowered her onto the mattress.

Carly's arms encircled his neck, directing his mouth to hers. She tasted his restraint the moment his mouth brushed past her lips.

"Brand," she whispered, hurt and confused. "What's wrong?"

He sat on the edge of the bed and leaned forward. The shadow of a dejected figure played against the opposite wall. He looked broken, tired, and intolerably sad. Carly propped herself up on one elbow and ran her hand along the curve of his spine. "Brand." She repeated her plea, not knowing what had prompted his actions. She was sure he desired her as much as she did him. Yet he'd called everything to an abrupt halt.

"Before we were married you suggested that we become lovers," Brand began. "I told you then that I wanted more out of our relationship than a few stolen hours in bed." His tone was heavy and tight. "I married you because I love you and need you emotionally, physically . . . every way that there is to need another person." He hesitated and straightened slightly. Wiping a hand over his tired eyes, he turned so he could watch her as he spoke. "My home is here—*our* home, our bedroom. I'm asking you to share that with me as your lover, your friend, your confidant, your husband. Someday I want to feel our child growing inside you. I won't accept just a small part of your life. I want it all. Maybe that's selfish of me, but I don't care anymore. All I know is that I can't continue living like this, praying every day you'll see all the love that's waiting for you right here. And worse, witnessing the battle going on inside you and knowing I'm losing. And when I lose, you lose. And Shawn and Sara lose."

Carly fell back against the mattress and stared at the ceiling. "Brand, please," she pleaded, in a soft, pain-filled voice. He couldn't believe that she *wanted* to be like this. She'd give anything to change and be different.

"I'll be your husband, Carly," he said flatly, "when you can be my wife."

Her heart cried out, but only a strangled sound came from her throat. Her emotions had been bared, and he'd known how desperately she'd needed him. There hadn't been any pretense in her coming to him tonight. She'd wanted his love and he was sending her away.

By some miracle, Carly managed to stumble out of the bedroom and the house. She didn't stop until she arrived back at the apartment. There were no more tears in her to cry as she paced the floor like a caged wild animal confined to the smallest of spaces. Mindless exhaustion claimed her in the early-morning hours, but even then she slept on the sofa rather than face the bedroom alone.

The following morning, Carly was able to avoid seeing Brand. Intuition told her that he was evading her as well.

At the end of what seemed like the longest day of her life, Carly drove to her apartment, parked the car, and, without going inside, decided to go for a walk. If she was able to exert herself physically, maybe she'd be tired enough to sleep tonight. With no set course in mind, she strode for what seemed miles. Her hands were buried deep in her pockets, her strides urgent. At every street she watched in amazement as long parades of boys and girls captured her attention. Never had she seen more children. It was the first week of June and the evenings were light. Young boys were riding their bikes. For a time a small band of bikers followed her, dashing in and out of the sidewalk along her chosen route. Ignoring them, Carly focused her attention directly ahead until her eyes found a group of young girls playing with cabbage-faced dolls in the front yard of a two-story white house.

Quickening her pace, she discovered that she was near the library. A good book would help her escape her problems. But once inside, Carly learned that the evening was one designated for the appearance of a prominent storyteller. The building was full of children Shawn's and Sara's ages. One glance inside and Carly hurried out. Her breath came in frantic gasps as she ran away.

For one insane moment Carly wanted to accuse Brand of planning the whole thing. She didn't need to be told her thoughts were outrageous, but the realization didn't help.

The remainder of the week passed in a blur. If she was staying away from Brand, then he had changed his strategy and was making every excuse to be near her.

"I don't mind telling you," George commented early Monday morning, "I've been worried about you and Brand. The air between you has seemed a mite thick lately."

Carly ignored him, centering her attention on the Pacific Alaska Maritime docking schedule. "We should get the Wilkens account to Nome by Thursday."

"I was worried," George continued, undaunted, "but the way Brand watches you, I know what brought you two together is still alive and well." He chuckled and rubbed the side of his unshaven cheek. "On his part, anyway."

Carly's fingers tightened around her pencil. "Have you looked over Primetime Gold's claim for the last shipment? Apparently, the dredging parts were damaged."

If George made one more comment on the way Brand was looking at her, Carly was sure the pencil would snap. Brand came into the office daily when he knew she'd be there. Often he poured himself coffee, looking for an excuse to linger and talk to her. He wasn't exactly subtle with what he had to say.

"Three more days" had been his comment this morning. He didn't need to elaborate. Shawn and Sara would be arriving on Thursday.

"I need longer than that," Carly had pleaded for the hundredth time. "I'm not ready for them. I want to be sure."

The pain in Brand's eyes mirrored her own. "Will you ever know? That's the question. Carly, how can you turn away from us when we love and need you?"

"I can't rush what I feel," she murmured miserably.

"If you're waiting for me to give up Shawn and Sara, set your mind straight right now. I won't."

"Oh, Brand," Carly cried softly, then lowered her head so that her chin was tucked against her shoulder. "I would never ask that of you."

"Then just what do you want? Three days, Carly," he repeated with grim impatience. "They're arriving in three days, and they expect a home and a mother."

"I won't be there. I can't," she cried on a soft sob.

The pain etched in Brand's eyes as he left the office haunted Carly for the remainder of the day.

George had already left for the afternoon when Brand checked in after a short flight. He filled out the information sheet and attached it to the clipboard for George's signature.

Although Carly attempted to ignore the suppressed anger in his movements, it was impossible. Silently, her eyes appealed to him. His gaze met hers boldly, and darkened.

"If you're through, I'd like to close up," she said, struggling to control the breathless quality in her voice. The office keys were clenched tightly in her hand. She'd seen that look on Brand's face before. Frustration hardened his eyes to a brilliant shade of brown, wary anger that all but flashed at her.

"Why should your likes concern me? Obviously my needs don't trouble you," he taunted softly. "Carly, I'm tired of playing the waiting game. I want a wife." With every word, he advanced toward her. An unfamiliar harshness stole into his features as he reached for her.

His mouth sought hers.

Carly tried to resist him, but she was weak and panting with need when he began kissing her. At first he was gentle, his mouth caressing and teasing hers until she responded, wrapping her arms around his neck and arching against him so that her body was intimately thrust against his.

"I should make love to you here and now," he whispered.

"Brand, no . . . not here," she pleaded. Still he kissed her again and again until she cried out, certain she heard someone approach. Whoever it was went into the hangar and thankfully not the office.

Brand must have heard the noise, too, because he broke away. Stepping back, he looked at her with wide, shock-filled eyes, as if he'd just woken from a trance and hadn't known what he'd been doing.

He released her.

If Carly was pale, Brand was more so. He looked for a moment as if he was going to be ill. He hesitated only long enough to jam his shirttails inside his pants. Without giving her another look, he turned toward the door.

"There was no excuse for that," he said, looking away from her. "It won't happen again."

"Brand . . ."

Halfway out the door, he stopped and glanced over his shoulder, but he made no attempt to come to her. His eyes met hers in quiet challenge. There were so many things she wanted to say, but no thought seemed clear in her mind.

"I . . . I understand," she murmured.

Chapter Thirteen

On Tuesday afternoon, another long letter from Jutta Hoverson was waiting for Carly. She held off opening the envelope until she had a cup of coffee. Carrying the mug to the kitchen table, she sat down and propped her bare feet on the opposite chair.

Of all the people in the world, Carly expected that Jutta would understand the hesitancy she felt toward Brand and the children. Diana, whom she loved and respected, hadn't come close to comprehending the heart-wrenching decision Carly faced. More than once during Diana's short visit, Carly felt that Diana had wanted to give her a hard shake. For once, Carly needed someone to identify with her needs, her insecurities. Jutta could do that.

Slipping the letter from the long envelope, she read:

Dear Carly,

My friend. Your letter arrived today and I've read it many times. You speak of your love for this man you have married. But you say that you are no longer living with him. I don't understand. In your last letter you wrote about his children and I sensed your discontent. You love, yet you fear. You battle against the things in life that are most natural. Reading your letter reminded me of the time when I was a young girl who dreamed of being a great runner. I worked very hard to accomplish this skill. My uncle coached me. And in his wisdom he explained that running demands complete coordination. He said that to be a good runner, I must let everything I'd learned, and everything I knew deep inside, come together and work for me. But I lost every race. Even when I knew I was the best, I couldn't win. Again and again, he said to me that once I quit trying so hard to win, I would. Of course, I didn't understand him at the time. I struggled, driving myself harder and harder. Then, one day at race time, my uncle threw up his hands at me. He said I would never win, and he walked away. And so I decided I wouldn't even try. When the race began, I ran, but every step still felt heavy, every breath an effort. Then something happened that I don't understand even now. Maybe because I wasn't trying, because I no longer cared to win, everything my uncle had tried to explain came together. My feet no longer dragged and every step seemed to only skim the surface. I no longer ran. I flew. I made no effort. I felt no strain. My rhythm was perfect, and I experienced a pure exhilaration and a joy I have never known since. I won the race, and for the only time in my life, maybe, I made my family proud.

My friend, in many ways we are alike.

Carly reread the letter three times. The message should have been clear, but it wasn't. Jutta had listened to the advice of an uncle and won a race. Carly couldn't see how that could relate to Brand and the children. The letter was a riddle Jutta expected Carly to understand. But Carly had never done well with word puzzles.

Not until Carly was in bed did she think again of Jutta's strange letter. The picture her mind conjured was of a young, dark-haired girl struggling against high odds to excel. In some ways, Carly saw herself. With her personality quirks, her chances for happiness had to be slim. Her thoughts drifted to the first few days of lightheartedness after she and Brand were married. Content in their love, they had lived in euphoric harmony.

Suddenly, Carly understood. Abruptly, she struggled to a sitting position and turned on the small lamp at the side of her bed. This kind of underlying accord was what Jutta had tried to explain in her letter. There was harmony in Jutta's steps as she ran because she no longer struggled. When something is right, really right, there is no strain, no effort. The harmony of body and soul supersedes the complications of life. There were rhythms and patterns to every aspect of human existence, and all Carly had to do was accept their flow and move with the even swell of their tides. Problems erupted only when she

struggled against this harmony. Once she reconciled herself to this flow, she could overcome the trap of always
fearing borrowed dreams.

Carly didn't know how she could explain any of this
to Brand, but she knew she had to try. The physical strain
that had marked her face over the last weeks relaxed as
she reached for her phone. He'd think she was crazy to
be calling him this late at night, particularly when she
didn't know what she was going to say. Probably the best
thing to do was blurt out the fact that she loved him and
that together they'd work out something. The love they
shared was the harmony in her life because it was right.
A lot of uncertainties remained; she hadn't reconciled
everything. But at least now she could see a light at the
end of the tunnel.

The phone rang ten times and Brand didn't answer.
Perplexed, Carly cut the call. A look at her wristwatch
confirmed that it was after midnight. Brand worked
hard, and he slept hard. It was possible he'd sleep through
the interruption, but not likely.

A quick mental review of the week's flight schedule
reminded her that Brand had been flying some Seattle
personnel to one of the Aleutian Islands that day. The
flight was as regular as clockwork. Brand had taken the
same route a thousand times. He hadn't checked in before she'd left work, she remembered. But then she'd left
a little early. She really didn't have anything to worry
about. If something had gone awry with Brand's flight,
George would have contacted her.

A long, body-stretching yawn convinced Carly to go
back to bed. In the morning she'd make a point of seek-

ing Brand out. Shawn and Sara were due to arrive the day after next, and she was hoping they could talk about that meeting.

Brand's Chevy was parked by the warehouse when Carly arrived at work the following morning. A smile lit up her face at the reassuring sight. Everything was fine.

"Where's Brand?" she asked her boss, as she breezed in the door. "I'd like to talk to him before he takes off."

George looked up from the report he was scanning. "He hasn't arrived yet."

Carly shook her head and gave George a bemused grin. Sometimes her boss could be the most forgetful person. "Of course he's here. His car's parked out back."

George glanced up and released an exaggerated sigh. "I tell you, he hasn't come in this morning." Glancing at the thick black watch on his wrist, George's brows rose suspiciously. Brand wasn't in the habit of arriving late.

"What time did he check in last night?" Carly questioned.

With deliberate care, George set the paper he was reading aside. "You tell me. I left early."

Carly discovered that her legs would no longer support her, and she sank into the swivel chair at her desk. "I thought he was checking in with you. I assumed . . ."

"You mean Brand didn't come back to the office yesterday?"

Carly felt her heart sink so low it seemed to land at her ankles. "You mean . . ." She couldn't voice the thought.

"His car's still here. He didn't come back." George

finished for her. He stood and grabbed the clipboard that held the flight schedules down from the wall. "Don't panic—everything's going to be fine. There's no cause for alarm." The rising uneasiness in his own voice wasn't reassuring. "I'll contact the airport and confirm his flight plan." George was out the door faster than she had seen him move in three months of working in Alaska.

Numbly, Carly sat. She couldn't have moved to save the world. Constant recriminations pounded at her from all sides until she wanted to bury her head in her hands. This was her fault. If Brand was hurt, no one would ever be able to convince her otherwise. Again and again George had told her that Brand was an excellent pilot. The best. Alaska Freight Forwarding was fortunate to have him on their team. Hiring Brand had been a coup for George.

But even excellent pilots made mistakes. Anyone was more prone toward error when his mind was preoccupied—and heaven knew that Brand had lots on his mind. He was working hard, and if he was anything like Carly, he hadn't been sleeping well. The combination of hard work and lack of sleep was enough to bring down the best pilots in the business.

When George returned forty-five minutes later, Carly knew her face was waxen. Her eyes searched his eagerly for information.

George cleared his throat, as if reluctant to speak. "There've been screwups everywhere, including the airport. They figure Brand has been missing close to fourteen hours."

"No . . . no." Carly felt as if someone had physically slammed a fist into her stomach. She didn't say anything.

The thoughts that flittered through her mind made no sense. She recalled that she had to go pick up some dry cleaning on her way home from work. Then she remembered that Diana had expected something horrible to happen once she'd decided to marry Barney. Happiness wasn't meant for people like her. Nor was it meant for someone like Carly.

"Carly, are you okay?" George was giving her a funny look, and she wondered how long he'd been trying to gain her attention.

"Search-and-rescue teams are in the air. They'll find him."

Carly was confident they would, sooner or later. The question neither of them was voicing was in what condition Brand would be found: dead or alive.

The entire day was like a nightmare. Only Carly discovered that, no matter what she did, she couldn't wake up. The amount of manpower and man-hours that went into finding a missing or downed pilot was staggering. Reports were coming in to the office from the command center at Anchorage Airport continually. If that was encouraging, the news wasn't. Brand hadn't been sighted, and a thick fog was hampering the search.

At ten that night, George put his hand over Carly's. "You might as well try to get a good night's sleep. I'll let you know the minute I hear anything."

Carly's answer was an abrupt shake of her head. "No. I won't leave. Not until I know."

George didn't try to persuade her further. But she noticed that he didn't leave. Both were determined to see this through, no matter what the outcome.

At some point during the long night, Carly fell asleep.

With her head leaning against the wall, she'd meant to rest her eyes for only a few minutes, but the next thing she knew, it was light outside and the sun was over the horizon. Immediately, she straightened and sought out George, who shook his head grimly.

Two hours later, with her nerves stretched taut, Carly forced herself to eat something for the first time since breakfast the day before. She ran a comb through her dark hair and brushed her teeth.

George was staring into the empty coffee cup he was holding when she approached him.

"I don't know when I'll be back."

He looked at her blankly. "Where are you going?"

"To the main terminal. Shawn and Sara are arriving in a half hour. I don't want them to know Brand's missing. If you hear anything, I'll be at the house." She let out a tired breath. "I'll phone as often as I can."

Squeezing her numb fingers, George offered Carly a smile and nodded.

It didn't seem possible that a day could be so full of sunshine and happiness—and that Carly's whole world could be dark with an unimaginable gloom.

As the Alaska Airlines flight with Shawn and Sara aboard touched down against the concrete runway, Carly felt an unreasonable surge of anger. Maybe Brand had planned this so she would be forced to deal with his children. If he'd wanted to find a way to punish her, he'd been highly successful.

As the flight attendant ushered Shawn and Sara out from the jetway, Carly straightened her shoulders and forced a smile. Her composure was eggshell fragile. She hadn't yet figured out what she was going to say to the children.

"Mom." A brilliant smile lit Sara's sky-blue eyes. She broke free from the young attendant and hurried toward Carly.

Scooting down, Carly was the wary recipient of a fierce hug from the little girl. Shawn was more restrained, but there was a happy light in his eyes she hadn't noticed during her visit to Oregon.

"Where's Dad?" Shawn was the first to notice that his father was missing.

Not quite meeting his inquisitive eyes, Carly managed a smile. "He told me to tell you how sorry he is that he couldn't meet the two of you today. But he's hoping you like the surprise he has waiting for you at the house."

"Can we go there now?" Sara asked. Her blond hair had been plaited into long pigtails that danced with the action of her head. The doll Carly had given her was clutched under her arm.

"I'll take you there now. Are you hungry?"

Both children bobbed their heads enthusiastically. Rather than find something to cook, Carly located a McDonald's. Shawn and Sara were delighted with the fact that their first meal in Alaska was to be a hamburger and milkshake.

When they reached the house, Shawn helped Carly unload the suitcases from the back of the car. "Grandma sent you a long letter. She said it was instructions."

"Then I should read it right away."

"Don't," Shawn returned soberly. "You can, if you want," he added, after a momentary lapse in conviction. "But you don't have to do everything she says."

"At least not the nap part. Right?" She gave him a conspiratorial wink.

"Right," Shawn confirmed with a nod.

"Mom, Mom." Sara rushed from her bedroom. "I've got a loose tooth. Look." She started pushing one of her front teeth back and forth. "Does the Tooth Fairy live in Alaska, too?"

"You bet," Carly answered, wiggling the tooth to satisfy Sara.

While Shawn and Sara investigated their new swing set, Carly unpacked their clothes. A quickly placed call to George confirmed that there hadn't been any word. A glance out of the window revealed that both Shawn and Sara had discovered neighborhood children their age.

"This is Lisa." Sara had brought her newfound friend into the house. "Can I show her my bedroom?"

"Go ahead."

Sara looked surprised, as though she'd expected Carly to refuse. "We won't make a mess."

"Good," Carly said, with a short laugh. "I'd hate to think of you spending your first day in Alaska cleaning your room."

"Sara's never messy," Shawn said, with a soft snicker. "At least, that's what Grandma says."

With a superior air, Sara led her friend down the hall to her bedroom. Lisa gave an appropriate sigh of appreciation at the beauty of the room, which immediately endeared her to Carly.

After the children had settled in, and Sara had taken a short nap, Carly drove them over to the apartment. Every night after work, she'd dreaded coming home. Now she understood the reason. She didn't belong here.

While she packed her things, Carly thought through the sober facts that faced her. Reality said that Brand could be dead. Her heart throbbed painfully at the thought, but it was a fact she couldn't ignore. If so, the question she had to deal with was what would happen to Shawn and Sara. Brand's mother was traveling. Her long vacation was well deserved. Kay St. Clair had done her best for these children, but she'd more than earned a life of her own. The state could remand Shawn and Sara as they had Carly. She'd been five when she'd gone to her first foster home. Sara's tender age.

Carly's fist tightened at the ferocity of her emotion. No matter what it took, she wouldn't allow that to happen. Not to Shawn and Sara. They would be hers, just as if she'd given them life. Nothing would separate the three of them. The path of her thoughts brought another realization. All these weeks that she'd battled within herself, she'd been fighting the even flow of her life's rhythm.

It wasn't that she couldn't give Brand something he didn't already have. It was what Brand, Shawn, and Sara could give her. Borrowed dreams were irrelevant. What they shared was new and vital. Brand had tried to tell her that in so many ways, and she hadn't understood.

"Mom." Sara stood in the open doorway, giving Carly a puzzled look. "I was talking to you."

Holding out her arms, Carly gave the small child a loving squeeze. "I'm sorry. I was thinking."

"Does thinking make you cry?"

Carly's fingers investigated her own face, unaware that tears had formed. She wiped the moisture from her cheeks and tried to laugh, but the sound couldn't be described as one of mirth. "Sometimes," she said with a

sniffle. "Hey, you know what I really need? A big hug."
Sweet Sara was eager to comply.

Both children wanted to listen to their favorite story
once they returned to the house. Carly promised them a
special dinner to go with the book. Somehow, she'd find
a way to cook "green eggs and ham." Luckily, neither
child seemed to find it out of the ordinary to see Carly
move her clothes from one house to another. At least,
they didn't mention it. But Carly wouldn't be moving
again. Her place was here.

The book was Shawn's favorite Dr. Seuss story. The
boy sat beside her while Sara occupied Carly's lap. The
thought slid through her mind as she opened the book
that, although Shawn and Sara resembled their mother,
they were amazingly like their father. The curious tilt of
Shawn's head was all Brand.

Carly was only a few pages into the book when a
movement caught her attention. The front door was
open and George stood just outside the closed screen.

A myriad of sensations assaulted Carly. Their eyes
met and Carly's clouded with emotion, begging him to
tell her everything was all right. Tears blurred his expression. But in her heart she knew the news wasn't good. If
Brand had been found alive, George would have phoned.

"You weren't here when I phoned," George said. "But
what I have has to be seen."

Carly's arms tightened around the children, drawing
them protectively close to her. Again she confirmed the
thought that nothing would separate Shawn and Sara
from her.

The screen door opened and Carly braced herself.

"Dad." Shawn flew off the love seat.

Carly jerked her head up to find Brand framed in the doorway. He scooped Shawn into his arms and reached down for Sara. Carly remained frozen.

"Mom said she didn't know what time you'd be home."

"Is that right?" Brand said, hugging his children close. "We'll have to make sure Mom knows from now on, won't we?" His eyes sought Carly's, bright with promise. "Isn't that right, Mom?"

"Yes." Carly nodded eagerly and walked into Brand's embrace. "Oh, Brand, tell me, tell me what happened? I was worried sick . . . I thought I'd lost you forever." She wept into his shoulder, knowing he probably couldn't understand anything she was saying. It didn't matter now that he was here. Not when he was holding her as if his very life depended on it. Later, when the children were in bed, he could fill in the details.

"Mom unpacked all the suitcases," Sara said happily. "Even hers."

Brand relaxed his hold so that he could lift Carly's chin and brush the wet strands of hair from her face. "Are you staying?" The husky question was so low Carly could barely hear him.

"Hey, kids," George said, clearing his throat. "Why don't you two show me your bedrooms? And wasn't that a swing set I saw outside?"

A grateful smile touched Carly's lips as George led the children from the living room.

"I'm never leaving. Oh, Brand, I know it all sounds crazy, but I realize I belong with you. Shawn and Sara are *our* children." She couldn't hide the breathlessness in her voice. "Everything's clear now. . . . I'm not borrowing anyone else's dreams, but living my own."

Sara skipped excitedly back into the room and squeezed her small body between Brand and Carly. Brand reached down and lifted her up. Two small arms shot out. One went around Carly and the other around Brand. "I'm so glad you're here."

"I'm home now," Brand murmured in a raw, husky voice and his eyes found Carly's. "We're all home."

The Trouble with Caasi

Chapter One

The majestic beauty of white-capped Mount Hood was unobstructed from the twentieth floor of the Empress Hotel in downtown Portland. Caasi Crane stood in front of the huge floor-to-ceiling window, her arms hugging her slim waist. Blake Sherrill's letter of resignation was clenched tightly in one hand.

Blake was the best general manager she'd ever hope to find. His resignation had caught her off guard. As far as Caasi knew, he had been perfectly content. His employee file was open on her computer, and Caasi moved across the plush office to study the information.

His salary was generous, she noted, but Caasi believed in paying her employees what they were worth. And Blake earned every cent. Maybe he'd reconsider if she offered him a raise. But according to the file, he'd received a healthy increase only three months earlier.

Scrolling down through the information, Caasi paused to read over the original employment application that included his photograph. He was six-three and at her guess around a hundred and eighty pounds. Dark hair and brown eyes. None of that had changed. At the time he was hired he was single and thirty. Certainly she would know if he'd married since then. He hadn't; she was sure of it. Had Blake been with Crane Enterprises that long? Six years?

Caasi pushed her wide-rimmed glasses up from the tip of her nose and sat in her cushioned white leather chair.

Her assistant buzzed, interrupting her thoughts. "Mr. Sherrill's here to see you."

Caasi pushed the intercom lever. "Please send him in." Mentally she prepared herself. Her father had groomed her well for this position. If Blake was displeased about something, she'd soon discover what it was. Employee performance and customer satisfaction were the name of the game. But an employee, even one as good as Blake, couldn't perform if he was unhappy. If so, Caasi wanted to know the reason. She pretended an interest in his computer file when the door opened. Looking up, she smiled brightly. "Sit down, Blake." Her hand indicated a chair on the other side of her desk.

He wasn't a handsome man. His features were rough and rugged, too craggy to be considered attractive. His chin projected stubbornly and the shadow of his beard was heavy. Caasi didn't doubt that he had to shave twice a day. He wore a dark business suit and silk tie, and his hair was coal dark. Could he be Italian with a name like Sherrill? Funny how she'd never really noticed Blake. At least, not the toughness in the lean, hard figure that stood in front of her.

"If you don't mind, I'd rather stand." With feet braced slightly apart, he joined his hands.

"Honestly," Caasi admonished with a soft smile, "you look like a recruit standing at attention."

"Sometimes I feel that way." The words were hardly above a whisper.

"Pardon?" Caasi looked up again.

"Nothing." The small lines about his eyes and mouth creased in a mirthless smile. "You're right. I'll sit down."

"How long have you been with us now, Blake?"

"Six years, six months, and five days," he replied drily.

"You counted the days?"

He shrugged. "Maybe I was hoping to gain your attention."

Caasi gave him a troubled look. Clearly something was wrong. Not in the five years since she'd taken over the company had Blake behaved like this.

"You have my attention now." She held up the resignation letter. "What's the problem?"

He looked away. "There's no problem. The time has come to move on, that's all."

"Is it the money?"

"No."

"Have you got another job offer?" That was the scenario that made the most sense.

"Not yet."

This wasn't going well, and she was fast losing her grip on the situation.

"All right, Blake, tell me what's up."

"Do you want a full report submitted? There's one due at the end of the month, as usual."

"I don't mean that and you know it." Angrily she glared at him.

"I thought you read every report," he muttered with an edge of sarcasm.

"I've never known you to be cynical," Caasi cut in.

"But then, you've never known me, have you?"

Caasi didn't know how to answer him. Maybe if she'd dated more often she'd be able to deal with men more effectively. That was one area in which her father had failed to instruct her. Sometimes she felt like a bungling teenager, and just as naïve.

"Take the rest of the week off, Blake. I would like you to reconsider this letter."

"I'm not going to change my mind." There was a determined look about him, unyielding and confident.

She didn't want to lose Blake. "Take it anyway, and let's talk again the first of the week."

He gave her a mocking salute. "As you wish."

Blake's resignation weighed heavily on Caasi the rest of the day. By the time her assistant left, she was in a rotten mood. It was due to far more than Blake, she realized. That night was the monthly get-together with Edie and June, her two BFFs.

The months passed so quickly that sometimes it seemed that they were meeting much too often—and at other times it wasn't nearly enough. Yet the two were her best friends . . . her only friends, Caasi admitted grudgingly, as she slid the key into the lock of her apartment door.

The penthouse suite on the twenty-first floor had been Caasi's home for as long as she could remember. She must have been eight before she realized that milk came from a cow and not the busboy who delivered all of the family's meals.

Daddy's little girl from the beginning, Caasi had known from the time she could walk that someday she would be president of Crane Enterprises and the string of hotels that ran down Oregon's coast and into California. Isaac Crane had tutored her for the position until his death five years earlier.

Daddy's little girl . . . The thought ran through her mind as Caasi opened her closet and took out a striped dress of teal, plum, and black. Everything about her reflected her father. A thousand times in her twenty-eight years Caasi had explained that her name hadn't been misspelled but was Isaac spelled backward.

Soaking in a bubble bath a few minutes later, Caasi lifted the sponge and drained the soothing water over her full breasts and flat stomach. Her big toe idly played with the faucet spout. Her medium-length chestnut hair was piled on top of her head as she lay back and let the hot water refresh her.

Steam swirled around the huge bathroom as Caasi got out of the tub, wrapped a thick cotton towel around herself, and moved into her bedroom. She didn't feel like going out tonight. A quiet dinner and television would be more to her liking, but she knew Edie and June well enough to realize they wouldn't easily let her forgo their monthly dinner.

An hour later, Caasi entered Brasserie Montmartre, a French restaurant Edie had raved about the previous month. Caasi didn't mind checking out the competition. The Empress's own small French restaurant served—in her opinion—some of the best food in town.

Edie waved when she saw Caasi. June apparently hadn't arrived yet, and Caasi wondered if she would, since June's baby was due any time.

"Greetings, fair one," the pert brunette said, as Caasi pulled out a chair and sat down. It was a standard joke among them that, of the three, Caasi was the most attractive. She accepted their good-natured teasing as part of the give-and-take in any friendship. They were her friends, and heaven knew she had few enough of those.

"You look pleased about something," Caasi said. Edie was grinning from ear to ear.

"I am." Edie took a sip of champagne and giggled like a sixteen-year-old. "I should probably wait until June's here, but if I don't tell someone soon, I think I'll bust."

"Come on, give," Caasi urged, and nodded at the waiter, who promptly delivered another glass and poured for her. Good service, she mused.

"I'm pregnant!"

Caasi nearly choked on the bubbly liquid. "Pregnant!" she spat back. Not both friends at the same time. It was too much!

"I don't think I've ever seen Freddy more excited."

"But you're the one who said—"

"I know, but I changed my mind. It's crazy, but I'm really happy about this. The doctor said there's no reason for me to lose my figure, and he's already put me on a high-protein diet. Freddy's agreed to the natural-childbirth classes. From what we've read, it's the best way for the baby. June's taking them now, and I'm hoping she can let me sit in on one of her sessions. And then there's the nursery to do. I think Freddy may make the cradle."

"Slow down," Caasi said with a light laugh. "My head's spinning already."

"What do you think?" Edie scooted her chair back and arched her shoulders.

"Think about what?" Caasi shook her head.

"Do I show?"

"Show? Good grief, Edie, you can't be more than a couple of months along!"

"You're right." She giggled, her dark eyes dancing. "And no more than a sip of champagne for me. I'm completely off alcohol and caffeine. I was just hoping . . ."

"Hoping what?" A tall blonde waddled up behind them. June's protruding stomach left little conjecture as to her condition. One hand rested against her rib cage as she lowered herself into the third chair. "Champagne?" Round blue eyes sought those of the others. "What are we celebrating?"

"Babies, in the plural," Edie supplied with a wide grin that lit up her whole face.

June looked blank for a minute.

"It seems our Edie has found herself with child," Caasi informed her.

"Edie?" June whispered disbelievingly. "Not the same Edie who marched in a rally for zero population growth when we were in high school?"

"One and the same." Edie laughed and motioned for the waiter, who produced a third glass.

"We're talking about the girl who was afraid to eat lettuce because it could ruin her perfect figure."

"Not the one who said, 'Lips that touch chocolate

shall never touch mine'?" June's eyes rounded with shock.

"'Fraid so," Caasi said.

"Would you two quit talking about me as if I wasn't here?" Edie demanded.

"A baby." Caasi looked from one to the other and shook her head. "Both of you. Wasn't it yesterday that I was your maid of honor, June? And Edie, remember how we argued over who got which bed our freshman year?"

"I always thought you'd be the first one to marry," June said to her in a somber tone. "Caasi the beauty. Blue-gray eyes to die for and a figure that was the envy of every girl in school."

"The fair one," Edie added.

"The aunt-to-be," Caasi murmured, in a poor attempt at humor. "Always the bridesmaid, never the bride."

"I find it more than just ironic," Edie said with conviction. "It's high time you came down from the lofty twentieth floor and joined us mortals."

"Edie!" June snapped. "What a terrible thing to say!"

"It's the champagne," Caasi said, excusing her friend. "In this instance it's a case of loose lips sinking ships."

"Ships?" Edie inquired.

"Friendships!"

"To friendship." Edie raised her glass and their former good mood was restored.

"To friendship." June and Caasi gently clicked their delicate crystal glasses against Edie's.

"By the way, who's paying for this?" June questioned.

"I don't know," Caasi joked, "but I'm only paying one-fifth, since both of you are drinking for two."

They all laughed and picked up their menus.

As Edie had promised, the food was superb. With observant eyes, Caasi noted the texture and quality of the food and the service. Such scrutiny had been ingrained in her since childhood. Caasi doubted that she could dine anywhere and not do a comparison to the food at her hotels.

"What about next month?" Caasi eyed June's stomach.

"No problem. Doc says I've got a good five weeks."

"Five weeks?" Edie looked shocked. "If I get that big, I'll die."

"You know, Edie, if your shoes are a little too tight, don't worry," Caasi teased.

"My shoes?" Edie looked up with a blank stare.

"After being in your mouth all night, they should fit fine."

Edie giggled and stared pointedly across the table. "I swear, the girl's a real wit tonight."

They divided up the check three ways. Although Caasi wanted to treat her friends, June and Edie wouldn't hear of it.

Sitting back, she watched as the waiter took their money. No matter what her mood at the beginning of these gatherings, Caasi always felt better afterward. Even Edie's remark had flowed off her like water from an oily surface. These two were like her sisters. She accepted their faults and loved them nonetheless.

Large drops of rain pounded against the street as the three emerged from the restaurant.

"How about an after-dinner dessert?" Edie suggested. "I'm in the mood for something sweet."

June and Caasi eyed each other and attempted to disguise a smile.

"Not me." June bowed out. "Burt's at home, anxiously awaiting my return. He worries if I'm out of his sight more than five minutes."

Edie raised both brows, seeking Caasi's response.

Caasi shrugged. "My feet hurt."

"I thought I was the one with tight shoes," Edie teased, looping her arm through Caasi's. "Come on, be a sport. If you're extra-nice I'll even let you take me up to your penthouse suite."

Caasi smiled. "I suppose something light and sweet would do wonders toward making me forget my problems."

"What about you, June? Come on, change your mind."

June shook her head and patted her rounded stomach. "Not tonight."

The hotel lobby at the Empress was peacefully quiet when Edie and Caasi came through the wide glass doors. The doorman tipped his hat politely, and Caasi gave him a bright smile. Old Aldo had been a grandfather when the hotel hired him twenty years before. Other employers would have retired him by now, but Caasi hadn't. The white-haired man had a way of greeting people that made them feel welcome. That quality wouldn't easily be replaced.

The sweet, soulful sounds of a ballad drifted from the lounge, and Edie paused to hum the tune as they waited for the elevator.

"Nice," she commented.

"The piano player's new this week. Would you rather we have our dessert down here?"

Edie's nod was eager. "I think I would. I'm in the mood for romance and music."

Caasi's laugh was sweet and light. "From the look of things, I'd say it's been a regular occurrence lately." Her eyes rested on her friend's still smooth abdomen. They chose to sit in the lounge in order to listen to the music.

The hostess seated them and saw to their order personally. The crowd was a good one. Caasi looked around and noted a few regulars, mostly salesmen who stayed at the hotel on a biweekly basis. The after-work crowd had thinned, but there were a few die-hards.

The middle-aged man at the piano was good. A portion of the bar was built around the piano, and Caasi watched as he interacted with the customers, took requests, and cracked a few jokes. She'd make sure he was invited back again.

Edie dipped her spoon into the glass of lemon sorbet while Caasi sampled her own. They didn't talk. They didn't need to. The piano music filled the room. A young couple at the bar started to sing and were joined by several others.

Edie's hand squeezed Caasi's forearm. "I'm sorry about what I said earlier."

"No need to apologize." Edie's gaze faltered slightly under Caasi's direct look. "I understand."

"I worry about you sometimes, Caasi."

"Worry about me? Whatever for?"

"I love you. You're more like a sister to me than my own. I don't know how you can be happy living the way you do. It's not natural."

"What's not natural?" Caasi realized she was beginning to sound like a worn echo.

"Your life."

Mildly disconcerted, Caasi looked away. "It's the only way I've ever known."

"That doesn't make it right. Haven't you ever yearned for someone to share your life? A man to cuddle up against on a cold night?"

Caasi's laugh was forced. "I've got my electric blanket."

"What about children?"

Although content with her lifestyle, Caasi had to admit that seeing both June and Edie pregnant was having a peculiar effect on her. She'd never thought much about being a mother, but she found the idea appealing. "I . . . I think I'd like that, but I'm not so keen on a husband."

"If it's a baby you want, then find yourself a man. You don't need a wedding ring and a march down the aisle in order to have a baby. Not these days."

Caasi tugged a strand of hair behind her ear, a nervous habit she rarely indulged. "I can't believe we're having this conversation."

"I mean it," Edie said with a serious look.

"What am I supposed to do? Find a good-looking man, saunter up, and suggest children?"

Edie's full laugh attracted the attention of others. "No, silly, don't say a word. Just let things happen naturally."

How could Caasi explain that she wasn't into casual affairs? Had never had a fling, and at twenty-eight remained a virgin? Edie would be sick laughing. Lack of experience wasn't the only thing holding her back; when would Caasi find the time for relationships and/or motherhood? Every waking minute was centered on Crane Enterprises. Even if she did find herself attracted to a man, she'd have to squeeze him in between meetings and conferences. Few men would be willing to accept that kind of relationship. And what man wouldn't be intimidated by her wealth? No, the die had been cast and she . . .

"Caasi." Edie's hushed whisper broke into Caasi's thoughts. "What you need is a man like the one who just walked in."

Caasi's gray eyes searched the crowd for the newcomer. "Where?" she murmured.

"There, by the piano. He just sat down."

The blood exploded in Caasi's cheeks, rushing up from her neck until she felt her face shining like a lighthouse on a foggy night. Blake Sherrill was the man Edie had pointed out. Pressing a tentative hand to her face, Caasi wondered at her reaction.

"Now, that's blatant masculinity if ever I've seen it."

"He's not that good-looking," Caasi felt obliged to say, grateful that Edie hadn't noticed the way the color had invaded her face.

"Of course not. His type never is. There's a lean hardness to him, an inborn arrogance that attracts women like flies to honey."

"Oh, honestly."

"Notice his mouth," Edie continued.

Caasi already had. Blake looked troubled about something, a surprising occurrence, since he'd always presented a controlled aura when he met with her. She watched as he ordered a drink, then emptied the shot glass in one gulp. That wasn't like Blake, either. As far as she knew, he stayed away from liquor.

"See how his lips are pressed together? The tight, chiseled effect. Women go for that."

There was a slight tremor in Caasi's hands as her friend spoke. "Maybe some women. But not me."

"Caasi." Edie groaned. "You can't be that oblivious. You're staring at an unqualified hunk. My blood's hot just looking at him."

"He's not my type," Caasi muttered under her breath, at the same time thinking she'd never really seen Blake. For years they'd worked together, and not once had she ever thought of him except as an exceptionally good general manager.

"That man is every woman's type. I've seen women threaten to kill for less."

Caasi knew her friend was teasing and offered a half-hearted smile. "Maybe he is my type, I don't know."

"Maybe?" Edie shot back disbelievingly. "Go over and introduce yourself. It can't hurt, and it may do you a lot of good."

"Do you think I should?"

"I wouldn't have said so if I didn't."

"This is crazy." Caasi shoved back her chair. Really, what did she hope to accomplish? Blake was more man than she'd ever recognized before, but the idea of a casual affair with him was crazy. More than crazy, it was ludicrous.

"Hurry up before he leaves," Edie whispered encouragingly.

Caasi didn't understand why she didn't want her friend to know she was already acquainted with Blake.

Edie stood with her.

"Are you coming, too?" Caasi cast her a challenging glare.

"Not this time, although I'm tempted. I just noticed the time. Freddy will be worried. I'll call you tomorrow."

"Fine." Caasi's spirits lifted. She could leave without saying a word to Blake and Edie need never know.

"I'll just wait by the door to see how you do. Once you've made the contact, I'll just slip away."

Caasi's spirits plummeted.

The stool beside Blake was vacant. Caasi strolled across the room, her heart pounding so loudly it drowned out the piano man. As casually as possible she perched herself atop the tall stool.

Blake looked over at her, surprise widening his eyes momentarily. He turned back without a greeting.

"Evening," she muttered, shocked at how strange her voice sounded. "I thought you were taking the rest of the week off."

"Something came up."

Caasi straightened. "What?"

"It's taken care of—don't worry about it."

"Blake." Her tone was crisp and businesslike.

Pointedly he turned his wrist and looked at his watch. "I was off duty hours ago. If you don't mind, I'd like to leave the office behind and enjoy some good scotch." He raised his shot glass in a mocking toast.

Caasi's throat constricted. "I've had one of those days myself." She didn't mention that his letter had brought it on, but that understanding hung oppressively in the air between them.

The bartender strolled past and braced both hands against the bar. "Can I get you anything?" He directed the question at Caasi.

Obviously he didn't know who she was, which was just as well; she could observe him at work. "I'll have the same as the gentleman."

Blake arched both brows. "It must have been a harder day than I thought."

"It was."

His lips came together in a severe line. "Drink it slowly," he cautioned.

"I can hold my liquor as well as any man," she said, surprised by how defensive she sounded. She didn't want to be. What she wanted was an honest, frank discussion of the reason or reasons he'd decided to leave Crane Enterprises.

"As you say." The corners of his mouth curved upward in challenge.

When Caasi's drink arrived she raised it tentatively to her lips and took an experimental sip. To her horror, she started coughing and choking.

"You all right?" he questioned with a rare smile.

As if she wasn't embarrassed enough, his hand pounded vigorously against her back.

"Stop it," she insisted, her eyes watering.

"I thought you said you could handle your scotch."

"I can!" she choked out between gasps of air. "It just went down wrong, that's all."

Blake rotated the stool so that she was given a profile of his compelling features. She turned back around, aware that half the lounge was watching her. "I'm fine, I'm fine," she felt obliged to say.

"So you are," Blake murmured.

"Aren't you worried about leaving your job?" she asked, even though he'd basically said he didn't want to discuss business. He turned to her then, his eyes dark and glittering as his taut gaze ran over her. "No, as a matter of fact, I'm not."

"Why not?" she queried, her hand curling around the small glass. "At least you owe me the courtesy of telling me why after all these years you want out."

"It's not a marriage, Cupcake."

Caasi bristled. "Don't call me that. Don't ever call me that." Cupcake had been her father's pet name for her. Only Isaac Crane had ever called her that. "I'm not a little girl anymore."

His laugh was short and derisive. "That you're not."

She took another sip of her drink. It burned all the way down her throat and seared a path through her stomach. But she didn't cough and felt pleased with herself.

"What do you want from me?" he asked, as he shoved the empty scotch glass aside.

Feeling slightly tipsy and more than a little reckless, she placed her hand gently over the crook in his elbow. "I want to dance."

His head jerked up, and the color seemed to flow from his face. "Not with me."

"Yes, with you," she said softly, surprised at how angry he sounded. Who else did he think she meant? The piano player?

"No."

The word was issued with such force that Caasi felt as if he'd physically struck her. How embarrassing and humiliating. All at once Caasi knew she had to get out of there before disgracing herself further. "Thanks anyway."

Her hands trembled as she slid off the stool. Wordlessly she turned and walked out of the lounge. She made it as far as the elevator before she felt her entire body start to shake.

The penthouse was dark. Very dark. Even the million lights of the city couldn't illuminate the room. Leaning against the door, Caasi heaved her shoulders in a long, shuddering sigh. She'd had too much to drink that night, far more than normal. That was what was wrong. Not Edie. Not Blake. Not even her. Only the alcohol.

Undressing, she pulled the long satin gown over her head. Accidentally, her hand hit against her abdomen and she paused, inhaling deeply. Lightly her fingers traced her breasts, then fell lifelessly to her sides as she hung her head in defeat.

"I am a woman," she whispered. "I am a woman," she repeated, and fell across the bed.

Chapter Two

Caasi's head throbbed the next morning when the alarm rang. She rolled over and moaned. She'd made a complete idiot of herself the night before. She couldn't believe that she'd actually suggested that Blake dance with her. Heavens, she hadn't been on a dance floor since her college days. The temptation was to bury her head under a pillow and go back to sleep, but the meeting with Pacific Contractors was scheduled for that morning, plus a labor-relations conference for that afternoon.

Laurie, the paragon of virtue who served as Caasi's assistant, was already at her desk when Caasi arrived.

"Morning," Caasi greeted her crisply.

"Schuster's been on the phone twice. He said it's important." Laurie held out several pink message slips.

Caasi groaned inwardly. Every time Schuster phoned it was important. She didn't want to deal with him. Not today. Not ever, if she could help it.

"Is Mr. Sherrill in yet?" Caasi would give the pesky

troublemaker to Blake to handle. He'd deal with Schuster quickly and efficiently. Then she remembered that she'd given Blake the rest of the week off.

"He's been in and out," Laurie announced, following Caasi into the inner office. "He left something on your desk."

A silver tray with a large pot and cup rested on the clean surface of her desk. Beside the cup was a large bottle of aspirin. Caasi managed just a hint of a smile.

"Thanks, Laurie," she murmured, and waited until the short, plump woman left the office.

A folded piece of paper lay on the tray beside the aspirin. Slowly, Caasi picked it up, her heart hammering. A single note and her heart was reacting more to that than any profit-and-loss statement.

The large, bold handwriting matched the man. How often had she read his messages and not noticed that his penmanship personified him? The note read: Thought you could use these this morning. B.

Caasi realized that she could. After snapping the cap off the bottle, she shook two tablets into the palm of her hand and poured the steaming coffee into the cup. She lifted her hand to touch the chestnut hair gathered primly at the base of her neck as she lazily walked across the carpet.

Everything last night hadn't been a fluke. Edie had raised questions that Caasi had long refused to voice. She was a woman, with a woman's desires and a woman's needs. Home, husband, children—these were things she had conveniently shelved. Seeing June and Edie happily married, in love and expecting children, was bringing all these feelings to an eruptive head. Her father hadn't counted on that. Caasi was the only child, the last of the Cranes, who were now an endangered species. With Isaac gone, and her mother dead before she had any memories of her, now there was only Caasi. Alone. Against the world.

Caasi wanted to be protected and loved, cherished and worried about. Like Edie and June. But at the same time, she wanted to be proud, independent, strong . . . everything her father had worked so hard to ingrain in her. Sometimes she felt as though a tug-of-war were going on inside her, with her heart at stake. Some days she looked in the mirror only to discover that a stranger was staring back at her.

The phone buzzed, interrupting her musings. Another day was about to begin, and her doubts would be pushed aside and shelved again.

Saturday morning Caasi woke, sat up in bed, and sighed heavily. The past two days, she'd crawled out of bed more tired than she'd been the night before, as if she hadn't slept at all. Now her eyes burned and she felt as if the problems of the world were pressing against her shoulders.

The company helicopter was flying in that day, and Caasi was scheduled to officiate at a ground-breaking ceremony at Seaside. Another Empress Hotel, the tenth, was about to be launched. She should be feeling a sense of pride and accomplishment, yet all she felt was tired and miserable. The day would be filled with false smiles and promotional hype.

She dressed in a navy-blue linen suit, double-breasted. Her father would approve.

Her breakfast tray was waiting for her, but she pushed it aside. The silver pot of coffee reminded her of Blake. Absent two days and she missed him like crazy. He was scheduled to have gone with her on this little jaunt. Somehow, having Blake along would have made the outing far more endurable.

Caasi was back at her suite by four. Exhausted, she kicked off her shoes and pulled the pins from her hair. The weather was fantastic, a glorious, sunny April afternoon. How could she have felt anything but exhilarated by the crisp ocean breeze? Everything had run smoothly— thanks to Blake, who had been responsible for setting up the ceremony.

The instant his name floated through her mind, the heaviness she'd experienced that morning returned. For years she'd taken him for granted. In rethinking the situation, Caasi realized that he had cause to resign. He was invaluable to her. He couldn't leave; she wouldn't let him. She'd find a way to convince him to stay.

Slouching against the deep, cushioned couch, Caasi propped her feet on the shining surface of the glass coffee table. She'd talk to him. Explain Crane Enterprises' position. And the sooner, the better. Now. Why not?

After changing into a three-piece pantsuit, Caasi sailed into her office to look through his personnel file. They'd worked together for years and she didn't even know where he lived. There were so many things she didn't know about Blake.

She scanned the computer file until she located the Gresham address, a few miles outside of Portland.

Her silver Mercedes had been a gift from her father. Caasi had little need to drive it. Usually she made a point of taking it for a spin once a month. It had been longer than that since she'd last driven it, but the maintenance men kept it tuned and the battery charged for her.

It took almost thirty minutes to find the address. She drove down a long, winding road that seemed to lead nowhere. Although there were several houses around, they were separated by wide spaces. Blake . . . in the country. The mental image of him tilling the fields flitted into her mind. The picture fit.

She stopped at the side of the road and, before pulling into Blake's driveway, checked the nearest house number against the one she'd scribbled down in her office. The house was an older two-story with a wide front porch, the kind Caasi would picture having an old-fashioned swing. A large weeping willow tree dominated one side of the front yard. Caasi had always loved weeping willows.

By the time she opened the car door and climbed out, Blake had come out of the garage, wiping his hands on an oily rag.

"Caasi." His voice was deep and irritated.

"Afternoon," she replied, sounding falsely cheerful. "This is beautiful country out here."

"I like it." He came to a halt, keeping several feet of distance from her.

"Everything went fine today."

"I knew it would."

Caasi untied the lemon-colored chiffon scarf from her throat and stuffed it into her purse. "Can we talk?"

His gaze traveled over her before he lifted one shoulder. "Okay."

Caasi felt some of the tension ease out of her. At least he was willing to discuss things.

"Go in the house; I'll wash up and be there in a minute."

"All right," she agreed.

"The back door's unlocked," he called to her, as he returned to the garage.

Caasi let herself into the rear of the house. An enclosed porch and pantry contained a thick braided rug, on which she wiped her feet. The door off the porch led into a huge kitchen decorated with checkered red-and-white curtains on its large windows.

The glass coffeepot was half full, and Caasi poured herself a mug, hugging it to keep her hands occupied.

With her purse clutched under her arm, she wandered out of the kitchen. A large formal dining room contained built-in china cabinets. An array of photographs filled the open wall space. Caasi stopped to examine each one. They left her wondering if Blake had once been married. Nervous apprehension creased her brow. Several pictures of children who vaguely resembled Blake dominated the grouping. Another of an older couple, dark and earthy, captured her attention. Caasi lifted the wooden frame to examine the two faces more closely. These must be his parents. They both had round, dark eyes—wonderful eyes that said so much. Warm, good people. If Caasi ever had the opportunity to meet them, she knew she would enjoy knowing them. They looked to be salt-of-the-earth kind of people.

Another picture rested behind the others; this one

was of a large family gathering outside what appeared to be the very house she was in. The willow tree was there, only smaller. The two adults were shown with six children. Blake's family. He stood out prominently, obviously the eldest.

"My parents," he explained from behind her.

Caasi hadn't heard him come in and gave a startled gasp, feeling much like a child caught looking at something she shouldn't. Her hand shook slightly as she replaced the photograph.

"The children?" she asked hesitatingly.

"My nieces and nephews."

"You've never married?"

Blake's mouth thinned slightly. "No." He ran a hand through his dark hair. "You said you wanted to talk?"

"Yes." Her head bobbed.

"Sit down." His open palm gestured toward the living room.

Caasi moved into the long, narrow living room. A huge fireplace took up an entire wall, and she paused momentarily to admire the oil painting above the mantel. Mount Hood was richly displayed in gray, white, and a forest of green against a backdrop of blue, blue skies.

"Wonderful painting," she commented casually, looking for the artist's name and finding none.

"Thanks."

Caasi sat in a chair where she could continue to study the mountain scene. On closer inspection she found minute details that weren't readily visible on casual notice. "I really like it. Who's the artist?"

The small lines about Blake's mouth hardened. "Me."

"You!" Caasi gasped. "I didn't know you did anything like this. Blake, it's lovely."

He dismissed the compliment with a short shake of his head. "There's a lot you don't know about me."

"I'm beginning to find that out," she said on a sober note.

His eyes pinned her to the chair.

Uncomfortable, she cleared her throat before continuing. "As I mentioned, the trip to Seaside went without a hitch. But it didn't seem right, not having you there."

"You'll get used to it."

"I don't want to have to do that."

Blake propelled himself out of the overstuffed chair he had sunk into and stalked to the far side of the room. "My decision's been made."

"Change it."

"No."

"Blake, listen." She set her coffee aside and stood. "Today I realized how inconsiderate I've been the last few years. Putting it simply, I've taken you for granted. You were Dad's right-hand man. Now you're mine. I don't know that I can do the job without you."

His laugh was sarcastic, cruel. "I have no doubts regarding your ability. More than once I've been amazed at your insight and discernment. You're a magnificent businesswoman, and don't let anyone tell you different."

"If I'm so wonderful, why am I losing you?"

He didn't answer her.

"I'm prepared to double your salary."

"You overpay me as it is."

She clenched her fist at her side and stared at the oil

painting, searching for some clue to the man she once thought she knew. "Then it isn't the money."

"I told you it wasn't."

"Then clearly someone else has made you a better offer. Holiday Inn? Hilton?"

"No." His voice was loud and insistent.

Don't yell at me, she wanted to shout back, but held her tongue. They'd never argued. For months on end they'd worked together without saying more than a few necessary words to each other. And suddenly everything had changed.

"Caasi." Her name was issued softly. "I wouldn't do that to you. I don't know what I'm planning yet, but I won't go to work for the competition."

"What is it you want?" Angrily she hugged her stomach with both arms and whirled around. "I've never known you to be unreasonable."

He was silent for so long, she didn't know whether he intended to answer.

"You can't give me what I want."

"Try me." She turned back to him, almost desperate. Blake was right; she could manage without him. A replacement could come in, be trained, and suffice, but she wanted him. Trusted him.

His dark gaze fell to her mouth. They stood so close that Caasi could see the flecks of gold in his dark irises. A strange hurt she didn't understand seemed to show in them. A desire welled in her to ease that pain, but she didn't know how. Wasn't that a woman's job, to comfort? But then, she was a complete failure as a woman.

He reached out and gently touched the side of her face. A warmth radiated from his light caress. "I was planning to take the summer off. Do some hiking. I've always wanted to climb mountains, especially Rainier."

Sadly, Caasi nodded, her eyes captured by his. "I've never hiked." She laughed nervously. "Or climbed."

"There are lots of things you haven't done, aren't there?" His soft voice contained a note of tenderness. He dropped his hand.

Caasi forced her eyes away. Blake didn't know the half of it. Her gaze fell on the rows of family pictures. "Do . . . do you like children?" What a ridiculous question, and yet it was one she'd asked of him.

"Very much."

"Why haven't you married and raised a houseful? You've got the room for it here."

"The same reason you haven't, Cupcake."

Caasi bit her tongue to keep from reminding him not to call her that. The name itself didn't bother her. Nor did she care if he reminded her of her father. What she didn't like was Blake thinking of her as a child.

"For the last several years," he elaborated, "the two of us have been married to Crane Enterprises."

"But you could have a family and still work for me." She was grasping at straws and knew it.

"I'm a little too old to start now."

"Old," she scoffed. "At thirty-six?"

Blake looked surprised that she knew his age.

"I don't want to lose you."

His expression hardened as if her words had displeased him. "I'll walk you to your car."

Perplexed, she watched him move across the room and pull open the front door.

"You're angry."

He forced a long breath. "Yes."

"But why? What did I say?"

"You wouldn't understand."

Her hand sliced through the air. "You keep saying that. I'm well above the age of reason. I have even been known to exhibit some intelligence—"

"And in other ways you're incredibly stupid," he interrupted. "Now go before I say something I'll regret."

Caasi sucked in her breath. Her shoes made a clicking rattle against the wooden steps as she hurried to her car. She couldn't get away from Blake fast enough.

Thirty minutes later, still angry and upset, Caasi let herself into the penthouse suite and threw her purse on the bed. Her shoes went next, first the right and then the left. She felt like shouting with frustration.

Dinner arrived and she stared at it with no appetite. No breakfast, a meager lunch, and now dinner held no appeal. She should be starved. Steak, potato, baby white asparagus, and a roll, eaten alone, might as well be over-baked, dried-out macaroni and cheese. Eating alone hadn't bothered her until that night. Why it should now remained a mystery.

The portrait of Blake's parents came into her mind. How easy it was to picture his mother standing in the kitchen with fresh bread dough rising on the counter. Kids eating breakfast and laughing. How could something she'd never known bother her so much? Children. Family. Home. Each word was as foreign to her as the moon. Yet she felt a terrible, gnawing loss.

Determinedly she took the crusty French roll and bit into it. Hard on the outside, tender inside, exactly right. It was the only thing in her life that was exactly right.

The phone buzzed, which usually meant trouble. Caasi lifted the receiver.

"Mr. Sherrill's on his way up," the hotel receptionist informed her cheerfully.

"Thank you," Caasi answered in a shaky voice. Blake coming here? He'd never been to her private quarters. Maybe when her father was alive, but not since she'd taken over.

Hurriedly she rushed into the bathroom and ran a brush through her hair. Halfway out the door, she whirled around and added a fresh layer of light pink gloss to her lips. Her hands shook, she was rushing so much. She unscrewed the cap from a perfume bottle and added a touch of the expensive French fragrance behind each ear and to the pulse points at her wrists.

Caasi started at the sound of his knock. Pausing to take in a deep, calming breath, she sauntered to the door.

"Why, Blake, what a pleasant surprise," she said sweetly.

He didn't look pleased. In fact, he looked much the same as he had when she'd left him earlier.

The feeling of happy surprise drained out of her.

"Go on, change."

"Change?" She stared at him blankly as he walked inside.

"Clothes," he supplied.

"You're not making any sense."

"Yes, I am," he refuted. "What you had on last night will do."

"Do for what?" His attitude was beginning to spark her anger.

"Dancing. That's what you said you wanted."

Hot color extended all the way down her neck. "That was after several drinks."

"You don't want to dance? Fine." He lowered himself onto the long couch. "We can sit and drink."

The dark scowl intimidated her. She'd stood up to angry union leaders, pesky reporters, and a thousand unpleasant situations. Yet one dark glower from Blake and she felt as though she could cry. Her gaze was centered on the carpet, and she noted that in her rush she'd forgotten to put on shoes.

"Caasi?" His voice pounded around the room like thunder.

"I don't know how to dance," she shouted. "And don't yell at me. Understand? The last time I went to a dance I was a college sophomore. Things . . . have . . . changed."

She moved to the window and pretended an interest in the city lights.

Blake moved behind her and gently laid a hand on her shoulder. "What you need is a few lessons."

"Lessons?" she repeated softly. The image that came to her mind was of the times the hotel had booked the ballroom for the students of several local dance studios.

"I'll be your teacher." The words were husky and low-pitched. The gentle pressure of his hand turned her toward him.

Submissively, Caasi's arms dangled at her sides. "What about music?"

"We'll make our own." He began to hum softly, a gentle ballad that the piano man had played the night before. "First, place your arms around my neck." His hands rested lightly on the curve of her hip just below her waist.

Caasi linked her fingers behind his neck. "Like this?"

Their eyes met and he nodded slowly—very slowly, as if the simple action had cost him a great deal. The grooves at the sides of his mouth deepened and he drew her close. His hands slid around to the small of her back, his touch feather-light.

Caasi had to stand on the tips of her toes to fit her body to his. When she eased her weight against him, he went rigid.

"Did I do something wrong?" she asked in a whisper.

"No." His breath stirred her hair. "You're doing fine."

"Why aren't we moving?"

"Because it feels good just to hold you," he said in a strange, husky voice.

A flood of warmth filled every pore, and when she raised her eyes she saw that his angry look had been replaced by a gaze so warm and sensuous that she went completely still. She didn't breathe. She didn't move. She didn't blink.

He moved his hand up her back in a slow, rotating action that brought her even closer, more intimately, against him.

"Blake?" Her voice was treacherously low.

His other hand slid behind her neck, and he wove his fingers into her hair. "Yes?" Slowly, Blake lowered his mouth, claiming the trembling softness of hers.

His lips were undemanding, the pressure light and deliciously seductive. But soon the pressure deepened, as if the gentle caress wasn't enough to satisfy him.

Caasi's body surged with a warm, glowing excitement. She'd been kissed before, but never had she experienced such a deep, overwhelming response. Her arms locked around his neck.

"Caasi . . ." He ground out her name on a husky breath. He kissed her again, and she parted her lips in eager welcome. Their mouths strained against each other, seeking a deeper contact.

Blake tore his mouth away and buried his face in her soft throat.

"My goodness," she whispered breathlessly, "that's some dance step."

Blake shuddered lightly and broke the contact. "Go change, or we'll be late."

"Be late?" she asked, and blinked.

His fingers traced the questioning creases in her brow, then slid lightly down the side of her cheek and under her chin. "My cousin's wedding is tonight. If we hurry, we'll make it to the reception."

"Will I meet your family?" Somehow that seemed important.

"Everyone. Even a few I'd rather you didn't know."

"Oh Blake, I'd like that," she cried excitedly. "I'd like that very much."

Blake smiled, one of those rare smiles that came from the eyes. He had beautiful eyes, like his parents, and Caasi couldn't move. His look held her softly against him.

"Hurry," he urged.

Reluctantly she let him go and took a step in retreat. "Are you sure what I wore last night will be all right? I have plenty of more formal outfits."

"It's fine. But whatever you wear, make sure it has a high neckline."

"Why?" she asked with a light laugh.

"Because I don't want any of my relatives ogling you." He sounded half angry.

Hands on her hips, her mood gay and excited, Caasi laughed. "Honestly, there isn't that much to ogle at."

Boldly, his gaze dropped to her rounded fullness as he studied her with silent amusement. "You have ten minutes. If you haven't appeared by that time, I'll come in and personally see to your dress."

The threat was tempting, and with a happy sigh, Caasi hurried out of the room.

Sorting through her wardrobe, she took out a pink-and-green skirt and top. The blouse had a button front, so the option of how much cleavage to reveal was strictly up to her. Purposely she left the top three buttons unfastened, blatantly revealing the hollow between her breasts. Caasi realized she was openly flirting with Blake, but she hadn't flirted with anyone in so long.

Blake was standing at the window, looking out, when she appeared. He turned and froze, his gaze meeting hers.

"Will I do?" Suddenly she felt uncertain. Idly her fingers played with the buttons of her blouse, fastening the most provocative one.

"You're beautiful."

Caasi felt a throb of excitement pulsate through her. "So are you."

His look deepened, and he glanced at his watch. Caasi had the impression he couldn't have told her the time if she'd asked.

"We'd better go."

"I'll get a jacket." Caasi returned to her bedroom and took a sweater from the hanger.

Blake took it out of her hand and held it open, gliding the soft material up her arms. His hands cupped her shoulders and brought her back against him. His breath stirred the hair at the crown of her head.

The sensations Blake was causing were new. So new that Caasi hadn't time to properly examine them. Not then. Not when his hand held her close to his side as they took her private elevator to the parking garage. Not when he opened the passenger door of the '57 T-Bird with the convertible top down. Not when he leaned over and lightly brushed his mouth across hers.

The recepion was held in a VFW hall off Sandy Boulevard. The lot was full of cars, the doors to the huge building open while loud music poured into the night.

"Once you meet my relatives you might consider yourself fortunate to be getting rid of me."

Caasi wished he hadn't mentioned his resignation, but forced herself to smile in response. "Do you think I could find your replacement here?"

Either he didn't hear the question or chose to ignore it.

"Hey, Blake, who's the pretty lady?" A couple of young people strolled toward them. Caasi could remember trying to walk in the same "cool" manner.

The boy who had spoken was chewing a mouthful of gum.

"You toucha my lady and I breaka your head." Blake's teasing voice carried a thread of warning.

Caasi doubted that either boy took him seriously.

"These two are my baby cousins."

"Baby cousins." The boys groaned. "Hey, man, give us a break."

"You taking your lady to Rocky Butte?" The second youth was walking backward in front of Blake and Caasi, his arms swinging at his sides.

"Rocky Butte?" Caasi glanced up at Blake.

"The local necking place." His hand found hers, and Caasi enjoyed the sensation of being linked to this powerful man. "You game?"

"No," she said, teasing. "I want more dancing lessons first."

His chuckle brought an exchange of curious glances between the youths.

"You're not going to dance, are you, Blake? That's for sissies."

"Wait a few years," he advised. "It has its advantages."

They paused in the open doorway. The polished wooden floor was crowded with dancing couples. A five-piece band was playing from a stage at the far right-hand side of the hall. Long tables containing food were against another wall, and several younger children were helping themselves to the trays of sweets. Older couples sat talking in rows of folding chairs.

A sense of wonder filled Caasi. This was a part of Blake. A part of life she had never experienced. "Are you related to all these people?"

"Most of them."

"But you know everyone here?"

"Everyone." He looked down at her and smiled. "Come on, I want you to meet my parents."

As soon as people were aware that Blake had arrived, there were shouts of welcome and raised hands. He responded with his own shouts, then gave Caasi a whispered explanation as to various identities.

"How many uncles do you have?" she asked, astonished.

"Ten uncles and twice as many aunts. I gave up counting cousins."

"Wow. I love it." Her face beamed with excitement and the laughter flowed from her, warm and easy.

Blake stopped once and turned her around, placing a hand on each shoulder. "I don't think I've ever heard you laugh. Really laugh."

She smiled up at him. "I don't know that I have. Not in a long time."

The bride, in a long, white, flowing gown, the train wrapped around her forearm, giggled and hurried to Blake. "I didn't think you'd ever get here," she admonished, and stood on tiptoes to kiss his cheek. "Now you have to dance with me."

Blake laughed and cast a questioning glance at Caasi. "Do you mind?"

"No, of course not." She stepped aside as Blake took the young woman in his arms. A wide path was cleared as the couple approached the dance floor. People began to clap their hands in time to the music.

Someone bumped against Caasi, and she turned to apologize. "Sorry," she murmured.

The dark eyes that met hers were cold and unfriendly. The lack of welcome surprised Caasi.

"So you're the one who's ruined my brother's life!"

Chapter Three

⁓

"Ruined your brother's life?" Caasi repeated incredulously. "I'm Caasi Crane." The girl obviously had her confused with someone else. A curious sensation attacked the pit of Caasi's stomach at the thought of Blake with another woman.

"I know who you are," the woman continued in angry, hissing tones. "And I know what you've done."

What I've done? Caasi's mind repeated. Those same wonderful eyes that had mesmerized her when she had studied the photo of Blake's parents were narrowed and hard in the tall woman beside her. Blake's own eyes darkened with the same deep intensity when he was angry.

"Are you sure you're talking to the right woman?"

"Oh yes, there's no doubt. I'd know you . . ."

Loud applause prevented Caasi from hearing the rest of what the woman was saying.

Caasi watched as the young bride, laughing and breathless, hugged Blake. He was flushed and laughing, but when his gaze found Caasi and saw who was with her, the humor quickly vanished. He kissed the bride, handed her off to the waiting groom, and hurried across the crowded dance floor to Caasi's side.

"I see Gina has introduced herself," Blake said, as he folded an arm around Caasi's shoulders. He smiled down at her, but there was a guarded quality in his gaze.

The eyes of the two women clashed. Something unreadable flickered in Gina's. Surprise? Warning? Caasi didn't know.

"We didn't get around to exchanging names," Caasi said, as she held out her hand to Blake's sister. It was important to clear away the misconception Gina had about her.

The hesitation was only minimal before Gina took her hand and shook it lightly.

"If you'll excuse us," Blake said, directing his comment to his sister, "I want to introduce Caasi to Mom and Dad."

"Sure," Gina said, her voice husky. She cleared her throat and shook her head as if to dispel the picture before her. Her look was confused as she glanced from her brother to Caasi. "I'm sure they'd like that."

"I know I would." Caasi didn't need to be a psychic to feel the finely honed tension between brother and sister. That Gina adored him was obvious just by the way she looked at him. That same reverence had been in the eyes of the young bride. Blake was an integral part of this family, loved and respected. Caasi, on the other hand, belonged to no one; her life had never appeared so empty—just a shell. She'd give everything she owned— the hotels, her money, anything—to be a part of something like this, to experience that overwhelming feeling of belonging and being loved.

Blake was watching her. "You look a hundred miles away."

"Sorry," she answered with a feeble smile.

He escorted her to a row of folding chairs. Several older women were gathered in a circle and were leaning forward, chatting busily.

"Mom." Blake tapped one of the women gently on the shoulder and kissed her cheek affectionately.

"Blake!" his mother cried in a burst of enthusiasm as she stood and embraced her son. "You did come! I knew you wouldn't disappoint Kathleen."

The gray-haired woman had changed little from the photo Caasi had seen. Although several years older and plumper, Blake's mother was almost exactly the same. Warmth, love, and acceptance radiated from every part of her. Caasi had recognized those wonderful qualities in the photo; in person, they became even more evident.

Blake broke the embrace. "I'd like you to meet Caasi Crane." He turned to Caasi. "My mother, Anne Sherrill."

"Miss Crane." Two large hands eagerly enveloped Caasi's. "We've heard so much about you. Meeting you is a long-overdue pleasure."

"Thank you," Caasi replied with a wide smile. "I feel the same way." She couldn't take her eyes from the older woman. "You're very like your photo."

Anne Sherrill looked blank.

"I should explain," Caasi inserted quickly. "I was at Blake's house this afternoon."

"Where's Dad?" Blake's arm continued to hold Caasi

to his side. She enjoyed the feeling of being coupled with him, the sense of belonging.

Anne Sherrill clucked with mock displeasure. "In the parking lot with two of your uncles."

Fleetingly Caasi wondered what they were doing in the parking lot but didn't ask.

Blake's rich laughter followed. "Do you want me to check on him for you?"

"And have you abandon Miss Crane?" Mrs. Sherrill sounded outraged.

"Please, call me Caasi" was Caasi's gentle request. "I don't mind." The latter comment was directed at Blake. "I'll stay here and visit with your mother. I wouldn't mind in the least."

"I'll only be a few minutes," Blake promised. "Mom, keep Caasi company, and don't let anyone walk away with her." He kissed his mother on the cheek and whispered something about lambs and wolves. With a knowing smile, his mother nodded.

Caasi had to bite her tongue to keep from asking what the comment had been about.

"Have you eaten?" Anne wanted to know. "With that son of mine, you probably haven't had a chance to breathe since you walked in the door. Let's fix you a plate. Not fancy food, mind you."

Caasi started to protest but realized she was hungry. No, starved. "I'd like that," she said as she followed Blake's mother to the row of tables against the wall. The variety of food was amazing, and all home-cooked, from the look of the dishes. It was probably a pot-luck supper, with each family contributing. Thick slices of ham, sausage, and turkey and a dozen huge salads were set out, along with several dishes Caasi didn't recognize.

Anne handed Caasi a plate and poured herself a cup of punch.

"This looks fantastic," Caasi murmured, as she surveyed the long tables. She helped herself to a slice of ham and a couple small sausage links. The German-style potato salad was thick with bacon and onions, and Caasi spooned a small serving of it alongside the ham. "This should be plenty."

"Take as much as you like. There's always food left over, and I hate having to take anything home with me."

"No, no, this is fine. Thank you."

They sat down again. Caasi balanced her plate on her knees and took a bite of the potato salad. "This is really delicious." The delicate blend of flavors wasn't like anything she'd ever tasted.

"Anne's German potato salad is the best this side of heaven," the middle-aged woman on the other side of Caasi commented.

"You made this?" Caasi looked at Anne.

Anne nodded with a pleased grin. "It's an old family recipe. My mother taught me, and now I've handed it down to my daughters."

Anne Sherrill's heritage to her daughters included warmth, love, and recipes. Caasi's was a famous father and a string of hotels, but given the chance she'd gladly have traded.

"No one makes German-style potato salad like Anne," the other woman continued. When she paused, Anne introduced the woman as Blake's cousin's wife.

"What's in it?" Caasi questioned, before she lifted the fork to her mouth. Her interest was genuine.

Anne ran down a list of ingredients with specific instructions. Nothing was listed in teaspoons; it was all in dashes and sprinkles. Caasi doubted that the family recipe had ever been written down. Caasi had never known her own mother, and at times when growing up had felt a deep sense of loss—but never more than right then. Her father had tutored her so thoroughly in the ways of business and finance. It was only at times like this that Caasi realized how much she missed a mother's loving influence.

"It's best to let the flavors blend overnight."

Caasi picked up on the last bit of information and nodded absently, her thoughts a million miles away.

"You must come to dinner some Sunday."

"I'd like that," Caasi said. "I'd like it very much."

"This is the first time Blake's brought a woman to a family get-together, isn't it?" The cousin's comment came in the form of a question. "Handsome devil, Blake Sherrill. I've seen the way women chase after him. Yet he's never married."

"No, Blake's my independent one."

Caasi paid an inordinate amount of attention to cutting her ham slice. "Why hasn't he married?"

The hesitation was slight. "I'm not really sure," Anne supplied thoughtfully. "He loves children. I think he'd like a wife and family, but he just hasn't found the right woman, that's all."

Caasi nodded and lifted a bite of meat to her mouth.

"Is tomorrow too soon?" Anne questioned, and at Caasi's blank look continued, "For dinner, I mean."

Mentally Caasi went over Sunday's schedule. It didn't matter; she could change whatever had been planned. "I'd enjoy nothing more. What time would you like me?"

Anne wrote the address and time on the back of one of Caasi's business cards. She wasn't sure why Blake's mother had invited her, but it didn't matter—she was going. Being with his family, Caasi couldn't help but learn more about the enigmatic man who was leaving her just when she was beginning to know him.

"I think I see Blake coming now," Anne murmured with a tender smile. "With his father in tow."

Caasi studied the gentle look on the older woman's face before scanning the room for Blake. She could barely make out his figure through the crowd of dancers. The faint stirrings of awareness he awakened within her surprised Caasi. She was proud to be with Blake, to meet his family, to be included in this celebration.

Their eyes sought each other's when he stepped into full view. Hers were soft and welcoming; his, slightly guarded.

"Dad, this is Caasi."

Blake's father reached down and took Caasi's hand, his dark eyes twinkling. "Pretty thing." The comment was made to no one directly.

"Thank you," Caasi murmured and blushed.

"Fine bone structure, but a little on the thin side. Always did like high foreheads. It's a sign of intelligence."

"Dad." Blake's low voice contained a thin note of warning.

"George." Anne slipped an arm around her husband's waist. "His tongue gets loose after a beer or two," Blake's mother explained to Caasi.

"Would you like to dance?" A corner of Blake's mouth tilted upward. He looked as if dancing was the last thing he wanted.

"Okay." Caasi would have preferred to stay and talk more with his parents, but she recognized the wisdom of following Blake onto the polished floor.

The band was playing a polka, and with a quick turn, Blake pulled her into his arms.

Caasi let out a small cry of surprise. She didn't know how to dance, especially the polka.

"Just follow me," he instructed. "And pity's sake, don't step on my toes with those high heels."

"Blake," she pleaded breathlessly. "I can't dance. I don't know how to do this."

"You're doing fine." He whirled her around again and again until she was dizzy, her head spinning with the man and the music.

They stopped after the first dance, and Blake brought her a glass of punch. Caasi took one sip and widened her eyes at the potency of the drink.

"Rum?" she quizzed.

"And probably a dab of this and that."

"Old family recipe," she said with a teasing smile. "I'm getting in on several of those tonight. Oh Blake, I like your family."

"They're an unusual breed, I'll say that." His voice was lazy and deep.

"Is Sherrill a German name?"

"No. Dad's English, or once was. Mom's the one with the German heritage."

The band started playing a slow waltz, and Caasi's eyes were drawn to the dance floor again.

Blake took the cup from her and set it aside. "Shall we?" His eyes met hers, the laughter gone, as he skillfully turned her into his arms.

A confused mixture of emotions whirled in her mind as he slid his arms around her waist, the gentle pressure at the small of her back guiding her movements.

A warmth flowed through her, beginning at his touch and fanning out until she could no longer resist and closed her eyes to its potency.

Caasi placed her head on his shoulder, her face against his neck. The scent of his aftershave attacked her senses. She was filled with the feel and the smell of Blake. It seemed the most natural thing in the world for her tongue to make a lazy foray against his neck, to taste him.

"Caasi." He groaned. "You don't know what you're doing to me."

"I do," she murmured. "And I like it. Don't make me stop."

He brought her closer, the intimate feel of his body sensuously moving with hers enough to steal her breath.

"Enough," Blake ground out hoarsely, as if her touch was causing him pain.

Gently his mouth nibbled at her earlobe, and sensations shot through her like a bolt of lightning. "Blake," she pleaded. "Oh Blake, this feels so good."

Right away he broke the contact and led her off the dance floor. "Just how much have you had to drink?" he demanded.

Caasi was too stunned to answer. She opened her mouth but found herself speechless.

"Apparently not nearly enough." She didn't know

why Blake was acting like this. She didn't know how he could turn from a gentle lover to a tormenting inquisitor in a matter of seconds, either.

They stood only a few feet apart, glaring at each other. Neither spoke.

"Hey, Blake, when are you going to introduce me to your lady?" A low masculine voice broke into the palpable silence that stretched between them.

A tall man with a thick mustache over a wide smile came into view. He was about Blake's age and good-looking in a stylish sport coat. His tie had been loosened, revealing curling black hairs at the base of his throat.

"Johnnie—Caasi. Caasi—Johnnie. My cousin."

Johnnie chuckled, his eyes roaming over Caasi with obvious interest. "You don't sound so thrilled that we're cousins." The comment was directed at Blake, but his eyes openly assessed Caasi.

"I'm not," Blake stated bluntly. "Now, if you don't mind, Caasi and I are having a serious discussion."

"We are?" she interrupted sweetly. "I thought we were through. I was just saying how thirsty I am and how delicious the punch is."

Johnnie cocked his head in gentlemanly fashion. "In which case, allow me to escort you to the punch bowl."

"I'd like that."

"Caasi." Blake's low voice was filled with challenge. "I wouldn't."

"Excuse me a minute, Blake," she returned, ignoring his dark, narrowed look. She placed her arm through Johnnie's offered elbow and strolled away. She didn't need to turn around to see that Blake's eyes were boring holes into her back.

"Like to live dangerously, don't you?" Johnnie quizzed with a good-natured grin.

Caasi's lower lip was quivering, and she drew in a shaky breath. "Not really."

"Then I'd say you enjoy placing others in terminal danger. My life wouldn't be worth a plugged nickel if Blake could find a way of getting hold of me without causing a scene."

The thought was so outrageous that Caasi felt her mouth curve with amusement. "Then why are you smiling?" she asked. Johnnie was obviously a charmer, and she found that she liked him.

"I have to admit," he said with a low chuckle, "it feels good to do one up on Blake. He's the family hero. Everyone looks up to him. Frankly, I'm jealous." Johnnie said it with such devilish charm that Caasi couldn't prevent a small laugh.

"Are you thirsty, or was that an excuse to put Blake in his place?" he queried.

"An excuse," she murmured wickedly.

"Then let's dance."

Caasi hesitated; dancing with Johnnie was another matter altogether. "I'm not sure."

"Come on," he said encouragingly. "Let's give Blake a real taste of the green-eyed monster."

By this time Caasi was beginning to regret her behavior. She was acting like a child, which undoubtedly confirmed what Blake thought of her.

"I don't think so. Another time."

"Don't look now," Johnnie whispered, "but Blake's

making his way over here, and he doesn't look pleased. No," he amended, "he looks downright violent."

Caasi shifted. The sound of Blake's footsteps seemed to be magnified a hundred times until it was all she could do not to cover her ears.

"Excuse us," Blake said to Johnnie, and gripped Caasi's upper arm in a punishing hold, "but this dance is ours."

Caasi glanced at him nervously, resisting the temptation to bite her lip as he half dragged her onto the dance floor.

When he placed his arms around her, the delicious sensations didn't warm her, nor did she feel that special communication that had existed between them only a few minutes earlier.

Caasi slid her arms around his neck, her body moving instinctively with his to the rhythm of the slow beat. She studied him through a screen of thick lashes. His mouth was pinched. His dark eyes were as intense as she'd ever seen them, and his clenched jaw seemed to be carved in stone.

Swallowing her pride, Caasi murmured, "I've only had the one glass of punch. I apologize for going off with your cousin. That was a childish thing to do."

Blake said nothing, but she felt some of the anger flow out of him. His arm tightened around her back. "One drink?" he retorted, his mouth moving disturbingly close to her ear.

"Honest."

"You were playing with fire, touching me like that. The way your body was moving against mine . . ." He paused. "If you aren't drunk, then explain the seduction scene." The harshness in his voice brought her head up and their eyes met, his gaze trapping hers.

"'Seduction scene'?"

"Come on, Caasi, you can't be that naïve," he muttered drily. "The looks you were giving me were meant for the bedroom, not the dance floor."

Her eyes fell and she lost her rhythm, faltering slightly. "Let me assure you," she whispered, hating the telltale color that suffused her face, "that was not my intention."

"Exactly," Blake retorted. "You don't need to explain, because I know you."

"You know me?" she repeated in a disbelieving whisper.

"That's right. You're a cool, suave, sophisticated businesswoman. Primed from an early age to take over Crane Enterprises. It's all you know. That isn't red blood that flows in your veins—it's ink from profit-and-loss statements."

They stopped the pretense of dancing. Caasi had never felt so cold. Myriad emotions came at her from every direction.

Wordlessly she dropped her hands and took a few steps in retreat. Her knees were trembling so badly she was afraid to move. The silence between them was charged like the still air before a storm. It was all she could do to turn away and disguise her reaction to his cruel words. Blindly she walked off the dance floor.

Somehow she made her way into the ladies' room. Her reflection in the mirror was deathly pale, her blue-gray eyes haunted.

Her hands trembled as she turned on the cold water. A wet paper towel pressed to her cheeks seemed to help.

Blake was right. She should have recognized as much herself. She wasn't a woman, she was a machine, an effectively programmed, well-oiled machine. Her father had repeatedly warned her against mixing business with pleasure. He'd said it often enough for her to know better than to become involved with Blake. Even now she wasn't sure why she had agreed to accompany him. She had to ask herself where the common sense her father had instilled in her was. Furthermore, she wanted to know why Blake's accusations hurt so much. The sound of someone coming into the room caused Caasi to straighten and make a pretense of washing her hands. She didn't turn around, not wanting to talk to anyone.

"I'm glad I found you." The soft, apologetic voice spoke from behind.

Caasi raised her head and her eyes met Gina's in the mirror. The dark-haired girl looked embarrassed and disturbed. Caasi looked away; she wasn't up to another confrontation.

"I'd like to apologize for what I said earlier," Blake's sister said softly. "It was rude of me."

Caasi nodded, having difficulty finding her voice. "I understand. It's fine." She forced a wan smile.

"Mom said you're coming to dinner tomorrow."

Caasi's eyes widened; she'd forgotten the invitation. "Yes, I'm looking forward to it."

"I hope we can be friends. Maybe we'll get a chance to visit more tomorrow." Gina offered her a genuine smile as Caasi dried her hands.

With most of her poise restored, Caasi returned to

the crowded hall. She saw Blake almost immediately. He stood by the exit. Caasi made her way across the room to Blake's mother. Anne looked up and a frown marred her brow.

"I enjoyed meeting you, Mrs. Sherrill."

"Anne," the woman corrected softly. "Call me Anne."

"Okay."

"Is something wrong, Caasi?"

Caasi had always prided herself on her ability to disguise her emotions. Yet this woman had intuitively known there was something troubling her.

"It's nothing. I'll be at your home tomorrow if the invitation's still open."

"Of course it is."

"Say good night to your husband for me, won't you?"

Anne's eyes were bright with concern. "You do look pale, dear. I hope you're not coming down with something."

Caasi dismissed the older woman's concern with a weak shake of her head. "I'm fine."

Blake had straightened by the time she came to the front door.

"You're ready to go?" he asked, his tone curt.

"I'm more than ready."

He led the way to his car, opened her door, and promptly walked around the front and climbed into the driver's side. The engine roared to life even before Caasi could strap her seat belt into place.

The night had grown cold, and Caasi wrapped her arms around herself to ward off the chill. Maybe it wasn't the night, Caasi mused, but the result of sitting next to Blake. If this cold war continued, she'd soon have frostbite.

They hadn't said a word since they'd left the reception. Caasi couldn't bear to look at him and closed her eyes, resting her head against the seat back.

The wind whipped through her hair and buffeted her face, but she didn't mind—and wouldn't have complained if she had.

The car slowed and Caasi straightened, looking around her. They were traveling in the opposite direction from the Empress. The road was narrow and curving.

"Where are we going?" she asked stiffly.

"To Rocky Butte."

"Rocky Butte?" she shot back incredulously. "Are you crazy?"

"Yes," he ground out angrily. "I've been crazy for six years, and just as stupid."

Caasi watched as his eyes narrowed on the road. "You're taking me to the local necking place? Are you out of your mind?"

Blake ignored her.

"Why are you bringing me here?" she demanded in frustration. "Do you want to make fun of me again? Is that how you get your thrills? Belittling me?"

Blake pulled off to the side of the road and shoved the gears into park. The challenge in his chiseled jaw couldn't be ignored.

"Remember me?" she said bravely. "I'm the girl without emotions. The company robot. I don't have blood, that's ink flowing through me," she informed him, as unemotionally as possible. To her horror, her voice cracked.

She jerked around and folded her arms across her chest, refusing to look at him.

Blake got out of the car and walked around to the front, apparently admiring the view of the flickering lights of Portland. Caasi stayed exactly where she was, her arms the only defense against the chill of the night.

Blake opened her car door. "Come on."

Caasi ignored him, staring straight ahead.

"Have it your way," he said tightly, slamming the door and walking away.

Stunned, Caasi didn't move. Not for a full ten seconds. He wouldn't just leave her, would he?

"Blake?" She threw open the door and hurried after him. Running in her heels was nearly impossible.

He paused and waited for her.

"Where are you going?" she asked, once she reached him.

"To the park. Come with me, Caasi." The invitation was strangely entreating. Would she ever understand this man? She should be screaming in outrage at the things he'd said to her and the way he'd acted.

A hand at her elbow guided her up two flights of hewn-rock steps to a castle-like fortress. The area was small and enclosed by a parapet. There were no picnic tables, and Caasi wondered how anyone could refer to this as a park. Even the ground had only a few patchy areas of grass.

The light of the full moon illuminated the Columbia River Gorge far below.

"It's beautiful, isn't it?" Caasi whispered, not really sure why she felt the need to keep her voice low.

"I love this place," Blake murmured. "It was too dark

for you to notice the rock embankment on the way up here. Each piece fits into the hillside perfectly without a hair's space between the rocks. That old-world craftsmanship is a lost art. There are only a few masons who know how to do that kind of stonework today."

"When was it built?" Caasi questioned.

"Sometime during the Depression, when President Roosevelt implemented the public-works projects."

Despite her best efforts, her voice trembled slightly. "Why did you bring me here . . . especially tonight?"

He shot her a disturbing look, as if unaware he'd said as much. "I don't know." He spoke softly, his gaze resting on her slightly parted lips. He turned toward her, his eyes holding her captive. "I should take you home."

Caasi heard the reluctance in his voice. She didn't want to go back to the empty apartment, the empty shell of her life. Blake was here and now, and she wanted him more than she'd ever wanted anything in her life.

"Blake . . ." His name came as a tormented whisper.

A breathless, timeless silence followed as he slipped his arms around her. Ever so tenderly, with a gentleness she hadn't expected from him, Blake fit his mouth over hers. Again and again, his mouth sought hers until Caasi was heady with the taste of him.

He moaned when her tongue outlined the curve of his mouth, and his grip tightened. Caasi melted against him as his hands slid down her hips, holding her intimately to his hard body.

Her hands were pressed against the firm wall of his chest and his heartbeat drummed against her open palm, telling her that he was just as affected as she was. He felt warm and strong, and Caasi wanted to cry with the wonder of it.

Reluctantly, he tilted his head back, and his warm gaze caressed her almost as effectively as his lips had.

"We should go."

Caasi fought the catch in her voice by shaking her head. If it was up to her they'd stay right there, exactly as they were, for the rest of their lives.

His hand at her waist, he led her back to the parked car. He lingered for a moment longer than necessary after opening her door and helping her inside.

Blake dropped her off in front of the Empress. "I won't see you inside," he stated flatly.

"Why?" She tried to disguise the disappointment in her voice.

His fingers bit into the steering wheel. "Because the way I feel right now, I wouldn't be leaving until the morning. Does that shock you, Caasi?"

Chapter Four

Caasi checked the house number written on the back of her business card with the one on the red brick above the front door. Several cars were in the driveway as well as along the tree-lined street. Caasi pulled her silver Mercedes to the curb, uneasily aware that her vehicle looked incongruous beside the Fords and Volkswagens.

This was a family neighborhood, with the wide sidewalks for bicycle riding and gnarled trees meant for climbing. Caasi looked around her with a sense of unfamiliarity. Her childhood sidewalks had been the elevators at the Empress.

Children were playing a game of tag in the front yard; they stopped to watch as she rang the doorbell, her arms loaded with a huge floral bouquet.

"Hi," a small boy called out. His two front teeth were missing and he had a thick thatch of dark hair and round brown eyes.

"Hi," Caasi said with a wide smile.

"I'm Todd."

"I'm Caasi."

"Are you coming to visit my grandma?"

"I sure am."

The door opened and Gina called into the kitchen, "Mom, it's Caasi." Gina held open the screen door for her. "Come on in, we've been waiting for you."

"I'm not late, am I?" Caasi glanced at her watch.

"No, no."

Anne Sherrill came into the living room from the large kitchen in the back of the house. She was wiping her hands on a flowered terry-cloth apron. "Caasi, we're so pleased you came."

"Here." Caasi handed her the flowers. "I wanted you to have these."

Anne looked impressed at the huge variety of flowers. "They're beautiful. Thank you."

For all the cars parked in front of the house, the living room was empty. Caasi glanced around as Anne took down a vase from the fireplace mantel. The décor was surprisingly modern, with a sofa and matching love seat. The polished oak coffee table was littered with several magazines.

"Come back and meet everyone," Anne said encouragingly. "The men are involved in their card game and the women are visiting."

"Which is a polite way of saying we're gossiping," Gina inserted with a small laugh.

Caasi followed both women into the kitchen, immediately adjacent to a family room which was filled to capacity. Children were playing a game of Monopoly on the floor while the men were seated at a table absorbed in a game of cards.

A flurry of introductions followed. Caasi didn't have trouble remembering names or faces; she dealt with so many people in a hundred capacities that she'd acquired skill for such things.

Five of the six Sherrill children were present. Only Blake was missing. Caasi talked briefly with each one and after a few questions learned who was married to whom and which child belonged to which set of parents. Blake and Gina were the two unmarried Sherrill children. But Gina proudly displayed an engagement ring. Caasi's eyes met Gina's. Whatever animosity had existed between them in the beginning was gone. Several grandchildren crowded around Anne and Caasi, following them as Anne led the way outside so that she could show off her prize garden.

"Roses," Gina supplied. "My mother and her roses. Sometimes I swear she cares as much about them as she does about us kids."

"Portland is the City of Roses," Anne said, as she strolled through the grounds, pointing out each bush and variety of rose as if these, too, were her children.

The older grandchildren followed them, while Gina carried a two-year-old on her hip. Young Tommy had just gotten up from his nap and was hiding his sleepy face against his aunt's shoulder.

Todd, the eight-year-old who had introduced himself at the front of the house, linked his hand with Caasi's.

"You're pretty," he commented, watching her closely. "Are you my aunt?"

"Does this mean only pretty girls are your aunts?"

Caasi teased him, enjoying the feeling of being a part of this gathering.

Todd looked flustered. "Aunt Gina's pretty, and Aunt Barbara's pretty."

"Then you can call me Aunt if you want to," Caasi told him tenderly. "But I'll have to be a special aunt."

"Okay," he agreed readily. They heard another boy calling him, wanting Todd to play. Todd looked uncertain.

"You can go," Caasi assured him. "I'll stay with your grandma, and you can come see me later."

The brown eyes brightened. "You'll be here for dinner?"

"Yup."

"Will you play a game of Yahtzee with me afterward?"

"Sure."

"Bye, Aunt Caasi."

Todd's words sent a warm feeling through her. She watched him run off and her heart swelled. This was the first time anyone had ever called her Aunt.

The baby in Gina's arms peeked at Caasi, eyeing her curiously.

"Do you think he'll let me hold him?" she asked Gina, putting her hands out to the baby. Immediately, Tommy buried his face in Gina's shoulder.

"Give him a few minutes to become used to you. He's not normally shy, but he just woke up and needs to be held a few minutes."

"Is Donald coming?" Anne asked Gina.

"He'll be here, Mom—you know Donald. He'll probably be late for his own wedding, but I love him anyway."

"Have you set a date?" Caasi questioned, as they strolled back to the house.

"In two months."

"The wedding shower's here in a couple of weeks, Caasi. We'd be honored if you came." Anne extended the invitation with an easy grace that came from including everyone, as she probably had all her life, Caasi realized.

"I'd love to. In fact, if you'd like, I could arrange to have the shower at the hotel. I mean, I wouldn't want to take over everything, but that way . . ." She hesitated; maybe she was offending Anne by making the offer.

"You'd do that?" Gina asked disbelievingly.

"We wouldn't want you to go through all that trouble." Anne looked more concerned than dismayed that Caasi would take on the project.

"It's something I'd enjoy doing, and it would be my way of thanking you for today."

"But we can't let you—"

"Nonsense," Caasi interrupted brightly, enthusiasm lighting up her expression. "This will give Gina and me a better chance to get acquainted."

"Oh Mom," Gina said happily. "A wedding shower at the Empress."

"We'll get together soon and make the arrangements," Caasi promised.

Tommy was studying her more intently now. "Can you come and see me, Tommy?" Caasi asked encouragingly. The little boy glanced from Caasi to Gina, then back to Caasi, before holding out both arms to her.

"You are such a good boy." Caasi lifted him into her arms. She was sure that at one time or another in her life she'd held a small child, but she couldn't remember when, and she thrilled to the way his tiny hands came around her neck.

"I think you've got yourself a friend for life." Anne laughed and held open the back door for Caasi to come inside. Donald had arrived, and Gina hurried into the living room to greet her fiancé.

Tommy's mother was busy making the salad at the sink, and she smiled shyly when Caasi entered the house carrying Tommy.

"Here." Anne pushed out a tall stool for Caasi to sit on while she put the finishing touches on the meal.

Although Caasi joined in the conversation around her, she was enjoying playing peekaboo and patty-cake with Tommy. The little boy's giggles rang through the house.

With her face flushed and happy, Caasi glanced up and saw Blake standing in the doorway of the kitchen. He was watching her, and her breath caught at the intensity of his gaze. At first she thought he was angry. His eyes had narrowed, but the glint that was shining from them couldn't be anger. A muscle worked in his jaw and his eyes seemed to take in every detail of her sitting in his mother's kitchen, bouncing a baby on her lap.

One of his brothers slapped Blake across the back and started chatting, but still Blake didn't take his eyes off her.

She broke the contact first as Tommy reached for her hair, not liking the fact that her attention had drifted elsewhere. Suddenly a dampness spread through her linen skirt and onto her thighs. She gave a small cry when she realized what had just happened. Laughing, she handed Tommy to his embarrassed mother, who was apologizing profusely.

Anne led Caasi into the bathroom and gave her a dampened cloth to wipe off her teal-blue skirt. Someone called Anne and she left Caasi standing just inside the open bathroom door. Caasi couldn't keep from smiling.

"What are you doing here?" Blake was leaning against the doorjamb. That warm, sensuous look was gone, replaced with something less welcoming.

"Your mom invited me last night," she told him, her eyes avoiding his as she continued to rub at her skirt. "Do you mind? I'll leave if you do. I wouldn't want to interfere with your family. I'm the outsider here."

He was silent for a long moment.

"No," he murmured. "I don't mind."

Some of the tension eased out of her. "If you'll excuse me, I'll see if I can help in the kitchen." She laid the cloth on top of the clothes hamper and started out the door. But Blake's arm stopped her.

"How'd you sleep last night?" A strange smile touched the curve of his mouth.

Caasi didn't know what he wanted her to say. "Fine. Why?" she asked tightly.

He shrugged, giving the impression of nonchalance. "No reason." But he didn't look pleased.

Anne gave her the job of dishing up the home-canned applesauce, dill pickles, and spicy beets. All the women were in the kitchen, helping in one capacity or another. Laughing and joking with everyone, Caasi didn't feel the least like a stranger. She was accepted, she was one of them. It was the most beautiful feeling in the world.

After the meal, everyone pitched in and helped with

the dishes. As promised, Caasi played Yahtzee with Todd and a couple of the other children. Blake was playing cards with his father and brothers and future brother-in-law.

While the children watched TV, Caasi joined the women, who were discussing knitting patterns and recipes. Caasi listened with interest, but her gaze was on Blake. He looked up once, caught her eye, and winked. Her heart did a somersault and she hurriedly glanced away.

"What game are the men playing?" Caasi asked Gina, who was sitting beside her.

"Pinochle. Have you ever played?"

Card playing was unheard of in the Crane family; even as a child Caasi had never indulged in something her father considered a waste of time.

"No." Caasi shook her head with a sad smile.

"You've never played pinochle?" Gina repeated incredulously. "I thought everyone did. It's a family institution. Come on, let Dad and Blake teach you."

"No . . . no, I couldn't."

"Sure you could," Gina insisted. "Donald, would you mind letting Caasi sit in? She's never played."

Blond-headed Donald immediately vacated his chair, holding it out for Caasi.

Standing, Caasi looked uncertain. Her eyes met Blake's: he didn't want her to play, and his eyes said as much. He scooted out of his seat, offering to let another of his brothers take his place.

Caasi felt terrible. The other women hadn't played.

"Come on. I'll coach you," Gina persisted, and straddled a chair beside Caasi's at the table.

The other men didn't look half as obliging as Donald had, but one look told her he had been losing. Slowly she lowered herself into the vacant seat opposite Blake's father, who was to be her partner.

The cards were dealt after a thorough review of the rules. Gina wrote down the necessary card combinations on a piece of paper as a ready reminder for Caasi. The bid, the meld, and the passing of cards were all gone over in careful detail until Caasi's head was swimming.

They played a practice hand to let Caasi get the feel of the game. Her eyes met Gina's before every move. Once she threw down the wrong card and witnessed her partner's scowl. Caasi's stomach instantly tightened, but George glanced up and offered her an encouraging smile. They made the bid without the point she had carelessly tossed the opponent, and all was well again.

Soon Caasi found herself relaxing enough to enjoy the game. Although playing cards was new to her, the basic principle behind the game was something she'd been working with for years. She studied her opponent's faces when they bid and instinctively recognized what cards were out and which ones she needed to draw. By the time they finished playing, almost everyone else had left—including Blake—and it was almost midnight.

Anne and George walked Caasi to her car, extending an open invitation for her to come again the next week.

"You do this every Sunday?"

"Not everyone makes it every week," Anne was quick to inform her. "This week was more the exception. Everyone was home because of Kathleen's wedding."

Caasi was glad Anne had reminded her. She snapped open her purse and took out an envelope. "Would you give this to Kathleen and her husband for me?" She had written out a check and a letter of congratulations.

"You didn't need to do this," Anne said, fingering the envelope.

"I know," Caasi admitted freely, "but I wanted to."

"I'll see that she gets it."

Caasi could see the elderly couple in her rearview mirror as she drove away. Their arms were around each other as they stood in the light of the golden moon as if they had always been together and always would be. A love that spanned the years.

Caasi was humming as she walked into her office the following morning. Laurie, her secretary, gave her a funny look and handed her the mail.

Caasi sorted through several pieces as she sauntered into her portion of the office. Pivoting, she came back to Laurie's desk.

"I'd like you to make arrangements for a wedding shower in the Blue Room a week from Thursday. Also, would you send the chef up? I'd like to talk to him personally about the cake and hors d'oeuvres."

Laurie looked even more perplexed. "I'll see to it right away."

"Thanks, Laurie," Caasi said, as she strolled back into her office.

The morning passed quickly, and Caasi ate a sandwich for lunch while at her desk. She hadn't seen Blake all morning, which wasn't unusual, but she discovered that her thoughts drifted to him. She wondered what he'd say when she did see him. Would he be all business, or would he make a comment about her visit with his family?

She stared down at the half-eaten sandwich and nibbled briefly on her bottom lip. His mother and sister had been discussing a quiche recipe that had been in Wednesday's paper. Caasi hadn't thought much about it at the time, but the urge to bake something was suddenly overwhelming. She'd taken a cooking class with Edie once simply because her friend didn't want to attend the session alone, but that seemed a hundred years ago. There was a kitchenette in her suite, although she'd never used the stove for much of anything. The oven had never been used, at least not by her. There hadn't been any reason to. And even if she did make the quiche, she'd be eating it all week.

Still . . .

Impulsively she buzzed her secretary. "Laurie, go online and get me the living section from last Wednesday's paper. I'm looking for a quiche recipe."

Laurie returned a few minutes later and handed Caasi the printout.

Reading over the list of ingredients, she realized that not only would it be necessary to shop for the groceries, but she would need to buy all the equipment, including pots, pans, and dishes. Quickly she made out a list and handed it to Laurie, who stared at it, dumbfounded.

"What you can't find and have delivered to my suite, get from Chef," Caasi instructed on her way out the door to a meeting.

Laurie opened and just as quickly closed her mouth, then nodded.

"Thanks," Caasi said.

Caasi was late getting back to her office. Laurie had left for the day, but Caasi wanted to check over the list of phone messages before heading upstairs. She was shuffling through the pink slips when she walked into her office and found Blake pacing the floor.

He took one look at her and frowned.

"Blake." She smiled nervously, avoiding his glare. "Is something the matter?" The atmosphere in the room was cool. He turned away, his back rigid. "Blake?"

He spun around, obviously upset. "I got a call from my mother this afternoon. She dropped off the card you gave her for Kathleen." His words were harsh. "What is the idea of giving them a check for two thousand dollars?" The challenge in his eyes was as hard as flint.

Caasi swallowed tightly. "What do you mean?"

"They're strangers to you."

"They're not strangers," she contradicted him sharply. "I met them when I was with you Saturday night. Don't you remember?"

"Kathleen and Bob don't need your charity." His eyes were as somber as they were dark.

"It wasn't charity," she returned. Her hands shook, and she clenched them into hard fists at her sides. "I have the money—in fact, I have lots of money. What does it matter to you what I do with it?"

"It matters," he shouted in return. "Do you think you can buy yourself a family? Is that it? Are you so naïve as to believe that people are going to love and respect you because of your money?"

Caasi blanched, her hand shooting out behind her to grip the edge of her desk. She suddenly needed its support to stand upright. From somewhere she found the courage to speak. "I don't need anyone, least of all you. Now I suggest you get out. I'll send a letter of apology to your cousin. It wasn't my intent to offend her or you or anyone. Now kindly leave."

He hesitated as if he wanted to say something more, but then he pivoted sharply and stalked out of the room.

Caasi lowered herself into her desk chair and covered her face with her hands. She took several deep breaths and managed to keep the tears stinging the back of her eyes at bay. It mortified her that Blake thought she was looking to buy herself a family. His family. The thought was too humiliating to consider. She wouldn't go to the next Sunday family dinner. Maybe keeping her away had been Blake's intent all along.

She stayed a few minutes longer in her office, but any thoughts of returning her phone messages had been sabotaged by Blake's anger. She leaned against the elevator wall on the ride to the penthouse suite, weary and defeated. Blake was right in some ways. That was what hurt so much. No matter how much she tried, she wasn't going to fit into the homey family scene with love and acceptance. She didn't belong. A lump had formed in her throat by the time she let herself into the empty suite. What she needed was a hot bath, an early dinner, and bed.

Dinner . . . Her mind stumbled over the word. She'd canceled her meal for the evening because she'd planned to bake the quiche. The laugh that followed was brittle. Well, why not? She could cook if she wanted to. Who was to care?

Laurie had done her job well, and the kitchen was filled with the necessary equipment. After a quick survey, Caasi slipped off her high heels and tucked her feet into slippers. Fearing she'd spill something on her suit, she used an old shirt as an apron, tying the sleeves around her waist. Rolling her sleeves up to her elbows, she braced both hands on the counter and read over the recipe list a second time. Last, she lined the ingredients up on the short countertop in the order in which she was to use them.

The piecrust was going to be the most difficult; everything else looked fairly simple.

Blending the flour and shortening together with a fork wasn't working, so Caasi decided to mix it with her fingers, kneading the shortening and flour together in the palms of her hands.

The phone rang; she stared at the gooey mixture on her hands and decided to let it ring. Ten minutes later, just as she'd spread a light dusting of flour across the counter and was ready to roll out the dough, there was a loud knock on her door.

"Come on, Caasi, I know you're in there."

Blake.

Panic filled her. He was the last person she wanted to see, especially now.

"Aldo says you haven't left. Your car's in the garage and there's no one in the office, so either let me in or I'll break down the door."

He didn't sound as though he was in a better mood than he had been in when she'd last seen him.

"Go away," she shouted.

"Caasi." His low voice held a note of warning.

"I'm . . ." She faltered slightly with the lie. "I'm not decent."

"Well, I suggest you cover yourself, because I'm coming through this door in exactly fifteen seconds."

She caught her lower lip in her teeth and breathed in deeply. Why was it that everything in her life had to end up like this?

"It's unlocked," she muttered in defeat.

Blake let himself in, then stopped when he saw her framed in the small kitchen.

"What are you doing?" he asked, hands on his hips.

"What are you thinking, coming up to my suite like this? I should have Security toss you out."

"Why didn't you?" he challenged.

"Because . . . because I had dough on my hands and would have gotten it all over the phone."

"That's a flimsy excuse."

Caasi released a low, frustrated groan. "Listen, Blake, go ahead and laugh. I seem to be an excellent source of amusement where you're concerned."

"I'm not laughing at you." The humor drained out of his eyes, and he dropped his hands.

"Then say what you came for and be done with it. I'm not up to another confrontation with you." Her voice trembled. Blake had the ability to hurt her, and that was frightening.

"To be honest," he murmured gently, as he took several deliberate steps toward her, "I can't recall a time I've seen you look more beautiful."

For every step he advanced, she took one in retreat, until she bumped against the oven door. The handle cut into the backs of her thighs.

"There's flour on your nose," Blake told her softly.

Caasi attempted to brush it aside and in the process spread more over her cheek.

His gaze swept over her and he shook his head in dismay. "Here, let me."

"No." She refused adamantly. "Don't touch me, Blake. Don't touch me again."

He looked as though she'd struck him. "I've hurt you, haven't I, Cupcake?" he asked gently.

"You can't hurt me," she lied. "Only people who mean something to me have that power."

He frowned, his dark eyes clouding with some unreadable emotion. Surely not pain, Caasi mused.

"For what it's worth," he said quietly, "I came to apologize."

She shrugged, hoping to give the impression of indifference.

"I got halfway home and couldn't get that stricken look in your eyes out of my mind."

"You're mistaken, Blake," she said pointedly, struggling to keep her voice steady. "That wasn't shock, or hurt, or anything else. It was . . ." She stopped abruptly when he placed the tips of his fingers over her lips. Helplessly, she stared at him, hating her own weakness. By all rights she should have him thrown out after the terrible things he'd said.

His hands slid around her waist and she tried to push him away, getting dough on his suit jacket.

"I told you not to touch me," she cried. "I knew something like this would happen. Here, I'll get something to clean that."

"There's only one thing I want," Blake murmured softly, pulling her back into his arms. His mouth settled hungrily over hers.

Caasi's soft body yielded to the firm hardness of his without a struggle. His arms tightened around her waist until every part of her came into contact with him. For pride's sake, Caasi wanted to struggle, but she was lost in a swirling vortex of emotion. She could feel the hunger in him and knew her own was as strong.

His teeth gently nibbled on her bottom lip, working his way from one corner of her mouth to the other. Caasi wanted to cry at the pure sensuous attack. No one had ever kissed her like that. What had she missed? All these years, what had she missed? Her breath came in quick, short gasps as she broke out of his arms. Tears filled her eyes until he became a watery blur.

"Don't," she whispered achingly, and jerked around, her back to him as she placed her hands on the counter to steady herself.

His ragged breathing sounded in her ear as he placed a comforting hand on her shoulder. "That's the problem," he said quietly. "Every time I touch you it nearly kills me to let you go. Someday you won't send me away, Cupcake."

"Don't call me that. I told you that before."

The phone rang and she glanced at it guiltily, not able to answer it with her dough-covered hands.

"Aren't you going to answer it?" Blake demanded.

She waved a floury hand in his direction.

"Wash your hands. I'll get it for you."

Because the water was running in the sink, Caasi didn't hear what Blake said or who was on the line.

"It's someone by the name of June. She sounded shocked that a man would answer your phone."

Caasi threw him an angry glare and picked up the receiver. "Yes, June."

"Who was that?" June demanded in low tones.

"My general manager. No one important." Caasi smiled at Blake sweetly, hoping the dig had hit its mark.

"I just got out of the doctor's office and he said that everything is looking great. He also said that I could have someone in the delivery room with me when my time came, and I was wondering if you'd like to be there."

Caasi didn't even have to think twice. "I'd love to, but what about Burt?"

"Oh, he doesn't mind. I can have two people with me, and I wanted you to be one of them."

"I'm honored."

"I'm going to be touring the hospital facilities on Friday. Could you come?"

"Yes; that shouldn't be any problem. I'll phone you in the morning once I've had a chance to check my schedule."

"I'll let you get back to that unimportant, sexy-sounding manager."

Caasi laughed lightly, knowing she hadn't fooled her intuitive friend. "Talk to you tomorrow," Caasi promised, and hung up.

When she returned to the kitchen, she discovered that Blake had taken off his jacket, rolled up his sleeves, and was placing the piecrust into the pan with the ease of an expert.

"Just what do you think you're doing?" she demanded righteously.

"I figured you couldn't possibly eat all this yourself and you'd probably want to invite me to dinner."

"You have a high opinion of yourself, Blake Sherrill."

His boyish smile would have disarmed a battalion. "And if you plan to invite me to dinner, the very least I can do is offer a hand in its making."

Chapter Five

"Well, don't just stand there," Blake insisted. "Beat the eggs."

Caasi hesitated, her feelings ambivalent. She wanted to tell Blake to leave, to get out of her life. He had hurt her in a way she had never expected. But at the same time he had awakened her to what it meant to be a woman, and she wanted him with her. He made her laugh, and when he touched her she felt more alive than she had in all her twenty-eight years.

Not fully understanding the reasons why, Caasi decided to swallow her pride and let him stay. She took the eggs and cracked them against the side of the bowl one by one. Silently they worked together. Caasi whipped the eggs until they were light and frothy while Blake chopped onion and green pepper and sliced zucchini.

"I'm going to the hospital Friday," Caasi mentioned casually.

Blake paused and turned toward her. "Is something wrong?"

"No," she assured him. "It's one of the most natural things in the world. Babies usually are."

A stunned silence crackled in the tension-filled room. "Did you say 'baby'?"

Caasi was enjoying this. "Yes," she murmured without looking up, pouring the milk into the measuring cup.

"Are you trying to tell me you're pregnant?" Blake demanded.

Caasi had trouble keeping a smile from forming. "I'm not trying to tell you anything. All I did was make a casual comment about going to the hospital Friday."

"Because of a baby?"

Caasi nodded. She could see the exasperation in his expression.

Blake's eyes raked over her, and she noticed the way the paring knife was savagely attacking the green pepper. "Who's the father?"

"Burt."

"Who's Burt?"

"June's husband."

"But that was June on the phone and . . ." Blake stopped in mid-sentence, as understanding leapt into his eyes. "You little tease," he said deeply. "I should make you pay for that."

"Tease? Me?" Caasi feigned shock. "How could you accuse me of something like that? You have to remember, I'm not a real woman, with real blood."

Blake linked his arms around her waist and nuzzled her neck. "I don't know, you're becoming more woman-like by the minute."

"You think so, do you?" A throb of excitement ran through her at his touch. Fleetingly Caasi wondered why she hadn't experienced these sensations with other men.

"Yes, I do." He turned her into his arms, linking his hands at the small of her back. Hungrily, his gaze studied her.

Caasi gave a nervous laugh and broke free. These feelings Blake was creating within her were all too new, too strong. They frightened her.

"I want you to know," Caasi began, taking a shaky breath, "I thought about what you said at the dance—about having ink in my veins."

A silence seemed to fill the small kitchen. "And?" Blake asked her softly.

"And I think you're probably right. Ever since Dad died, I've been so busy with Crane Enterprises that I've allowed that role to dominate my life." She slipped the onion and other vegetables he had chopped into the egg mixture and poured it over the thinly sliced zucchini already in the piecrust. "June and Edie tried to tell me the same thing," she said, and gave a weak laugh. "Edie said what I needed was an affair."

"An affair," Blake repeated slowly, his dark eyes unreadable. "So that's what this is all about."

"What?"

"You heard me. What happened then? Did you suddenly look at me and see the most likely candidate?" His words went cold.

"Of course not. I thought Edie was nuts. I'm not the type of woman who would have an affair. Do you honestly think I'd do something like that?"

"Why not? I won't be around much longer. You can have your fling and be done with me."

Words momentarily failed her as she struggled to control her outrage. "Why do you do this to me? I started out by telling you that you were right in what you'd said about me and suddenly I'm on the defensive again." One hand gripped the oven door, and she knotted the other until the long nails bit into her palm. "June and Edie had noticed that I have no life except the business. All I'm saying is that I'm trying to change that." Irritated with her inability to explain herself in simpler terms, Caasi walked across the suite to stand in front of the large picture window. Her arms hugged her stomach. These changes made her vulnerable to Blake. If these changes only brought pain, then she wanted no part of it.

He came to stand beside her but made no attempt to touch her. "Have you noticed how we can't seem to be together anymore without disagreeing about one thing or another?"

"Oh yes, I've noticed." Her hands dropped to fists at her side.

"By all rights you should throw me out."

Caasi knew that, but she didn't want him to leave. He might have the power to wound, but just as strong was his ability to comfort and heal.

"That wouldn't be fair." A wry smile twisted her mouth. "You made half the dinner." It didn't make sense, Caasi realized, but she wanted him with her, liked having him around.

"Truce, Caasi?" His voice was soft and gruff at the same time.

"For how long?" They hadn't gone without fighting for more than a few minutes lately.

"Just tonight. We can get through one night without arguing."

Caasi resisted the temptation to slip her arms around him. "Working together, we can manage it." They'd been a team for years—but soon that, too, would change. The thought was a forceful reminder that Blake had turned in his resignation and would be leaving soon. She wondered if she'd ever see him again after he left the Empress. The realization produced a painful sensation in the area of her heart. Blake had always been there. She relied on him. Nothing would be the same after he left. But she couldn't mention that now. Not when they'd agreed on a truce. Every time she said something about him leaving, they argued.

"The quiche has to bake for an hour. Let's listen to some music," he suggested.

"And have a glass of wine."

Caasi kept a supply of her favorite Chablis available and brought down two crystal glasses. While she poured, Blake reached for his phone and music started to play.

Music filled the suite as Caasi brought their drinks into the living room.

Blake sat on the couch, holding out his arm to indicate he wanted her at his side. Caasi handed him the wine and sat next to him on the plush leather sofa, leaning her head against his shoulder. A hand cupping her upper arm kept her close. Not that Caasi wanted to be anyplace else.

The music was mellow and soft, the ballad a love song. Oftentimes, after a long day, Caasi would sit with her feet propped up on the coffee table, close her eyes, and let the music work its magic on her tired body. But the only magic she needed that night was Blake.

"June asked me to go into the delivery room with her when her baby is born," Caasi said, elaborating on the earlier conversation. "That's why I'm going to the hospital this Friday. They want to familiarize the three of us with the procedures."

"Three of you?"

"Four, actually," Caasi said, correcting herself. "Burt, June, baby, and me."

"You're sure you want to do this?" Caasi felt his gaze wandering over her as if in assessment. "From what I understand, labor is no picnic, and for someone who's never had a baby, it may be more than you can handle."

Caasi stiffened. "I want to be there and nothing's going to stop me."

Blake glanced at his wristwatch. "Twenty minutes."

"What's twenty minutes?"

"How long we lasted without arguing."

"We didn't fight. I was tempted, but being the mature woman I am, I managed to avoid telling you that I found that remark unnecessarily condescending."

Blake chuckled and took a sip of his wine. "I'm glad. Because then I can admit that sometimes I say things purposely just to see the anger spark in your eyes. You're beautiful when you let that invisible guard down, and sometimes anger is the only thing that lowers it."

Every part of her was conscious of Blake. Pressed close to his side, she ached for the feel of his arms around her and the taste of his mouth. But their truce wasn't limited to arguments, although they hadn't stated as much. They needed to find a level plane, a happy medium between the fighting and the loving.

"I'm working to change that about myself," Caasi admitted softly. "When Dad was in charge he was firm in his belief about mixing business with pleasure. When he was in the office he was one man, and outside the office, another. In some ways I'm a lot like my father. We've worked together five years, Blake, but I never saw you as anything more than my general manager."

"And you do now?"

Her voice was becoming huskier as she strove to keep the emotion out of it. "Yes."

"Because I'm leaving?"

"Say . . ." She laughed shakily. "Why am I doing all the talking? Shouldn't you make some deep revelation about yourself?"

Blake's answering grin was dry. "I like fine wine"—he raised the glass to his lips and took a sip—"and the challenge of climbing mountains. I love the Pacific and enjoy walks along the beach in the early hours of the morning before the sun rises. Sometimes when the mood comes over me, I paint." He paused. "Does that satisfy your curiosity?"

"In some ways." But he didn't offer to reveal more, and the point was well noted.

The timer on the stove rang and Caasi reluctantly broke from his arms. "I'll check our dinner."

She set the quiche on top of the stove to cool and returned to the living room. Blake was looking out the window at the view.

"Some nights, especially when things are troubling

me," Caasi admitted softly, as she joined him, "I'll stand here and think."

"So that's why there's a worn spot in the carpet," Blake teased.

"I've been here a lot lately."

"Why?" Blake turned and took a step toward her. Only a few inches separated them.

Caasi lowered her gaze to the floor and shrugged. "Lots of things."

"Anything in particular?"

She ignored the question. "The quiche is ready if you are."

Blake brushed a strand of hair from her face. When his hand grazed her cheek, Caasi swallowed her gasp of pleasure.

"No," Blake said slowly, his words barely audible. "I'm not ready." His hand worked its way around the back of her neck, his fingers twining into her hair as he brought her mouth up to meet his.

With a small whisper of welcome, Caasi swayed into him, melting against him, her arms reaching instinctively for him. Her response was so automatic she didn't have time to question it.

As his mouth plundered hers, Caasi felt as though she were on fire, the burning heat spreading down her legs until she was weak and clinging.

This wasn't supposed to happen, they'd promised each other it wouldn't, but they were like two climbers waiting to explore a mountain and would no longer be denied the thrill of the challenge.

Her hands reveled in the feel of the hard muscles and

smooth skin of his back. A languor spread through her, and her breath came in short, soft gasps.

Blake buried his face in the hollow of her throat and shuddered. "Let's eat," he whispered, and Caasi smiled at the husky timbre of his voice as she realized he was experiencing the same sensations she was.

Neither showed much interest in the meal. Blake commented that she'd done a good job and Caasi was pleased with her efforts, but her mind wasn't on the food.

They hardly spoke, but each intuitively seemed to know what the other was thinking. Caasi wished she had her wine, and without a word Blake stood and brought it to her.

Simultaneously they set their forks across half-full plates, their interest in food entirely gone. Blake stood and held out his hand to her.

Heedless of where he was taking her, Caasi realized she would have followed him to Mars. She placed her hand in his. Blake reached for his phone and once more the music played as he led her back to the sofa.

Caasi slid an arm around him and rested the side of her face close to his heart. Blake rubbed his jaw against the top of her head in a slow, rotating action that was faintly hypnotic. His fingers were in her hair.

Caasi didn't need to look to know that his eyes were closed. This was like a dream, a trance from which she never wanted to wake. The barriers were down.

Caasi didn't know how long he had held her. The music had faded long ago, but they made their own. She didn't even need to close her eyes to hear the violins.

Blake shifted and Caasi was shocked to look at her watch and see that it was almost midnight.

"Walk me to the door," he whispered, and kissed the crown of her head, his breath stirring her dark hair.

She nodded, not finding the words to release him readily.

"Our truce lasted," she said softly, and added, with a warm smile, "sort of."

"If we're going to fight, let's do it like this. Agreed?" He took her in his arms, gazing down at her upturned face with a warmth that reached all the way to the soles of her feet.

"Yes, I agree." Her hand lovingly stroked his thick, unruly hair. "Are you really going to leave me, Blake?"

He went completely still. "How do you mean?"

Did he think she was asking him to spend the night? If she was honest, she'd admit the thought wasn't an alien one. But she had been sincere when she explained that she wasn't one to indulge in casual affairs. She wanted Blake; Caasi couldn't deny it. But she wanted him forever.

"The Empress," she explained. "You're not going to leave, are you?" The minute the words were out, she knew she'd said the wrong thing.

Blake looked as if she'd physically struck him. He pulled her arms away, severing the contact. "So that was what this was all about." Impatience shadowed his face.

"Blake, no!" But he wasn't listening as he sharply turned, opened the door, and left.

————

"There's a Gina Sherrill to see you," Laurie announced the following Monday.

"Send her in," Caasi replied. "And, Laurie, could you see to it that we're not disturbed?"

"Of course."

Gina stepped into the office a moment later.

"Hi, Caasi." She looked uncertain, her eyes taking in the expensive décor of the room. "Wow, you've got a great view from up here, haven't you? How do you ever get anything done?"

"It's hard, especially on a sunny day like today when it seems that the whole world is outside this window and ready to be explored."

"We missed you Sunday."

Caasi rolled a pen between her palms. "I had a previous engagement." The lie was a small one.

"Everyone likes you, and we were hoping you'd come again."

"I will," Caasi assured her, but secretly doubted that she could. Not with Blake in his present state of mind. Another confrontation with him was to be avoided at all costs. Since the night they'd cooked together they treated each other like polite strangers. Blake had hired his replacement and was training the middle-aged man now. Caasi liked Brian Harris and had recognized almost instantly that she wouldn't have any trouble working with him.

Blake's last day was scheduled for the end of the month, less than ten days away.

"Let's go down to the Blue Room and you can tell me what kind of decorations you want. Are the other women coming?" Caasi asked. Gina had asked to include her maid of honor and bridesmaids in the shower planning.

"They're in the lobby. We didn't feel like we should all descend on you."

"Why not?" Caasi asked, setting the pen aside. "I'm looking forward to meeting them."

"Blake's leaving, isn't he?" Gina's question came as a surprise.

Caasi nodded with forced calm. "Yes; he handed in his resignation not long ago."

"I'm surprised." Gina wrinkled her nose. "I didn't think Blake would ever leave you."

That was the crux of the problem—Caasi hadn't thought so, either.

"Shall we go now?" Caasi wanted to divert the conversation from Blake.

"Sure," Gina answered eagerly.

Riding the elevator down to the lobby, Gina announced, "All the invitations have been mailed. Everyone is impressed that the shower's at the Empress. I'm still having problems believing it myself."

"I'm glad to do it." Caasi meant that.

"You'll be there, won't you? I know it's in the middle of the day and everything, but you wouldn't have to stay long and I'd really like everyone to meet you."

Caasi hesitated. There was an important meeting scheduled with architects the afternoon of the shower, and if past experience was anything to go by, she could be held up for hours.

"I won't make any promises, but I'll see what I can do."

"Great," Gina enthused.

They met the others in the lobby, and the small party took the broad, winding stairs built against a mirrored wall to the second floor, where the Blue Room was situated.

"Oh." Gina exclaimed with excitement. "It's perfect, just perfect."

Caasi stayed only a few minutes longer. She wanted to have some time to herself before she had to leave for a luncheon engagement that was scheduled with the Portland Chamber of Commerce; they would be discussing plans for a basketball players' convention that winter.

Briefly Caasi explained that she'd ordered the flowers delivered Thursday morning and had asked the chef to provide a sketch of the cake.

"The cake," Gina said happily, "is larger than the one for the wedding."

Glancing at her wristwatch, Caasi groaned. "I've got to run, but I'll see you Thursday afternoon."

"Oh thanks, Caasi. I can't tell you how excited I am about this."

"To be honest, I'm having as much fun as you, doing it."

Caasi took the elevator back to her office. As the huge doors glided open, Caasi stepped into the wide hallway—and nearly bumped into Blake.

His hands shot out to help her maintain her balance and their eyes clashed. "Are you all right?"

Caasi couldn't take her eyes off him. For the first time in days there was a faint flicker of something more than polite disregard. Every angle of his jaw was lovingly familiar, and she longed to ease the lines of strain from his eyes and mouth.

"Caasi," he said sharply.

Her eyes studied the floor, and she struggled to maintain the thin thread of her composure. "I'm fine."

He released her slowly. "Will you have time this afternoon to go over the Wilson figures?"

"Yes, that shouldn't be any problem. I'll be back around two."

"Fine," he said in clipped tones. "I'll send Harris into your office then."

"Harris." She repeated the name. She knew the man was replacing Blake, but she had yet to deal with him directly. "Yes." Her voice faltered a bit. "That'll be fine."

Caasi stepped into her office and retrieved her purse. "I'm leaving now."

Laurie looked up at her blankly. The luncheon wasn't scheduled for another hour. "But Mr. Gains is due to see you in twenty minutes."

"Send him in to Blake," Caasi said curtly. "You know where to reach him."

Caasi took the Mercedes, heading east down Sandy Boulevard until she located Broadway. She drove around for several fruitless minutes. It had to be around here somewhere. Finally she recalled seeing that small mom-and-pop grocery and knew she was headed in the right direction. For all her years in Portland, she'd been to Rocky Butte only once. With Blake, the night of his cousin's wedding.

She parked her car in the same area Blake had. The scene was all the more magnificent during the day. The snow-capped mountain peaks of the Cascade Range and the flowing Columbia and Willamette Rivers could all be seen from there. Washington state was just on the other side of the Columbia River Gorge, and once powerful Mount Saint Helens was in full view. No wonder Blake loved it up here so much.

The park itself was a different matter. Someone had broken beer bottles against the steps, and Caasi avoided the sharp pieces of glass as she climbed the flights of hewn-rock stairs for the second time. Walking to the parapet, she studied the view again. Faint stirrings of love and appreciation for what lay before her brought an involuntary smile. Caasi, born and raised in Portland, Oregon, was unaware of her city's charm and beauty. A shame, she mused dejectedly.

Caasi sauntered into the office a little after two, having decided to send Harris to the luncheon. Laurie glanced up at her nervously.

"Mr. Sherrill's in your office."

"Thanks, Laurie." Her assistant's tone told her Blake wasn't in a mood to exchange pleasantries.

"Problems, Blake?" she quizzed, as she entered.

He swiveled and jammed his hands into his pockets. His gaze hardened. "Gains had the appointment with you. Where were you?"

"Out," she snapped.

"You don't give important people like Gains the brush-off like that. The banker was furious, and with good reason."

Perfectly calm, Caasi sat at her desk and glared at him. "Do you presume to tell me how to run Crane Enterprises now? Criticizing my personal life isn't enough?"

Blake clamped his mouth closed. "You're in no mood to discuss this rationally."

Caasi's laugh was sarcastic and brittle. "This is getting better every minute," she said, refusing to let him talk down to her. "Send Harry in with the Wilson figures, please."

"The man's name is Harris." The contempt in Blake's eyes was enough to make her cry. Maybe tears would dissolve the lump of loneliness within her. Maybe tears would take away the pain of what Blake was doing. But somehow Caasi doubted it.

Thursday afternoon, fifteen minutes before her scheduled meeting with the architects, Caasi took the elevator to the Blue Room, where Gina's wedding shower was in progress.

She stood in the entry, watching the young woman open her gifts. The turnout was a good one, and Caasi recognized several people from Kathleen's wedding.

The bouquets of blue and white flowers harmonized beautifully with the room's décor. The chef had outdone himself with the huge sheet cake.

Gina saw Caasi just inside the doorway and gave a squeal of delight. The young bride-to-be hurried to proudly introduce Caasi to her friends.

Caasi's appearance was only a token one, and she made her farewells, sorry to learn that she'd missed Anne. She would have enjoyed seeing Blake's mother again.

Laurie smiled when Caasi returned to the office. "There was a Mrs. Sherrill here to see you. I told her you'd gone down to the Blue Room."

Caasi smiled sadly. She'd just missed Anne again. But that was the way her life was headed. Always close, but never close enough.

She'd barely sat down at her desk when Blake

slammed into her office, nearly taking her door off the hinges when he closed it.

"What was my mother doing here?" he demanded.

"Your mother was here because of Gina's shower," Caasi replied calmly.

"Gina's wedding shower?" He was pacing the floor like a caged lion eager for the opportunity to escape and hunt the closest victim.

"Yes. It's in the Blue Room."

"My family can't afford the Blue Room."

"But I can. I'm doing this for Gina."

Blake froze, and his anger burned from every pore. "You did what?"

"I would have said something earlier if we'd been on better terms. Everything I do lately angers you. There are only a few days left until you're free of me. Must you fight me at every turn?"

Blake marched to the far side of the office and raked his hand through his hair. "I want you to add up every cent that this fiasco has cost and take it out of my next paycheck."

"What?" Caasi exploded, bolting out of her chair.

"You heard me. Every cent."

Tears sprang from her eyes, blinding her. She lowered her gaze so Blake wouldn't notice.

"Why?" she asked, amazed that her voice could remain so steady when she felt as though the world was crumbling apart beneath her.

"I told you before that you couldn't buy yourself a family. Least of all mine."

"Yes, of course." She swallowed at the painful hoarseness in her throat. "Now, if you'll excuse me."

She left the office and nearly walked into Laurie. "Conference Room A is ready for—" Laurie stopped sharply. "Miss Crane, are you all right? Do you need a doctor?" The woman looked flabbergasted to see Caasi in tears. Hurriedly she supplied Caasi with a tissue.

"Cancel the meeting, Laurie." Her voice trembling, Caasi fought down a sob. "Please extend my sincere apologies." With as much self-possession as she could muster, Caasi walked out of the office.

Blake came up behind her. "Caasi." Her name was issued grimly.

She ignored him and stepped into the elevator. When she turned around, their eyes met. The tall, lean figure swam in and out of her vision.

"You have so much, Blake. Is it that difficult to share just this little bit with me?" The huge metal doors swished shut and Caasi broke into sobs that heaved her shoulders and shook her whole body.

Chapter Six

Caasi leaned against the penthouse door, her shoulders shaking. If this horrible ache was part of being a woman, she wanted none of it. Ink in her veins was preferable to the pain in her heart. But it was too late, and Caasi recognized that.

With her arms hugging her stomach, she tilted her face to the ceiling to keep the tears from spilling. She was tired. The weariness came from deep within.

Blake was leaving; why shouldn't she? She hadn't been on a real vacation in years, not since she took over Crane Enterprises.

Wiping the moisture from her cheeks, she took a quivering breath and stood at her favorite place by the window. She'd be fine. All she needed was a few days away to gain perspective.

Her leather luggage was stored in the spare bedroom. Caasi wasn't exactly sure where she'd go. It would be fun just to drive down the coast. Oregon had some of the most beautiful coastline in the world.

The soft knock on the door surprised her. Probably Laurie. The secretary had been shocked to see Caasi cry . . . and little wonder. Caasi wasn't the weeping-female type.

"Yes," Caasi called softly, striving to sound composed and confident. "Come in."

When Blake strolled into the living room, Caasi felt ice form in the pit of her stomach. "These are my private quarters," she told him in a voice that was dipped in acid. "I don't know who or what has given you the impression that you may come up here, but that has got to change. Now get out before I call Security." She marched out of the room and into her bedroom, carelessly tossing her clothes into the suitcase.

"Caasi, listen." There was an unfamiliar pleading quality to his voice as he followed her. "Let me apologize."

"Okay," she said, without looking up. "You're sorry. Now leave."

"What are you doing?" His eyes followed her as she moved from the closet to the suitcase, then back to the closet.

"That's none of your business."

"If you're going someplace, I need to know."

"I'll leave the details of my trip with Laurie." She didn't look at him; she was having enough trouble just keeping her composure intact.

"Isn't this trip a bit sudden?"

"Since when do you have the authority to question

me?" She whirled around, placing her hands challeng-
ingly on her hips.

"Since you started acting like an irrational female,"
he returned sarcastically.

"Me?" Caasi exploded. "Of all the nerve!" She
stormed across the room and picked up the phone. "Security, please."

"I'm not leaving," Blake threatened. "Call out the
National Guard, but I'm not leaving until we understand
each other."

"Understand?" Caasi cried. "What's there to understand? I'm the boss, you're the employee. Now get out."

"No."

"Yes." Caasi spoke into the receiver. "This is Miss
Crane. I'm having a problem here. Could you send up
Security?" She hung up the phone and tossed Blake a
hard look. "Oh, before I forget," she said, and gave him
a saccharine smile, "be sure and have Accounting give
you an employee discount on the Blue Room." She
slammed the lid of her suitcase closed and dragged it off
the top of the bed.

Taking a smaller case, she entered the master bathroom and impatiently stuffed a brush, a comb, shampoo,
a hair dryer, and an entire cupboard of cosmetics into it.
When she whirled around, Blake was blocking the doorway.

"Will you kindly step out of the way?"

"Not until we talk."

Giving the impression of boredom, Caasi crossed her
arms and glared at him. "All right, you win. Say what
you want to say and be done with it."

Blake looked surprised but determined. He paused and ran his hand over his jaw.

"What's the matter, has the cat got your tongue?" she taunted unfairly.

Confusion flickered across his brow. "There's something about you, Caasi, that makes me say and do things I know are going to hurt you. Yet I do them."

"This is supposed to be an apology?" She faked a yawn.

Blake's thick brows drew together in a pained, confused expression. Caasi doubted that her feigned indifference could create a fissure in the hard wall of his defenses.

The phone rang, diverting her attention to the other room.

"If you'll excuse me."

"No, not now." His arm across the door prevented her from leaving.

"Blake." She groaned in frustration. "This is ridiculous. Look at you. Will you kindly move so I can answer the phone?"

He didn't budge.

"Please," she added.

Blake dropped his hand and turned his back to her. As she hurried past him, Caasi noted fleetingly that he looked as weary and defeated as she felt.

"Hello," she answered on the fourth ring, her voice slightly breathless.

"Caasi?" The male voice on the other end was only faintly recognizable.

"Burt?" Caasi felt all the blood drain from her face.

"It's June. She's in labor. She said I should phone you now."

"Now?" Caasi repeated with a sense of unreality. "Isn't this early?"

"Only ten days. The doctor assured us it wasn't anything to worry about. I'm at the hospital; the nurse is checking June and said she'd prefer I stepped out for a few minutes." Burt sounded worried and unsure.

"I'll be there in five minutes." Caasi's heart was singing with excitement as she replaced the telephone receiver.

"Who was it?"

Caasi had forgotten Blake was there. "Burt. June's in labor." She grabbed her purse from the end of the bed and hurried out of the suite. A security man met her just outside the door.

"You wanted me, Miss Crane?"

"Yes," she shouted, and shot past him to the elevator. "I mean no, everything's been taken care of. I'm sorry to have troubled you."

"No trouble, miss." He touched the brim of his hat with his index finger.

"Caasi," Blake called, as he followed her out of the suite. "I'll meet with the architects and we can talk about it in the morning."

"Fine." She'd have agreed to anything as long as it didn't delay her.

The car engine roared to life when she turned the key. Caasi wondered if June was experiencing this same kind of exhilarated excitement. Burt and June wanted this baby so much and had planned carefully for it. For her,

Caasi corrected her thoughts. June's deepest desire was for a little girl.

The visitors' parking lot was full, and Caasi spent several frustrating minutes until she found a space on the street. On her visit the previous Friday, she had learned that once Burt phoned she was to go directly to the labor room on the third floor. Stepping off the elevator, her shoes clapped against the polished, squeaky-clean floor.

"I'm Caasi Crane," she announced at the nurses' station. "Can you tell me which labor room Mrs. Kauffman is in?"

The uniformed nurse with white hair and a wide smile glanced at the chart. "Number 304. I believe her husband is with her."

"Thanks," Caasi said with a smile.

The room was the second one on the left side of the hall. The door was closed, so Caasi knocked lightly.

Burt opened it for her, looking pale and worried.

"Is anything wrong?" Caasi asked anxiously.

"No, everything's fine, or so I've been assured." He ran his hand through his hair. "June's doing great."

Caasi smiled. "How come you look like you're the one in labor?"

"I don't know, Caasi, I can hardly stand to see June in pain like this."

"Caasi?" June looked flushed against the white sheets. "Is that you?"

"I'm here."

"I suppose I got you out of some important meeting."

"Nothing I wasn't glad to escape from," Caasi assured her, and pulled up a chair so she could sit beside the bed. "I've read that babies aren't particularly known for their sense of timing."

June laughed weakly. "At least not this one. The pains woke me up this morning, but I wasn't really sure this was the real thing. I didn't want to trouble you if it wasn't."

Burt came around to the other side of the bed and took his wife's hand in both of his. "How do you feel?" His eyes were filled with such tenderness that it hurt Caasi to look at him. Would any man ever look at her like that? The only thing she'd seen in Blake's eyes lately was disdain.

"I'm fine, so quit worrying about me. Women have been having babies since the beginning of time."

Burt looked up at Caasi. "I'll say one thing: Having a baby is a lot different than I thought."

Caasi smiled reassuringly. "I don't imagine it's much what June thought, either." She glanced down to note that June's face was twisted with pain. Instinctively, Caasi gave June her hand. Her friend gripped it the way a drowning man would a life preserver. After a few moments her face relaxed.

"The pains last about thirty seconds, but it's the longest thirty seconds of my life," June whispered.

"The last time the nurse checked, she'd dilated to five centimeters. She has to get to ten centimeters in the first stage of labor."

Caasi had been reading the book the doctor had given her in preparation for the big event. Once June was fully dilated, the second stage of labor, when the baby entered the birth canal, would begin.

"The nurse said that won't be for hours yet," June told her.

"Not to worry, I've got all day. What about you?"

"Well, if the truth be known, I'm missing a big sale at Lloyd Center," June joked.

The hours passed quickly. Caasi was shocked to look up from timing a contraction to note that it was after seven, and she hadn't eaten lunch. But she was too busy to care about food.

When the hard contractions came, Burt coached his wife, while Caasi, her hand on June's abdomen, counted out the seconds. Time and again Caasi was astonished at her friend's fortitude. June and Burt had decided in the beginning that they wanted a natural childbirth, and although the pains were excruciating, June's resolve didn't waver. Burt didn't look as confident.

When the time came to move into the delivery room, Caasi and Burt were asked to don surgical gowns.

"I didn't realize I would have to dress for the occasion," Caasi joked, as June reached for her hand.

A small cry slipped from June as the pain crescendoed. As it ebbed, June lay back on the pillow, panting.

Burt carried June's fingers to his lips. Then, tenderly, he wiped the moisture from her brow.

"I love you," June whispered, the soft light of love shining in her eyes.

Strangely, Caasi didn't feel like an intruder on the touching scene; she felt she was a part of it—a wonderful, important part.

"I've never loved you more than I do right this minute," Burt whispered in return.

Another pain came and June bit into her lip with the grinding agony, panting and breathless when it waned.

"One more pain and you should be able to see the head," the doctor told them. A round mirror was positioned near the ceiling, and all eyes focused on the reflection as another pain came and passed. June gave Caasi a happy but weak smile.

The baby started crying once the head was free of the birth canal, the doctor supporting the tiny skull.

"Good pair of lungs," Burt said excitedly. "It must be a girl."

One final contraction and the baby slipped into the doctor's waiting hands.

"It's a girl," he announced.

June gave an exhilarated cry. "Oh, I wanted a girl so badly. Burt . . . a girl." Laughing and crying at the same time, she threw her arms around her husband's neck, hugging him fiercely.

"Seven pounds, twelve ounces," the nurse said, as she lifted the squalling baby from the scale.

Unabashed tears of happiness flowed down Caasi's cheeks. She had never felt such wondrous joy in her life. To have had even a small part in the baby's birth produced warm emotions that touched the softest core of her heart.

"Caasi." June gripped her hand. "You're crying. I don't think I've ever seen you cry."

"It's all so beautiful. And your daughter's beautiful."

"Should I tell her?" Burt looked down with love at his wife. At June's confirming nod, he glanced up. "June and I decided if we had a daughter we would name her Cassi—two s's, one a."

"After a lifelong friend we both love and respect," June added.

Caasi couldn't push the words of love and appreciation past the lump of happiness in her throat.

"And, of course, we want you to be her godmother," Burt continued.

"Of course," Caasi confirmed, tears winding a crooked path down her face.

An hour later, Caasi walked to her car parked on the deserted street. A look at her watch confirmed that it was almost ten. She felt like skipping and singing. Tiny, sweet baby Cassi was adorable, and Caasi couldn't love her any more if she were her own.

Caasi pulled onto the avenue and merged with the flow of traffic. She felt wonderful and rolled down the window, singing as she cheerfully missed the turn that would lead her back to the downtown area and the Empress.

Before she could reconsider, she took the turnoff for Gresham and Blake's house. He'd said something about wanting to talk to her after the meeting that afternoon, but that wasn't the reason she had to see him. If she didn't tell someone about the baby, she'd burst.

There wasn't a streetlight to guide her as she drove down the winding road. She had to pull over to the side of the road a couple times, having difficulty finding her way in the night. Finally she pulled into the driveway, the old weeping willow the only reminder she required.

The kitchen lights were on, and Caasi paused before climbing out of the car and slowly closing the door. Maybe coming to Blake's wasn't such a good idea after all. They'd been fighting when she left.

The back door opened and Blake came down the steps. "Caasi." He sounded shocked. "Is anything wrong?"

She shook her head. "June had a baby girl."

"That's wonderful. Come inside and I'll make you a cup of coffee."

"I'd like that."

A hand at her elbow guided her up the stairs. The coffeepot was on the kitchen counter. Caasi glanced into the living room and saw an open book lying across the arm of an overstuffed chair. Blake had been spending a quiet evening at home reading.

He handed her a mug and Caasi took it, leaning against the kitchen counter as she hugged the coffee cup with both hands.

"June and Burt are naming her Cassi—two s's, one a. She's so beautiful, all pink and with the tiniest hands. She's perfect, just perfect. Before they moved her out of the delivery room, the nurse let me hold her for a few minutes. It was the most incredible feeling I've ever experienced, holding this new life. I still can't believe it," she finished breathlessly.

A warm smile appeared on his face and was reflected in his eyes as he watched her. "Come and sit down in the living room. You can tell me all about it."

"I don't even know where to start." She sat in the chair opposite his and lifted the lid from a candy jar nearby, popping a couple pieces of hard candy into her mouth. "I'm starved. I hope you don't mind if I help myself."

"Didn't you eat dinner?"

Caasi shook her head. "Not lunch, either. No time,"

she explained, while sucking the lemon drops. The sugary sweetness filled her mouth, making her hunger more pronounced.

"Let me fix you something."

"No, I'll be fine, really," she asserted.

Blake ignored her, returning to the kitchen and opening the refrigerator as Caasi trailed after him. "There are leftover pork chops, eggs, bacon. What's your pleasure?"

Caasi bit into the side of her mouth to keep from saying: You. The thought nearly squeezed the oxygen from her lungs. Never had she wanted a home and husband more than she did at that moment. They even looked like an old married couple, standing in the kitchen, roaming through the fridge and looking for leftovers.

"Caasi?" Blake glanced up, his look questioning.

She shook her head. "Anything's fine. Don't worry about a meal, a sandwich would do as well."

"Bacon and eggs," he decided for her, taking both from the refrigerator and setting them on top of the counter.

Caasi pulled out a chair and sat at the table while Blake peeled off thick slices of bacon and laid them across a skillet.

"June was incredible," Caasi continued. "She was a real trooper. Burt and June had decided they wanted natural childbirth, and she did it. She refused to give up. Burt tried to talk her into using the anesthesiologist a couple of times, but June refused." She paused and smiled. "Instead of watching, he closed his eyes along with her. Don't get me wrong—he was wonderful, too. I don't know how any woman can have a baby without her husband's help. I know I couldn't." Caasi swallowed tightly. But then, she probably wouldn't have a child. Some of the enthusiasm left her and she stared into the coffee mug.

Silence filled the kitchen.

"The meeting with Schultz and Schultz went fine. But they'd like you to make a trip to Seaside next Tuesday, if you can."

"I don't see why not." Eagerly Caasi picked up the conversation. "I don't remember that anything's scheduled. I'll check with Laurie in the morning." Her index finger made a lazy circle on the tabletop. "Will you be coming?" Blake sometimes traveled with her, depending on the circumstances.

"It looks as if I'll have to. We'll leave Harris in the office, which will be good experience for him."

"Sure," she agreed, feeling somewhat guilty. Not once in the past week had she made an effort to meet or talk to Brian Harris. The man served only to remind her that Blake was leaving, and she hadn't accepted that. Couldn't accept it. Not yet.

The bacon grease was sizzling in the frying pan when Blake cracked two eggs against the side and let them slide into the hot fat. With the dexterity of an accomplished chef he flipped down the toaster switch.

"Hey, I didn't realize you were that skilled in the kitchen," Caasi murmured, uneasy with the fact that he could cook and she couldn't.

"Practice makes perfect, and I've cooked plenty of solitary meals in my time," he said, as he slid the fried eggs onto a plate. He set the meal in front of her and straddled a chair, drinking his coffee while she ate.

Everything was delicious, and she said as much. "I

don't remember a time I've enjoyed a meal more." At his skeptical look, Caasi laughed and crossed her heart with her finger. "Honest."

"Then I suggest you have a talk with that expensive chef you imported."

Blake had never approved of her hiring the Frenchman who ran the Empress kitchen.

"I'd be willing to do away with the whole kitchen staff if you'd agree to stay."

Forcefully Blake expelled his breath, and Caasi realized that she'd done it again.

Lowering her gaze to the empty plate, she tore a piece of crust from her toast. "That was a dumb joke. I didn't mean it." For once, just tonight, when she was so happy, she didn't want to say or do anything that would start a disagreement.

"Didn't you?" he asked in a low, troubled voice.

Caasi peered at him through thick lashes. "Well, it's true I don't want you to go, but my reasons are entirely selfish."

"You don't need me anymore."

If only he knew. "I guess not," she agreed reluctantly, "but you've always been there, and it won't be the same when you're gone."

"Sure it will."

How could he sound so casual about leaving the place that had been his second home for six years? Apparently she didn't mean much to him. Instead of seeking answers to the nagging doubts, Caasi scooted out of her chair and stood.

"I'll do the dishes. Anyone who does the cooking shouldn't have to do the dishes."

"Caasi Crane doing dishes," Blake said mockingly. "This I've got to see."

"Well, just who do you think did them the night we baked the quiche?" she declared righteously. "I am a capable person, Blake, whether you care to admit it or not."

She washed while he dried and put away. Wordlessly they worked together, but it wasn't a strained silence.

When they finished, Caasi noted that it was late . . . they both had to be at work in the morning. There wasn't any reason to stay, but she didn't want to go.

"I suppose I should think about heading back," she murmured, as she dried her hands on a kitchen towel.

Blake agreed with a curt nod, but he didn't look as though he wanted her to leave, either.

Caasi glanced at the oil painting over the fireplace. "Have you done any artwork lately?" Maybe some small talk would delay her departure.

"Not much to speak of." He shrugged. "I'm thinking about concentrating more on my painting after the first of the month."

After the first—when he would no longer be at the Empress and wouldn't be troubled with her anymore.

"Let me know; I'd like to buy something from you."

Blake laughed outright. "I only dabble in art. The Empress displays paintings from some of the best in the country. Those artists would be insulted to have my work hanging beside theirs."

Caasi hadn't been thinking of hanging it in the hotel, but in her suite. It would give her something tangible to remember him by. But rather than admit it, she said nothing.

"We did it," Caasi murmured, as they strolled toward her car.

"Did what?"

"Went the whole night, or at least a portion of it, without fighting. That's a record, I think."

"You mentioned my resignation only once."

"I won't admit how many times I've had to bite my tongue," Caasi teased.

"Is my leaving that difficult for you to accept?" Blake leaned against the front of her car and folded his arms across his chest.

Caasi shrugged both delicate shoulders. "Yes," she admitted starkly. "But I'm beginning to understand how selfish I'm being toward you. There's something about having you with me. . . . I trust you, Blake—sometimes more than I do myself. Looking back, I can see the mistakes I've made in my enthusiasm to live up to Dad's expectations. I allowed Crane Enterprises to become everything to me."

For a long second he looked at her. "But not anymore?"

"I don't know," she admitted honestly. "But I'd do anything if you'd change your mind."

Indecision flickered in his narrowed gaze. "You're handing me a powerful weapon; you know that, don't you, Caasi?"

"You're worth it."

"To Crane Enterprises?"

She nodded. "And me," she told him softly.

He was silent for so long that Caasi wasn't sure if he'd heard her.

"Let me think about it," Blake said. Looking away, he took a deep breath, as if struggling within himself.

"How soon before you can give me an answer?" Her heart was beating double time. If Blake stayed she would have the opportunity to explore the relationship that was developing between them. The thought of losing him now—just when she was discovering Blake, the man—was intolerable.

"I'll let you know by the first of the week."

"Great," Caasi agreed. At least there was a chance.

Chapter Seven

Monday morning Caasi strolled into the outer office and greeted her secretary with a cheerful "Good morning."

Laurie glanced up. A frown drove deep grooves into her wide brow. "Good morning, Miss Crane."

Caasi was sure Laurie didn't know what to think of her anymore. Her secretary probably attributed the wide swings in her moods to Blake's resignation. Not immune to office gossip, Caasi was aware that there was heavy speculation as to his reasons.

Today she would know his decision. How could he refuse her after all that they'd shared recently? How could he walk away from her on a day as gorgeous and sunny as this one? He wouldn't, Caasi was sure of it.

In her office, she buzzed the intercom. "Laurie, would you ask Mr. Sherrill to come to my office when he arrives?"

"I think he's in now."

"Good."

Caasi released the switch and sauntered to the far side of the room. So much had changed between her and Blake in such a short time. Mostly there was Blake to thank for that. And he'd see that she was changing and that would be all the incentive he'd need to stay.

Friday she'd watched him, studied his body language as well as his speech. He didn't want to leave, she was sure of it. Her father had warned her of the hazards of being overconfident, but she didn't feel the necessity to heed his counsel this morning. Not this glorious morning.

Caasi had spent Sunday with June, Burt, and baby Cassi. June had come home from the hospital, and while Burt had fussed over his wife, Caasi had sat and held the baby. Cradling the tiny being in her arms had filled her heart with love. This was what it meant to be a woman, whole and complete. The overwhelming tenderness she'd experienced holding the baby lingered even now, a day later.

Sunday night Caasi had lain awake, staring at the ceiling, unable to sleep. So much depended on Blake's decision. Her father had taught her to hope for the best but plan for the worst. She'd asked herself over and over again what would change if Blake decided to leave. Ultimately nothing. Brian Harris seemed capable enough of assuming Blake's duties.

But losing Blake the man would be more than Caasi could bear. Not now, not when she was just coming into her own. Surely he'd see the changes in her and withdraw his resignation.

"Good morning," Blake said, as he entered the room. "You wanted to see me?"

"Yes." Caasi nodded, standing at her desk. One look at Blake and a nauseated feeling attacked her stomach. He looked terrible. "Blake, are you ill?"

"No," he denied. "I suspect you want to hear my decision."

"Of course I do," she said, somewhat sharply. What she wanted to do was scream at him to tell her what she needed to hear: the promise that he'd never leave her, that he'd stay with her all her life.

Blake rubbed a hand over his eyes. "This decision hasn't been easy," he said softly.

"I know," she whispered in return. Dear God, her mind screamed, don't let him leave me.

"I can't stay, Cupcake."

Caasi slumped into her chair, fighting to disguise the effect of his decision by squaring her shoulders and clamping her hands together in her lap. "Why?"

Blake lowered himself into the chair on the other side of her desk. "Not for the same reasons I originally resigned," he explained.

"I see," Caasi replied stiffly. "In other words—"

"In other words," Blake interrupted, "things have changed between us."

"For the better," she inserted, not easily dissuaded. "I've tried so hard."

"Too hard, Cupcake."

Caasi couldn't respond as the continued waves of disappointment rippled over her.

"In light of my decision, maybe it would be best if Brian Harris accompanied you tomorrow."

Somehow, with a determined effort, Caasi managed to nod.

"My last day is Wednesday, but if you think you'd like me to stay a few more days . . ."

"No," she whispered. "No," she repeated softly, a bit more in control of her voice now. "If you've made your decision, then don't prolong the inevitable."

"You're beginning to sound like your father again."

"Again?" Caasi asked with a dry smile. "I've always sounded like Dad. Why shouldn't I? After all, I am his daughter."

"Caasi . . ." Blake sounded unsure.

"If you'll excuse me, I've got a meeting to attend." She spoke crisply and centered her gaze just past him on the seascape hanging on the wall.

The door clicked and Caasi realized that Blake had left. Taking deep breaths helped to calm her pounding heart. She was stunned, completely and totally shocked.

"Laurie." Her hand was surprisingly steady as she held down the intercom switch. "Do I have anything pressing this morning?"

Her secretary ran down a list of appointments.

"Would you reschedule them at a more convenient time, please? I'm going out for a while."

"Going out?" Laurie repeated disbelievingly. "But there's the meeting with Jefferson at nine."

"I'll be here for that, but cancel everything else."

"The whole day?"

"No." Caasi pressed a hand to her forehead. She was overreacting. She had to come to grips with herself. "Just this morning."

An hour later Caasi couldn't have repeated one word of the meeting with Jefferson. The accountant seemed to be aware of her lack of attention and called their time short. Caasi didn't return to her office, but went directly to the parking garage and took out her Mercedes.

The drive to the Lloyd Center was accomplished in only a matter of minutes. Leaving her car in the underground parking garage, she took the escalator to the second-floor shopping level. Standing at the rail, she looked down at the ice-skating rink situated in the middle of the huge complex.

A sad smile touched her eyes as she watched the figures circle the silvery ice. Most of the skaters were senior citizens, loving couples with their arms around each other as they skillfully glided around the rink. Thirty years from now she could picture June and Burt skating like that. Thirty years from now and she would remain an observer, standing on the outside of life—exactly as she was now.

In the mood to spend money, Caasi went from store to store, buying whatever took her fancy. She bought baby Cassi enough clothes to see her into grade school. She also bought toys, blankets, shoes—whatever attracted her attention. Caasi held up one frilly outfit after another and understood why June had wanted a baby girl.

Returning to the hotel garage, she left instructions for the packages to be taken to her quarters. The last thing she needed was for Blake to see what she'd bought and accuse her of buying herself another family.

Laurie glanced up and smiled when Caasi stepped into the outer office.

"Happy Monday," Caasi said, and handed her secretary a small box.

"What's this for?" Laurie pulled the gold elastic ribbon off the box.

"Just a thank-you for rearranging the day."

Her announcement was followed by a short gasp of pleasure from Laurie. "Chocolates from How Sweet It Is. But they're fifty dollars a pound."

"You deserve only the best."

For the first time in years, Laurie looked completely flustered. "Thank you, Miss Crane."

"Thank you, Laurie," Caasi stated sincerely.

The stack of phone messages was thick. Caasi shuffled through them and paused at the one from Dirk Evans from the International Hotel chain. He'd phoned several times in the past few years, eager to talk to her about acquiring the Empress. International was interested not only in the Portland Empress, but also in several others in California and along the Oregon coast.

She stared at the pink slip for several moments while pacing the floor. Pausing at the window, she examined her options. Her father would turn over in his grave if she were to sell. But why did she need the hotels? Why did she need any of this? Even without the hotels, she was a wealthy woman. No, the thought of unburdening herself was tempting at the moment, but the Empress was her family, the only family she'd ever known, the only family she would ever know. She couldn't throw that away, not on a whim.

Laurie buzzed and broke into her thoughts. "Call from Edie Albright on line one."

"Thanks, Laurie." Caasi released one button and pushed down another. "Edie, how are you?"

"Fine."

"You don't sound fine. What's wrong?"

"Freddy's in New York and I'm bored. I don't suppose you'd be interested in dinner with me tonight? Nothing fancy. I could come to the Empress if you'd like."

"I would. I'm feeling down myself." That was a gross understatement, but if she admitted as much, they'd both be crying in their salads.

"Great." Edie cheered up immediately. "What time?"

"Any time you like."

Edie paused. "My goodness, you're accommodating today. I expected an argument at the very least. You don't go out that often."

Caasi smiled drily. "And how would you know that?"

"Honestly, Caasi, June and I are your best friends. We know you."

"Apparently not well enough," Caasi couldn't resist adding. "I'll meet you at seven in the main dining room."

"Wonderful. You don't know how much I appreciate this," Edie said. "I've got lots to tell you. This pregnancy stuff isn't all it's cracked up to be."

Caasi replaced the receiver and stared into space a while longer. Seeing Edie that night was just what she needed. Her friend, scheming and crazy, had a refreshing way of helping her see the bright side of things. And she'd need a lot of talking to see the pot of gold at the end of the rainbow as far as Blake's leaving was concerned.

The afternoon passed in a whirl of appointments and phone calls. By six Laurie had left, and although there were several items on Caasi's desk that needed her attention, she decided to deal with them Wednesday. The next day she'd be flying to Seaside with Brian Harris to meet with the architects. The time spent with Harris would help her become acquainted with the man. They'd be working together closely in the future, and there was no reason to delay. No reason, her mind repeated, and a curious pain attacked her heart.

Wednesday would be Blake's last day. As she pushed the elevator button, Caasi wondered how or where she would get the courage to relinquish him as unemotionally as possible.

Her living room was filled with packages from that morning's shopping spree. Caasi decided to ignore them until after her bath. She didn't want to keep Edie waiting.

The bathwater was running when there was a knock on her door.

Caasi wasn't sure it was someone at her door until the sound was repeated. "Just a minute," she called, and hurried to turn off the water. She was grateful that she hadn't completely undressed. Putting on a robe, she tied the sash as she walked across the living room carpet.

"I thought I said seven in the dining room," Caasi murmured good-naturedly as she opened the door. Her jaw must have sagged.

"Can I come in?" Blake looked at her, his eyes sparkling with amusement as he looked her over.

"I . . . I'm not dressed for visitors," Caasi stammered, her heart pounding wildly.

"Get dressed, then, if it'll make you feel more comfortable."

Numbly, she stepped aside, swinging open the door.

"I'll only take a minute of your time," Blake promised with a half-smile.

"I prefer to be dressed," she said. Naturally she was curious as to why he'd come, but she wasn't ready to deal with him. Not tonight, not after he'd announced his decision. "If you'll excuse me." She turned around and nearly choked. The packages from her shopping spree covered the sofa and chair. She closed her eyes and groaned inwardly. The only thing she could do was ignore them now. If she called Blake's attention to the parcels and boxes it would only invite comment.

She went into the bedroom and her fingers shook as she hurriedly grabbed a blouse, fumbling with the tiny buttons. Stuffing the silk tails into her skirt, she returned to the living room.

"Yes," she said crisply. "What is it?"

Blake turned around with a slightly guilty look. "I'd say this is a little small, wouldn't you?" He held up one of the dresses she'd purchased for June's baby.

"It's not for me," she said stiffly, refusing to meet his laughing eyes.

"I'd guessed as much," he returned seriously. "Is all this for little Cassi?"

Caasi jerked the dress out of his hands and stuffed it back into its paper sack. "That's none of your business," she told him. "And don't you dare . . ." She paused to inhale a quivering breath. "Don't you dare say I'm buying myself a family."

"You are their family, Cupcake," Blake said gently.

Caasi jerked her face up and their eyes met. His were warm and oddly indulgent. She wanted to yell at him not to look at her like that. How could he do this when only hours before he'd told her he wanted nothing more to do with her or the Empress. He was the one who wanted out, not her. Heaven knew she didn't want him to go.

Caasi turned away. "Was there something you wanted to tell me?" she asked.

"Yes." Blake walked to the other side of the room and ran his hand through his hair. "Harris won't be able to go with you tomorrow. His wife is having a medical procedure. So it looks like you're stuck with me for one last trip."

Terrific, her mind threw out sarcastically.

Some of her thoughts must have shown in her expression. "Don't look so pleased," Blake chided. "We'll be back by afternoon. I assume after all these years that we can manage to get along for a few hours."

"Sure." The word nearly stuck in her throat, then came out sounding scratchy and weak. "Why not?"

"You tell me," Blake said in a low voice.

Caasi pivoted sharply and walked to her favorite place by the window. "No reason," she said, and shrugged.

"I'll see you in the morning, then."

Without turning around, she answered, "It looks that way." She stood poised, waiting for the click of the door. When it didn't come, she turned to find Blake watching her.

"Caasi?"

"Was there something else?" she asked politely.

His searching eyes narrowed on her, and Caasi had the impression he wanted to say something more. "No." He shook his head. "I'll see you tomorrow."

"Fine."

Edie was already seated in the dining room when

Caasi arrived. Caasi returned her small wave as she entered the room.

"You look positively . . ." Edie paused and sighed longingly. "Skinny."

Caasi laughed. "You always did have a silver tongue."

"The only reason I'm so candid is that for every ounce you've lost, I've gained three." Elbows on the table, Edie leaned forward. "I'm telling you, Caasi, I'm going crazy."

"What's wrong?" Edie had always been the dramatic one, so Caasi wasn't overly concerned.

"Well, for one thing, I can't stop eating peanut butter. I woke up at two this morning and ate it straight out of the jar. Freddy couldn't believe it, and for that matter, neither could I."

"At least peanut butter is a high source of protein."

Edie groaned and closed her eyes. "That's what Freddy keeps telling me."

"Why the worry?"

"My dear Caasi, have you any idea how fattening peanut butter is?"

"I haven't checked out any calorie counters lately," Caasi responded, and fought to hide the smile that teased the corners of her mouth.

"Well, it's fattening, believe me. The shocking thing is I've hated the stuff since I was a kid."

"There are worse things." Caasi attempted to soothe a few of Edie's doubts.

"Okay," Edie agreed, and took a sip from her virgin cocktail. "Listen to this. I was watching the Blazers play basketball the other night. The center missed two free throws at the foul line and all of a sudden tears welled in my eyes and I started crying. Not just a few silent tears, but gigantic sobs. Freddy didn't know what to think. He was finishing up a report in his den and came rushing in. I'm sure he thought the telecast had been interrupted and someone had just announced that my mother had died or something."

The small laugh could no longer be contained. "Listen, Edie, I'm no expert on the subject, but isn't this all part of being pregnant?"

"I certainly hope so," Edie said fervently.

"Have you talked to June? She'd probably be more help than me."

"June," Edie repeated, and shook her head dramatically. "You know June; she's the salt of the earth. The entire time she was pregnant she acted as if she was in heaven. June's the kind of woman who would deliver her baby and go back to work in the fields an hour later. I'm going to need six months' rest on the Riviera to recover."

The maître d' handed them the menu and gave Caasi a polite nod of recognition.

Edie opened the menu, took one look, moaned, and folded it closed.

"What's the matter?" Caasi asked.

"I was afraid this would happen. Everything looks divine. I want the first four entrées and chocolate mousse for dessert."

"Edie!" Caasi couldn't prevent her small gasp of shock. Of the three, Edie had always been the most weight-conscious.

"I can't help it," Edie hissed.

"If you eat that much, I'll get sick."

"All right, all right," Edie said, "you choose for me. I don't trust myself."

The waiter took their order and filled their water glasses.

"Enough about me." Edie took a sip of the water. "I want to hear what's been going on in your life. I don't suppose you've picked up any tall, dark, handsome men lately, have you?"

Caasi shrugged and looked away uncomfortably. "Not recently. You know I went into the delivery room with June and Burt, don't you?"

"Don't tell me a thing about it. I don't want to hear." Edie shook her head and squinted her eyes closed.

"It was one of the most beautiful experiences of my life," Caasi reminisced softly.

"Sure—it wasn't you going through all that pain."

Caasi didn't bother to try to explain. Edie wouldn't understand. At least, not until her own baby was delivered.

"Have you had any thoughts about what I was saying the last time we were together?" At Caasi's blank look, Edie continued, "You know, about having an affair and maybe getting pregnant yourself?"

Caasi nearly choked on her wine. "Edie, I wish you wouldn't talk like that."

"Maybe not, but it's what you need. I bet you've lost five pounds since the last time I saw you. Believe me when I tell you a man can do wonders."

"Maybe," Caasi conceded, feeling the color seep up her neck.

"I take it that it didn't work out with the hunk you met here the last time?"

Caasi's hands surrounded her glass of wine. She felt

the cold move up her arm and stop directly at her heart. "No. It didn't work out."

"It was only your first try, so don't let it discourage you. Would you like me to pick out someone else?"

"No," Caasi returned forcefully. "I'm perfectly capable of finding a man myself. If I want one."

" 'If'?"

Their dinner arrived, and thankfully Caasi was able to steer the conversation from Edie's questions to the light banter they normally enjoyed.

After their dinner they decided to visit the lounge. The same piano player was at the keyboard and a fresh crowd was gathered around the bar.

The cocktail waitress brought Caasi a drink and Edie cranberry juice. They sat listening to the mellow sounds of a love song.

"Hey," Edie whispered excitedly. "Don't turn around now, but guess who just came in!"

"Who? The Easter Bunny?"

"No," Edie remarked seriously. Her eyes didn't waver. "Mr. Incredible."

"Who?" Caasi whispered.

"The same guy who was here the other night. You remember—you've got to," Edie admonished, her voice dipping incredulously.

Caasi moved her chair so that she could look at the newcomer. She didn't need a second guess to know it was Blake.

Edie's eyes widened appreciatively. "He really is something, isn't he?"

"If you go for that type," Caasi replied with a flippancy she wasn't feeling.

"Did you notice how every woman here perked up the minute he walked in?"

Caasi certainly had. Her stomach felt as if a hole was being seared through it. The burning sensation intensified when a tall, attractive blonde slid onto the empty stool beside Blake. Caasi's eyes narrowed as the woman leaned close and whispered something to Blake.

"Watch," Edie advised. "This blonde knows what she's doing. You might be able to pick up a few pointers."

Caasi smiled weakly, her hand a hard fist in her lap. For one crazy moment she felt like screaming in outrage. Blake was hers! But he wasn't, not really—he had made that clear this morning. Rather than watch the exchange between the two, she lowered her gaze to her fruity drink.

"Well, I'll be," Edie murmured unbelievingly.

"What?" Caasi demanded.

"Weren't you watching?"

"No," Caasi whispered, her voice shaking.

"As slick as a whistle, Mr. Incredible gave the blonde the brush-off. I wouldn't have believed it. This fellow is one tough character. Little wonder you didn't have any luck."

"Little wonder," Caasi repeated.

Edie continued to study Blake. "You know, just watching Mr. Incredible, I'm getting the distinct impression he's hurting."

"Hurting?" Caasi asked, and swallowed tightly.

"Yes. Look at the way he's leaning against the counter. See the way his elbows are positioned? He doesn't want to be disturbed and his body is saying as much, discouraging anyone from joining him."

"Why doesn't he just sit at a table?" Caasi whispered, revealing her curiosity.

"Because that would be an open invitation for company. No, this man wants to be left alone."

"Just because he wants his own company doesn't mean he's eating his heart out."

Thoughtfully, Edie shook her head. "That's true. But he's troubled. Look at the way he's hunched over his drink. He looks as if he's lost his best friend."

Caasi felt Edie's slow appraisal turn to her. "So do you, for that matter."

"So do I—what?" Caasi feigned ignorance on a falsely cheerful note.

"Never mind," Edie murmured thoughtfully.

"I was looking through some travel brochures the other day. . . ." Caasi quickly changed the subject before Edie managed to stumble onto something she could only escape by blatantly lying. "Do you realize I haven't had a vacation, a real vacation," she amended, "in over five years? I was thinking of a cruise."

"I'll believe it when I see it." Edie tilted her chin mockingly. "You wouldn't know what to do with yourself with empty time on your hands."

"Sure I would," Caasi argued. "I'd take a few classes. I've always wanted to learn how to do calligraphy. And get back to reading. I bet there are a hundred books I haven't had time to read in the last five years. They're stacked to the ceiling in my bedroom just waiting for me. I'd bake, and learn how to sew, and volunteer some time at the local—" She stopped at the peculiar look Edie gave her.

"I can't believe this is Caasi Crane speaking!" Edie looked shocked.

Caasi laughed, hoping to make light of her own enthusiasm and squelch Edie's growing curiosity. "It's been on my mind a lot, that's all."

"What's been on your mind?" Edie asked. "Those weren't things you'd do on vacation. They're things an everyday housewife does."

"A housewife?" She gave Edie a surprised look. "And what's wrong with a housewife and mother?"

"Nothing." Edie was quick to amend her attitude. "Heavens, June's one, and I'll be one shortly. Think about it, Caasi. You, a housewife? A baby on each hip, diapers that need to be changed with dinner boiling on top of the stove. Can you picture yourself in that scene?"

Caasi pressed her mouth tightly closed. She longed to cry out that she'd never wanted anything more. If she could run ten hotels effectively, she could manage a single home. The only condition her mind demanded was that Blake share that loving picture with her.

Her eyes drifted across the room to the dejected figure sitting at the bar. It took everything within her not to go to him. But she couldn't see that it would do any good. She'd bared her heart and he'd rejected her. Just remembering the shock she'd felt at hearing his decision caused her to bite into her bottom lip.

"Caasi?" Edie's soft voice broke into her musings.

Gently Caasi shook her head. "Sorry." She turned her attention back to Edie. "What were you saying?"

Edie's attention was focused in the direction of the

bar. "Look who's coming our way," she whispered in shocked disbelief.

Blake strolled to their table and nodded politely at Edie. "We didn't set a time for tomorrow morning. Is eight too early?"

"Fine," Caasi managed to answer with some difficulty.

"I'll see you then."

Edie looked stunned as Blake turned and walked away. "All right, Caasi Crane," she whispered in a shocked voice, "you've got some explaining to do."

Chapter Eight

The whirling blades of the helicopter stirred the early-morning air. With her purse clutched under her arm and her head bowed, Caasi rushed across the landing pad. Blake supported her elbow as she climbed aboard.

The volume of swirling sound made conversation impossible, which was just as well. There was little Caasi had to say to Blake. Not anymore. A week before, even less, she would have been excited about this trip with him. It would have been a chance to talk, another opportunity to learn more about this man who had been invaluable to her. Now it would be torture to sit beside him and know that the next day he would be walking out of her life.

"Caasi."

Blake's hand against her forearm recalled her from her musings.

"It's not too late. We can make the drive in less than—"

"No," she interrupted him and, closing her eyes, leaned her head back against the seat cushion. When they'd met at eight that morning, the first thing Blake had done was propose that they drive instead of taking the helicopter. Caasi couldn't understand why he would make such a suggestion. He wasn't any more eager to spend time alone with her than she was to endure the stilted silence that would have existed in the comparative quiet of a car.

When they didn't take off immediately, Caasi opened her eyes and noted that Blake was talking to the pilot. A frown creased his brow before he nodded and climbed back aboard.

"Is everything all right?" she asked.

"Nothing to worry about," Blake assured her.

A wobbly sensation attacked her stomach as the helicopter rose. To hide her anxiety, Caasi clenched her hands, closed her eyes, and turned her head as if she were gazing out the window.

Blake placed his hand over hers; Caasi sat up and shook her hand free. She didn't want his comfort or assurance or anything else. The day was torture. If he was going to get out of her life, then he should go. Why prolong the agony?

They didn't say a word as Portland disappeared. A small smile flickered across Caasi's face at the memory of Edie's reaction when Blake had stopped at their table the night before. Her friend had been stunned speechless. Caasi couldn't remember a time in all the years they'd known each other that Edie didn't have an immediate comeback.

"You sly fox," Edie had gasped a full minute after Blake had sauntered away from the table.

"Don't get excited," Caasi returned with a nervous smile. "Blake works for me. He's been around for six years."

Edie shook her head in disbelief. "You have worked with that hunk all these years?"

"His last day is Wednesday." Something in Caasi's voice must have revealed the pain she felt at the thought.

Edie's look was thoughtful. "I noticed something was different almost from the moment you came into the dining room tonight. At first I was sure I was imagining things. Somehow, you're . . . softer. It's in your eyes, even in the way you walk, if that's possible. You have, my dear, dear Caasi, the look of a woman in love."

Caasi tried to laugh off Edie's announcement. "Who, me?"

"Yes, you!" Edie declared adamantly. "Now, tell me, why is Blake leaving?"

Sadly Caasi shook her head. "I don't know. I've tried everything I know to convince him to stay."

"Everything?"

Hot color suffused Caasi's face and she lowered her gaze, unable to meet Edie's probing eyes. "It wouldn't do any good. Blake's mind is set."

"Is there any chance of you two getting together?"

Caasi shook her head, unable to answer with words. A terrible sadness settled over her. The pain was potent. Blake would be lost to her.

"What about your baby hunger?" Edie asked.

"My what?" Caasi jerked her head up.

"The last time we were together we talked about you and a baby, don't you remember?"

"Yes, but a baby usually requires a father."

Edie gave a sophisticated shrug. "Not always. You're a successful career woman. You're strong, independent, and financially capable. Any child would be lucky to have you as a mother."

"I can't believe what I'm hearing." Caasi gripped her hands in her lap so that Edie wouldn't see how her fingers were trembling. "You're not really suggesting I get pregnant with Blake's child?"

"Of course I am. He's leaving, isn't he? You want a baby, not a husband. As far as I can see, the setup is perfect."

Even now, with Blake sitting beside her, Caasi couldn't help shaking her head in disbelief at her friend's suggestion. Sometimes it was astonishing that two women so completely different could be such good friends.

An hour later, with a cup of coffee in front of her, Caasi reviewed the architects' plans. The piece of beach was prime property, and Caasi realized how fortunate she was to have obtained it. No, she had Blake to thank for that. He was the one who had handled the negotiations.

Seaside was a tourist town. The economy depended on the business of travelers. With only a few weeks left until summer and a flux of vacationers, the community was preparing for the seasonal traffic.

The morning passed quickly. Leaving the architects' office, Caasi donned a hard hat and visited the building site. Everything was ahead of schedule; where she had pitched a shovelful of dirt only a few weeks before now stood the empty shell of the latest Empress Hotel.

Caasi walked around, examining each area. Once she would have experienced an intense satisfaction at the venture; now she was surprised to feel nothing. The lack of emotion shocked her. What did she care if there were ten or a hundred Empress Hotels? Would breaking ground for another hotel bring her happiness? Perhaps at one time it would have. But no longer. Blake was responsible for that. He was responsible for a lot of things.

Her smile felt frozen as she entered the restaurant where the Seaside Chamber of Commerce was holding its luncheon.

After they ate, Caasi stood before the group and spoke a few introductory words before turning the presentation over to Blake. As he was talking, Caasi observed the way the men in the room responded to him. In some ways their reactions were like those of the women in the cocktail lounge the night before. Blake was a man's man.

Caasi's fingers were tender from all the handshaking she'd done by the time they returned to the helicopter. The pilot, a middle-aged man with a receding hairline, removed his hat as they approached. He shook his head, seeking Blake's eyes.

"Is something wrong?" Caasi asked Blake.

"I don't know, but I'll find out."

Blake and the pilot talked for several minutes, and when Blake returned, his jaw was tight, his look disturbed.

"Well?"

"There's something wrong with the chopper. Dick

noticed that one of the gauges was malfunctioning when he revved it up this morning. That was why I suggested we drive."

Caasi closed her mouth tightly to bite back bitter words. Blake hadn't been eager for her company that morning. Had she been fooling herself with the belief that he would have enjoyed an intimate drive from Portland?

"How long will it take to check it out?"

"An hour, two at the most."

Unwilling to spend an extra minute in Blake's company, Caasi announced, "I'll wait for you on the beach, then."

Blake didn't acknowledge her as she turned and walked the block or so to the ocean.

Wind whipped her hair about her face as she stood, looking out over the pounding surf.

A flight of concrete stairs led to the beach. Caasi walked down to the sand, removed her heels, and strolled toward the water.

Once, when she was a little girl, her father had taken her to the ocean. A business trip, Caasi was sure. Very little in Isaac Crane's life had been done for pleasure. Caasi remembered how the thundering surf had frightened her and how she'd clung to her father's leg.

Funny, Caasi mused, she hadn't thought about that in years. She couldn't have been more than two, maybe three, at the time. The incident was her earliest memory.

Swinging her high heels in her hands, Caasi walked for what seemed like miles, enjoying the solitude; the fresh, salt-scented air; and the peace that came over her. Blake would go and she'd hurt for a time, suffer through the regrets for the love they could have shared. But the time would come when that, too, would pass. And she'd be better for having loved him.

When she turned around to return to the street, she noticed Blake standing at the top of the concrete steps, watching her. He was a solitary figure silhouetted against the bright sun, hands in his pockets and at ease with the world. That disturbed her somehow. He was leaving her without a second thought, without regrets, without looking back.

As she neared the steps, Blake came down to meet her. "I just talked to Dick."

"And?" she prompted.

"The problem is more extensive than he thought. It looks as if we'll have to spend the night."

"Spend the night?" she cried in frustration. "I won't do that."

"There isn't much choice," Blake returned with limited patience.

"Rent a car. And if you can't do that, then buy one! I'm not spending the night here."

"Caasi." Blake drew in a slow, angry breath.

"You're still my employee," she said bitterly, and glanced at her watch. "For another twenty-three and a half hours I expect you to do what I ask. After that, I don't care what you do."

Caasi regretted the words the minute they slipped out. She watched Blake's struggle to hide his anger.

"I didn't mean that," she said in a low voice, and released her breath slowly. "Make what arrangements you can. I'll phone Laurie and answer any necessary calls from here."

Fifteen minutes later Caasi walked across her hotel room, carrying her cell with her as she spoke. A knock on her door interrupted the conversation.

"Could you hold a minute, Laurie?" she asked, before unlocking the door and letting Blake into the rented quarters.

"It's Blake," she said into the receiver. "I'll give you a call in the morning before we leave." She hung up and turned to him. "Yes?"

"I thought you might need a few things." He handed her a small sack that contained a toothbrush and toothpaste.

"Thanks." She smiled her appreciation. "But what I could really use is a good martini."

"Dry, of course."

"Very dry," Caasi agreed.

The cocktail lounge was deserted; it was too early for the pre-dinner crowd and too late for the business-luncheon group.

It amazed Caasi that they could sit companionably at a minuscule table and not say a word. It was almost as if they were an old married couple who no longer needed words to communicate. Caasi focused her attention on the ocean scene outside the window. The view was lovely, but she had seen so much breathtaking scenery in her life. That day it failed to stir the familiar chord of appreciation.

Without asking, Blake ordered another round. Slowly, Caasi sipped her drink. The bitter liquid seared its way down her throat. The lounge was quickly filling now; after two martinis, Caasi could feel the coiled tension ease out of her.

"Are you ready for dinner?" Blake asked.

"Sure," she agreed readily. "Why not?"

His hand cupped her elbow as he escorted her into the dining room. The food was good, though not excellent.

"Chef would be appalled," Caasi remarked, as she set her fork aside.

"You and that chef. I don't know when I was more upset with you than when you imported him."

Caasi's smile didn't quite reach her eyes. "Oh, I can tell you. Several times you've looked as if you wanted to wring my neck, all within the last couple of weeks, too."

Blake's expression was weary and he conceded with a short shake of his head.

The soulful sounds of a singer drifted into the dining room from the lounge.

"Shall we?" Blake asked softly.

Caasi couldn't find an excuse to refuse. All there was to do in her room was watch television. "All right," she agreed, somewhat reluctantly. When they reentered the lounge, she saw that a few couples occupied the tiny dance floor, which was little bigger than a tabletop.

They sat for a long time, so close their thighs touched, listening to the music and not speaking. For the first time, Caasi admitted to herself how glad she was that the helicopter needed work. The repairs afforded her this last chance to be with Blake. She didn't speak for a long time, fearing words would destroy the moment.

"Caasi."

Their eyes met and she drew a shaky breath at the intensity of his look.

"Dance with me, Blake," she whispered urgently. "Hold me one last time."

He answered her by standing and giving her his hand. They didn't take their eyes from each other as Caasi slid her arms around his neck, her body's movement joining his in a rhythm that was uniquely theirs.

His fingers were pressed against the small of her back as he molded her body to him. His mouth was mere inches from hers as his warm breath fanned her cheek.

The music stopped—but they didn't. If Blake released her now, she'd die, Caasi mused.

The singer began a love song. Caasi bit into the corner of her bottom lip. Tomorrow Blake would go—but for tonight, he was hers.

Caasi lost track of how long Blake held her, how many songs they danced to, barely moving, oblivious to the world surrounding them.

When the music stopped, Caasi led the way off the dance floor, but instead of stopping at their table she continued out of the lounge and down the wide hall to their rooms, which were opposite each other.

Her hands shook as she inserted the key and opened the door to her room. It was dark and silent.

Blake's eyes bore into hers as she stepped inside the room and extended her hand to him. A look of indecision passed across his face. Caasi's eyes pleaded with him, and gradually the expression on his face softened as his look became potent enough for her to drown in.

He took one step inside and Caasi smiled softly. He couldn't turn away from her. Not now. Not tonight.

She slid her arms around his neck and stood on the tips of her toes as she melted against him.

He groaned her name, reaching out to close the door as she fit her body to his.

She wouldn't let him talk, her open mouth seeking his. He hadn't kissed her in so long, so very long.

"Caasi." He groaned, repeatedly rubbing his mouth over hers. "You don't know what you're doing." His voice was husky and hungry.

"I do," she insisted in a low murmur. "Oh Blake, I do."

Again and again his mouth cherished hers, eager, hungry, seeking, demanding, giving, taking. The soft, gentle sounds of their lovemaking filled the silence. They whispered phrases of awe as passion took control of their bodies.

Caasi paused long enough to tug the shirt free at Blake's waist. Her eager fingers fumbled with the buttons until she could slip her palms over his chest. The sensations were so exquisite she wanted to cry.

"Caasi, no," Blake whispered gruffly. "Not now, not like this." The shirt fell to the floor.

"Yes, like this," she pleaded. "Only tonight, it's all I want." She felt the tears well in her eyes. Her body trembled against his, and Blake released an anguished groan as he swung her off her feet and carried her across the room.

Caasi wanted him so desperately, she could no longer think. Pressing her face to his neck, she gave him tiny, biting kisses and felt his shudder as he laid her on the bed.

Her arms around his neck, Caasi refused to release him, half lifting herself as she kissed him long and hard, her mouth slanting under his.

His eyes looked tortured in the golden glow of the moon as he pulled her arms from his neck. "Caasi," he whispered, in a voice she hardly recognized. "Are you drunk? Is this the liquor?"

"Yes, I'm drunk," she whispered, "but not from the martinis. You do this to me, Blake. Only you."

"This isn't the way I wanted it, but heaven knows I haven't got the strength to let you go," he murmured, his lips above hers. His hands ran down her smooth body, exploring, touching, until Caasi was sure she would die if he didn't take her. She arched against him and sighed with a longing so intense that it sounded like a mournful cry.

Impatiently he worked at her clothing, freeing her from the constricting material. The feel of his hands against her bare skin was an exquisite torture.

"Tonight," she whispered in a quivering breath. "For tonight, I'm yours."

"Yes," he agreed, his mouth seeking hers again.

"I'm freeing you from any . . . consequences," she stammered slightly.

He froze. For a moment he didn't even breathe. "You're what?" He sat up, holding her away from him, a rough hand against each bare shoulder.

"I'm freeing you from any responsibility," she murmured, confused. What had she said that upset him so much? Wasn't that something a man wanted to hear?

Sitting on the edge of the bed, Blake leaned forward and buried his face in his hands as if he needed time to compose himself.

"Blake," she pleaded in a soft whisper, "what did I say?"

He didn't answer as he reached for his shirt and rammed his arms into the sleeves. Not bothering to fasten the buttons, he started across the room.

"Blake," she begged, "don't do this to me. Please don't do this to me."

He turned to her in the moonlight. She had never seen a man look more upset. His face was contorted with anger, his mouth twisted, his eyes as hard as flint.

Caasi sagged against the bed, closing her eyes against the pain that went through her heart, a pain so deep that it was beyond tears.

For hours Caasi lay exactly as she was, staring dry-eyed at the ceiling. She had offered Blake everything she had to give and he had rejected it all.

Even her makeup couldn't camouflage the dark circles under her eyes the next morning. The mirror revealed pale, colorless cheeks, as if she were recovering from a long illness. Caasi doubted that she would ever recover. Not really. She'd go on with her life, would probably even laugh again, but something deep inside her had died last night. In some respects she would never be the same.

It gave her little satisfaction to note that Blake looked as if he hadn't slept, either.

Dick was at the helicopter when they arrived, assuring them that everything was fixed and ready to go.

Blake didn't offer her his hand when she climbed inside, which was just as well, since she would have refused it. They sat as far apart from each other as possible.

The atmosphere was so thick that even Dick was affected, glancing anxiously from one to the other, then concentrating on the flight.

As Caasi ran the bathwater in her quarters back at the Empress, she realized there was nothing about the short flight home that she could remember. The pain of being so close to Blake was almost more than she could bear. Her mind had blotted it from her memory.

Blake had stepped out of the helicopter and announced stiffly that he was going home to change and would be back later to clear out his desk and pack up what remained of his personal items. It was Wednesday. His last day with Crane Enterprises.

Caasi hadn't bothered to answer him but had turned and gone directly to her suite.

Some of the staff had planned a small farewell party for Blake, but she hadn't contributed anything. Not when seeing him go was so painful. There would be an obligatory statement of good wishes she would make. Somehow she'd manage that. Somehow.

A hot bath relieved some of the tiredness in her bones, but it had little effect on her heart.

Dressed in a prim business suit, Caasi walked briskly into the office and offered Laurie a short nod before entering her own.

Her desk was stacked with mail, telephone messages, and a variety of items that needed her immediate attention.

"Laurie," she called to her secretary, "send in Brian Harris."

"Right away."

If the man was there to take Blake's place, she had best start working with him now.

By noon Caasi's head was pounding. She wasn't one

to suffer from headaches, but the pain was quickly becoming unbearable.

"Are you all right?" Laurie asked, as she came into Caasi's office for dictation.

"I'm fine," Caasi murmured. She stood at the window, her fingertips massaging her temples as she shot off one letter after another, scarcely pausing between items of correspondence.

Laurie sat on the edge of her chair, her glasses delicately balanced on the bridge of her nose as her pencil flew across the steno pad.

"That'll be all." Caasi paused. "No; get me Dirk Evans of International on the phone."

Laurie returned to her office and buzzed Caasi a minute later. "Mr. Evans is on line two."

"Thanks, Laurie," Caasi said. "Would it be possible for you to find me some aspirin?"

"Of course."

"Thanks." Five years since she took over for her father, and this was the second time she'd needed something to help her through the day. And both times it could be directly related to Blake.

The aspirin had little effect on the pounding sensation that persisted at her temples well into the afternoon.

Laurie came into her office around four to tell her that the farewell party for Blake was in progress.

"I'll be there in a minute," Caasi said without looking up, her fingers tightening around her pen.

Hands braced against the side of her desk, Caasi inhaled deeply, closing her eyes and forcing herself to absorb the silence for a couple moments before rising and going to join the party.

Someone had opened a bottle of champagne. Caasi stood on the outskirts of the small crowd and watched as everyone toasted Blake and wished him success. One of the women had made a farewell cake and was serving thin slices. Caasi recognized her as Blake's personal assistant but couldn't recall her being so attractive.

Caasi felt far removed from the joking banter that existed between Blake and his staff. There wasn't one who didn't regret his leaving. Yet he had chosen to do exactly that.

Someone slapped him across the back and he laughed but stopped short as his eyes met hers.

Quickly Caasi looked away. A hush fell over the room as she walked to the center, Blake at her side.

"I think we can all agree that you'll be missed," she said in a voice that was surprisingly steady. "If my father were here, I'm sure he would say how much he appreciated the excellent job you have done for Crane Enterprises for the past six years. I'm sure he'd extend to you his personal best wishes."

"But not yours?" Blake whispered, for her ears alone.

Stiffening, Caasi continued somewhat defiantly, "My own are extended to you in whatever you pursue. If there's ever a time you feel you'd like to return, you know that there will always be a place for you here. Goodbye, Blake."

"What? No gold watch?" he mumbled under his breath, as he stepped forward and shook her hand. "Thank you, Miss Crane." Those dark, unreadable eyes stared into hers, and Caasi could barely breathe.

Grateful for the opportunity to escape, she nodded and stepped aside as Blake's assistant approached with a small wrapped package. Hoping to give the impression she was needed elsewhere, Caasi glanced at her watch. "If you'll excuse me, please."

"Of course," Blake answered for the group.

Without another word, she turned and walked away, not stopping until she reached her desk.

Caasi forced herself to eat dinner. For two days she hadn't been able to force down more than a few bites of any meal.

The headache was now forty-eight hours old. Nothing seemed to relieve the throbbing pain. She hadn't slept well, either. After several hours of tossing fitfully, she would fall into an uneasy slumber, only to wake an hour or two later more tired than when she'd gone to bed.

The phone rang Saturday when she returned from a spot-check at the Sacramento Empress.

"Hello," she said, with little enthusiasm.

"Is this Caasi?"

Faintly, Caasi recognized the voice over the phone. Her home phone had a private listing and she seldom gave out the number.

"Yes, it is."

"Caasi." The young voice sounded relieved. "This is Gina. Gina Sherrill."

"Hello, Gina. What can I do for you?" Caasi's hand tightened around the receiver. The woman had phoned three times in the last few days, and Caasi hadn't returned the calls. She had completely severed herself from Blake and wanted every painful reminder of him removed from her life.

"I'm sorry to bother you like this, but I haven't been able to get hold of you at your office."

"I've been busy." She hoped the tone of her voice would effectively convey the message. She didn't want to be purposely rude.

"I knew that, and I hope you'll forgive me for being so forward, but I did want to tell you that everyone would like it if you could come to dinner on Sunday."

Everyone but Blake, Caasi added silently. "I'm sure I'd like that very much, but I'm sorry, it's impossible this week. Perhaps another time."

Caasi heard a sigh of disappointment come over the line. "I understand."

Maybe she did, Caasi mused.

"I'd like to talk to you someday when you've got the time."

"I'd enjoy that, Gina, but I really am busy. Thank you for calling. Give my love to your family."

"I will. Goodbye, Caasi."

Caasi heard the drone of the disconnected line sound in her ear. Replacing the receiver, she walked to the window and studied the view of miniature people and miniature cars far below.

Someone knocked on her door, and she wanted to cry out in irritation. Why couldn't people just leave her alone? Everything would be fine if she could have some peace and quiet in her life.

"Just a minute," she answered shortly, as she strode across the floor. She opened the door to discover . . . Blake. Her heart leapt into her throat, and she was too stunned to move.

"I hope you haven't eaten yet. By the way, where were you all afternoon?" he asked, as he walked past her into the living room.

Chapter Nine

"Where was I?" Caasi repeated, nonplussed. What was Blake doing here? Hadn't he left her, decided to sever his relationship with her and Crane Enterprises?

"Yes—I've been trying to get you all day."

Her hand on the doorknob, Caasi watched his relaxed movements as he sauntered to the sofa, sat back, and positioned his ankle on his knee.

"I do have a business to run." She hated the telltale way her voice shook, revealing her shock.

"Yes, but it wasn't business that kept you out. I know, because I checked."

"You checked?" Caasi demanded. "Then I suggest you question your sources, because it most certainly was business."

"Instead of standing all the way over there and arguing, why don't you come and sit with me?" He held out his hand invitingly. "I certainly hope you're hungry, because I'm starved."

Caasi closed the door but didn't sit with him as he requested. Instead she walked to the window, her arms cradling her waist.

"What you're wearing is fine," he assured her. "Don't bother to change."

Her gaze shot to him. The friendly, almost gentle light in his eyes was enough to steal her breath. His ready smile was warm and encouraging.

"I thought you wanted out of Crane Enterprises."

"I did."

"Then why are you here? Why come back? Don't you know how hard it was for me to let you walk away? Are you really that insensitive, Blake? I don't want you flitting in and out of my life when the mood strikes you. I haven't seen you in—"

"Three days," he supplied. "I know. I wanted you to have time to think things through, but I can see you haven't figured anything out yet."

Caasi's hands became knotted fists and fell to her sides. "I hate it when people play these kinds of games with me. If you have something to say, just say it."

Blake groaned in frustration. "Are you really so dense you can't see?"

"I don't need to stand in my own home and be insulted by you, Blake Sherrill." She stalked across the room and opened the door. "Perhaps it would be best if you left."

"Caasi, I didn't come here to argue."

"Well, you seem to be doing a bang-up job of it."

He stood and rammed his hands into his pockets. He strode to the window, his back to her as he gazed at the panorama.

Caasi could see and feel the frustration in the rigid set of his shoulders. She didn't want to fight. The desire to walk to him and slip her arms around his waist and press her face to his back was almost overwhelming. The headache that had persisted since Blake left was her body's method of telling her how miserable she had been without him.

A hundred times since Wednesday she'd had to stop herself from consulting him, remembering that Blake was no longer available to ask. Softly she exhaled and closed the door.

At the sound of the click, Blake turned around. "Can we start again, Cupcake? Pretend I'm an old friend who's come to town for the weekend."

Caasi lowered her gaze. "Don't call me Cupcake," she murmured stiffly. "I'm not a little girl. That's the last way I want you to think of me."

The sound of his robust laugh filled the room. "There's no worry of that."

Indecision gripped Caasi. All her life she'd been in control of every situation. She had always known what to expect and how to react. But not with Blake and this new ground he seemed to want to travel with her. Of one thing Caasi was sure: She couldn't tolerate much more of the pain she'd felt when he walked away.

"Dinner, Caasi?" His arched brow contained a challenging lift.

Her compliant nod was as weak as her resolve. She would accept what little Blake was willing to offer and be grateful.

His smile crinkled the lines at his eyes. "Come on. I've got fat steaks ready for the grill."

Caasi took a light jacket out of the closet. "Where are we going?"

"To my place."

"Your place?"

"Then after dinner I thought we'd try our luck at the horse races."

"Horse races?" she repeated.

Blake looked around, stared at the ceiling, and shook his head. "This room seems to have developed an echo all of a sudden."

Caasi smiled. It was the first time she could remember smiling since Monday, when Blake had announced he would be leaving her and Crane Enterprises.

They rode in his T-Bird convertible with the top down. The wind ruffled her sleekly styled curls, and Caasi closed her eyes to savor the delicious sensations that flowed through her. She was with Blake, and it felt right.

The grill could be seen in the backyard, a bag of briquettes leaning against its base, when Blake pulled into the driveway. He came around and opened her car door for her. Leaning over the rolled-down window, he lightly brushed his mouth across hers. He straightened and his eyes looked deeply into hers. With a groan, his arms surrounded her, half lifting her from the car as she arched against his chest. Caasi slipped her arms around his neck and surrendered to his kiss. Gradually his grip relaxed and he tenderly brushed the tangled hair from her temple. "I've missed you."

Still caught in the rush of emotion he could evoke, Caasi didn't speak. A happy smile lifted the corners of her mouth. "I've missed you, too."

"I'll cook the steaks if you fix the salad. Agreed?"

Eagerly, Caasi nodded. He helped her out of the car, his arm cupping her shoulder as he led her up the back stairs and into the kitchen.

"I'll get the grill going and leave you to your task," he instructed.

Almost immediately he was out the back door. Taking off her jacket, Caasi draped it over a chair and looked around. She really loved this house. A gentle feeling warmed her. Any woman would be proud to be a part of this.

The ingredients for the salad were in the refrigerator, and she laid them on the counter. Next she searched through the cupboards for a large bowl. A salad shouldn't be difficult, she mused happily. Her culinary skills were limited, but a salad would be easy enough.

She was at the cutting board chopping lettuce when Blake came back for the steaks and a variety of spices.

He paused, watching her as she slid the knife across the fresh lettuce.

"Is something the matter?" She tensed and looped a strand of hair behind her ear. What could she possibly be doing wrong in making a salad? It was the simplest job he could have given her.

"No. It's just that it's better to tear apart the lettuce leaves instead of cutting them."

"Okay." Feeling incredibly naïve in the kitchen, Caasi set the knife aside.

"Did you wash it?" Blake asked her next.

Caasi swallowed at the painful lump that filled her throat. With tight-lipped grimness she answered him with a negative shake of her head. Dumping the cut lettuce into the bowl, she carried it to the sink and filled the bowl with water. Pure pique caused her to pour dish-washing liquid over the green leaves. "Like this?" She batted her long lashes at him innocently.

Not waiting for his reaction, she moved into the living room and stared sightlessly out the front window. A hand over her mouth, she took in several deep breaths. What was she doing here with Blake? This wonderful homey scene wasn't meant for someone like her. She was about as undomesticated as they came.

The sound of footsteps told her Blake had moved behind her. His hand on her shoulder sent a silky warmth sliding down her arm.

"I apologize," she whispered. "That was a stupid thing to do."

"No—I should be the one to apologize." The pressure of his hands turned her around. Gently he pulled her into his arms, his chin resting against the top of her head.

"It's just that I'm so incredibly dumb." Her voice was thick with self-derision.

"You, stupid?" Soft laughter tumbled from his throat, stirring the hair at the crown of her head. "Maybe you won't be competing in the same class as Chef, but not because you lack intelligence. You've just never learned, that's all."

"But will I ever?"

"That's up to you, Cupcake."

Caasi winced. "You're using that name again when I've asked you repeatedly not to."

He didn't comment for several tense moments. "I don't think I'll ever forget the first time I saw you. I'd been working with your father for several months. Isaac didn't talk much about his private life. I think I was at the Empress six months before I even knew he had a daughter. We were in his office one day and you came floating in as fresh as spring and so breathtakingly beautiful I nearly fell out of my chair." He stopped and gently eased her away so that he could look at her as he spoke. "I watched this hard-nosed businessman light up like a sparkler on the Fourth of July. His eyes softened as he held out his arms to you and called you Cupcake. I've never thought of you as anything else since."

"I was barely twenty-two."

A finger under her chin lifted her face to his. "The amazing part is that you're even more beautiful now." Ever so gently, he placed his mouth over hers.

No kiss had ever been so incredibly sweet. Caasi swayed toward him when he released her. "I hope you've got another head of lettuce. I'm afraid I've ruined the first one."

"I'll start cooking the steaks now." He kissed her on the tip of her nose and released her. "How do you want your steak cooked? Rare?"

"No, medium."

Blake looked dissatisfied. "You honestly should try it cooked a little less sometime."

"Blake." She placed her hands on her hips and shook her head. "We seem doomed for one confrontation after another. I happen to prefer my meat medium. If you'd rather, I can cook my own."

"I'd like to see that."

"Steak," she asserted, "I can do. There's nothing to it but flopping it over the grill a couple of times."

"It's an art."

"You overrate yourself," Caasi insisted. "How about I cook the steaks and you make the salad?"

Blake chuckled, shaking his head. "I hate to see good meat wasted, but it'll be worth it just to prove my point."

Caasi was in the backyard, readjusting the grill so that it was closer to the fire, when Blake walked out.

"I thought you were making the salad."

"I did," he said teasingly, his eyes twinkling. "I slapped a hunk of lettuce on a plate, added a slice of tomato, and poured dressing over the top. What's happening to my steak is of much more interest to me."

"On second thought . . ." Caasi moistened her dry lips. "I'd hate to ruin your meal. Why don't we each cook our own?"

"That sounds fair," Blake agreed with a smile.

The thick steaks sizzled when placed across the grill, flames curling around the edges of fat.

"Who lowered this? It's too close to the fire," he said irritably.

Guiltily, Caasi handed him the potholders. "Sorry," she muttered.

Blake didn't look pleased. He obviously took his grilling seriously. He'd flipped his steak over before Caasi had a chance to add salt and pepper to hers.

When he lifted the barely warmed meat from the grill, Caasi dropped her jaw in disbelief. "That couldn't possibly be done."

"This is a rare steak."

"That's not rare," she declared. "It's raw. A good vet would have it back on its feet in fifteen minutes."

What had been a light, teasing air was suddenly cold and sober.

"You cook your meat the way you like it and I'll have mine my way. As far as I can see, you're not in any position to tell me what's right or wrong in the kitchen."

Caasi felt the color drain out of her face.

"Caasi," Blake said, forcefully expelling his breath. "I didn't mean that."

"Why not?" she said. "It's true. You go and eat. I'll join you in a few minutes."

Caasi ate little of her dinner and noted that Blake didn't, either. Her steak was burned crisp around the edges and was far more well done than she normally enjoyed. The whole time they were eating she waited for Blake to make some sarcastic comment about her cooking. She was grateful that he didn't.

Blake didn't say anything when she left the table and took her plate to the sink. The bowlful of sudsy lettuce leaves was there to remind her of her childish prank. This new relationship Blake apparently wanted to build wasn't going to work; she couldn't be with him more than ten minutes without the two of them fighting. She didn't know how to respond to him on unfamiliar ground. Crane Enterprises had been a common denominator, but now that was gone.

Gathering the wilted greens in her hands, she dumped them into the garbage.

"You could use the disposal instead of—"

"I think I've had enough of your 'instead ofs' to last me a lifetime." She made a show of glancing at her watch. "On second thought, maybe we should forgo the races for another time."

"I couldn't agree with you more," he snapped. He stood so fast he almost knocked over his chair in the process. Pointedly he took the car keys from his pocket.

They didn't say a word during the drive back to the Empress. Caasi sat upright, her arms crossed determinedly in front of her. From start to finish, the evening had been a fiasco.

Blake pulled up to the curb in front of the hotel. His hands clenched the steering wheel as he stared straight ahead. "We need to talk, but now isn't the time. Neither one of us is in the mood for a serious discussion."

Caasi couldn't agree more. "What do you want from me, Blake? When you worked for the hotel I knew exactly where we stood, but now all I feel is an uncertainty I can't explain." She watched as Blake's hand tightened on the wheel until his knuckles were white.

"You haven't figured it out yet? After all these years you still don't know, do you?" He was so angry that Caasi knew any kind of response would only fuel his irritation. "Maybe it is too late, maybe you're so impossibly wrapped up in Crane Enterprises that you'll never know."

She'd barely closed the car door before he drove away. As the car sped down the street, she stood alone on the sidewalk. Blake was always leaving her.

Later that night, as she lay in bed staring at the dark ceiling, Caasi thought about his parting comment. Obviously she had been horribly wrong not to recognize his motives.

Rather than suffer through another day of self-recrimination over her relationship with Blake, Caasi drove to June and Burt's on Sunday afternoon.

"Welcome," June said, greeting Caasi with a hug. "I'm glad you came. The first pictures of Cassi have arrived. You wouldn't believe how much she's changed already."

"Sure I would." Caasi walked into the house and handed June a small gift she'd picked up for the baby while in Sacramento.

"Caasi," June protested, "you've got to stop buying Cassi all these gifts. Otherwise, she'll grow up and not appreciate anything."

"Let me spoil her," Caasi pleaded, and lifted the sleeping baby from the bassinet. "She's probably the closest thing I'll ever have to a daughter. And I love her so much, it's hard not to."

"I know." June shook her head in defeat. "But try to hold it down. There isn't any more room in her bedroom to hold all your gifts."

"I hope that's not true."

"Almost," June said. "She's due to wake up any minute and will probably want to eat. I'll get you a cup of coffee now. Burt's working in the back, building one of those aluminum storage sheds."

Cradling the sleeping baby in her arms, Caasi sat in the rocking chair. Her eyes misted as she watched the angelic face. It never failed to materialize, the powerful, overwhelming surge of love she experienced every time she held this child. If this was what she felt with June's baby, how much more would she feel for her own? The question had been on her mind ever since her dinner with Edie. What had Edie called it? Baby hunger. But it was more than that, far more than a passing fancy because her two best friends were having children. When

June and Edie had married she hadn't had the urge to go out and find herself a husband. These feelings were different.

A home and family would be worth more than all the accumulated riches of Crane Enterprises. Her father had worked himself into an early grave, and for what reason? All those years he had slaved to build a fortune for her. But she didn't want wealth. The greatest desires of her heart were for a simple life. A home and family, maybe a dog or two. Certainly, money alone couldn't provide all that.

The baby stirred and, opening her tiny mouth, arched her back and yawned.

"Diaper-changing time," Caasi announced, as she carried little Cassi into the bedroom and laid her across the changing table. Within a matter of minutes Caasi handed the baby to her mother.

June sat in a rocking chair and unbuttoned her blouse to nurse. "Every time I see you with the baby I'm amazed at how natural you are with her," June said, as she smoothed the soft hairs away from her daughter's face. "To be honest, I was afraid you wouldn't do well around children, but I was wrong. You're a natural. I wish you'd marry and have children of your own."

The coffee cup sat on the end table, and Caasi's hand tightened around it. "I've been giving some serious thought to exactly that."

"Caasi, that's wonderful!" June exclaimed. "You don't know how glad I'll be to see you get away from that hotel. It's dominated your life. I swear, it's been like a monster that's eaten away at you more and more until you were hardly yourself. Who's the lucky man?"

Caasi shifted uncomfortably, crossed and uncrossed her legs, then set her cup aside. "I wasn't thinking of getting married."

June's eyes widened incredulously. "You mean . . ." She stopped and looked flustered. "You're just going to have a baby?"

"Something like that," Caasi explained cheerfully. "A husband is a nice extra, but not necessary."

"I don't get it. Why not marry? You're an attractive woman, and you have so much to offer."

"Maybe," Caasi returned, "but in this case a husband would be an encumbrance I can live without."

"What about the baby? Doesn't he—or she—have a right to a father?"

"That's something I'm thinking about now."

"This whole idea doesn't even sound like you. Where did you come up with—" June stopped, a knowing look lighting her eyes. "Edie. This sounds exactly like one of her crazy schemes."

"Maybe." A smile tugged at Caasi's mouth. "And when you think about it, the idea isn't all that crazy. Single women are raising children all the time."

"Yes, but . . ." Slowly June shook her head. "Have you chosen the father? I mean, have you said anything to him?"

"Not yet."

"Then you have chosen someone?"

"Oh yes. You've never met him, but he . . ." Caasi paused and swallowed. "He used to work for me. Actually, I think my method is a better idea than Edie's. She suggested I pick up someone in a bar. I swear, that woman is loony sometimes."

"I'm going to have a talk with her," June muttered between tight lips.

"Don't. To be honest, I think she was only kidding. She didn't expect me to take it seriously, but I have and I am."

"You know, Caasi, I've never advised you about anything. You've never needed my advice. There's confidence in everything about you—the way you talk, the way you stand, the way you look. Think about this, think very seriously before you do something you might regret."

"I will," Caasi assured her with a warm smile. "I've never done anything haphazardly in my well-ordered existence, and I'm not about to start now."

Monday's mail included an invitation to Gina and Donald's wedding. She felt bad at having snubbed Blake's sister the past Saturday. Gina was a warm and loving young woman. Caasi took her checkbook and wrote out a generous check. Staring at the amount, she pictured her confrontation with Blake after she'd sent his cousin a wedding gift. She could imagine what he'd accuse her of if he saw this. Defeated, Caasi tore the check in two and wrote another for half of what she had before.

"What the heck," she muttered with frustration. What gave Blake Sherrill the right to dictate the kind of gift she gave anyone? Angrily she tore out another check and wrote it for the amount of the original one. After scribbling an apologetic letter declining the invitation, she added her congratulations and hoped the couple could put the money to good use.

The letter and money went out in the afternoon mail.

Tuesday Caasi met with her lawyer. If he thought her request was unusual, he said nothing, at least not to her. He did admit, however, that he hadn't handled anything like that in the past and would have to get back to her. Caasi told him there wasn't any rush. She hadn't heard from Blake since their Saturday-night clash.

Wednesday morning Caasi was in her office giving dictation to Laurie when Blake burst in.

"There'd better be a good explanation for this." He slapped a newspaper on top of her desk.

Completely calm, Caasi turned to Laurie. "Maybe it would be best if you excused us for a few moments, Laurie. It seems Mr. Sherrill has something he'd like to say."

The secretary stood up, left the office, and closed the door behind her. Blake waited until they were alone.

"Well," he demanded, and stalked to the far side of the room.

"I knew this would happen." Her hand gestured impatiently. "I knew the minute I put the money in the mail that you'd come storming in here as if I'd done some terrible deed. Quite frankly, Blake Sherrill, I'm growing weary of your attempts to dictate my life."

"Dictate your life!" he repeated, and rammed both hands into his pants pockets, then just as quickly pulled them out again and smoothed back his hair. Even when angry, Blake was a fine male figure. His body was rock hard as he continued to pace the carpet. "I couldn't believe it. I still am having trouble." He stared at her as if he'd never seen her before. "Caasi, what would your father say?" He was deadly serious.

"My father?" She shook her head in bewilderment. "My father has been dead for years. I don't think he'd care one way or another if I sent your sister a generous wedding present."

"My sister?" he said, confused. "What has Gina got to do with this?" He spread the newspaper across her desk and pointed to the headlines in the business section: "International Rumored to Buy Empress Hotels."

"Oh, that." Caasi said with relief. "I thought you were talking about—"

"I know what you thought," he shouted. "I want to ask you about this article. Is it true?"

She gestured toward the chair on the other side of her desk. "Will you sit down?" she requested calmly, belying her pounding heart. "We need to talk, and there's no better time than the present."

Blake lowered himself into the soft leather chair, but he sat on the edge of the seat as if ready to spring up at the slightest provocation.

"Well?" he demanded again. "Is it true?"

"Yes," she said, confirming his suspicions. "But I'm only selling eight hotels. I'm keeping the Portland Empress and the Seaside Empress."

"Caasi." He groaned in frustration. "Do you know what you're doing?"

"Yes." She nodded. "I've never been more sure of anything in my life. I don't have the time to manage the hotels and everything else."

"Everything else? What?" he demanded. "What could possibly be more important to you than Crane Enterprises?"

Sitting opposite him, Caasi watched his face intently as she spoke. "A baby," she murmured softly.

"A baby," he exploded, and shot to his feet.

"Blake, I wanted to have a nice logical discussion with you. But if you insist on overreacting like this, then I'm simply going to have to ask you to leave."

"You don't say things like that and expect me to react as if you've asked for the sugar bowl."

"Okay, okay," she agreed. "When you've cooled down I'd like to have a calm, rational discussion."

He sat back down and said nothing for several moments as though trying to calm himself. After a while he asked, "Are you pregnant?"

"Not yet."

"Not yet?" Impatience showed in the set of his mouth.

Caasi lowered her gaze and struggled to keep a firm grip on her composure. "I've met with a real estate agent and have started looking at houses. I don't want my baby growing up in a hotel the way I did."

Blake straightened in the chair, his back ramrod stiff.

"I've also talked with an attorney, and he's drawing up the necessary papers. I think . . . the father . . . should have some rights, but I'd be foolish not to protect myself and the baby legally."

Blake's face was hard, his eyes blazing. Yet he was pale, as if his grip on his temper was fragile. "And the father?" he asked curtly.

"Yes, well . . ." Caasi felt the muscles of her throat tighten as the words slipped out. "I'd like you to be my baby's father."

Chapter Ten

Blake's razor-sharp gaze ripped into her. "What did you say?"

Caasi had trouble meeting his eyes. "You heard me right."

Blake propelled himself out of the chair and stalked to the far side of the room. "Have you seen a doctor?" He ground out the question, his back to her.

"No, not yet. I didn't feel that would be necessary until I was fairly certain I was pregnant," she explained tightly.

Blake swiveled around, his brow knit with questioning concern. "I'm not talking about that kind of doctor."

"Honestly, Blake. Do you think I need a psychiatrist?" Her smile was tense and nervous.

"Yes," he insisted. "Quite frankly, that's exactly what I think. You've been working too hard."

Caasi's spirits sank and she lowered her head. Her fingers toyed with a stack of papers on her desk. "I'm not working any harder now than I have for the past five years."

"Exactly." His hand sliced through the air.

"Blake, the Empress has nothing to do with this. I woke up, that's all. I've decided I want something more out of life than money and an empty suite." She didn't elaborate that he was the one responsible for awakening her. "I'm a woman. Is it so wrong to want to be a mother? I can assure you I'll be a good one." She inhaled deeply. "June says I'm a natural with the baby and I'd make—"

"Why pick me?" he interrupted, a grim set to his jaw.

"Why not?" she said, and shrugged. The heat seeped into her face, reddening her cheeks. "You're tall, good-looking, and possess certain characteristics I admire." Nervously she stood up and walked around to the front of the desk. Leaning her thighs against the flat top, she crossed her arms.

"Just how do you propose to get pregnant? By osmosis?" Blake taunted.

"No . . . of course not," she stammered. "Listen, Blake, I'm not doing a very good job of explaining this. I really wish I hadn't said anything. At least, not until I'd heard from the lawyer. But aside from anything else, I'd like you to know I'm willing to make this venture worth your while."

His mouth twisted into a cynical smile. "You don't have enough money to pay me for what you're asking. I'd like to tell you what to do with your proposition, Cupcake, but your face would burn for a week." Slowly he turned and walked to the door.

"Don't go, Blake. Please."

With his hand on the doorknob, he turned; his gaze

was concentrated on her, disturbing her even more. "There's nothing you can say. Goodbye, Cupcake."

Just the way he said it made her blood run cold. His voice expressed so many things in those few words. Frustration. Disappointment. Contempt. Disbelief.

Caasi sagged against the desk as the door closed. Blake couldn't be feeling any more confused than she was. He had been angry. Blazingly angry. She'd seen him express myriad emotions over the years. And plenty of anger. But never like this. This kind of anger went beyond raised voices and lost tempers. This time it came from Blake's heart.

The thought of working was almost impossible. Caasi tried for the remainder of the morning, but her concentration drifted, and every page seemed to mirror Blake's look as he walked out the door. At lunchtime she announced to Laurie that she didn't know when she'd be back. Laurie's eyes rounded with frustration but said nothing.

Caasi let herself into the penthouse suite and slowly sauntered around the empty quarters. She shouldn't have approached Blake that day. Even the most naïve business graduate would have recognized that this wasn't the time to propose anything to him. He'd been upset even before she'd opened her mouth. Her sense of timing couldn't have been more off-kilter. That wasn't like her. She knew better.

Staring out the window, Caasi blinked uncertainly. She needed to get away. Think. Reconsider.

After changing out of her smart linen business suit into capris and a pink sweater, she took her car out of the garage and drove around for a while. It was true that she wanted a baby. But what she hadn't realized until that morning was that she wanted Blake's child. If he wouldn't agree, then she would have to abandon the idea completely.

She had to talk to Blake and make him understand. All the way to Gresham, she practiced what she wanted to say, the assurances she would give him. Nothing in her life had ever been so important.

His driveway was empty when she turned into it. She had counted on his being there. Just as she climbed out of her car, it started to rain. Staring at the skies in defeat, Caasi raised the collar of her jacket and hurried up the back steps, pounding on the door on the off chance he was inside. Nothing.

Rushing back to her car, she climbed inside and listened to the pelting rain dance on the roof. An arc of lightning flashed across the dark sky. Wonderful, she reflected disconsolately. Even nature responded to Blake's moods.

Ten minutes passed and it seemed like ten years. But Caasi was determined to stay until she'd had the chance to explain things to Blake.

Half an hour later, when the storm was beginning to abate, she got out of the car a second time. Maybe Blake had left his back door unlocked and she could go inside.

The door was tightly locked, but Caasi found a key under a ceramic flowerpot. It looked old and slightly rusted. Briefly Caasi wondered if Blake even knew it was there. After several minutes spent trying to work the key into the lock, she managed to open the door.

Wiping her feet on the mat, she let herself into the kitchen. Blake's dirty breakfast dishes were on the table and she carried them to the sink. It looked as if he'd been reading the morning paper, found the article about the rumored sale of the Empress, and rushed out the door, newspaper in hand.

To fill the time, she leafed through several magazines. But nothing held her interest, so she straightened up the living room and ran warm, sudsy water into the kitchen sink to wash the breakfast dishes. She had just finished scrubbing the frying pan when she heard a car in the driveway.

Her heart thumped as though she'd just run a marathon when Blake walked in the door. Turning, her hands braced on the edge of the sink behind her, Caasi smiled weakly.

"Who let you in?"

Involuntarily, Caasi flinched at the hard edge in his voice.

"There was a key under the flowerpot." Her voice nearly failed her. Turning back to the sink, she jerked the kitchen towel from the drawer and started drying the few dishes she'd washed. At least she could hide how badly her hands were shaking.

"Okay, we'll abort that how and go directly to why. Why are you here?" His dry sarcasm knotted her stomach.

"Would you like a cup of coffee?" she asked brightly. "I know I would."

"No!" he nearly shouted. "I don't want any coffee. What I'd like is a simple explanation." His hard gaze followed her as she took a mug from the cupboard and helped herself to a cup.

"Caasi?" The tone of his voice as he spoke her name revealed the depth of his frustration.

After pulling out a chair, she sat down, her eyes issuing a silent invitation for him to do the same.

He ignored her and leaned against the kitchen counter.

She didn't look at him as she spoke. "You once accused me of having ink in my veins. At the time you were right. But the ink is gone and there's blood flowing there now." Briefly her gaze slid to him. His stance didn't encourage her to continue.

"So?" His arms were crossed as if to block her out. He drew his head back, pride dictating the indifference he so vividly portrayed.

"So?" she repeated with bitter mockery. "You did this to me. You're the one responsible. . . ."

Blake straightened slightly. "Does that make it my duty to fall in with these loony plans of yours? Do you have any idea of how crazy you sound? You want to pay me to father your child, so you can be a mother. What do you have against marriage?"

"Nothing. I . . . I think marriage is wonderful."

"Then if you're so hot for a family, why don't we get married?"

She stiffened with angry pride as she met his glare. "Is this a proposal?"

"Yes," he snapped.

Caasi felt as if someone had punched her in the stomach. Tears brimmed in her eyes.

"Well?" His voice softened perceptibly.

One tear slid down her cheek and she wiped it aside. "Every girl dreams about having a man ask her to marry him. I never thought my proposal would be shouted at me from across a kitchen."

"I'm not exactly in a romantic mood. Do you want to get married or don't you?" he barked. "And while we're on the subject, let's get something else straight. We'll live right here in this house and on my income. Whatever money is yours will be put into a trust fund for the children."

Her hair fell forward to cover her face as she stared into the steaming coffee. "My mother died before I knew her," she began weakly. "Maybe if she'd lived I would know a better way to say these things. To me, marriage means more than producing children. There's love and commitment and a hundred different things I don't even know how to explain. The quiet communication I witnessed between your mother and father. That look in Burt's eyes as June was delivering their child. Do you see what I'm trying to say?"

Blake was quiet for so long, she wondered if he'd heard her. "Maybe as time goes by you could learn to love me," Blake said with slow deliberation. "I think we should give it a try."

"Learn to love you?" Caasi repeated incredulously. "I love you already." She raised her eyes to his, her gaze level and clear. "I don't want any baby unless it's yours. I don't want any other man but you . . . ever."

In the next instant, she was hauled out of the chair and into his arms. "You love me?" Roughly he pushed the hair from her eyes, as if he had to see it himself, couldn't believe what she was saying and had to read it in her face.

Her hands were braced against his chest. "Of course

I do. Could I have made it any more obvious in Seaside?" Her lashes fluttered closed as she struggled to disguise the pain that his rejection still had the power to inflict. "But you . . . you . . ."

"I know what I did," he interrupted. "I walked out. It was the hardest thing I'd ever done in my life, but I turned away and left you." He released her and twined his fingers through his hair. "I was half a breath from telling you how much I loved you. Then I heard you say that you were absolving me from any responsibility. Here I was, ready to give you my heart, and you were talking to me like a one-night stand."

"Oh Blake." She moaned, lifting the hair from her forehead with one hand. "I wanted you to understand that I didn't expect anything of you. You didn't have to love me, not when I loved you so much."

Tenderly, his eyes caressed her. "How can any two people misunderstand each other the way we have?"

Sadly, Caasi shook her head. "Why did you resign? Why did you leave when I wanted you so desperately to stay?"

He took her back into his arms, and his lips softly brushed her cheek. "Because loving you and working with you were becoming impossible. I've loved you almost from the moment you floated into your father's office that day. I kept waiting for you to wake up to that fact. Then one day I realized you never would."

"Why didn't you say something? Why didn't you let me know?"

"Caasi, I couldn't have been any more obvious. All the times I made excuses to touch you, be with you. Anything. But you were so caught up in Crane Enterprises you didn't notice. And to be truthful, your money in-timidated me. One day I decided: Why torture myself anymore? You were already married to the company, and I was never going to be rich enough for you to believe I wasn't attracted to you for your money."

"But, Blake, I didn't think that. Not once."

"Then you didn't realize I loved you, either."

Smiling, Caasi slid her arms over his shoulders and looked at him with all the love in her heart. "But now that I know, Blake Sherrill, I'm not letting you go. Not for a minute."

Tenderly he kissed her as if she were a fragile flower and held her close as if he'd never release her.

"I love you so much." She curled tighter into his em-brace. "And, Blake, we're going to have the most beauti-ful children."

"Yes," he murmured, his lips seeking hers. "But not for a year. I want you to myself for that long. Under-stood?"

"Oh yes," she agreed eagerly, her eyes glowing with the soft light of happiness. "Anything you say."

Five months later, Caasi stood on the back porch as Blake drove into the driveway. Even after three months of marriage, just seeing her husband climb out of the car at the end of the day produced a wealth of emotions.

"Hi—how was your afternoon?" she greeted him, wrapping her arms around his neck and kissing him. She worked mornings at the Empress but gradually was turn-ing her responsibilities over to Blake so that the time would come when she could pursue some of the things she wanted.

Lifting her off the floor, Blake swung her around, his mouth locating the sensitive area at the hollow of her throat, knowing the tingling reaction he'd evoke.

"You're being mighty brave for five-thirty in the afternoon," she teased.

"It doesn't seem to matter what time of the day it is. I don't think I'll ever stop wanting you," he whispered in her ear. "Fifty years from now, I'll probably be chasing you around the bedroom." His voice was deep and emotion-filled.

"I don't think you'll have to chase too hard."

"Good thing," he said, as he set his briefcase aside so he could hold her tightly against him. "Your cooking is improving, because whatever it is smells delicious."

"Yes—that reminds me." Caasi groaned and broke from his embrace. "I have good news and bad news. Which do you want first?"

Blake's eyes narrowed fractionally. "Knowing you, I think I'd better hear the bad news first."

"Promise you won't get angry?"

"I'm not making any promises." He pulled her back into his arms and nuzzled her throat playfully.

Giggling and happy, Caasi blurted out, "The bad news is I burnt the roast. The good news is I went out and got Kentucky Fried Chicken."

"Caasi, that's twice this month." Blake groaned, but there was no anger in the way his eyes caressed her.

"That's not all," she added, lowering her eyes. "Honey, I tried, but I can't make Ekalb into a decent name for a boy or a girl."

Blake laughed. "What are you talking about now?"

"Your name spelled backward, silly. I wanted to name the baby after you, and Ekalb just isn't going to do it."

Silence fell over the room. "Baby?" Blake repeated. "What baby?"

"The one right here." She took his hand and pressed it against her flat stomach. "I know you said a year, but eight months from now it will be almost that long."

"Caasi," Blake murmured, as if he couldn't believe what he was hearing. "Why didn't you say something sooner?"

"I couldn't. Not until I was sure. Are you upset?"

"Upset?" He chuckled. "No, never that. Just surprised, that's all." His smile was filled with satisfaction as he pulled her into his arms.

Closing her eyes, Caasi slid her arms around her husband's neck and released a contented sigh as she drew his mouth to hers.